BRAZILIAN ADVENTURES

JUNGLES, CAIMANS, PIRANHAS, AND GAUCHOS

AUTHOR: DR. TOM LATHAM

EDITOR: DAVE CARLSON

DynoTech Publishing, Colorado Springs, Colorado, USA

Edited and published by Dave Carlson at DynoTech Publishing,
Colorado Springs, Colorado, USA.
(www.dynotech.com)

The title font, Brasilêro (a vernacular typeface), is free. The author
and publisher recognize the talented Australian designer, Crystian
Cruz with a respectful hat-tip.

Scripture quotations are from the King James Version (KJV) of the
Bible.

ISBN: 978-1-885708-25-0 (Paperback)
        978-1-885708-26-7 (EPUB)

Library of Congress Control Number: 2026907888

Print information is available on the last page.

First Printing: May 2026

Contents

INTRODUCTION...v

SHANE WOODS SERIES Characters.................................vii

CHAPTER 1   Getting a Visa 1

CHAPTER 2   Stranded in the Atlantic Ocean 13

CHAPTER 3   Caimans and Tucans 25

CHAPTER 4   Amazon Jungle 35

CHAPTER 5   Shaman Training.......................................43

CHAPTER 6   Rejecting Wickedness...............................49

CHAPTER 7   Hunting Caimans......................................55

CHAPTER 8   Fishing for Piranhas.................................63

CHAPTER 9   Jungle Wrestling Tournament....................69

CHAPTER 10   Jungle Evangelism 75

CHAPTER 11   Caiman Attack...83

CHAPTER 12   Fortaleza in Northeast Brazil.....................93

CHAPTER 13   Erin to the Rescue 101

CHAPTER 14   Finding an Ape 109

CHAPTER 15   A Cardboard House...................................119

CHAPTER 16   Church Service in Portuguese 125

CHAPTER 17   Semi-Desert in Brazil.................................131

CHAPTER 18   The Opposition 137

CHAPTER 19   Street Evangelism......................................145

CHAPTER 20   Genuine Conversions 149

CHAPTER 21   Kidnapped...157

CHAPTER 22   Rescued 165

CHAPTER 23   Introduction to Southern Brazil............175

CHAPTER 24   Clunked in the Noggin 183

CHAPTER 25   Rocky's Arrival...................................191

CHAPTER 26   Lost in the City 201

CHAPTER 27   Creative Thieves................................ 209

CHAPTER 28   Bowie's Back.....................................217

CHAPTER 29   Mafia Closing In 225

CHAPTER 30   A Gaucho Gets Saved.........................231

CHAPTER 31   A Scary Thought 241

CHAPTER 32   Vini's End 247

About the Author: Dr. Tom Latham............................ 255

Acknowledgment & Thanks.....................................257

BOOKS by Dr. Tom Latham 259

INTRODUCTION

I love storytelling. In my books, I aim to bring readers joy, encourage reflection on faith, and share real emotions inspired by true experiences—enhanced fictionally. My goal is to show Christ as the only true Savior and illustrate how sincere faith leads to a vibrant Christian life.

The *SHANE WOODS SERIES* has fourty books, most of which are still unpublished. After spending time in the Northwestern United States, the characters leave Crabtree Creek near Lebanon, Oregon, and head to Brazil for new adventures. In the next section, you'll find a backstory to help you familiarize yourself with the characters in this book. While the backstory and what follows contain minor spoilers for some of the *SHANE WOODS SERIES* books, this story stands alone, making it easy for new readers to follow the characters' adventures.

I've always tried to follow traditional writing rules, but I recently discovered the concept of "poetic license." I like that concept. While I'll follow most accepted grammatical rules, I understand, many times, it's my choice what to do with commas and when to insert or remove the word "that" into or from a sentence. I also understand most novels have no illustrations. I like pictures and the way they amplify my words, so my books have images. There are some images on, otherwise blank pages, not directly related to the storyline. Some represent ture-life events or objeccts that inspired many of my stories.

I also like vibrant colors, but my publisher vetoed my choice for the interior, so I agreed to settle for B&W. OK, so "Poetic license" is NOT a blank check. If you're a professional reviewer, I understand you need to do your thing. I'm a professional writer, and I do my thing. I trust you'll enjoy the unique things that make me, me.

If you are unsure of your spiritual status, I pray this fictional story (inspired by many true events) encourages you to accept Christ as your Savior and commit your life to Him. My own journey began on May 6, 1964, when my friend and fellow sailor, Richard Edwards, invited me to Calvary Baptist Church in San Francisco. As we served in the U.S. Navy, our friendship grew, and we shared our faith with others on the ship.

Before I accepted Christ, I often felt lost, like a ship without a rudder. I remember several nights when a sudden storm hit: the wind howled, the ship pitched, and I was bedridden with seasickness. After coming to Christ, I turned to the Scriptures for guidance and comfort and to His church for support and spiritual growth. Trusting God brought purpose and calmness even in hard times, and even shaped how I handled life's challenges. I'll share that same hope with you through these stories.

As you read, I invite you to pause and consider: Is there a moment in Shane's journey that mirrors a crossroads in your own life? How might his challenges and choices speak to your experiences? I pray these stories not only entertain you but also help you reflect on your own path and relationship with Christ.

If my stories awaken your emotions, then I've achieved my goal. As fellow virtual travelers, observing these stories, we are connected—passing tales along, encouraging one another, and sharing discoveries. At the end, only you know if they made a difference in your life. Reflect on what moments or truths resonate with you.

Many images and illustrations in this book were generated or enhanced using artificial intelligence (AI) to enrich your reading experience.

Get comfortable, move to the next page, and let's begin the adventure together.

Dr. Tom Latham
Missionary and Wrestling Coach
www.brazilwrestler.com

SHANE WOODS SERIES
Characters

This cover image for "The Show Peak Robbers," Book One in the SHANE WOODS SERIES by Dr. Tom Latham, sets the scene for the series, which is the basis for this book.

A howler monkey screamed overhead as red mud splashed Shane's boots—what he'd anticipated about a Brazilian Adventure. Before you meet the group of friends swept into this adventure, it helps to understand how their paths crossed. The main characters developed in the first eleven books of the SHANE WOODS SERIES spring to life during their journey to Brazil. As you read, learning their individual and connected backgrounds will help you relate to them. The author's real-life experiences inspired this fictional account.

Because of their mom, Loretta's, sinful choices, Thomas, Shane, and Kosette (Kosy) Woods were often uprooted as she indulged her vices. As a result, when Loretta was in prison, they lived with Grandpa Woods on his farm in Lacomb, Oregon, along Crabtree Creek. Residents were known as Lacombites.

Grandpa's farm was the Woods kids' only refuge, where they enjoyed swimming and fishing in Crabtree Creek, hunting in fields and woods near the farm, and returning home to the aroma of Grandma Julia's homemade chicken and dumplings. The pungent smell of cedar-scented sawdust from local private mills drifted across the property. They felt loved and safe under Grandpa Woods's watchful eyes, comforted by the sounds of distant chainsaws and the chorus of frogs at dusk. Grandpa Woods worked at Snow Peak Lumber Company, located behind the farm. Julia, his housekeeper wife, helped with the food bills by hunting white-tailed deer and catching rainbow trout.

When Loretta abandoned them again, Thomas (17), Shane (15), and Kosy (11) faced even more upheaval. With their mother on the run from loan sharks and her whereabouts unknown, the kids were alone again.

Thomas had already enlisted in the Navy with his mother's permission, as he was under 18. Before he left for U.S. Navy basic training, he gave Shane and Kosy a plan for the near future, but was unable to help them execute it. He spent the night at a friend's house. The next day, this friend took him to the bus station so he could catch a bus to the Portland airport and fly to San Diego to report for Navy boot camp.

Shane, fiercely protective, guided young Kosy on a difficult journey from California to their grandfather's farm in Oregon. Despite her youth and the lack of maternal support in the late 50s and early 60s, Kosy remained remarkably emotionally secure.

Once settled at Grandpa's farm for their first summer, Shane and Kosy helped cover living costs by working in strawberry and bean fields, waking at 5:00 AM each day during summer months. When school was in session, they joined their friends Marty and Erin as Lacomb Detectives, assisting local police in solving crimes.

Meanwhile, Loretta faced her own ordeals, nearly drowning twice in the North Pacific while fleeing her enemy, Vini the Fin. Her journey led her to a Russian concentration camp in Siberia, where she met a fellow prisoner—a Baptist pastor's wife—who led her to Christ. Following her release, a surprise invitation brought her to meet President Kennedy at the White House. She finally returned, under mysterious circumstances, to her family at the Crabtree Creek farm. Thomas, who had taken leave from the

Navy to support her return home, was at her side.

In Lacomb, Shane and Kosy became good friends with Marty Lynch and his sister, Erin, who lived on Rocking L Ranch near them. Shane and Marty became best of friends; Marty was Shane's wrestling teacher, who learned how much of a natural Shane was at the sport.

Shane and Erin found each other very interesting and started spending time together. Their connection deepened as the months marched on, and they became best friends. Shane even taught Erin to enjoy "yucky" fishing. In fact, the local newspaper printed a front-page story about her fishing prowess.

Shane's blind childhood friend, Billy Evans, joined the Lacomb gang during their first high school year. He had helped Shane and the gang solve a telescope mystery. Because he was an atheist, like his Jewish parents, Billy questioned everything they said about God and salvation. Finally, he admitted that God was looking after the passengers, of which he was one, during a plane crash in Montana. After telling his parents about his salvation experience, his father cast him out of his home. Billy found refuge with the Lynch's, his friends. While staying at Lynch's Rocking L Ranch, he grew in his faith.

Bowie Pinetree is a Native American, a Nez Perce, and decendent of Chief Joseph, known as one of the best Native American military leaders. Even though Bowie followed the teachings of Spiritism his entire life, he became a part of the Lacomb detectives. His dad, Travis Pinetree, owned a gas station (T.P. Oil Company) where Bowie and Shane worked. Bowie had several exciting adventures, including finding the elusive Nez Perce treasure, which funded their Brazilian Adventure. He eventually reached a turning point, accepted Christ as his Savior, and began a campaign to see his whole family come to Christ.

Shane, Marty, Bowie, and Billy are all skilled wrestlers. As training partners, they supported one another in competitions. Even Billy— whom Shane called "Blind Billy"—excelled at the sport despite his visual impairment. For Shane, the wrestling mat became a place where he knew he belonged. The partners supported each other on and off the mat, especially during moments of struggle. The team forged a fierce loyalty, suporting one another through challenging moments.

Engelbert Farnsworth III (Bert) was privileged and spoiled. He, too, was a very good wrestler and used his physical abilities to consistently bully others. He exploited his wealthy father's resources to satisfy his desire for possessions and repeatedly tried to get the group of believers he called "goody-two-shoes" in trouble, though these efforts failed. Ultimately, his attitude and criminal actions led to jail time. At that low point in his life, he responded to the Holy Spirit's promptings and reached out to Shane from his cell.

After accepting Jesus, Bert experienced a dramatic personal change. Yet, Shane and friends, especially Marty, were hesitant to believe him. Shane thought Bert had stolen his favorite pocket knife, but lacked proof.

Linda McCarn, Bert's girlfriend and a high school cheerleader, fell under his influence before his conversion. She struggled with alcohol addiction and depression. On the night she nearly lost hope at Waterloo Bridge, the icy metal railing pressed into Linda's palms as she gazed down at the swirling water below. With a rope tied to the railing and to her neck, she jumped before anyone could stop her. Shane cut the rope just after she jumped, Bowie threw her an inflated car tire, and Erin jumped in to save her. After that moment, Linda found support and encouragement. Step by step, she overcame her drinking problem.

Pastor John Ballentine, pastor of Lacomb Baptist Church, the kids' home church in Lacomb, Oregon, had a brother, Tom, a missionary in Gravataí, Brazil. They frequently kept in touch over their ham radios.

Harriet, an orangutan, was part of the adventurous gang since Kosy discovered her in the farm's barn. The gang found out Tina Swanson was the ape's owner. She had asked Grandpa Woods if his family would care for Harriet over the summer while she recovered from double knee replacement surgery. The Woods family decided to do that because Harriet's good-natured antics during the gang's adventures had provided everyone a lot of laughs and a feeling of safety as she filled her self-appointed role as their muscular bodyguard.

See the end of this book for information about the SHANE WOODS SERIES books to read more about the characters and stories mentioned above.

Ready to find out what dangers and discoveries await Shane and his friends in the heart of Brazil? Unravel the mystery, face jungle secrets, and walk with these unforgettable characters as faith and friendship are put to the ultimate test. Your adventure begins on the very next page.

CHAPTER 1
Getting a Visa

BELÉM, BRAZIL

School was out, Kosy had celebrated her 12th birthday, and Crabtree Creek was swimmable again. The air lingered with the cool, sharp scent of wet cedar and earth, and just beneath the drone of insects, there was the metallic whir of a reel casting into the water. The rainbow trout were still trying to resist colorful red devil spinners. The ones that couldn't were condemned to Grandma's skillet, and the ones that could would have to be careful all summer, or they would eventually join the condemned.

As the trout dodged lures in the creek, the white-tailed deer that survived the hunting season were looking for lush places to eat and dead, brown needles to arrange with their feet for a soft place to lie down. They were biding their time until the corn stalks grew higher. Then they could act like "huge rats," as the local residents called them, devouring soft corn on the cob, leaving the hard-working farmers with dwindling profits.

The strawberry fields buzzed with pickers, while Shane and Kosy, unlike past summers, watched from afar. Migrant workers, living in one-room shacks built by the farmers, came from Oklahoma, Mississippi, and New Mexico. Shane and Kosy would not rise at 5:00 AM, work until 5:00 PM, and cool off in the creek at sunset, as before.

Loretta Woods was home—her return from a Siberian concentration camp marked a new start. She reminisced on how a Russian pastor's wife had explained salvation to her in a way she finally understood. When people asked about her salvation experience, she answered, "I was condemned until the Lord intervened for me. At that time, I was not His child. He was saving me for a purpose, so I could eventually understand His salvation."

The day she returned to Oregon and stepped off the plane with Thomas, many doubts overwhelmed her mind: Would she see disappointment in her father's eyes? Would she sense anger from her brothers, Walter and Jackie, whom she had failed so many times? Would her children be revolted by her presence, unable to forget and forgive her various abandonments?

She moved forward and saw her children running toward her. Their arms wide, and their faces bright with hope. They wrapped her in a tight embrace. Loretta felt the warmth of their skin; their tears mingled with her own. Their hugs left her breathless with relief and a lump in her throat.

This was what coming home meant: laughter pressed against her coat and forgiveness pulsing in every heartbeat. Her heart paused as her eyes locked with theirs. The euphoric surprise of their unconditional love beaming from each of their faces calmed her soul.

Speaking her regrets out loud exposed her inner self, but it felt strangely carthartic—each confession vaporized a rusted shackle from her soul. She knew she was truly welcomed home when her dad's strong arms surrounded her. Without hesitation, her brothers each gave her a lumberjack's hug. Her children's forgiveness was the most emotional to accept because every glimmer of trust in their eyes humbled her to tears.

She felt like a daughter, a sister, a mom, and a loved member of a family again. She realized in that moment how long she had yearned for this kind of grace. Even this, she owed to her Savior. Without His redemption, she would never have experienced such a moment of healing.

Later, during the drive south, she took in a deep breath of the welcoming smell of home. The air, filled with hints of cedar and hay, rekindled many happy memories, hidden for so long.

Fortunately, these feelings were not overshadowed by the harsh arguments, long absences, and silent disappointments that had once shaped her days. The hint of regret still lingered in the back of her mind, but now she was beginning to feel happiness again.

Her late teen years had been spent in rebellion, and adulthood was consumed by addiction to liquor and gambling, but she changed in an instant. It felt as if a heavy weight had been lifted from her soul. She did not need to resolve to be different. That never worked—she always fell back into old patterns, feeling as if there was no escape.

From the moment she accepted Christ, Loretta felt a shift.

That shift is what brought her home, where she was now unpacking her meager belongings and placing them in the dresser drawers. There she found a faded sweater she had worn long ago, triggering memories she regretted having while wearing it.

But the regrets were different as a Christian. Her thoughts were not only centered on the suffering SHE endured, but also on how her choices had disappointed her Savior. She vowed not to repeat the mistakes of her past. She recalled the words she held onto during her long flight home: "If any man be in Christ, he is a new creature, old things have passed away, behold all things are become new." Her desires changed. The weight she once carried was replaced by a calm she couldn't explain. Guided by the Holy Spirit, she understood a belonging she'd never known before.

For the first time, the kids truly loved their ex-runaway mom. Before, none would have called it love—children's love for parents is different, conditional in a way. Parents are meant to earn it. Now, Loretta was the mother they wanted. Now, the family could truly begin; now they could have what they had always missed.

Grandpa had built them a house on his property. This meant Shane and Kosy would not only have a permanent home, they would also be able to attend the same school each year, instead of bouncing around and hating every minute of it. No more boarding homes, no more drinking, and certainly no more gambling. It's what a family was supposed to be.

It seemed almost like Thomas said "hello" and "goodbye" in the same sentence. After a good night's rest and a hearty farm breakfast, he stepped into a taxi and returned to the Navy before his ship departed.

As summer approached, the family settled into their new life together and began making plans. A few months ago, they had received an invitation from Pastor Ballentine's brother in Brazil. They would explore many regions of the vast country, mostly south of the Equator. With a full season of travel ahead, their anticipation grew. Loretta, happily agreed to join as their adult leader responsible for safety and coordination, delighting everyone.

Just as excitement was building, a snag appeared. When Shane double-checked the paperwork, he discovered their visa application was missing a critical document—a simple parents' authorization for travel abroad for minors. Even though they thought the application was complete, a call to the Brazilian consulate revealed someone had overlooked the required *Autorização de Viagem para o Exterior de Menor / Travel Consent for Minor* form. Their entry would be denied during the customs check in Brazil.

Everyone scavenged through kitchen drawers and desk piles. The authorization had to be on an official form—Brazilian customs officials would turn them away without it. Time was running short; the deadline was looming. Without the proper signed form for everybody who needed one, there would be no trip. For a few tense days, hope stretched thin.

Sleepless nights, a last-minute cross-town trip, and many pleas with officials led to the required form, translated into Portuguese, signed, and notorized. The group returned to planning their adventure, with a renewed enthusiasm, determined that nothing else would slip past them.

The list of travelers soon grew. Bowie, Marty, and Erin were also among those planning to travel. Since Blind Billy Evans was still staying on Rocking L Ranch, without a permanent home, he was invited to join them. He liked the idea. "I'm going to experience the Amazon. Even if I can't see it, I'll feel the heat and humidity just like everyone else can."

On Sunday morning, Pastor Ballentine spoke clearly, as always. "When someone accepts Christ, their life changes. The Holy Spirit gives a new Christian the desire and power to do God's will daily.

"How long does it take for a new Christian to start walking the walk? Let me ask you this: How long does it take a newborn baby to start breathing? If there is no change in desires and lifestyle, then this person really didn't accept Christ. Therefore, he has no motive or power to do right. And that's exactly why he's NOT doing the right thing. This isn't my opinion; it's what the Holy Scripture teaches, what God said about it.

"There are many reasons why people may say a prayer of salvation and not really be saved. They may be doing it to please someone else, win a person's heart, or consider it another important step upward on the ladder of good works to get them into heaven. I've seen some make these kinds of decisions, and it never amounts to a hill of beans. Their lives don't change because they don't have the Holy Spirit living within them.

"There are many biblical accounts of what I'm talking about, but we don't have to look any further than our own congregation to find such an example. The conversion of Loretta Woods and her lifestyle change is enough of an example for us. This is what salvation is all about. You can talk to her, and she'll fill you in on the details. You'll come to the same conclusions I have about what it means to be a 'born-again Christian'."

After the service, Marty was thinking about how Engelbert Farnsworth III's life changed after his arrest. His unexpected conversion to Christianity was a miracle that changed others' view of him. Marty stood at the edge of the group of friends, observing Bert speaking to Shane. Marty avoided eye contact with Bert. Even Marty, once Bert's harshest critic, sensed change despite his guarded approval.

But trust, as everyone knew, was not built in a day; it had to be proven, not just declared. That Sunday after the service, Bert did something no one saw coming. He stood up in front of the dozen or so lingering congregants and reached into his coat pocket, pulling out a small pocketknife. Holding it up, his voice shook as he spoke, "This knife belonged to Shane. I took it last fall. I wanted to keep it, but I knew it was wrong. I'm sorry I stole from you. Here—it's yours."

For a moment, the room was pin-drop silent. Shane accepted the knife and met Bert's eyes. Bert's shoulders sagged with relief. Marty watched, arms crossed, reconsidering how he felt about Bert after observing this humble act of restitution. In that moment, Marty's impression of Bert began to change, and the cynicism he harbored began to crumble.

Bert addressed Shane and Marty. "I know trust has to be earned, and I have a lot to prove to all of you. That's why I'll show I'm trustworthy by following through on my commitments. What the pastor described is exactly what I'm going through. Even my parents are surprised—they've acknowledged I'm a different person."

"My dad, who you know is very wealthy, gave me every advantage possible: money, cars, clothes, and even super expensive vacations. But I was lost, dark and doomed inside my soul. I was a bully and a thief. I was the one who tied Sergeant Kochian's police car deferential to the light pole. I was the one who put the whiskey bottle in your car. I tried to ruin you, and you knew it was me. I want to make it up to all of you, but it'll take some time for you to trust me—especially Marty.

"I know you're planning a summer trip to Brazil. I'd love to go with you. It will allow me to show all of you that I've really changed, or as the pastor says, the Holy Spirit of God has changed me. What do you say, can I go with you? I promise you won't regret it if you let me go."

His request moved Shane. Marty was still a doubter, but was willing to listen to the rest of the Lacombites. Shane spoke up, "Listen, Bert, we'll get our heads together today and let you know by tonight. I'll call you. I can't speak for the rest of them, but as for me: you're forgiven. However, you're right about the confidence thing; it has to be earned. It doesn't just come with the territory."

The gang spent the afternoon on the banks of Crabtree Creek below Snow Peak Bridge, chasing rainbow trout, catching crawdads, and braving the snowmelt-chilled water. Most adults found it too cold, but not so for bored teens in the area. After a group vote—almost unanimous with 6.5 in favor—Bert was allowed to join the trip to Brazil. Because of Bert's previous action of returning the knife and his apparent genuine change, the half-vote carried the weight of something genuinely earned.

Kosy's vote was a full yes—she wanted Bert to come, hoping to observe his behavior and see if it matched his words. Marty's vote was the half-vote; he was still uncertain and wanted more proof of Bert's transformation.

Loretta didn't want to vote because she hardly knew Bert. She was trusting the others to make a good decision.

Meanwhile, another unexpected opportunity arose. Kosy had discovered Harriet, an orangutan, in the farm's barn. She told the family, but they didn't believe her until they DID! Tina Swanson had asked Grandpa Woods if his family would care for Harriet over the summer while she recovered from double knee replacement surgery. She explained that Harriet insisted on eating bananas with every meal and snack. To help, she promised to provide a train car full of bananas for her care. Grandpa Woods agreed and added Harriet to the list of those traveling to Brazil. They were wondering if she needed a passport and a visa, too!

During this time, Bert was also dealing with matters of the heart. Since becoming a Christian, he had a deep concern for his ex-girlfriend, Linda McCarn. He went to see the only person he thought could help him—Pastor John Ballentine.

John asked him what his main concern for her was. Bert didn't hesitate, "I dated her when I was a rebel, drinking and such. I was a very bad influence on her, and some of her problems with liquor are my fault. But, my main concern is that she would realize her lost spiritual condition and come to Christ to remedy it, as I did."

The pastor was very impressed by his motives and told him this attitude towards Linda was definite proof of the Holy Spirit's presence in his life. This is the proof the Lacomb kids were looking for. He suggested Bert ask them for permission to invite her on the Brazilian trip. Possibly getting her away from negative influences would be just what she needed to turn to Christ and be saved. It certainly was worth a try!

Bert had a lengthy conversation with Linda and convinced her a summer in Brazil would "broaden her horizons." They spoke to her parents; Mom and Dad were happy about her plans for the summer. They secretly wanted time away from their daughter; she had worn them out with her antics. Now all Bert had to do was convince the group it was a good idea to take her along and try to win her to Christ by getting her away from other bad influences. He succeeded, and she was added to the travel list.

So, after a quick request with justification, the list of travelers to Brazil grew by one more. They were going to the Amazon jungle first, then to the semi-desert area of the northeast corner. For a finale, they were expecting to spend about three weeks in Gaucho territory in Rio Grande do Sul, the southernmost state of Brazil.

The erratic scramble for paperwork became an urgent mission. With passports and photographs in hand, the whole group piled into Shane and Bert's cars and made a beeline for the Brazilian consulate in Portland. The waiting room was stifling, filled with the nervous energy of many travelers and the distinct scent of floor polish.

While Loretta rifled desperately through her purse for Shane's misplaced birth certificate, Bert tried, unsuccessfully, to coax Harriet the orangutan to sit quietly in the corner. He had volunteered to keep Harriet in line. But Harriet's curiosity often led to problems; she sneaked into off-limits locations to see what was inside, climbed wobbly shelves to grab shiny trinkets, and sometimes annoyed people with her playfulness. She always meant well, though her kindness could be hard to notice.

Finally, with a flurry of anxious whispers and hurried signatures, they made it to the consulate window just before closing time. The official peered over his glasses at the stack of forms, frowned at Harriet's passport photo (actually, she had official, government-enorsed health documents, but the kids liked to call her travel packt a 'passport'), and stamped everything with resignation. "As long as you promise to bring her back with you," he warned. "Brazil already has enough banana-lovers." The group signed the official documents with nervous grins, grateful to have cleared what they thought was the last hurdle.

Back at Rocking L Ranch, they were still double-checking every detail, watching for any more disasters, when a sudden racket erupted on the front porch. Conversation hiccupped, then trailed off as everyone turned toward the noise. Footsteps pounded up the steps. The front door swung wide open with a bang. Every head swiveled. The kids froze, eyes wide, and Loretta's hands gripped her travel itinerary so tightly the pages crinkled.

Bert appeared, but not alone. Behind him strode a stranger in a pilot's jacket. For a long heartbeat, no one spoke. Erin's jaw dropped. Shane blinked in confusion. Kosy flashed a stunned look toward Billy, then felt self-conscious when she remembered he couldn't see. For a moment, the excitement in the room turned into a hush broken only by the squeak of Bert's shoes and the tap of the stranger's boots across the threshold. Marty was the first to find his voice, whispering, "Who's that guy with Bert?"

Bert stopped just inside the door, unable to suppress a broad grin. He looked around at everyone's startled faces before clearing his throat. "You all probably should sit down right now. (Of course, everyone was too excited to sit down. They just moved forward in anticipation.) My parents have offered us ... well, a ride for our trip to Brazil." He gestured toward the man standing beside him, "They're loaning us their private, twelve-passenger airplane, along with Fernando Garcia, the pilot. It's a Grumman Albatross flying boat. They purchased it a few years ago from a U.S. Navy surplus sale and refurbished it for civilian use."

Everyone seemed stunned for a moment longer, as if unable to process what they'd heard. Then laughter erupted, shouts of disbelief mixed with delighted yells, and even a couple of shocked gasps. Shane collapsed onto the sofa, his eyes round as saucers. Kosy and Erin started talking over each other. Loretta blinked and then broke into a smile of pure amazement.

As hands enthusiastically slapped Bert on the back and excited questions tumbled out, a surge of overwhelming gratitude and joy washed over them. The moment felt almost unreal, as the details began to fall into place. Loretta immediately called Bert's dad to thank him. On the phone, Bert's dad explained they'd only need to pay for fuel—the pilot's salary would be his heartfelt gift to help realize their dream. As an extra sign of support, he would also cover the cost of a special inspection and any maintenance needed. With this help, the airplane would be ready to land safely on the Amazon River. Mr. Farnsworth II explained he was doing this because Bert had finally become the son his bewildered and suffering parents always wanted him to be.

This really put the gears into motion. They were packing bags and getting malaria shots all in the same day. Harriet didn't need a shot. That was a good thing because they thought she wouldn't like it, and no one wanted to show up in Brazil sporting black eyes. They left the Portland harbor on June 1, 1963, at 5:00 AM, expecting to be in Belém, Brazil later the same day. Belém was at the mouth of the mighty Amazon River, about sixteen hours of total flying time away. They would have to stop in Miami to refuel, which would add about 30 minutes to their trip.

People stared as the group moved through the airport toward the private terminal. The reactions were funny. Harriet, a step ahead, flashed a big, toothy grin, deliberately showing her heavily stained teeth. They dressed her in a Lebanon Union High School sweater and Bermuda shorts to make her more presentable, but the outfit only made the scene funnier.

When they finally boarded the plane and put on their seatbelts, Harriet was a real pain. She took it off. They put it back on. She took it off. They put it back on and used duct tape to secure it. She picked at it for a little while, but finally accepted the belt as part of her travel attire.

The whole group noted Bert's excessive pampering of Linda. He helped her up the stairs, carried her bag, stowed the bag in the overhead bin, made sure her seat belt was fastened properly, and even located and delilivered a blanket and pillow. No one knew about his meeting with Pastor Ballentine. His demeanor even surprised Marty, the group's doubter.

Loretta was sitting between Blind Billy and Kosette. She leaned a bit closer to his ear. "Does flying bother you, Billy?" The teenager did not respond untill she gently elbowed him.

Finally, he shook his head and turned toward Loretta. The grappler was sporting a medium-sized grin, "Not really. I've done quite a bit of flying with my parents. We went to Hawaii every year on vacation. I miss those family times."

Sometimes it took a little while to get his attention. Since he wore sunglasses, no one could really tell when he was in a daze, his mind in outer space. Now had been one of those times. He had deep feelings about his parents and rarely shared them with anyone. They had thrown him out when he accepted Jesus Christ as the Messiah and his Savior. He thought the separation would be short-lived, but even he had underestimated his father's wrath.

Solomon Evans, Billy's dad, was an atheistic Jew. He had hidden his heritage from the community for reasons he thought were very logical. He concluded the jewelry stores he owned would suffer loss if everyone knew he had descended from the Israelites.

Billy always thought this was not correct, but he would never disobey his parents by revealing their family's secret. He, for one, was extremely proud to be related to the authors of the Bible and Jesus, too.

The Jewish kid desperately wanted to go home, everyone knew it, even his parents. He liked the Lynches well enough, but as he often mentioned, "There's no place like home." His family never really celebrated Jewish holidays because they were trying to keep a low profile. Instead, they conformed and participated in all the Christian ones. His parents had always been very generous with him.

He decided to confide in Shane's mom, who had been reunited with her family. Maybe she had experienced some of these same deep feelings, too. "I was just thinking about how much I missed my family. We did so many wonderful things together, like vacations and holidays. My mom was never a happy cook. She usually catered all our meals, even on special days like July 4th and Christmas. Thanksgiving was wonderful with all the trimmings, including pumpkin pie with a mountain of whipped cream."

Loretta felt sorry for this throw-away kid. She knew by experience how he must be feeling. Not by her personal experience, but by the horrible lifestyle she had put her own children through. "My fine friend, I believe I know exactly what you mean. My kids had the same complaint, year after year, and I paid no attention to them. They wanted family, traditions, and time with their cousins.

"An invisible force more powerful than I gripped my throat. My whole existence was an egotistical trip that caused me to put my own sinful desires ahead of the well-being of my children. They suffered a lot because of my bad lifestyle choices. I'm glad the Lord not only forgives, but He also forgets our sins. That's what He promised, and I believe Him.

"I heard a radio preacher say the Lord doesn't have a 'catch and release program,' and I'm thankful for this. When He catches us, He keeps us eternally. He also said the Lord forgives us but doesn't forget us. I loved that idea. I adore Him for this and will for eternity.

"It's wonderful to know that at our judgment, God won't hold me accountable for even one of my sins. This gives me a reason to lay my head on my pillow at night and sleep in peace. That wasn't an experience I had over the past 28 years. It's something I want my brothers to have, so I'm praying they'll see the changes in my life and come to understand what true Christianity is all about."

The pint-sized wrestler just sighed deeply. He was extremely happy for Shane and Kosy. Even though they had some very bad experiences in the past, at least right now, at this very moment, they were 'in the gravy.' Having their mom back and being a Christian to boot. WOW, how utterly wonderful that must be. He envied them and wanted the same thing for himself and his parents. Only a miracle would ever produce this.

After refueling in the Miami harbor, the Albatross flying boat took off, pointing towards Belém, on the northern coast of Brazil. The skies were clear midday as they crossed the Florida Keys. No one expected any problems with the remainder of the flight, especially Fernando, the pilot. He was abreast of the weather conditions and was not concerned.

But things can change quickly and drastically over Caribbean waters. After passing Cuba a few hours ago, they still had more than three hours of flight time to the Brazilian coast. The sky began to fill with dark, threatening clouds that appeared from nowhere, as far as the pilot was concerned. He pulled back on the yoke and tried to get above the cloud cover. Since the refurbished plane had a height restriction, he couldn't fly as high as he wanted to.

Inside the plane's cabin, a hush fell over the passengers (even Harriet sensed something was not normal), and the steady drone of the engines seemed anxious. Kosy stared out her window, gripping the armrest, her thoughts racing between silent prayers and an ache of doubt. Shane watched the sky darken, feeling the weight of so many changes behind and so much unknown ahead. An uneasy awe bloomed in his chest with every flash of distant lightning. As the storm grew more intense, the mood inside the plane shifted with the weather, every heart bracing for whatever formidable surprise might come.

About an hour from their scheduled landing, the plane slipped into a menacing cloud. Fernando's calm voice remained steady and unshaken as he directed everyone to fasten seatbelts, stow trays, and brace themselves with heads down and arms wrapped around their legs. Passengers snapped into action, but Harriet hesitated. She watched those around her, struggling to copy their movements; her rounded belly made it impossible for her to bend forward or grasp her legs as they did.

Bowie shifted uneasily in his seat, his voice trembling with worry. "Unbelievable! Only my second flight, and here we are again, staring down another disaster. I'd gladly trade places with anyone on firm ground right now. I'm praying, just like the rest of you, I'm sure."

They all hoped and prayed the plane would reach the coastline. But their 'luck,' as Linda would later call it, ran out. A sudden blinding flash exploded outside the windows, filling the cabin with harsh, white light. The sharp smell of burnt metal and ozone rushed in, and the roar of thunder shook their seats. They had been struck by a monstrous bolt of lightning and were going down, faster than the pilot wanted to—faster than anyone wanted to!

As they plunged through terrifying storm clouds toward the vast Atlantic off Brazil's northeast coast, one thought echoed through all minds: reaching Brazil was slipping out of grasp.

The Grumman HU-16 Albatross flying boat was an amphibious aircraft used by the U.S. Military and Royal Canadian Air Force in the 1950s. Bert's dad purchased one from Navy Surplus. He added enhancements and refit the plane for civilian use.

CHAPTER 2
Stranded in the Atlantic Ocean

Atlantic Ocean storms can be very violent.

The pilot gripped the controls, scanning the clouds for a break. Ten people and an ape jostled behind him as the small plane shuddered, descending rapidly.

What he didn't know was that all but two of the passengers sat silently with eyes squeezed shut, each lost in their own appeal to God for protection. The squeak of hands gripping armrests and the almost imperceptible murmur of whispered prayers filled the small cabin. Teens, wrestlers, an ex-alcoholic, a kid with a white cane, a pilot, and a mom all held their breath, each seeking help in their own way, as the storm tossed them through the sky.

The powerful lightning bolt had burned out the radio and many other electrical components. Fortunately, the plane still had functioning flight controls, allowing Fernando to control the aircraft safely. The normally calm, fully-in-control pilot now realized he had no way of sending a

MAYDAY or an SOS. He knew a landing on a tempestuous ocean could mean immediate disaster. The Albatross was designed to withstand landing in rough ocean conditions. But, he knew the waves they were going to see could reach 30 feet, far beyond the optimal 4-foot seas the rugged flying boat was designed to handle, making survival unlikely.

If the waves were that rough, the pilot knew he wouldn't be able to set the seaplane's hull flat on the water. His knuckles whitened on the yoke, and sweat oozed down his forehead, blurring the edges of his vision. He could almost feel the plane hurling through the air, battered like a ping-pong ball in a wind tunnel, doomed to sink beneath a monstrous swell the instant they touched the water. He looked at the passengers, searching their faces for glimmers of hope. "All of you should pray to whatever god you think could help us and start asking for a miracle. I've never been more serious, folks. It's NOW we need this prayer," he announced, his voice calm, yet conveying urgency.

Linda McCarn was crossing her fingers and repeating some prayers she had heard others use in distress. The rest of the group knew exactly what to do—they were spiritually calm at the Throne of Grace, pleading for mercy and time for Linda and Fernando to become part of the family of God. In their hearts, they believed the Bible promise found in James 5:16: "the effectual fervent prayer of a righteous man availeth much."

Kosy prayed silently, "Lord, give us mercy and save us from this certain death. We want to see Linda and Fernando come to know You as we do." Does the Lord Almighty, the Creator of all humanity and animals, bend his ear to the desperate cry of a twelve-year-old? Of course, He does. There's abundant evidence of this throughout the Bible, both the Old and New Testaments.

Loretta bowed her head and prayed quietly: "My Lord and Savior. I've just begun to be the mother I should have always been to these wonderful children You gave me. Please let us live so I can see them grow up to be great servants of Your grace and mercy. Save us, Lord of the sky and the sea. AMEN."

Even though the pilot and Linda expected to perish, they relied on luck and hoped for the best. God had His guardian angels over the aircraft, protecting His children seeking miraculous rescue, as demonstrated many times in the Bible. The Albatross was full of these heirs. Yet, as Bert prayed, a flicker of doubt crept in. What if his prayer was not answered; what if no miracle came? For a split second, he wondered whether his fledgling faith could really rescue them from tragedy. He fought to suppress the thought, holding more tightly to his developing faith, but the shadow of uncertainty lingered in his heart as he continued to plead for rescue.

Bert, sensing Linda's terror, carefully wrapped his arm around the trembling cheerleader. Panic appeared to consume her as she imagined her future slipping away. Desperation pounded in her chest; her father's weather lessons had left no illusions: death was looming close today. Her heart hammered with certainty: this was the end.

The ex-bully, recently saved and sitting among his friends, was making good progress in his newfound faith. He, who had once scoffed at religion as "nonsense," now watched for any sign of spiritual meaning—even in this moment of danger. While he had not yet studied theology (that would come later), he was attentive to the spiritual significance of their situation.

What he did know, from the small time he had to study the Bible, was that the Creator of the ocean was now His spiritual Father, and He was interested in his well-being. Bert had read some stories in the Old Testament about miraculous rescues, and he was asking for one now. "God, give us some grace and mercy, even though we don't deserve it. We have souls here who need to know You before they cross over to the other side." He resolved in his heart to overcome the lingering doubt that seemed to erode his faith. "God, I need Your help NOW, more than ever."

Shane had his head between his knees as instructed by the pilot. He still grasped Erin's hand and prayed, knowing she did the same. Contrary to what some thought, even though they were dating, they weren't into the serious stuff, like exchanging class rings and the like.

Erin was not parading a big gold "S" around her neck or displaying any obvious going-steady tokens. Their relationship spoke of promises to each other and to God: both were fully committed to God's will and did not need to prove it to anyone.

Marty, now in the co-pilot's seat (the same seat Bowie had occupied during a plane crash they had in Montana), looked at the cramped space and realized he couldn't fit his head into his lap because of the yoke in front of him. Instead, he shut his eyes tightly and began to pray after observing the clouds outside, finding their formation extremely threatening. He relied on his Christian upbringing and his parents' example to help him trust God, even now.

Billy was oblivious to the visual dangers but sensed the urgency through the sounds around him. The blind wrestler remained cooler and calmer than most, certain his life was in God's hands. He had accepted Christ and knew he was immortal until God was finished with him. If he crossed over today, he knew he would gain the gift of sight as an upgrade in his next life.

Harriet, the ape, sat motionless in her seat. Lacking an understanding of the danger, she interpreted the tension around her as a new human game. She wriggled slightly, but her seat belt was too snug for her to join in. Too round in the middle, she couldn't mimic the others' head-between-knees position. Instead, she looked around, giving everyone a toothy, green smile.

Bowie had quit "thanking his lucky stars" a few months ago, after he put his trust in "the white man's Savior," as all of his Spiritist relatives in Eastern Oregon called Jesus. They could call Him whatever they found appropriate in their Spiritist thinking, but he found Jesus to be the Savior of all humanity, not just the white man. Now the heavyweight wrestler was on his knees in prayer to the Almighty all the time, not just when he was standing on an ancient burial site, as his Nez Perce family practiced.

Fernando remained professionally calm and had no time to think through theology or philosophy. That's why he ordered all passengers to call upon their god, whoever that was. His main concern and total attention were focused on maintaining the plane in a level position and getting below the cloud cover. However, he was certain about one thing: whatever awaited them at the surface of the ocean, below the high-velocity storm clouds that engulfed them, was not at all a pleasant thought.

He had no problem relaying his unpleasant feelings to the rest of the passengers; they were not paying his salary, and no salary was big enough to cover this present danger. He gave them a final warning before he thought they would hit the water and be thrust into eternity. "Prepare yourselves for a violent crash. We're about to descend low enough to break free of the cloud cover."

When the plane dropped below the storm clouds (100 feet, according to the altimeter), he expected tumultuous waters with 30-foot waves, not navigable in any stretch of the imagination. What he actually observed made him shake his head and jerk backwards in utter amazement. "Well, cut my legs off and call me shorty.

"Never in my thirty years of flying have I ever seen anything like this," the pilot whispered, almost to himself. He stared at the sea below, his voice trailing off as if not wanting to disturb the hush that had fallen over the cabin. The waters, which should have been a cauldron of riotous foam, lay calm and gleaming all the way to the edge of the horizon.

Behind him, an unidentifiable quiet voice whispered, "This must be what peace looks like." For a long heartbeat, no one dared to speak. The awe was heavy, uncertain, and strangely gentle, contemplating that invisible hands were holding back the storm itself. The pilot shook his head, unable to explain or even try. Whatever force was at work left them all suspended between fear and gratitude. A mystery settled over them more powerful than any explanation from physics teachers, weather forecasters, or lucky rabbits' feet.

Everyone eventually accepted what their eyes showed them: the sea was calm, almost glass-like. To have a raging storm above and a calm sea below was a miracle on par with the parting of the Red Sea—totally unnatural. The pilot was utterly flabbergasted and relieved, no longer fearful that the end of his life would be reported in a sorrowful obituary about his unfortunate and untimely demise.

He happily set the seaplane down on the astonishingly calm water, creating a huge splash and a frothy white-water plume. As they glided to a stop, the substantial wake extended almost 300 feet behind the plane. The wake gently dissipated as the amphibious aircraft rocked gently to a stop, and the water resumed its tranquil, mirror-like appearance. The passengers, relieved and grateful, sat up, exchanging backslaps and thumbs-up. Harriet, not wanting to be left out, clapped her hands, oblivious to how narrowly she had avoided a reunion with her kind in the big banana orchard in the sky.

The delighted pilot opened the cockpit windows and leaned out to assess the damage on each side of the plane. He also reviewed an image from a maintenance observation camera, one of the few electrical systems that had survived the lightning strike. He could see damage to the lower right portion of the front engine cowling, stained by leaking coolant. When he finished his examination, he exited the cockpit to inform all the stunned passengers that both engines were in good condition. They still had no radio communications, though. It appeared the lightning strike had blown a small hole in the bottom of their cooling system radiator located on the right side of the engine. They had lost all of the water and coolant necessary to cool the engine.

Linda knew a little about weather conditions but absolutely nothing about mechanical principles. "Why don't you just scoop some water out of the ocean and put it in the radiator?"

The suggestion seemed ludicrous to anyone who knew the reason engines had radiators and how they worked. Bowie knew because he worked on them at the T.P. Oil Company, which his dad owned. "That won't work, Linda. We have to patch the hole in the radiator, or all the water we put in will leak out again. Besides, we don't have any coolant fluid to add to the water." He thought she should have been smart enough to know this simple fact.

She was defensive, "I knew that, big guy. I was testing your knowledge. I knew we'd have to plug the hole first. I have some duct tape in my purse. Will that work, Fernando?" Now she was doing it again, and, this time, no one wanted to correct her.

Billy wanted to know how big the hole was. The pilot said it was about the size of a BB, but explained that under pressure, even a tiny hole could let all the water out in a few minutes. He expanded on what Bowie had told everyone, saying that once the engine started, the system would pressurize, and water would spurt out of any hole with force.

They really needed to patch it with a soldering gun and solder. All of them knew, without even asking, that they didn't have this kind of equipment on board.

Fernando said he could repair most of the electrical damage, but they had to resolve the radiator issue before they could take off again. The original engines were air-cooled, but the renovations added a water-cooled system. Despite the new cooling system increasing weight and fuel consumption, Bert's dad had decided the benefits were worth the extra weight. It improved heat management, reduced hot spots, and enabled tighter engine tolerances. These improvements extended overhaul intervals by reducing thermal stress. Equipment for these renovations blocked a portion of the original air-cooling ports on both sides, so during flight, the engines would not last even 15 minutes without water.

Billy asked if any of them had a transistor radio. Three of them did. He then asked for them, and all three complied. He told the pilot he could talk someone through radiator repair if they followed his instructions to the "T." Marty volunteered.

The Jewish grappler had the solution to fixing the radiator, but he needed the sun at its full strength. That would not happen today, and maybe not tomorrow. They knew spending the night in the aircraft, floating on the Atlantic, was not optional; it was their reality.

They assessed their food and drink situation. No one had brought bottles of water because they thought the flight would be only a few hours from Miami. The pilot said the plane didn't carry a tank for drinking water because of the weight limit. Between them, they only had two small bottles of Coke. Suddenly, everyone felt the desperate gnaw of thirst. They imagined burned and cracked lips concealing thick and swollen tongues; every swallow scratching parched throats. Their mouths seemed glued shut. As the sticky hunger for water intensified, even the thought of not having access to a single cool drop made their skin crawl.

When the sun started setting in the west, they would not have the privilege of seeing its glorious demise. The ceiling was still overcast, dark, and ominous. They hoped all the cloud cover would be gone by morning so Billy could talk Marty through the leaky-radiator repairs.

To alleviate the perceived sensation of dying of thirst, they passed the Coke bottle around, allowing each person to sip just a little. They let Harriet use the bottle last, for obvious reasons no one needed to explain. (She didn't look like she had hurt feelings about being last.) That would leave one bottle left for the remainder of their excursion in the Atlantic Floating Aerospace Motel.

The food they consolidated was: 2 apples, 3 oranges, 12 bananas, 5 packs of Twinkies, 7 packs of David Sunflower Seeds, 5 Heath Bars, 4 Snickers Bars, and 14 packs of Hubba Bubba Chewing Gum. After a second, extensive search, no more water or soda pop was discovered aboard the aircraft. They discounted the salty sunflower seeds as a food item for now. No one needed another reason to have their mouth screaming for liquids.

Before the sun went down and it became blacker than the inside of a cow, they all gathered on the plane's emergency raft and dangled their feet in the water. Getting salt water on their feet would be refreshing compared to being cramped in the cabin all night.

Loretta took a cup and scooped up some seawater to rinse her mouth. It was intensely salty and slightly bitter—it was NOT a good idea, and actually did more harm than good. "Pitooey," she uttered as she quickly spat out the nasty water.

"Yuck!" Kosy exclaimed. "Do you know what fish do in this water?"

At last, the sun must have set over the Brazilian Amazon jungle, because darkness fell quickly. They climbed back into the aircraft. It was a unanimous decision: the ape would sit in the pilot's seat during the night, because no one wanted to sleep beside her. After she was strapped in for the safety of all inside, she didn't give them a pouty lip or make it seem like she had her feelings hurt. She quickly settled in for a relaxing night's sleep, remaining oblivious to their current plight.

Erin suggested a round of prayer before they tried to drift off to sleep. Linda was a bit taken aback. "I suppose we can ask The Good Lord to help us, but what I want to know is WHY did The Man Upstairs even let us get into this mess anyway. Couldn't He have prevented it from happening in the first place, just saying? I hope I'm not offending anyone here."

There was a 15-watt bulb, powered by a dwindling battery, lighting the interior of the plane; not enough to see in all the crevices, but sufficient illumination to notice the strange looks on all of their faces, except for Harriett. The ape always had a strange look on her face.

They didn't know who should answer her question. None of the Christians EVER referred to the Almighty as "The Good Lord" or "The Man Upstairs." These terms were used by people who didn't know Him personally. It is the same kind of irreverence as calling one's dad, "My Old Man." But that correction was for another day, not this one.

During the uneasy moment of silence, the group glanced at each other. Shane, after a pause, gently asked, "Linda, what sort of answer would really satisfy you?" His voice was soft, not arguing, not trying to lecture— just opening a space for the question to linger. "Some things are hard to understand no matter how you look at them." Tension softened a bit, and for a moment, the weight of uncertainty faded a little.

Shane had limited knowledge and was thankful he didn't have a habit of sleeping during church services. He glanced around at everyone, his voice wavering as he continued. "Um ... I think ... well, the rain falls on the heads of Christians just like it does on everyone else's head," he said, not quite sure if he got the words right. He faltered, rubbing his palms together. "If nothing bad ever happened to believers, then ... uh, everyone would want to be one, you know, just to make life easier." He paused, searching his memory for something else, but could only manage, "I guess, I mean, that's how I've heard it." He wondered whether he had gotten off to a good start.

"Old Testament saints were not spared horrendous experiences just because they had a personal relationship with Jehovah. Daniel was put in the lion's den because he refused to pray to the king instead of God. But the lions didn't bother him. He was still alive when the king called out for him in the morning. BUT, the lions were very hungry, because they devoured Daniel's enemies before they even hit the floor of the den.

"Shadrach, Meshach, and Abednego were thrown into a fiery furnace heated up seven times the normal temperature, just because they would not bow down to the golden idol of King Nebuchadnezzar. The fire was so hot it killed the guards who threw them inside. But the king saw four men walking around in the flames. When he had them brought out of the furnace, they didn't even have the smell of smoke on their clothes."

Linda was not too impressed. "I've heard these bedtime stories before. But what do they have to do with our situation? We know why they were persecuted; that's clear. But WHY are we the ones out here floating? Is there any purpose to this, or are we just unlucky?" Her tone sharpened with a mix of frustration and challenge, but no one took offense. They had all been praying for her since they left the States. They knew she was not a Christian and believed she needed more light to see her way to the cross. They were all hoping she would not reject the light that would soon be offered to her, as so many do.

Loretta thought she would assist her son. She was proud of him and his measured answer. "I'll tell you the whole story some other time, but I was totally to blame for a situation when I was thrown into the freezing waters of the North Pacific. I thought I was a goner for sure. Even though it was all my fault, God, the Almighty, had my rescue planned. He was looking after me even when I didn't believe in Him. I call that pretty awesome, don't you think?"

Still unconvinced, Linda responded, forcing a wary smile. "If He's really looking after us, then maybe He'll send a boat out of nowhere, stocked with lots of water and snacks. Otherwise, I guess we'll watch the sun rise while we dehydrate out here, and someone can write our stories from whatever's left behind." The group quickly recognized no answer would quiet her doubts tonight.

They all agreed to call it a day and go to sleep. Throughout the night, they could feel the plane bobbing as it floated, surrounded by a slight breeze. Fernando got up twice during the night and tried to get a bearing. Still, without the use of any of the plane's navigational equipment, and with stars obscured by dense storm clouds, he could not even get an old-fashioned seaman's navigational bearing. No matter what he tried, he had no idea of the direction or distance they had drifted, nor where they might end up by morning when the light returned.

The next day started early for anyone who wanted some fresh air. Being cooped up in the aircraft with ten others all night was bad enough, but having the orangutan sitting in the pilot's seat scratching herself all night until she rocked the plane was too much. Kosy and Erin, rubbing the sleep from their eyes, were the first to get up, open the door, and lean out of the plane.

Dark grey clouds still hid the sky. This was good news and bad news. The good news: the blazing sun was not going to worsen their already parched tongues. The bad news: they couldn't fix the radiator without heat from the blazing sun.

The other, really bad news: no one guarded the last bottle of Coke overnight. Somehow, the ape got her long arm back to the second row, absconded with the bottle, found a way to open it, and drank it dry without any shame. She had doomed them to spend the rest of their bobbing existence without a drop of liquid to drink.

Most of the survivors started a new day outside the plane. A heavy hush settled over them. Everyone stared at the endless water under the dark, cloudy sky. The last bottle of Coke was gone, leaving no hope of immediate relief for their dry, cracked lips and parched tongues. Each person silently wondered if rescue might never come. They were trapped, unable to fix the plane or signal for rescue. The only sounds came from Harriet, quietly rustling in the cockpit, and an occasional wave lapping against the plane. Doubt hovered in the air, thick as the humidity.

Into that silence, Bowie cleared his throat. Sensing the weight pressing down on all of them, he decided to pray for their breakfast and include a petition for some heavy-duty rays from the sun, pronto. "Lord of heaven and earth, we thank You for this food we brought along. We need some intense sunlight to get us out of here. You know I turned my back on our tribal customs when I accepted Your Son, Jesus Christ, as my Savior. I've never been disappointed and don't expect to be now. Amen." His prayer was short and wonderful, to the point.

Just before noon, the clouds thinned and faded away as quickly as they had appeared, revealing the blazing equatorial sun. It was very humid. Billy took over, "Bowie, give me your magnifying glass, please. You mentioned to me you were going to bring it."

Everyone raised their eyebrows in questioning disbelief.

"What are all the surprise looks about. I brought it along to start fires. We're going to be in the jungle, right? We're going to have to start fires, right? Well, I'm not up on that spinning the pointed stick between the palms stuff to start a fire. I'm a Native American, not a prehistoric barbarian." With that explanation, he handed Billy the glass.

Marty took the small portable radios apart, as Billy had instructed. He then held them up and used the magnifying glass to melt all the solder off the components, allowing it to run into a stainless steel cup. While Marty collected the reclaimed solder, Shane used Erin's nail file to clean around the hole in the radiator, so the solder would have the best chance of sticking to the metal. When Marty finished, he ensured them that all the solder in the radios was melted. He gave it to Fernando, who spread it in and over the hole in the radiator. According to the pilot, it was repaired enough to fly. All they needed now was water to fill the radiator and any empty cooling tubes.

That didn't seem to be a problem, Linda noted. "We're sitting on an ocean of water, for Pete's sake. Let's fill 'er up and zoom outa here before I melt or drop over dead with heat stroke ... or BOTH."

The pilot never wanted to be the bearer of bad news, but saltwater was unusable. Its boiling point was different, it was highly corrosive, and it contained minerals that could block essential cooling passages. It would simply not work. They might get airborne only to be forced down again, and this time over rocky coastal areas, which would not allow a landing as soft as the water did last time. They all wanted to know why he hadn't told them this before. He said he wanted to be more optimistic, hoping to catch some fresh rainwater and get by without coolant until they reached their destination.

With this additional bad news compounding the bad news she already knew, Linda's parched delirium took over. She began to react erratically. She had already threatened to drink seawater, anything to take the dryness out of her mouth and throat. "My tongue is completely dry, sticking to the roof of my mouth. We're all going to die out here, aren't we? Die a horrible death we will, and then our bodies are going to fall helplessly into the water and be devoured by man-eating sharks. It's a dreadful demise and a miserable end. I can't take it anymore. They'll write a nice story about all of us in the *Lebanon Express*, saying we perished at sea and our bodies were never found. I have to have some water, or I'll perish like a desert fool. Maybe they'll name an elementary school after me."

Panic overwhelmed her, and she threw herself into the water, disappearing under its darkness.

Bowie was about to dive in and save her, but he didn't have to. She appeared quickly and spouted water out of her mouth like a humpback whale.

When her mouth was empty, she blurted out, "IT'S FRESH WATER!"

The Albatross busted through the dark clouds and found the ocean to be calm. This was not physically possible but it was the reality they faced and accepted with thanks to their God. At least most of them did!

CHAPTER 3
Caimans and Tucans

The black caiman and toucan both live in the Amazon jungle. Caimans, related to alligators, are apex predators in Brazil.

Kosette plunged in after Linda and came up shouting, "IT REALLY IS FRESH WATER!" Crisp drops splashed around her. Expecting salt, she tasted pure freshness and sweetness instead. Mimicking Linda, she surfaced and spat water. "It IS fresh water!" she exclaimed. Loretta leapt in too, gulping water like a fish. As Kosette paddled around, she noticed something odd. The water tasted fresh, but it wasn't as clear as she expected. Sometimes, when she looked down, sunlight caught a faint muddiness swirling near her fingers. A slightly brownish cloud in the water swept by. She wiped her eyes and looked again, wondering if she had just imagined it.

Everyone rejoiced. Bowie's face showed relief and amazement as he grabbed a cup and dipped it in the ocean. He held the cup, hands trembling. He stared at the clear liquid, knowing everyone was watching his next move. Thoughts raced through his mind. Was this a miracle? Slowly, he raised the cup and took a cautious sip. He paused in disbelief, then finished the cup in one gulp, looking confused and awed. "I know Jesus turned water into wine, but I've never heard of Him transforming salt water into fresh. Are we witnessing a miracle or not?" he asked the group, searching their faces. Blank stares were unable to answer his question. Nobody knew.

Billy wanted a drink, his curiosity evident. Bowie handed him the cup. Billy's brow furrowed with skepticism and awe. "There has to be some logical answer. Surely God didn't change the Atlantic Ocean into fresh water for us. That would be a bit egotistical, don't you think?" He scratched his head, and an expression of frustration flickered across his face as he searched for a physics explanation, but found none. He shrugged and drank the sweet water.

Fernando, ignoring the water's mystery, shouted to the group, "Quick, get some into the radiator so we can 'zoom out of here' as Linda wanted!" The group immediately began collecting water and filling the radiator while Fernando completed his pre-checks to start the engines. Filling complete, they all scrambled back into the plane, anticipating success.

Above them, the hole in the sky closed, and dark, heavy clouds gathered overhead. The wind picked up. As the pilot, Fernando, activated the ignition. The engines first gave a weak rumble, then sputtered and fell silent. Fear flickered through the group—what if the miracle had run out? A tense hush filled the cabin. Fernando adjusted the controls and tried again. This time, the propellers roared to life. With the radiator full, the cooling system functioning as expected, and everyone safely on board, they took off. No one yet understood how fresh water had appeared where the salty Atlantic Ocean should be.

The drone of the plane's two mighty engines and its shadow on the water, visible outside their windows, assured everyone aboard: the detoured Albatross had resumed its journey. The drama of the flight faded as Linda's giddiness grew. "We've got lucky leprechauns on our side! Man, who woulda thunk it? At least we're alive to tell the story."

Fernando nodded in agreement with Linda. As the rest of the group exchanged wry glances at her explanation, the ape longed for another ripe banana, which she could smell in the cabin. With spirits lifted, the travelers gave Harriet the last banana and relaxed in their seats, confident they were on the last short leg of their journey.

Their journey quickly led them to Belém (Bethlehem), on the Tocantins River, near the mouth of the vast Amazon River. As the city came into view through the plane's windows, Kosy nudged Shane, wondering why some Brazilians had such long names.

Not expecting that out-of-nowhere subject, Shane turned and grinned at his little sister. "Brazilians have interesting surnames. The governor of Amazonas is Gilberto Mestrinho de Medeiros Raposo—Raposo means 'fox' in English. You'll meet people named Rabbit, Horse, Olive Tree, Saints, or Cross. I'm not sure why, but sometimes names run as long as seven words! Signatures on documents can span the page, from margin to margin. Even street signs have to shrink the letters or grow to fit famous names."

The Amazon River stretches an astonishing 4,345 miles from its source in the Mantaro River in Southeastern Peru. If you could straighten it and put it on the United States, it would extend from New York City to Los Angeles, then continue 1,566 miles past the West Coast. If you want to keep the massive virtual object connected to Brazil, it would extend from Porto Seguro, Brazil, to Boston, Massachusetts, in the USA. Some argue this makes it the world's longest river, though the debate continues, especially in Egypt. The river's fish, of course, have their own silent opinions.

When the group heard these facts, their faces pressed eagerly to the glass, jaws dropping at the scale of the mighty river below. Even Loretta, usually unimpressed and stoic, felt a surprising humility and awe, shrinking a little in her seat. The grandeur left her feeling incredibly small, unmoved by any Egyptian debate, but deeply moved by the scene outside.

After their harrowing flight—one for the record books—the Albatross finally landed on the river within the city limits of Belém. With the challenging journey behind them, they now turned their attention to settling in for their brief stay. The transition from the cramped plane cabin to the wide-open city brought a new sense of excitement.

At the docks, as planned, missionary Fred McClanhan met them. Fred, a friend of Tom Ballentine (brother of the Lacomb pastor), was ready to serve as their tour guide. After they explained why they were late, Fred welcomed them to his city.

The first thing the ladies wanted to do was take a shower, desperate to wash off the tension and fatigue. The men, stomachs rumbling and feeling drained, wanted to get some good food. They unpacked the Albatross so Fernando, still feeling residual anxiety, could get a full look at the structure and assure himself the lightning bolt had not damaged any hidden areas of the plane.

The girls, eager for help with their luggage, exhausted yet mischievous, convinced Harriet to carry it. The ape loaded up: she tucked bags under each armpit, clutched two more in her hands, and balanced one on her head, showing pride in her strength. The others watched, amused admiration on their faces, as she managed it all, evidently motivated by the prospect of extra bananas—maybe even a few chocolate-covered ones—as a reward.

Fred lived in a spacious house on the edge of town. He built it with help from his church members and his wife. Susan was the daughter of an American architect known across the fruited plains. She insisted on arches in the hallways and a half-moon front porch. Roman columns supported the second-floor veranda. Upstairs, there were three bedrooms, three bathrooms, and 23 beds. Fred and Susan were used to hosting large groups. They were very hospitable, with a great housemaid and an excellent cook.

Fred beamed. "Groups that visit us are a blessing—and we hear our believers bless them too. It's a win-win. So, what are you looking forward to in Belém?"

Bert wanted to see the zoo, especially the parrots. Fred thought he would start the lesson at home. "Suppose you took a toucan, you know, the parrot with the long, colored nose," he said, while rummaging through the kitchen. Soon, Bert found himself with a puzzled expression, as Fred set two bowls on the table—a pile of juicy grapes in one, diced lightly-seared steak in the other. "Which food do you think the toucan will choose?"

Bert hesitated. "Grapes? But since you asked—steak? Right?"

"Let's see," Fred nodded toward the open window, where a curious toucan perched on the ledge, drawn by the commotion. Bert lifted the bowls and carefully placed them in front of the vibrant bird, the children crowding around to see what would happen next. For a moment, the toucan examined both options with a shrewd glint in its eye, then pecked eagerly at the grapes, ignoring the meat entirely. "How 'bout that," Bert muttered to himself.

Fred was a respected missionary in Brazil, but his proficiency in the language was poor. He scored 0 out of 100 on his language learning ability test. He joked, "They refused to mark me below zero out of kindness."

The four-hour test used a made-up language. Fred was content with the gifts God had given him, and he was sure language abilities were not among them. Gifted people pick up languages easily. He did not. He worked extra hard to meet the minimum passing score on his final language proficiency test.

After completing one year of language school in Belém, he hired a private tutor to continue his studies. Even though he had received a proficiency certificate from the language school, he knew he would need a tutor to master the national language enough to minister to the upper class. He would watch films in Portuguese and write down every new phrase, studying them with his tutor again and again.

The Brazilians cared nothing for his language test score. They valued other qualities. Although his Portuguese wasn't fluent, and he had an "amusing and entertaining" accent, his actions spoke volumes. He had lived among them for 42 years, and they loved him for his genuine devotion. That, not linguistic talent, mattered most. They'd had enough of missionaries fluent in Portuguese but lacking basic kindness.

One afternoon at the bustling Belém city market, tempers flared as two vendors disputed who would sell a customer a basket of fruit. Voices rose, hands waved, and a small crowd gathered. Fred, returning from his morning errands, stepped between the sparring parties with a gentle word and warm smile. He listened patiently to both sides, nodding at times, showing each man respect. Then, he reached into his own pocket, bought a basket from each vendor, and handed both baskets to the amused customer. "Let's share this blessing," he said, allowing both vendors to receive a profit. Of course, the customer was absolutely delighted with the outcome and went away in a better mood than when he arrived. The mood shifted. The two vendors shared a monstrous bear hug and a mutual back-slapping session. Laughter replaced shouting, and even the bystanders started to smile. Such was Fred's gift: wherever he went, he left calm in his wake, never making a show of it, just quietly earning his local title of "the legend."

Fred was an expert at allowing the Brazilians to save face. This "saving one's face" is very important to the people in Brazil. It allows them to bow out gracefully when they are not right. Saving face never highlights when someone is wrong, especially when the subject at hand is insignificant.

The senior missionary was a master of pleasing others and being flexible and available. That's why he was now asking his visitors what they wanted to do. He threw out the question again, "What do you want to do while you're in Belém?"

Kosy was the first to speak up, "I want to see some alligators."

Fred replied, "In Brazil, they're called caimans—close relatives of alligators. We don't even have to leave the city limits to see some."

Their Belém land adventure began in a rented, 15-passenger bus with a driver. Fred directed the driver to a spot where a narrow bridge crossed a polluted stream. He stopped on the bridge and urged everyone to look closely to the right.

Fred pointed down to the extremely polluted, smelly stream running under the bridge. "Do you see those two big, scary eyes among the plastic bottles? Look next to the three large, plastic gallon jugs." No one could see anything scary, so Fred got off the bus, picked up a stone, and threw it at the oily area. There, two beady eyes slowly emerged above the slime, right where he had indicated.

Linda squealed. "Yikes, it IS an alligator—well, a caiman—and huge! This is scary, right in the middle of the city. How did that ugly, dangerous reptile get in so far? It's absurd. Someone could get attacked and not even know the danger. Bitten, mauled—what a horrible way to go. I heard they latch on, pull people under—in this case, the slime—and twist them until they drown. It's beyond the worst nightmare."

"Where'd you get the drama teacher?" Fred joked. He had no idea how the wild, scary, flesh-eating caiman ended up here, in a busy city neighborhood. The residents, duly warned, now avoided the bridge. Local authorities, always slow, seemed unmotivated to capture or move the beast. Maybe, after someone was mauled, they'd act quickly, only to save their political reputations!

Loretta, Billy, and Erin wanted to go to the zoo. They were interested in seeing more local wildlife. So, to the zoo they went. The admission was only three cruzeiros, about thirty cents in American money. The zoo boasted of animals not found in Brazil, such as the African elephant. Kosy wanted to know how a huge, powerful beast could be held captive by a cord tied to a small stake in the ground. "It seems absolutely physically impossible," she duly noted.

Then, a thoughtful look crossed her face. She wondered how strange and lonely it must feel for an animal that big, brought from another continent, to be kept behind a fence for people to stare at. "I wonder if the elephant misses home or feels sad sometimes," she murmured, a quiet note of sympathy in her voice. As Kosy watched the elephant tug feebly against its thin restraint, a wave of sympathy washed over her. She couldn't help but think of their own group—far from home, at the mercy of strange events and forces beyond their control. For a moment, Kosy wondered if they, too, in some way, were learning what it meant to feel both longing and restraint in a world much bigger than themselves.

Billy, the blind wrestler, was glad to finally be able to contribute. "I'll explain, my fine young lady, why a huge beast can be constrained by a thin cord. When the animal is young, they chain it to something it can't possibly move. It jerks as hard as it can, but never budges the huge post nor challenges the strong chain. After a few months of this senseless jerking without any success, it stops trying and gives up. Thus, when it now tugs on the thin rope, it determines there's no way it will move; therefore, it gives up. Is this enough of a logical explanation, Kosy?" He thought this could be the source of a very good sermon illustration. He'd have to talk to Pastor Ballentine about it.

The tenderhearted preteen remained concerned about the plight of the huge, powerful mammal. She asked Billy another question. "I suppose then, if an elephant really gets mad, it can burst loose and cause a lot of scary times and damage, right, Billy?"

The history buff was ready to give her an answer. "You're correct, my fine little friend. It has happened many times, usually in India or Africa. When they get really agitated, the rope is useless for holding them back. Out-of-control elephants have destroyed buildings, turned over cars and trucks, and trampled residents to death. It's not a pleasant thought. Sometimes it even happens in a circus setting, where many people are packed closely together. Imagine that!"

When they got to the building containing an explanation of the history and utter awesomeness of the mighty Amazon River, Bowie started reading the information to himself and finally let out a Nez Perce yelp, "WOW, for Pete's sake. I finally know how we escaped from the clutches of the Atlantic Ocean. Come over here, all you guys. Look at this!" He was pointing to a map of the coastline, where the Amazon pours into the ocean.

He continued reading, this time out loud, so everyone could hear, "The water, being forced by the humongous volume behind it, causes the river to push its fresh liquid 100 miles out into the ocean. Do you understand now? We were floating in the fresh water that the Amazon pushed out into the Atlantic. Isn't that utterly amazing? One can see only 12 miles to the horizon, so we didn't know how far we were from land."

Billy piped in, "I knew there was a logical reason for the weird water phenomenon. I just KNEW it, but didn't understand it until now."

Linda thought it was time to promote her ideas. "And all that time praying to 'the Man Upstairs' was actually wasted. It was just a physical happening, not a spiritual rescue as all of you thought."

Marty was at the limit of his tolerance of her disrespect. "My dear cheerleader, you need to change your vocabulary in reference to the Almighty. He's not 'the Man Upstairs' as you've called Him since we left the USA. This is not a respectful name for the King of Kings, the Lord of Lords. Does He live on the second floor of your house? We need to give Him all the respect and honor due Him, and the name you've been using doesn't meet that criteria."

Loretta was chomping at the bit to enter the conversation. Marty noticed it and nodded for her to take over. "I don't know much about science, but this I do know. When we landed on the surface of the water, it was calm, even though the storm raged above us. This was contrary to any laws of physics. The ocean should've been in turmoil. We should've been smashed to pieces the minute we touched down. Now, THAT was a miracle no one could deny. You, being the daughter of a meteorologist, should know that. You even admitted it to all of us, remember?"

Shane affirmed his mother's assessment of the situation. "We landed smoothly on salt water. Everyone knows this because you, Linda, tried to quench your thirst with it. Remember?" She nodded affirmatively. "Well, during the night, the Albatross drifted over fresh water, right?" She nodded again. "This is another gift from God.

"The water being pushed into the sea normally wouldn't allow anything to move upstream, against that mighty current. Do you acknowledge this, at least?" She was getting straightened out now; it looked like it, anyway. "This would be another act contrary to the laws of nature, and would be considered a miracle. We all know that for sure." Case closed! They were all praying for Linda to come to know Christ as they did. She was going to be a hard nut to crack, though.

Harriet was on a leash; this was the only way to ensure she wouldn't wander off and become a nuisance to the general public. The ape was docile until they reached the monkey cage. Then she started jumping around, scratching herself, and making ape sounds. The Brazilian tree swingers were so interested in her, they all came to the thick, wire-mesh fence. One put his hand on his forehead like he was saying, "Mama Mia, I've never seen a relative this big, and a redhead to boot!" If this is what really happened, it was probably because they had never seen an anthropoid this large.

Harriet put her face up to the fence, and they exchanged a few jungle kisses, or whatever you would call the facial contact. It was all quite amusing to watch. The Brazilians gathered and took pictures with their 35mm cameras. They, too, had never seen an ape as large and as red as Harriet. She was a star!

Fred was the perfect host. On Sunday, he took the group to Faith Baptist Church for the morning service. Of course, all the singing and preaching were in Portuguese. As the pastor, he preached the morning message in the native tongue. But to give the visitors a little break, he taught a Sunday school class in English. Well, it was almost English. Fred was from Alabama, so he spoke with a thick southern accent and used "y'all" a lot.

The official greeting across Brazil was a brush of cheeks, with a "smack" sound from the lips. This was from men to women and women to women. The greeting between men was a big bear hug, with lots of backslaps. Erin asked Susan McClanahan to explain the kissy greeting.

"The first brush of the cheek means 'Hello', the second means 'How are you'; these two are for the ladies. Teenage girls get three brushes. They are: 'Hello, How are you,' and 'I hope you get married.' If a young girl is engaged to be married, she gets four brushes: 'Hello, How are you, I'm glad you are getting married,' and the fourth one is: 'I hope you don't have to live with your mother-in-law,' which is quite common here. No Brazilian married couple really wants to live with either mother-in-law, but the economic conditions sometimes require it."

All the Americans thought it was quite amusing, to say the least. The teenage boys really got excited about this wonderful Brazilian custom. There were lines of girls in front of each one of them, waiting to give the Gringos a hearty, warm Brazilian welcome.

Billy was enjoying it even more than the rest of them. Some of the girls even allowed him to read their faces. They thought the blind grappler was very interesting. "Legal" is the exact Portuguese word they used, which means "cool" in English.

The line in front of Shane was twice as long as the rest. Erin didn't know how to react, so she kept her jealousy in check and said nothing, which kept her eyes from turning green. This was quite unusual for the Montana cowgirl. There was no line in front of Harriet, but she didn't appear to have her feelings hurt. She just enjoyed the happy time, giving all of the greeters a friendly, green-toothed grin. One of the German immigrants said that Harriet had a smile just like her grandfather!

After the morning service, the missionary took all his guests to a local restaurant. They had a huge buffet with all the salad, finger food, pizza, lasagna, and spaghetti they could eat; all for only $3.00, American money. It was a good deal in anybody's opinion. They were also introduced to the most famous Brazilian drink, "Guaraná." It's a lot like ginger ale, made from a red berry native to the Amazon region. The ape took all the bananas on the fruit bar, but she was limited to using the tables outside, next to the concrete walkway, where the flies congregated.

These are guaraná berries. They appear to be looking at you!

After church, Bowie, Erin, and Shane fill their trays with food at a local restaurant.

CHAPTER 4
Amazon Jungle

The Amazon rainforest is often very foggy due to extreme humidity.

Pre-flight maintenance on the Albatross was complete. It was fueled and ready to go. As the group prepared to board the plane, Loretta wrapped her arms around her Brazilian friend, leaving the outline of her grasp pressed into his shirt—a perfect dark ring of sweat blooming where her face had rested for one last hug. Brazilians quickly form strong friendships, and departures hit hard. Some Americans clutched paper napkins to their faces, waving soggy farewells as they climbed aboard. Saying goodbye stung; the ache carried on in the small, vivid marks their presence left behind.

Linda, ever dramatic, sighed, "Parting is always agony—not for the weak at heart. I'm sorry to be departing now."

After heartfelt farewells, the plane roared to life and sped down the river. As anticipation grew, Fernando pulled back on the yoke—they were off to the heart of the mighty, dangerous Amazon. The adventurers soon gazed in wonderment as the Albatross climbed high above the jungle, revealing a new perspective on the Amazon's vastness.

Loretta pressed her face against the window, her voice soft and awed. "This river looks like it's consuming the land. It just keeps going."

Shane, his voice still shaky with amazement, tried to put it into words. "You know, the Amazon dumps enough water into the Atlantic Ocean every second to fill about 20,000 swimming pools. I mean, that's every single second. It's almost impossible to believe, but there it is."

Linda, always skeptical, stretched her neck for a better look and shook her head with disbelief. "That's like emptying an Olympic pool before you can even finish your sentence."

Bowie, sounding thoughtful and a bit showy, chimed in with a memory. "A pilot once told me the Amazon holds more water than the Mississippi, Nile, and Yangtze combined, and it carries a fifth of the planet's fresh water." Through the plane's small windows, the magnitude started to feel real in the scale of the green and the glittering river.

Their journey would take four hours to Manaus, 930 miles upriver from the mouth. In this region, the climate barely changes: hot and humid—always. It rains every day. Here, people plan around the rain: "I'll meet you after the rain," or "let's play soccer before the rain."

As they flew, the plane made several dips near the river's surface so the passengers could get a good look at its massive size; more than 200 miles wide at the delta. At many places, before it surges into the ocean, it's 50 miles wide, if one's mind can even fathom that. At Manaus, it's only about five miles wide, which is still hard to imagine. Shane had read that the difference between the rainy and dry seasons is 36 feet of water level.

This dramatic change in water levels affects daily life in Manaus. All docks must float to adjust to shifting water. At the docks, high water marks are 36 feet above your head. The islands three miles out are underwater in the rainy season. No permanent homes exist on these islands, and no one in Manaus has a standard riverside home.

When they landed and stepped outside the air-conditioned plane, the humidity immediately enveloped them like a heavy, invisible blanket, making shirts cling to their backs. Long hair captured the humidity and adhered to warm, sticky skin. Beads of sweat pooled in the crook of an elbow and the small of a back. Stepping outside, even for a moment, left everyone wanting to rush and find a shower to wash the clinging film away again and again ... and again.

Within twenty minutes of showering, one needs another. In relentless humidity, mold thrives. It coats books, leather, and anything left untouched. It ruins clothes and furniture. Sometimes, it's so toxic that allergy sufferers could die from contact or even just proximity.

The Gringos were already sweltering in the sticky heat. No one gets used to it, especially on a short visit. Bowie, wiping sweat from his brow and fanning his face in exaggerated misery, complained, "Man, it's so hot I think I'm going to melt, and so humid, I think I've already melted." Yes, it can get hot enough in Manaus, Brazil, for asphalt to become soft and sticky, particularly during the peak of the dry season.

Amid the sweltering heat, the travelers noticed another unique aspect of the city as they trudged past a row of warehouses near the waterfront. Shane wiped his brow and asked Fernando, "Why are there so many factories out here in the middle of the jungle? I thought everything had to be brought by boat."

Fernando smiled, "Manaus is a duty-free city. That means companies can make things here or just assemble things without paying the twenty-five percent federal tax you'd pay elsewhere."

Bowie, eyes wide with curiosity, leaned forward. "So that's why all these American companies have factories here? No tax, huh?"

Fernando nodded. "Right. But remember, most of the merchandise still has to be shipped in and out by boat. Manaus is the main transport hub for the whole upper Amazon basin, and it can take weeks for ships to get here from the coast."

The group exchanged glances, quietly impressed by how this jungle city had become a crossroads for South American commerce.

The Oregon visitors wanted to see the city's world-famous Opera House. Tourism would end soon, with Indian village visits set for the last weeks.

Their stay in Manaus also brought them into contact with locals dedicated to helping others. Fred McClanahan had missionary friends in Manaus who planned trips to remote villages few white men had visited. Patricia and Lori Sheldon, single missionary twin sisters, had worked in Brazil for over 30 years and were legends. They would brief the visitors on 'dos and don'ts' for visiting tribes; knowing this was vital: offending someone makes it harder to reach them with the gospel.

Taking showers was a real experience. The water is heated by an electrical unit that activates only when a minimum water pressure is reached. Turn on the water first, then lift the 220-volt power switch. If it's too hot, turn off the power, adjust it at the top, then turn the power back on. When you're finished, turn off the electricity, then shut off the water. If you get mixed up and do it wrong, you may learn a nice little 220-volt dance step.

The girls went first. Since the water was heated as it flowed through the unit, there was no risk of running out of hot water, unless power failed while you were in the shower. Since that wasn't likely to happen today, the boys thought it would be fun to turn it off while Shane was rinsing off all the soap. They talked Harriet into doing it so none of them would take the blame.

Harriet understood, and when she got the signal, she cut power to that part of the house. From the bathroom, Shane bellowed, voice rising in mock outrage, "YEOW, who did that? I don't get mad, I get even. Someone will pay for this. BRRRR, now turn it back on so I can get this soap out of my eyes; it's burning."

Loretta heard his yelp, checked the switch box, and identified the culprit. By the time she arrived, the real culprits had fled, leaving the innocent party behind. Mom found it funny but, instinctively, helped her son by turning the power back on. He thanked her later with a kiss.

Eager to continue exploring, the group planned its next outing. A visit to the world-famous Manaus Opera House was next on the tourist agenda. As they circled the domed theater, Linda, ever vigilant, muttered just loud enough for Loretta to hear, "Somebody's practically breathing down my neck—are they after my purse or my perfume?" She shot a sharp glance behind her, eyeing a twitchy figure hovering near her bag. Before she could voice a warning, the group started to go inside the air-conditioned building for a break from the heat. A teenager had taken his time to get very close to her. He shoved her a bit and yanked her purse hard off her shoulder.

He dashed down the street, much too quickly for any American or Brazilian to catch him.

But the thief had not counted on a warm body from Borneo catching up with him. Harriet shot forward, using her long, powerful arms to swing from tree to tree, true to her ancient custom. Before the thief could turn the corner and disappear, the anthropoid dropped right on top of him, knocking the kid for a loop.

It was quite a sight to see Harriet leading him back, dragging him across the uneven street. He protested loudly, but she didn't speak Portuguese, nor was she interested in listening. He had stolen the wrong purse—the one full of Harriet's bananas. Stealing from an orangutan was never a good idea; it was a costly mistake that might require an ambulance call.

She dropped him at Linda's feet. Linda cheered, drawing locals. They knew the thief and were glad. A policeman, seeing it all, arrested him.

At a café, Loretta tried her Portuguese. The waiter grinned, "Your accent is too cute! You need to teach me English, yes?"

A teen at the next table stood up. "You're from America? I want to visit New York. Maybe you can help with my English?" Locals eager to practice English often surrounded the group. Brazilians were happy to be around their American friends, offering help and friendly smiles, and weren't shy about asking for an English lesson or a new slang. Their warmth, mixed with genuine curiosity, left the visitors honored and amused by the attention.

Patricia and Lori were friends with local politicians, including Governor Raposo. He had invited the visitors to a gathering of influential people to meet Brazilians responsible for running the government.

The president of all the indigenous tribes of the Amazon area was in the city to meet with the Governor. His aide informed him that Bootte Mathee, the representative of the Indians, had arrived at the hotel. The governor sent a three-piece suit for the native to wear, insisting he put it on before coming to the meeting. Bootte stared at the suit. "Why is my own skin not good enough for them?" he wondered. The demands of these meetings always seemed to come with invisible strings, as if respect had to be worn like a costume.

The representative was taken aback. He had never worn such a ridiculous outfit in his whole life and wasn't about to start now. The governor didn't budge. If he didn't wear the suit, there would be no meeting between them. The Indian was also immovable; he returned to the tribe without meeting with the politician.

Bowie thought the whole ordeal was a bit childish on the governor's part and told his tourist guides, "I find it hard to believe the governor would make such a demand on a person who never wore more than a loincloth his whole life."

This cultural clash lingered in their minds as they departed. The Americans left the meeting feeling a bit strange. They thought the Indians needed to be given a little slack, considering they were the ones being run off their land by miners and farmers. It appeared to be the wild west all over again, and the Indians were taking it on the chin here just like they did in the United States during the past century.

There are about 400 different tribes in the Amazon area with a population of almost 800,000. Most Indians live in settled villages along rivers and grow plants such as bananas, beans, corn, and manioc. They also hunt and fish, using plant-based poisons to stun the fish. Some tribes use shotguns for hunting, while others use bows and arrows, spears, or blowguns with poison-tipped darts.

Few Amazonian tribes are nomadic; they usually live close to a river, so they can have transportation in and out. They grow some crops to supplement hunting and gathering. Almost all the Indians' problems revolve around land: outsiders either want their land or something on or underneath it.

Bobby, their contact in the village, shared the story of his cousin Marcos, whose family's orchard once covered many acres. One morning, the tranquility-shattering buzz of chainsaws overpowered the usual bird songs. By noon, all the trees marked with red paint were gone, making way for trucks and machinery. Marcos pleaded with the overseer to leave the old Brazil nut trees standing, but talking to them was ineffective. That evening, Marcos sadly sat watching smoke rise from smoldering piles. His father's and grandfather's land was now stripped bare for timber. In a single day, decades of shade, fruit, and medicine were lost.

The key threats to these villages are not distant or abstract, but come in the form of relentless logging crews, oil and gas explorers, and the rapid spread of ranching and farming. For families like Marcos's, what outsiders call economic opportunity can feel more like the earth shifting under their feet, leaving little behind but splinters and sorrow.

Fernando advised the group that the plane was fueled and ready to fly to the tribe in the morning. As night settled in, the whir of a ceiling fan, along with the sounds of insects and other night critters outside open windows, reminded them how far they were from home. Loretta found a quiet corner to pen a letter to her dad in Lacomb, telling him everything was going well. She described their day and tomorrow's plans, and suppressed the hollow feeling that rose as she mentioned the upcoming departure.

Since they would be away from the plane most of the time, there would be little chance to communicate with them. She ended the letter with, "We're doing well, Dad, don't worry about us. Kosette is okay. She's the biggest attraction we have, if you don't count the ape." She stuffed the letter into an envelope and put it on the nightstand. She would take it to the post office on the way to the plane. She fell asleep almost the instant she lay on the bed, despite the sweltering humidity.

The next morning at 5:00 AM, the group left Manaus for the tribe's location. It was an exciting time for them. This would be a once-in-a-lifetime experience for all the Oregonians. No one ever thought they would get another chance to visit a few tribes within the Amazon jungle. This was it.

The further the plane went into the jungle, the denser the foliage became. There are 2.3 million square miles of jungle in the Amazon, the largest jungle on planet Earth. The Amazon rainforest is often called the "Lungs of the Earth" and has been credited with producing 20 percent of the world's oxygen. Shane had read in National Geographic that this figure is likely an overestimate, and some scientists suggest the actual number is much lower—maybe closer to 6 percent—while others point out that the forest itself uses up most of the oxygen produced. "People still debate how much oxygen the Amazon really contributes," Shane said in his best tour-guide voice. They noticed some fog, caused by high humidity, hovering over the trees.

After three hours of flying, the plane landed on a river, with only 100 yards of clearance on each side of the plane. Bowie noted this was four times the space to work with than he had when he flew a Cessna through a ravine and landed on a ledge in the Montana mountains.

Three canoes came to the boat's side to take the visitors onto land. The Indians were all wearing loincloths; some had feathers on their heads, held there by brightly colored bands of cloth. Some had bows in their hands, with long arrows lying in the canoe. They rowed to the bank and let the group disembark in shallow water. Everyone got their tennis shoes wet, but that was not a problem. With this intense heat, the PF Flyers would dry out quickly.

Their contact with the tribes was an Indian who had become a Christian about five years ago. For simplicity's sake, he told them to call him Bobby. He and his wife were the only believers in this area.

The first thing that greeted them upon entering the huts they were assigned to was the sweet, earthy scent of damp grass and wood smoke, drifting through the open slats in the walls. The lazy whirring of insects seemed to pulse right through the woven matting of the floor, as somewhere outside a parrot gave a loud, raspy squawk. Light filtered in softly through the windows, painting dappled patterns on the hammocks strung from post to post. They would have to sleep in two grass huts, on hammocks nailed to the posts. Their bathing would have to be in a makeshift shower using river water, at ambient temperature. They brought soap and towels as instructed. The niceties of modern living would have to be set aside for a few weeks. Linda looked like she was in shock! The ape was fine with all the arrangements. She felt right at home, because she WAS at home.

Bobby informed them that the local spiritual leader was not very excited about their visit. He was a very hard man who opposed Bobby at every attempt to start any Christian work in this village. They would all have to keep very low profiles if their stay were to be pleasant.

Breakfast would be a piece of fruit and possibly a slice of bread made from manioc root, but that would be rare. Their lunch would be some vegetables, possibly with a piece of wild boar. The supper would be a mixture of the two meals, if they were lucky. Indians were not used to eating three meals a day. They just ate whenever they were hungry. That's why they had very low obesity rates. All the grapplers thought they might leave the tribe at, or at least near, their wrestling weight.

After taking showers in shifts, they met in one of the huts to say goodbye to Bobby, who was called away and wouldn't return until after they left the village. Marty led a prayer for Bobby to have a safe journey. After Bobby left, Bert prayed before they all headed off to bed.

He started, "God, these people live much more primitively than we do. They are Spiritists who worship nature and seek help from the spirit world. We want Your Holy Spirit to use us to bring some understanding to their minds. This has to be done through doors only He can open for us. We're looking to You for help so we can explain who Jesus Christ is in a manner they can understand. In His name we pray, Amen."

As Bert finished, the hush lingered—but outside, a distant howl rose from the darkness beyond the hut—a monkey called out to the jungle, echoed by the low rumble of frogs. For a moment, it seemed the very air trembled between the prayers and all that waited outside.

Marty noted that the prayer seemed to come from someone walking closer to God than he had imagined Engelbert Farnsworth III could in so short a time as a Christian. He was impressed, but kept it to himself lest he be wrong and disappoint the whole group with unfounded optimism. Time would tell how Bert was spiritually, and this trip might be the time needed.

CHAPTER 5
Shaman Training

Amazonian shamans (pajé in Portuguese), believe they are a bridge between the spirit world and things on this plane of existance. Early European visitors called them "witch doctors," which may be offensive to many indiginous persons.

Batubo, the shaman and spiritual leader of the tribe, felt angry and threatened by how well his fellow tribe members got along with the Gringos. His hatred for all Gringos, especially these Christian ones, simmered, feeding his frustration. He was jealous and resentful, feeling his spiritual leadership was being undermined. They wanted everyone to abandon his teachings and embrace the teachings of a Jewish man named Jesus. Batubo was confused and irritated—how could a man who died over 2,000 years ago matter to his people now?

His distrust of outsiders went much deeper than simple rivalry. Batubo remembered many years ago, when a group of explorers brought gifts wrapped in shiny plastic. Their actions and promises seemed friendly at the time, but they left behind loss and confusion. Many tribe members, including one of his uncles, had died shortly afterwards from a fever no healer could cure. The grief and anger he felt never left him. Each encounter with an outsider made him more distrustful. If their ways could warp his world, how could he risk letting more outsiders shape his people's beliefs?

His great hope was Esterdo, his only son. Esterdo was 18, handsome, tall, friendly, and intelligent. Everyone in the village liked him. It was obvious that the young prodigy should follow in his powerful, political, and spiritual father's footsteps. It only seemed logical and sensible. This son would continue his father's work: controlling the whole area with blessings and curses.

Esterdo was closest to his mother, Agather, daughter of the last shaman. With no brother, her father's authority ended. Girls couldn't be shamans in this part of the Amazon, though some other tribes allowed it. Not the Natubi.

Batubo introduced cruelty early. From age 4, Esterdo was forced to cage rodents and provoke rage by poking them, with his father watching sternly. Disgust and sadness overwhelmed him, and the hated task filled him with dread. Many times, Esterdo flung the stick away, fleeing his father's demanding approval.

His mother also led spiritually, without Batubo's cruelty. She wanted Esterdo to be the next shaman but preferred a humane approach. When she saw his distress during training, her heart ached with helplessness. She wanted to comfort him and protect his gentle nature, but she was not in charge.

Whenever training became intense, Agather escaped with their five-year-old son to her relatives, a day's journey away. During these escapes, Esterdo's bond with his mother strengthened, deepening his preference for her over his strict father.

While visiting the other tribe, Esterdo played with the children. They always gathered in the middle of the communal living area to play stickball. They used strips of cloth to form the ball and bent branches as sticks. The game's goal was to get the ball into the other team's net. It was an Amazon version of hockey, reimagined for the rainforest: no ice, no fighting, and no showmanship before play began.

Talita, the chief's daughter, was the best player. The chief also had three sons, but Talita, at five years old, like Esterdo, stood out. Her skill in stickball earned her respect among the children. Because she was shorter than the others, she sometimes stood on a brick to match Esterdo's height when they were just talking.

The only other sport this tribe played was wrestling. It was used more to settle disputes and win courtships than as a sport. The wrestling was not like the kind Shane and Bowie did, but similar. There were no rules except no biting or pulling hair. Everything else was allowed. It hurt much more to be thrown onto the ground than onto a foam mat. Matches were held on thick grass when possible. But the grassy ground hid jiggers, fleas, and fire ants. Losing was humiliating and painful. Fire ants are serious. Jiggers can be brought into the bed and easily spread.

At six, Esterdo's training escalated. He had to tie three monkeys' tails and hang them over a rope, forcing them to fight. Witnessing their distress and pain made him feel sick to his stomach and deeply disturbed. Unable to bear the guilt and revulsion, he never touched a monkey again as a boy.

Animal cruelty was only one lesson; power was central. Alongside his father's orders, Esterdo snatched balls from the other children, casting them deep into the jungle. Only when rewarded—sometimes with a piece of fruit or a worn stick—would he return them. The ransom never truly mattered. Redemption was the point. Each episode left Esterdo uneasy; he knew, deep down, these acts conflicted with his nature. Every required ransom felt corrosive, eating away at his soul. He dreamed of refusing these games entirely. This longing disturbed him. Disobedience, however, always meant harsh punishment from his shaman father.

Revenge came next. Esterdo needed to instill fear to maintain control, but he was too well-liked. So his father attempted to make someone mad at him. Batubo's obsession defied reason.

His wife's voice trembled with rage and desperation. Her words cut like a knife: "This campaign to raise a monster instead of a son will backfire on you. Stop and consider: all your training to make him like you has not worked. He's just the opposite of who you are. Aren't we very lucky for that! Also, remember this: if you succeed in making him just like you, imagine what a nightmare our lives will be. Can you imagine the kind of wife he'll find, and what monsters our grandchildren might become?"

She glared at him, pain and fear written in every line of her face. "Our relatives hate you, and I'll no longer help you become a legend at our son's expense. You're on your own on this journey. The tribe fears you, and our relatives despise you. Is this the life you want? Even the monkeys have it better than us."

After this rather tart conversation with the most powerful man in the area, she kept her word and never once supported him in his quest to be a legend in his own time. But that did not detour him from his obsession. He continued paddling his canoe against the current, as his wife had once made the comparison.

The training dragged on for years without his wife's support until Esterdo reached adolescence. By then, Batubo expected to see pride and satisfaction reflected in his son. However, Esterdo didn't mirror his father at all. Instead, he felt the weight of disappointment and confusion. Years of shaman boot camp were wasted, leaving Batubo angry and resentful. Esterdo, meanwhile, silently struggled with the disconnect between his gentle nature and his father's vision.

The shaman started Esterdo's training when he was very young. He believed a sapling could become a great tree if cultivated and watched closely. When Esterdo was 12, his dad gave him a blue-feathered toucan hat and painted his face. To his father, the son was that growing tree. Batubo would tutor him, aiming to make him a greater shaman than he himself had ever been. This would secure his legacy in the tribe's history. He was a dedicated politician to everyone.

Training was vital for acceptance by the tribe. Esterdo had to be convincing, demanding, brutal, and quick to retaliate. But his gentle, friendly nature unsettled Batubo, who reacted with frustration and disappointment. Once, when an older child shoved a little boy out of a game, Esterdo intervened. He helped the boy to his feet and stood between him and the bully. He said nothing, but his steady eyes made the older child back down. All the children recognized Esterdo's quiet strength beneath his kindness. Even Batubo noticed, but instead of pride, he felt irritated and worried that Esterdo would never be harsh enough.

Although his father spoke proudly of these plans to make his son a copy of himself, Esterdo sometimes wondered what his life might look like if his father had taken a divergent path. He wished to be freed from the weight of so many expectations. Deep down, he worried he would disappoint his father, or worse, lose himself in the transformation process.

Batubo was infuriated by the Gringos' presence. His son acted more like them than his own leaders or father. This was unacceptable. Esterdo was training to become the tribe's next leader, but things weren't going well. Batubo had to discredit the Gringos and turn his son against them.

The shaman devised a plan: make the Gringos look bad, and his son look good. Tribal people could tolerate much, but not theft. Property seemed communal, but a thief was unwelcome.

They could not tolerate a thief—or "waltina" (lightning hands). Anyone so nicknamed was ostracized and denied leadership roles. Theft was simply intolerable.

The one possession his son prized the most was the beautiful, handcrafted bow his great-grandfather had passed down to him. It was the most revered object of Esterdo's childhood. It still occupied a very special place in his heart. For many years, the bow had hung above his cot in their grass hut, right above the carved wooden plaque his Uncle Tifario, from the adjoining tribe, gave him. It was a carefully crafted plaque of Esterdo's favorite dog. If the bow disappeared, his son would go bananas. Theft was uncommon in this part of Brazil.

The shaman planned to hide the bow in the Gringo guys' grass hut. He had heard that the biggest one, the Native American, was an expert with the bow. This would be the perfect setup to discredit them and drive a rift between his son and the unwanted, despised Gringos. Maybe this might even get them kicked out of the villages. This was his best idea yet.

Batubo knelt next to a smoky fire. He scooped some red clay from a small gourd and pressed his thumb hard against his forehead, leaving an impression in his skin. He confidently traced a spiral into the dirt next to the fire. Quietly chanting words passed down for generations, he flicked bits of clay into the fire, watching embers flare. As smoke rose, he looked up and offered a final desperate plea to the spirits, seeking their guidance and cunning.

Esterdo's tribe moved rocks to build a dam, blocking the fish in and making it easier to catch them.

AMAZONAS INDIGENOUS PEOPLE'S FLAG

Esterdo loved the bow his great-grandfather gave him. It was his most prized possession.

CHAPTER 6
Rejecting Wickedness

Esterdo and Bowie had a contest to see who could put the most arrows in the swinging bananas.

Although Esterdo was trained to be a cruel, powerful shaman, he was far from it. This frustrated his demanding father. Years of intense instruction had not made him like his father. He remained the opposite. His mother was delighted.

Over the years, she repeatedly told Batubo he was wasting his time. Their son would never be a cruel, powerful shaman. She often said, "That monkey won't swing," "That canoe won't paddle," and most often, "That greased pole can't be climbed!"

Unbeknownst to his parents, Esterdo admired the Americans visiting his village. He secretly liked Patricia and Lori, the two white women who frequently visited. They always brought supplies and medical care, taught the children to read, and led well-received classes on hygiene and farming. They also helped the Indians endure the measles outbreak.

The village didn't pay them. He asked and found that the government didn't pay them either, not even offering supplies. Esterdo couldn't fathom how these people, whom his father scorned, found reasons for kindness. Did they simply want to help? Or did they have hidden motives? How could they afford supplies? These doubts haunted him. No one in the village understood. Some tribe members speculated but found no answers.

It baffled his young mind why anyone would do these charitable things on their own. Did they hope to help others or prove something to themselves? Why journey so far, live with heat and humidity, and stay in grass huts for weeks? He wondered what could possibly motivate them when they could be enjoying luxury in the large villages he knew existed. He had never visited these villages, but books had shown him wonderful buildings, clean water, and sparkling artificial pools, all common sights there.

His father forbade him from spending time with the white ladies or any outsiders. Esterdo felt anxious and confused about this rule, especially since he found these people kind and different from the tribe, who could be disconnected or even cruel. He struggled with doubt, questioning whether his father's approach could foster a good society. Deep down, he felt certain that fear, cruelty, and vengeance were not the answers for anyone.

Although forbidden to approach the women, Esterdo could never forget being six, covered in red spots and high with fever. He'd felt overwhelmed by fear and pain, desperate for anyone's help. His mother insisted he needed the medical help the women always provided to children, and Esterdo had clung to that hope in his feverish state.

Batubo was steadfast in his refusal to allow any contact with the white devils, as he called them. "If those ladies were worth anything, they'd have been married, had children, and worked as cooks and housekeepers for some unlucky white man. Obviously, there was something wrong with them. That's why they were punished and sent to work here in this miserable village, with these sick and ungrateful people."

Esterdo's mother ignored the shaman's opinion; she was terrified for her son's life and went against her husband's wishes to seek medical help for their only child. Hiding her fear and determination, she secretly planned to take the suffering boy to a nearby village where Patricia and Lori treated the red-dotted sickness. After witnessing other children die from the same plague, her anxiety transformed into a fierce resolve. She refused to let her only son suffer the same fate. Defying her husband and braving the risks for Esterdo's sake, she rushed him to the place the ladies were at.

Apparently, she arrived just in time. When Patricia saw the boy, her eyebrows shot up. "Why didn't you bring him sooner? He's had a high fever for too long. I'm not sure we can help now. You'll have to leave him here at least a week, or he won't make it. I'm not kidding. This is serious. If you don't listen to me, he will die. Are you hearing me?" Gripped by fear and hope, the desperate mother left her son and rushed home.

He remained in a coma for several days. When he finally awoke, he recalled the details of his time in their hut. Both women took turns through the night, sponging his fevered body with cool rags. They never left him alone. Their faces showed genuine concern. Occasionally, he glimpsed them with bowed heads and moving lips. He assumed they were praying to their Spirits on his behalf.

After five days, he guessed, his fever broke. Patricia gave him a stainless-steel cup half-filled with liquid and told him to drink it. He felt relief and exhaustion mingling as he slowly sipped the liquid with a plastic straw. Gradually, he regained his strength, hope returning with each day. His mother sent daily messengers; her worry never faded until she knew his condition. She told his dad their son was visiting cousins, anxiety hidden behind the lie. After six days, she received word that she could come and get him if someone could transport him. He felt frustrated at being unable to walk home, and uncertainty crept in—if she didn't accept, he couldn't leave.

Agather paid someone to bring him back on a sled pulled by two donkeys borrowed from her cousin. When Batubo saw his son, a surge of dread filled him—he knew something was wrong. He questioned his wife anxiously until she told him a story he would accept: their son had fallen into a pit, was injured, and too weak to return, so he stayed with relatives until he was strong enough to come home. She said she hadn't told him earlier because she feared adding to his stress while he was so busy trying to be the powerful man he thought he was.

Esterdo knew she lied again, to protect him from punishment. Sometimes it worked, sometimes not. He wished for honesty, but fear forced her actions.

He was now 18 and needed to make some of his own decisions. He made gestures toward the Gringos that he wanted to talk with them, in secret, at night, SOON. Marty and Bowie arranged a meeting with him in their hut after the tribe's evening parley around their community fire in the middle of the village.

The young tribesman arrived about an hour after sundown. On the equator, the sun rose at 5:30 AM and set at 5:30 PM each day, with no daylight saving time. Annual time changes were meaningless here at the planet's midsection.

Esterdo sat on the straw mat and looked into Bowie's face. "I heards you are Indio, too. Is dis correcto." The young man had learned some English from Patricia and Lori when his dad was on trips, causing havoc in other parts of their tribal territory. He was actually doing quite well with this extremely difficult foreign language.

Bowie was proud to admit he was a Nez Perce Native American. "I certainly am. My roots go way back to the great Chief Joseph, a mighty warrior and an awesome leader of his people."

"Whats kind of leaper was he? Was he ... kruil and powersful liked my fader?" This was important to the young man. He wanted to know whether any political leaders were honest, kind, and had integrity. Bowie assured him there were many leaders like this in the world. "So, way ares you here? Ares you doink da sam works dat Patricas and Lorias ares doink? Do yu haves da sam ... medicinese and foodse day do?"

Shane took up the conversation. "We don't exactly have the same resources as those ladies do. We're just visiting, learning, and trying to share our belief in the Savior of the World—Jesus Christ. He was a Jewish man who was born to a virgin over 2,000 years ago. Have you ever heard of him?"

The humble teenager answered quickly, "Patricas an Lorias tole me a yiddle abut dis man. He vas claimed to bees da Son of God. He did died a cruel deaths, no?"

Billy added, "We have a Bible here in your language, with English on one side and your tribal tongue on the other. Do you know much about the Bible?" The grappler hoped he would say yes, but the boy only shook his head no.

The tribal Indian motioned towards his hut, across the communal center of the camp. It was about one block away. "I has to gets someting, I vills been rite bak." With that, he jumped up like a jack-in-the-box and took off like a lightning bolt. Within minutes, he returned carrying something in a blanket. When he unwrapped it, all of the boys gasped.

It was a beautifully hand-carved bow, engraved with jungle scenes, accompanied by 12 arrows. Only the handle wasn't engraved. The string looked store-bought, which was rare here. It was obviously his most prized possession.

Tribe members shot birds from the air, each arrow marked. The one who hit a bird got the food and hearty backslaps. Esterdo usually got the backslaps.

"I voods liked to ... teachs dis Indio to shot my bow. Does you vants to learned to shot my bow?"

The whole group knew this was a very rare offer in this part of the world. It would be almost an offense to refuse such an invitation. There was no need to be pressured by customs; Bowie was delighted to have a few archery lessons from a tribal expert.

Patricia and Lori were champion archers from the University of Minnesota. They both participated in Big Ten tournaments, earning medals every time. They had taught little Esterdo all they knew.

Bowie's lessons started early the next morning. Fortunately, Esterdo's father was away, drumming up support for his campaign against the Gringos, so far unsuccessfully.

The archery targets were coconuts hanging from tree limbs. The villagers had cut holes at the top and bottom, pushing a vine through the whole green ball. To make hitting the target more difficult, the jungle teenager asked someone to swing the balls in all directions. He took the bow and launched an arrow, striking one of the moving targets. On his second shot, he hit another coconut. He was definitely showing off.

Bowie just shook his head in disbelief. On his first three attempts, he managed to hit the same number of coconuts as he had girlfriends! The zero count for the Nez Perce was not embarrassing, as he knew he was up against an expert archer. Linda, Erin, Billy, and Kosy served as cheerleaders for the American, while Loretta, Shane, Bert and Harriet represented Jungle Boy.

The heavyweight wrestler asked for some pointers from his opposition, if he didn't mind. Turning more to the side, widening his stance, tilting the bow more, and adjusting his grip on the handle were the hints he received from the tribe member. His second attempt succeeded—he struck a coconut. His fans went wild, yelling and jumping around. The number of spectators grew, making a large circle, except at the place where the arrows were flying, of course.

The next challenge was a mango, which was about half the size of a coconut. Esterdo started with three arrows, and Bowie got four, to make it more evenly matched. It was called a jungle handicap. Smiling at all of his admirers, Jungle Boy hit two out of three. His cheering section was down a bit in total volume as one of them had five bananas in her mouth and one in each hand. Guess which cheerleader that was.

Bowie managed to hit one mango out of the four attempts he had. Personally, he thought that was very good, because he was sweating profusely and his jungle competition had not even broken a sweat yet. This gave the tribe member a definite advantage.

The last test was the most difficult, hitting a swinging banana. Bowie got five arrows. The cheers rose from the whole tribe when Esterdo hit just one banana out of four tries. The Nez Perce cheerleaders were making a lot of noise, just trying to hype up their hero for the competition. Bowie was fortunate to hit a banana with his fifth shot, so the last event ended in a tie.

They had to quit because a furry, redheaded anthropoid from the American group had eaten all of their targets!

Bowie was very thankful for the lessons and felt he had improved 100% in just a few hours of instruction and competition. The prized bow was ceremoniously hung back on its honored perch, just above Jungle Boy's bed. Esterdo thought Bowie didn't need any more teacher's time. Anyone who could hit even just ONE swinging banana was ready for every challenge that would come their way.

SEAL OF THE
STATE OF AMAZONAS

CHAPTER 7
Hunting Caimans

ANGRY BLACK CAIMAN

Linda McCarn wasn't used to this kind of self-denial. She suffered most from the primitive lifestyle. Sleeping in a hammock and under a mosquito net—never on her agenda. Why had she ever agreed to come along? She didn't know. Was she losing her ability to use common sense, to stay on easy street?

She snuck out of the hut at daybreak and went to the river's edge for fresh air and possibly a swim. It was their only way to shower. Using soap and shampoo in a river full of slimy creatures was not Linda's idea of daily hygiene. She never imagined agreeing to it. This cheerleader knew how to pamper herself, making this experience a complete reversal from her usual life.

The Oregonian knew she was breaking Esterdo's rule: NEVER GO TO THE RIVER BY YOURSELF. IT'S TOO DANGEROUS. ALWAYS TAKE SOMEONE TO WATCH FOR GATORS AND SNAKES. Rules, rules, and MORE rules tired her, especially from people who didn't know her. She felt old enough to make her own decisions, right or wrong. (This would be one of those WRONG times.)

As she sat on a rock, feet in the river, monkeys scampered from limb to limb, taking risky jumps. She had never seen them so excited. What made them run wild? They seemed to yell at her and threw bananas and manioc roots at her. She ducked a few. These monkeys were crazier than Harriet. Distracted by their antics, Linda failed to watch the river.

Suddenly, terror surged through her as the water rushed away in front of her and a huge anaconda clamped down on her left foot. Panic overwhelmed her as the creature yanked her toward the river, and she let out a scream—raw, desperate, and full of fear—that only amplified the chaos among the monkeys.

Bert, who had left the hut craving a moment of peace for his devotions, was startled into alarm by Linda's scream. Adrenaline surged, and dread gripped him as he saw her being dragged into the water. He couldn't make out the assailant—only that something terrible was unfolding before his eyes. Determination and fear collided as he realized her life was at risk, and rushed forward, resolute not to let her be harmed.

Bert carried his Bowie knife out of habit and was glad for it now. He pulled the large, sharp blade from its sheath and charged down the bank, jumping into the river without thought for his own safety. The water was up to his chest when he reached Linda. He grabbed her leg at the knee and lunged forward, throwing his weight onto the snake's head.

With his left hand gripping her leg, his right arm slammed the snake's head and slashed backward with the razor-sharp Bowie knife. The snake, thick as a basketball, endured several deep plunges before loosening its grip. Once it released Linda's foot, Bert kept hacking, finally severing its head from its long, muscular body.

When the head floated by, Bert was exhausted, feeling as if he had wrestled for six minutes straight. He sat on the bank, huffing to catch his breath. Linda, still terrified, rubbed her leg covered by teeth marks from the knee to the toes.

Horrified, she couldn't even muster a dramatic speech as usual. By then, Loretta had arrived, holding the cheerleader in her arms. Minutes later, the rest of the village, alerted by the commotion, gathered riverside.

Kosette stared at the scene with disbelief and agitation, anxiety prickling under her skin. "WOW, what in the world were you doing here by yourself, Linda? I'm only twelve years old, and even I know not to do something this risky." Her worry was evident, a mix of frustration and concern in her words.

Loretta motioned for Kosy to cool it. If Linda were to be scolded, it would have to wait until she was no longer in shock. Loretta would NOT forget to give the cheerleader a piece of her mind for being as dumb as dirt to risk both her life and drawing Bert into the fracas.

Kosette understood her mom's motion and agreed. It was wonderful to have a loving, respected mom to look up to. WONDERFUL INDEED. Loretta sat beside Linda, cleaning her wounds with a piece of her shirt sleeve.

The tribe members acted swiftly, plunging into the river to secure the snake's body before it drifted downstream. They kicked the grotesque head aside, unwilling to see it again. The jungle boys hauled the creature ashore and called for help. It was the largest anaconda they'd ever encountered; their eyes bulged in awe.

Roast snake appeared on the lunch and dinner menus—a rare treat. As Shane guessed, it was said to taste like chicken. Later, after Linda recovered, she grabbed Bert's hand and unleashed her signature theatrics. "My hero! You saved me from certain death! That giant reptile would've pulled me under, and I'd have drowned in minutes. Then he'd have swallowed me whole, taking a month to digest what was left. Friends in Lebanon would have mourned—well, at least three! I owe you everything!"

The more Erin heard these dramatic responses to Linda's traumatic experiences, the more she was convinced the cheerleader had spent too much time reading all the books of *Anne of Green Gables*. Honestly, no one could make it sound more theatrical than Linda could. She would have made an excellent actress; actually, maybe she already was one.

Batubo arrived after all the danger and hard work were over, his usual mode of operation (MO). He assessed the situation and was not at all happy. As far as he was concerned, the snake could have taken the Gringo girl downstream, and he would never have to see her again. He hated these

Americans. Everything they did made the simple tribe members admire them more.

This unusual bravery by the tall, handsome Bert was another nail in Batubo's coffin. The shaman could see his influence as the tribe's authoritative leader was waning. This made him more determined to destroy all these Americans, and the sooner the better, as far as he was concerned. It would have happened yesterday if he had had his way.

Hunting caimans (frequently called alligators or gators) is a nocturnal adventure. The tribe members wanted the Americans to have another experience they could write home to Mom about, so they added gator hunting to the night's agenda. Taking three canoes, the fifteen hunters left the shore after the sun's rays said goodbye to the tree tops. They had powerful flashlights to spotlight the critters, just like poachers did in Lacomb, Oregon, when they wanted to kill the elusive white-tailed deer out of season.

The hunters rowed upstream to where the huge lily pads were so thick they were hiding the surface of the water. Jungle Boy told Bowie to shine the flashlight on the shoreline, trying to locate the eyes that would reflect the beam. This is how poachers in Linn County would do it. The Nez Perce scanned the beach and immediately stopped when he spotted two sinister eyes gleaming back at him.

Bowie shouted excitedly, "There he is! We've got him. What now?"

The teenage tribe member asked, "Hows far aparted is his eyes? Like yous fist, Bowie?"

Everyone was mesmerized by the two wicked eyes glaring at them. The consensus was that Bowie could hold his fist between the eyes and not touch either one. Kosy wanted to know why Bowie would ever put his fist in front of a reptile that only wanted to bite it off.

Esterdo explained to everyone. If the distance between the eyes is as far apart as even Kosy's fist is wide, this would not be one they could even consider messing with—not if they wanted to keep all of their limbs intact. Erin mentioned she has always appreciated retaining all her appendages, which she has had since birth. "So, what's the next option?" she inquired. Linda agreed with her observation, declaring she had grown very fond of her arms and legs and had no intention of waving goodbye to any of them tonight.

Esterdo got the drift of their messages. In response to Kosy's question, Jungle Boy said the eyes could not be more than two fingers apart. A creature this small would ensure a pleasant experience for them rather than having to retrieve their arms and legs from a fast-moving, monster-sized, carnivorous predator.

It took them only five more minutes to find one that fit the bill. The canoe moved closer to the shore as the light beam focused on the eyes. This was a small gator. The "hunter" sits right behind the man with the light. When the boat gets alongside, the hunter swoops down with his hand and grips the reptile on the neck, right behind the eyes. The captured mini-beast is then pulled aboard so everyone can hold it.

Esterdo made sure everything was done right, so no one lost any fingers. They had to secure the animal behind its eyes with one hand and, with the other hand, grab its torso above the hind legs. After they ran out of 35mm film, they threw the lucky-duck creature back into the water. It unceremoniously swam away, thanking its lucky stars that these Gringos were the catch-and-release crew!

They returned to their hut, spent the night dreaming about pizza and swimming in a pool. The next day, after breakfast they began meandering around the area as they took in the new sights.

A caiman can run 11 miles per hour on a straight, flat surface. Normal humans can only run six miles per hour on the same ground. So, it's not a good idea to believe you can outrun a gator. This mistake may cost you a leg or two. The reptiles are not good at running uphill; humans have the advantage in this situation. The only problem is that the Amazon basin is not known for its elevation. In other words, there are NO hills to run up to get away from a toothy, hungry predator.

All the Gringos had been educated on jungle safety. One of the rules was never to go near a gator, especially not for a close-up photo. Billy was extremely careful in the jungle, ten times more than the rest of the Oregonians. This was for obvious reasons. His white cane was not much good out here because it didn't make any sound when it struck the soft Amazon soil. He could use it only to warn himself if he came upon a rock, log, or person on the ground in front of him.

All the villagers were aware of Billy's condition and kept a very close tab on him at all times. They could be heard yelling at him from all corners of the communal living area. They had set up a simple signal to warn him of obstacles in his path. It was the word "Billy," yes, his name. Only, they couldn't pronounce it correctly, and they ended up saying "Bullie." So, it was agreed on. If anyone saw him in danger of colliding with objects on the ground, they would yell it out, with all their lungs a-blasting.

It was a good setup. He had already been saved from what would have been several ugly tumbles. When he heard the BULLIE yell, he would stop dead in his tracks until someone came to his side and helped him around the object. Sometimes it was a log, a kid, a goat, a few chickens, a pig, or the campfire. He was getting used to their help and didn't show any displeasure. He was thankful they were so eager to assist him.

The blind grappler was walking with Edar, a tribe member. Both had just entered the large clearing at the north end of the village. When they were about 20 yards from the edge of the thick forest, a large black caiman divided the tall grass and headed straight for what he thought was an easy lunch.

The villagers at the other end of the clearing were screaming, "BULLIE, BUILLE," as they had promised they would when the Oregonian was in trouble.

The jungle teenager let out a yelp and grabbed Billy's hand. The wrestler didn't know what it was, but he definitely knew that running was the best solution. The two of them, hand in hand, would never outrun the gator; the Indian knew this. Therefore, with every intention of saving Billy's life, he turned him loose, yelling something the wrestler could not understand. Edar was watching Billy as he took off at "Mach speed" for wherever he thought was the opposite direction from whatever wanted to eat him.

Because of this distraction, the Indian didn't see the dead tree in front of him, which lay half-hidden in the tall grass. The jungle teenager tripped on the tree and fell face down in the grass. The gator lost sight of him. But that didn't keep the reptile from pursuing his other prey. Billy was running full speed towards the people yelling at him, assuming that was the best direction. Bowie entered the area. Using hand motions, he told the others to zip their lips. "Billy, turn to eleven o'clock and run faster."

The pint-sized wrestler understood perfectly what the Nez Perce was telling him to do. He threw down his white cane, angled slightly to the left, and put the pedal to the metal. His arms were going up and down like an oil rig pumps its precious liquid. Bowie yelled again, "Tree dead ahead, raise hands, grab limb, swing aboard. Count down to limb. One, two, THREE, GRAB."

Still running at breakneck speed, with raised arms, Billy followed Bowie's instructions to the letter. He felt the limb in his hands and swung upward with all his might. He felt something brush his boot as he lifted off. The gator had just missed his meal. Billy scampered onto the higher limbs and held on for dear life.

The villagers had already been running full speed for Billy, arms waving and spears in flight. The gator knew when he had been licked. It was his turn to be the hunted instead of the hunter. The hunter, turned hunted, did a 180° turn and lit off for the thick jungle brush. Even though he was faster than any of the tribe members, he was NOT faster than their spears. Pronto! More fresh meat for supper and more durable hide to make boots.

When Bowie and the villagers got to the base of the tree, they were amazed at how high the grappler had climbed. Marty gave him some instructions. "Hey there, Rocketman! Wow, you sure can run fast when you have a motive. Man, you must've been doing Olympic speed for the 100-yard dash with the gator on your heels!"

Billy was winded and a bit shaken as he started climbing down the tree. "I figured it must have been a gator, anacondas are not that fast, and nothing else is big enough to scare Edar that much. Carumba, he almost got my boot. Thanks for the help, Bowie. I would never have made it without your guiding voice."

Loretta and the girls had witnessed the whole ordeal and stood, stunned.

Everyone was backslapping and smiling except for Linda McCarn. She was fed up with this entire jungle experience. "When we're not running for our lives, we're being hunted for blood donations. This is a horrible place to live. LIVE? This isn't living. This is waking up at sunrise, running for your life all day, and fighting off bats and blood-sucking insects all night. Billy was almost toast. If it hadn't been for Bowie's quick thinking, he would've been mauled by that horrible reptile. That would have been an unspeakable tragedy of Shakespearean flavor. I, for one, am ready to leave this place where our lives are not worth a hill of beans, and our untimely deaths would add to the jungle food bank."

She was right, to a certain extent. The only difference is that she had no motive for staying. Patricia and Lori had been here for over 30 years. They had seen everything these Gringos had, but continually repeated over three long decades. The missionary ladies had survived. HOW? Because they were in God's hands and had guardian angels working overtime to preserve their lives. The ladies, as well as all of the Christians, knew they were immortal until their Creator and Savior were done with them, and their work on earth was over.

Loretta took note of Linda's words and decided to pray more for the cheerleader's salvation. When Loretta was alone with Erin and Kosette, she vented her feelings. "Linda isn't a Christian. She has no spiritual motivation to stay here. I'd have a difficult time adapting to this jungle life, but I'm certain God has chosen some very special children of His to come here, live here, and, if necessary, die here. They'll adapt and make a difference. Maybe He will even call someone from our group to make this sacrifice." Was she thinking of Erin or Kosette?

And the King shall answer and say unto them, Verily I say unto you, Inasmuch as ye have done it unto one of the least of these my brethren, ye have done it unto me. - Matthew 25:40

Patricia and Lori had been working in the jungle for a long time, making sure the tribes had some much needed medical help.

CHAPTER 8
Fishing for Piranhas

A piranha is a freshwater fish with razor-sharp interlocking teeth and powerful, bone-crushing jaws. They can be very dangerous when gathered together in large schools, called shoals, for protection.

The razor-toothed piranha is found only in the Amazon River but sometimes appears in aquariums, where a curious house cat might lose a paw and earn the name "Pegleg." Piranhas may also live in large public school aquariums, where mischievous students might feed them lab mice. Piranhas have been known to attack their own if wounded and bleeding. The smell of blood drives them into a frenzy, churning the water as if it's boiling. One drop of blood in a 200-quart tank turns them into a furious swarm seeking something to slice and dice.

There are 30 kinds of piranhas, all native to the Amazon River. Some have turned up in freshwater systems in the United States, China, Europe, and Africa only because owners, tired of feeding them meat and fearing an unexpected bite, flushed the predators down the toilet. Now these piranhas menace local waters and scare fishermen.

To move his cattle across a piranha-filled stream, an Amazon rancher sacrifices his sickest cow downstream and shoots it repeatedly. Blood fills the river, luring the piranhas away at once. They churn the water, stripping the cow until only bones remain—a chilling sight.

Matide, a chief from a tribe close to Esterdo's, was an expert fisherman. Even so, he was still capable of making a life-threatening mistake now and then. As his net snagged many piranhas and he threw them into his canoe, he spotted an enormous one. At that instant, a jungle cat tried to steal his catch. Matide threw his ax at it, and the cat scurried into the bush. Even for a veteran like Matide, this was a dangerous distraction.

Wanting to separate the extra-large piranha from the rest, which were normal size, he bit down on the piranha just past the eyes. He thought for sure he had killed it. The trapped piranha, wanting his liberty back, woke up and bit off the tip of Matide's tongue. The surprised fisherman spat out the attacker and took off running for the hut where Patricia and Lori were attending others. When the women saw him running full speed towards them with blood gushing out of his mouth, they couldn't even imagine what had caused it.

That didn't matter. If Patricia and Lori didn't stop the bleeding immediately, the unlucky Amazon fisherman would die in minutes. Patricia pulled Matide's tongue out and pinched the wound shut, while Lori stitched it with lightweight fishing line. Fortunately for Matide, these skilled medical assistants were good at procedures like these. Matide would sip soup for the next month, but he was saved to fish another day.

Fishing for piranhas was unlike anything the Oregonians had ever known. Worms and red devil spinners wouldn't work in the Amazon. Esterdo, the guide, explained, "To catchs da vicious piranha yous musk use red meat on da hook on dis bamboo poles. See dat da line is bery longe cause the piranha lives in deep vaters."

The girls were relieved they didn't have to work with a slimy, wiggling, uncooperative worm. Persuading a night crawler to give its life for humanity was never easy. Linda refused. "Imagine me fumbling with a wet, cold, nocturnal creature that won't cooperate. I shudder at the thought. It's as repulsive to me as it is to the worm. For me, it's an ordeal; for the worm, it's last rites. Curtains for him, or her. Whatever."

Esterdo explained that the next step in catching piranhas was to slap the water with the tip of the bamboo pole. This gets their attention. When the Gringos did this, the razor-toothed fish advanced en masse. The rest of the Amazon fishing ordeal was much like hooking a rainbow trout in Crabtree Creek.

Piranhas nibbled the raw meat. The fisherman jerked the pole to set the hook. They averaged a little bit wider than tennis-shoe size and, being small, most went straight into the campfire pot.

Once the Gringos had filled a few buckets with piranhas for the cooks, Esterdo decided to take a sack to the adjoining tribe, where his girlfriend Talita lived. He had been friends with her since they were kids. He wanted the Americans to meet his special friend, as he called her, and seemed very excited about this visit.

Leaving early as usual, they explored the jungle between villages. Jungle Boy, their guide, said, "Here are trees ve used to send messages. Tribe members beat da trunks vich stiks. Listen—dis is a message to my moder." He beat out a message; the echo was obvious.

They asked what the message was. He replied that it was a request for his favorite piranha soup when he returned. Kosy joked it was jungle Morse code and wondered whether anyone else could hear—a fair assumption.

But hearing isn't the same as understanding. Messages sent by Amazonian tribes are drummed on special tree trunks or logs (known as manguaré, "slit drum" in English). The messages are usually unique to each tribe. The drum codes are like a language or dialect. Expert percussionists of these "talking drums" try to mimic tones, rhythms, and key syllables of their specific spoken language.

The Natubi tribe was bigger in number than Esterdo's was. The Americans arrived there around noon, just in time to have some anaconda barbecue. The snake was about as big around as a basketball, spinning on a short iron bar that someone was turning slowly. None of the Americans knew if they really wanted to try this. Linda said it seemed a bit strange to be eating something that, if given the chance, would have eaten her! "I suppose it's just the survival of the fittest, as we have always been told. But I think I'll pass this time."

Bowie reminded her that the same scenario was possible when someone eats bear meat. "An Oregon brown bear will chomp on you, too, if you give it a chance." That didn't change her mind as she said bear meat had never touched her lips, and probably never would.

Erin, the only girl willing, asked for a piece. She tried it, masked her reaction, and declared, "It does taste just like chicken! Here, Loretta, try it, you'll like it."

The wrestler's mom agreed with Erin, so Loretta gave Kosette a small portion. "Try it, Daughter—it's as good as Kentucky Fried Chicken."

Talita was dressed in her tribal clothes, beads, and all. She was not wearing any objects having to do with Spiritism, duly noted by both Marty and Bert. The Farnsworth wrestler mentioned it to the rest of the Gringos. "I think it's interesting that Talita is not wearing anything to do with her tribe's spiritual beliefs. Maybe we should talk to her about that."

There was a pow-wow in the medical hut—Americans and one lovely, beautifully dressed Amazonian Indian princess, the chief's daughter. Kosy asked about her tribal dress. She was delighted to answer all of them. "I am so happys dat you liked my tradition dress. We takes gret proud in ours heritage."

Billy began with the intended main topic of the meeting, "We noticed you're not wearing anything linked to Spiritism—no religious beads or headdress. Can you tell us why?" Billy was always a gentleman.

Her warm smile made everyone feel at ease. "I ams glad yu asks. I has ben listened to vat Patricia and Lori haved ben saying in da meeting at da Jesus hut. I has reded a lots of da Bible, vat yus called The Vord of God. Last month, I asked this Jesus to comes into my hearts and saved me. He did dat and nuw I ams a differen perskon. I supposed all of yus new vat I ams talked abut, right?"

Now it was the Gringos' turn to smile. This was wonderful. A real jewel in the crown of a soul winner that Patricia and Lori would be able to lay at the feet of Jesus, as it says in Revelation.

Suddenly, the Princess had a dramatic change in her facial expression. Kosy was the first one to note it. "Is something bothering you, Talita? Can we do anything for you?" The twelve year old was very tenderhearted. Loretta noted it and was extremely proud of her daughter.

Talita continued her conversation, only this time she was not smiling. "I has know Esterdo for manys year. Ve has been friends for long times. I always taught ve vould sleep in da same hammock (this was their slang for getting married). But knows I am a followers of Jesus an he is note. Dis bother me a lots. I do not nows hows to do it all now."

Bert was impressed with her determination to follow Christ. He decided to mention Billy when he spoke to her. "Talita, you have a right to be concerned. Hitching up with someone who is not a Christian would be a terrible mistake. Billy accepted Christ and was immediately thrown out of his own home. The path of a true follower of Jesus is sometimes difficult to travel, but for someone who loves Him dearly and puts His interests first, there's NO other logical and spiritual path to take. God the Father, Christ the Son, and the Holy Spirit are all expecting 100% surrender to Them and Their will for your life.

"You remind me of a Bible verse. Proverbs 20:11 says, 'Even a child is known by his doings, whether his work be pure, and wether it be right.' We'll be praying for you and for Esterdo. You can put that in your canoe and paddle up stream with it."

Marty was listening with both ears fully attentive. He noted the dramatic statement to the Indian princess. This is the Engelbert Farnsworth III, whom he hoped to discover on this trip. A re-vote today to include Bert as a full-fledged member of their group would be 7 in favor and 0 against. Marty was duly impressed and told Bert that before they left the village.

When a rancher moved his herd across the river, he would sacrifice a sick cow downstream to keep piranhas away from his good ones.

> **AUTHOR NOTE**
>
> *The Nile River is 156 miles longer than the Amazon River but the Brazilian one holds the title for the largest volume of water discharged.*

Since Esterdo's birth, he had lived in a hut with his parents. But recently, Esterdo wanted his privacy, so he moved into his own smaller hut close by.

CHAPTER 9
Jungle Wrestling Tournament

Amazonian wrestling is not the same kind of sport as most of the rest of the world. Competitions are usually organized to settle tribal disputes; a much better option than going to war.

Fishing rights for the Jatuba River were brewing a storm between the four villages. Deciding who could use the river was always contentious. Having or lacking those rights mattered, especially if fish numbers were low at some point during the season.

Each village wanted the river, which flowed through all four. The tribe with the upper part got the best fish and game. Normally, they took turns, each tribe claiming the upper river for 90 moons—about three months.

Lately, squabbles at the riverbank have erupted too often.

Two tribes without upper river rights were still sending fishermen there. Since the government didn't have fishing wardens, as Oregon did, enforcing the tribal council's decisions was not easy. Something else had to be done. This plan was not working worth a hoot.

The shaman appointed the supposed chief of all the villages. This particular shaman, Batubo, was about as crooked as a dog's hind leg, or as they say here, as crooked as a boar's hind leg. Batubo, driven by personal gain, used his political and spiritual authority to manipulate decisions. No one could depend on him to make a fair and simple ruling. His greed motivated him, making him vulnerable to bribes. So, even though the council made the decision, his deeply corrupt involvement in all their affairs gave the fishing rights to whoever could arrange a deal that was in HIS best interest.

The villagers, normally very calm, were running out of patience and wanted another way to decide who got the coveted upper-river rights. Their frustration with ongoing disputes drove them to seek change. They finally put their painted faces together and decided to have a wrestling contest each year. The village that won would control the rights for the whole year. If they kept winning year after year, they could defer their rights to another village. Yeah, like that was ever going to happen! This involved a life-sustaining food supply chain, not whose turn it was to bring snacks to the next meeting.

The sporting event was scheduled two days following the unanimous agreement to the plan. Jungle Boy wanted to know if the Oregon grapplers would wrestle for his tribe. The standard rule was: anyone living in the village at the time of the contest could participate. All the high school students in Brazil on the Lebanon High School Warriors wrestling team were interested, including Billy.

This was going to be a grand event, attended by most residents of all four villages. The wrestling meet was to be in Esterdo's village because they had the best grass field to fall on. No one wanted hard or rocky ground.

The American wrestlers asked about the rules, the referee, and the match length. Esterdo tried not to laugh; he thought it would be insulting. Therefore, he just snickered a little to himself, but the whole group duly noted it. Shane put his hand on Jungle Boy's shoulder. "What's so funny? Did we say something comical? We don't want to be left out, fill us in." The Oregon grappler hoped it was not bad news he was about to hear.

The teenage Indian tried to be serious. "Yu ark very funnys. Der ark no rules cept can no bite vith teeth and can no pull har. Der is no judges, no ned one, cause each fights go util sombodi gived ups, gets back held to gras, or is like Patricas say 'out freezing'." (He meant 'out cold' but most of them understood that).

Bert, who liked standard procedures, asked, "When will it end? What do I have to do to win?" Esterdo, his smile obvious to all, replied, "Bert da terd, yu arek no a comic book, no can be. But yu ark funnys. For yors sake, I wils repeat myself. To wins yu halfs to put da utter perskons back on da grass or he halfs to cry outs, BAUMO which mens 'I quits' or he is kocke out, do yu understoods?"

Apparently, it was like a tap-out sport, as in some martial arts. If you're in pain or risk injury, you tap or yell, and the referee stops the match. It would be an interesting experience for the Lebanon Warriors. They just hoped they wouldn't have to tap out from too much pain.

Jungle Boy wanted to know if the blind kid would wrestle, thinking it unfair. They assured him Billy could take care of himself. Marty added, "He's our best wrestler. We'll ask to start the match holding hands."

Before the competition began, Bottee Mattee—the elected representative for all Amazon tribes—was introduced. He had just returned from the capital and stopped by to see the much-advertised meet. It was big news: GRINGOS JOIN RIVER DISPUTE WRESTLING TOURNAMENT.

Since many Amazon Indians would be at Esterdo's village, the governor decided to try mending fences after refusing to receive Bottee Mattee at the capital. The governor only accepted visitors who wore a three-piece suit, so he had one waiting in the hotel room. Bottee Mattee, who wore only a loincloth his entire life, refused to put on the suit, stormed out of the hotel, and returned back home, angry about the situation.

By council law, a governor's visit required an invitation from Bottee Mattee to enter Indian territory. The rep sent a message: Raposo must wait for a gift to signal an invitation. The governor eagerly awaited it, thinking it meant goodwill. He believed the Indians held no grudge, and maybe he'd misjudged them.

The gift was delivered. On the box was a note, in perfect Portuguese: "When you find the courage to wear this outfit, we will meet with you here." All five council members signed it.

He opened the box, jerked back, and dropped the gift—a skimpy, beaded loincloth. There was no meeting. Government officials had egg on their faces; the Indians smiled. It was Amazon karma—revenge for the "insignificant people"!

With political preliminaries over, the tournament began. The Gringos had five wrestlers—Shane, Marty, Bowie, Bert, and Billy—and Esterdo's tribe had five, including Jungle Boy. They had a full team. Ten grapplers would represent each tribe during competition.

There would be no weighing or height matching. The leaders did their best to pair wrestlers close in weight.

Bowie got the first match. His opponent looked about 20 pounds lighter. But, the Nez Perce had dealt with men like this before—strong as oxen, with cable strength from constant activity. It wasn't visible, but they would grab on and grip you until they got a pin.

The Indian circled and grabbed, knowing nothing of speed or single-leg takedowns. Bowie used this to his advantage, flattening his opponent to the grass in two minutes.

Marty didn't have it so easy. His opponent was at least 20 pounds heavier than he was; it was a struggle, with lots of pushing and shoving, panting and whizzing. Finally, the Indian caught the American off guard and threw him on his back. The Lacomb wrestler couldn't escape, and the match was over.

Bert was matched in weight, but his opponent was six inches shorter, giving Bert the advantage. When grabbed by the leg, Bert sprawled, landed on the Indian's back, flattening him to the ground, and finished the bout with a quick 180° spin and a half-nelson, pinning his opponent.

Shane's opponent had a 10-pound advantage, but Shane was stronger, especially up top. The jungle wrestler, a fast learner, attempted a single-leg takedown, but Shane countered. He underhooked and flipped him in one smooth movement—winning in 46 seconds, the fastest time ever recorded in a tournament like this.

Now came the awaited match: Blind Billy against their best wrestler. Weight and height were roughly even. Billy would start with their hands together—a style foreign to the Amazonian, but he agreed.

When someone whistled, the battle began. Billy threw the Indian's right arm in the air and did a duck under move so fast the jungle wrestler was stunned. He thought they would just waltz around a little first, holding hands until the blind Gringo got his bearings. Billy, on the other hand, knew if he didn't strike like lightning, it would be curtains for him. Billy was behind the Indian, with his left arm trapped in a vice-like grip around his waist. After a one-second adjustment, three seconds into the match, Billy launched the dazed champion wrestler overhead in a perfectly executed rear suplex; the poor man never knew what hit him. WHAMO, the match was over. They had grossly underestimated Billy, as many uninformed folks did. Oh, by the way, the officials had already entered Shane's 46-second win in the record book. Nobody could have anticipated Billy's RECORD SHATTERING 8-second victory. It's a good thing the officials used a pencil instead of a pen.

Two of the tribes tied for first place. There would have to be another match. Loretta suggested they challenge the other tribe to try to knock Harriet off her feet. If three wrestlers could not take her down in one minute, they lost. The adversaries got their headbands together. Everyone supposed it would be easy. They came to this unfortunate conclusion because they had no experience with monkeys this big. They had no idea what a mistake that assumption would prove to be!

The ape had already played this game at Marty's house, in the wrestling room, against four of them. She knew what to do. The Indians attacked her from three different sides. She swept two of them off their feet with a swinging blow from each long arm. They didn't even get close to her. The third was held at bay with one foot until an arm was free, and then he went flying north towards the river.

The jungle wrestlers thought it was the better part of valor to surrender now, while they still had all their body parts intact. It was a wise decision on their part. All the Oregonians and Jungle Boy rushed to the red-haired anthropoid and raised both of her hands in a victory sign.

The ape looked happy, too. She knew by experience that when the humans got this animated, more bananas would be coming down the food elevator for her, and maybe they would throw in a few huge cockroaches for dessert.

The best river fishing area would go to Esterdo's tribe for the entire year. This made Jungle Boy very happy. His American friends had done something very valuable for his tribe, and he would never forget it, nor would he let his people forget it. The tribe members gathered around the ape and began whooping and hollering to beat the band. They were so happy and proud of the Gringos.

BUT, this didn't sit well with Batubo. He was more interested in his control over the tribes than in their well-being. He wanted to humiliate the

Gringos not elevate them to the status of local heroes. This wrestling stuff was a bad idea. He didn't give a lick about their fishing rights, never did. He got his funding by extorting and threatening victimized and innocent souls. He was really hot under the collar now, actually, it would be more accurate to say "hot under the neck beads." He was about to turn GREEN.

As leader of the village, the shaman settles disputes, punishes those who don't follow the rules, and passes on infomation or guidance. Batubo had many chats with the tribe. Everyone was required to be present.

CHAPTER 10
Jungle Evangelism

Kosy became close friends with the village children.

Sneaking around behind the shaman's back had become a habit, but it was not easy. So far, Batubo had not noticed changes in his son's behavior. The once-cruel and powerful man was losing his grip on authority in the tribal area. He blamed this on the arrival and continued presence of the Gringos. To him, they were a bad influence, weakening his importance.

He had a plan, a sinister plot to make the Gringos look bad and regain his son's trust. He also wanted to win back his wife and other members of his tribe. His plot involved his son's prized possession—the handcrafted bow from his great-grandfather. It hung above his cot like a Van Gogh or Picasso.

It had never been used, only admired. He was sure his son would never use it like a common bow. (He would really be hot under the beads if he knew it had just been used while he was out of the village and there would be an atom bomb explosion if Batubo ever found it that was to honor Bowie because he was also an Indian.) Batubo was very upset by the latest wrestling tournament results. No one in the tribe would mention it to him. They valued the few teeth they had and wanted to keep them, if possible.

The next Gringo group discussion was set for 4:00 in the morning. That was an hour and a half before the sun rose. Batubo and his wife would not be up that early, they were still in their hammocks above the hard dirt floor.

The Oregonians rubbed the sleep from their eyes and gathered for prayer before Esterdo stumbled into their hut. Carrying his spiritual beads, he approached with questions about these artifacts. Bowie began, "Let's start at the beginning, friend. God—Jehovah, worshipped by Jewish and Christian people—made the heavens and the earth. He is the creator of everything we see. Does this make sense to you?"

Esterdo replied, "Yes, I understoods, but hows does ve knos dis is true? Our peoples believes dat da spirits mad all dis and da spirits helps us, sometimes, and uddertimes day hurts us."

Billy jumped in feet first and responded, "Okay, friend, then who made the spirits? Someone has to have started it all, the whole creation. The Word of God is very clear that He is the Creator and the Sustainer of all living things, plants, animals, and humans. We believe the Bible, and there's no reason to believe all we see came from any other source or process of growth, that some call evolution."

Esterdo raised his eyebrows until they disappeared under the bangs of his jet black hair. He asked, "I has herds of dis nice story before. Patricias tolds me abut it, verly interlesting. But whys does you belives da Bible is God's writtun pages?"

Marty started his part of the lesson, answering, "There are many religious books in this world. BUT, no book has any prophecy, not one book and not one prophecy. The Bible has over 4,000 prophecies. Already 2,500 have been fulfilled; we still have 1,500 that are yet to come to pass. Jesus told his followers what would happen, so when it did, they would believe in him. He told them the rulers would try him, beat him, and then crucify him. He also told them three times that He would rise from the dead three days after He was killed. And all this happened just like he said it would."

"Dis is all verily interlesting. But hows do we nos He was da Son of God. Vhat is da proof dat no ones can says is a lie? Der is manys liars in da vorld, dis I nos for certainly." Esterdo pressed further, looking for evidence.

Shane added his part to the before-sunrise lesson, explaining, "Jesus performed many miracles to prove He was God's Son. He healed many sick people, walked on water, changed water to wine, calmed a raging storm, fed 5,000 people from two fish and a few pieces of bread, he raised some people from the dead, and most important of all, HE WAS RAISED FROM THE DEAD, just like He said would happen."

Esterdo was duly impressed. He wanted to know who Jesus' parents were. Bowie explained, "Over 1,000 years before he was born, a prophecy said where and how he would be born—through a pure virgin. Many prophecies described his life and death. He would be rejected by men and crucified between two criminals, but not a bone of his body would be broken. He would be buried in a rich man's tomb. He is alive today, sending missionaries worldwide to share this wonderful, true story."

Jungle Boy shook his head in amazement. "Dis is a goods stories but what doz dis has to do vith me. Is der someting elses to da stories dat yu has no tolds me yet?" Esterdo asked, looking curious.

Billy took over the witnessing and said, "This was not an ordinary man. He had no earthly father. God was his father. Mary was his mother. God made her with child. The child was born a perfect man. This is important. We need a perfect man to be sacrificed so we can be saved. Jesus Christ was a perfect man. He died for us and paid for our sins before a Holy God. Do you know what sin is, Esterdo?"

"Da ladies Patricias and Lorie tolds me. Sin is wens we do nots obeyed God's laws. We sin wens we lies or steals. We sin wens we kills. I has no killed anyone. But I has lied and I has stealed. Day tolds me I neds to asks Jesus in my hearts to has my sins forgived. Is dis whats yu belefes, too?" Esterdo asked, looking hopeful.

Back to Bowie. "It is not just what we believe. Our opinions are not worth a pile of bananas, if you know what I mean. We must read and study God's Word to know what He wants us to know about Him and His Son. That's how we can have eternal life. He offers it as a free gift if we put our faith in Him and ask Him into our hearts. This is called being 'born again' or 'saved.' Have you ever heard these terms?" Bowie asked, emphasizing the point.

It was getting light, and his parents would soon be falling out of their hammocks. He needed to get back before they did. "I ded heard diz words befores. Patrictas tolds dem to me a few time. I wants to nos more about dis. I vell comes back tomorrow, OK?" Esterdo said, making his plan to return clear.

That was fine with the Gringos. They bid him goodbye, and all of them crawled back into their hammocks to return to never-never land.

There were only a few days left until the Albatross would depart, and their Amazon adventure would become history. There were still a few things to do. The boys wanted to kill a wild boar. All the girls wanted to paint the fingernails of the girls and ladies in the tribe. Everyone began making plans.

The guides for the boar hunt would be Esterdo and his uncle Ratnele. Ratnele was the best at finding boars and the most accurate with a spear. It was tough for a hunter to take down a wild boar with an arrow while he was making tracks to get away from the on-coming, well-tusked fury. They carried bows but relied more on long poles with steel tips. They traded fresh pork for these tips at a store downriver, about two miles away.

Most villagers were still asleep, counting bananas as they flew over jungle bushes. Esterdo didn't want to wake his parents, so he hung his hammock outside the Gringos' hut. He watched the ape try to balance on flimsy limbs above the hut. She did well despite her large size. He didn't hang his hammock directly below her, just in case she slipped off the limbs at night.

Harriet was not invited to join the hunt, she stayed to guard the banana trees in front of the huts. She wasn't upset about being left behind. Instead, she entertained herself by throwing bananas at monkeys swinging in the foliage at the edge of the camp.

To hunt the wild boar, you have to outsmart it. Boars hid in mudflats and bushes during the heat of the day. That made it a bad time to try bringing home the bacon. Early birds may get the worm, but early hunters get the boar. Ratnele convinced them to get up at 4:00 a.m. and leave camp early. Bert was not used to this life. "Man, you have to get up before breakfast just to hunt for breakfast." He hoped to bring something back to eat.

Camp trails were well-worn, for obvious reasons, but the wild boars avoided them. Taking the usual paths led to fewer boars. Instead of following human paths, the boars chose to hide in wild areas where snakes and poisonous frogs lived.

Morning fog hovered over the treetops. It was really just thick humidity. The temperature never dropped below 80° in this part of the equatorial jungle. No one here knew what it was like to be cold. They never had numb fingers or toes from bad weather. They never scraped ice off canoes or chipped ice from the river.

They packed dried fish and cornbread to avoid empty stomachs. Billy decided to stay behind, so he rested in the red hammock above the dirt floor. Hammocks were a smart idea. Crawling things had a harder time reaching you that way.

But mosquitoes still got through. Sometimes, tarantulas would fall from the straw ceiling. To prevent this, the locals always hung a net over each hammock while they were sleeping in it. The blood-suckers would gather outside the net. With over 100 trying to get in, their steady hum could put you to sleep. Billy heard them better than the others. He even had nightmares about them using nose extensions, like in a Craftsman socket set, to reach him, no matter how he crouched in the hammock.

The smarter, more experienced mosquitoes would even attack from the bottom of the hammock. Their long, sharp, straw-like beaks could actually pass through the hammock, and one would be scratching all day where the sun did not shine. The only way to prevent this was to put a layer of plastic under you, so you could sleep and visit the sauna all night long. It was a lose-lose situation. You lost sleep and lost weight at the same time. If you didn't take any of these preventative measures, it was still a lose-lose situation. You still lost sleep and lost blood to the local insect blood bank.

The mosquito bites were different here. It seemed like these mean Amazon insects wanted some kind of revenge for being hatched here. They would hunt you down and suck your blood, making you miserable for days, scratching and putting mud packs on--at least that was the remedy here. The Oregonians were prime targets, and those with a warm body would be singled out, while the fortunate ones with a cold body would get a pass.

Back to boar hunting. After cutting their way through the foliage, the hunting party came to a clearing, about the size of a baseball field. Jungle Boy saw it first. Across the way, he spotted a boar about the size of a small calf or a big dog. It was enough to feed his whole village for one enormous meal.

Bowie strung the bow, but Esterdo put his hand on the shoulder of the Nez Perce. "Don'ts shoot naw, he is too long away. Da arrow not kill him, wust makes he mad. We neds to get him to come overs here, so I cans killed him wis dis spear. Den he wills be really dead, as you say, 'deader dan a doorlatch'." He got it wrong, but no one had the guts to correct him because he had the spear in his hand.

Jungle Boy hunched down in the grass, hiding his head. The others followed suit. He started making noises with his nose and throat. They were weird whistles and snorts. The grapplers weren't sure this would work, but they had some trust in this kid's abilities; after all, he had lived his whole life here. He should know what he was doing, shouldn't he? You would think so, wouldn't you?

Well, it didn't turn out as they had originally planned. The huge boar wasn't alone. He had three sows with him and some piglets. This was not a good recipe for a happy ending. The boar thought these humans were going to harm his herd, and that gave him a very dark and dangerous attitude.

He charged the group, bellowing and snorting. His fangs were aimed right at their leader, Esterdo. He wasn't worried. He had seen this attack tactic before. They all had the same agenda: make a lot of noise, snort up a storm, and charge at the intruders with the intent to cause bodily harm.

Jungle Boy stood up and drew back his spear with the intention of causing bodily harm to the attacker. Just as he was about to launch the death-dealing blow, a parrot came out of nowhere and landed on the spear. Apparently, the feathered friend thought the spear was a limb. Perhaps its eyesight had been waning in the last year, or it was just plain stupid. Whatever the reason, the spear took a dive and missed the boar by a few yards.

It was every man, boy, and coward for himself now. Luckily, Billy was not with them. They scattered, each one according to his best ability. The boar couldn't chase all of them at the same time, so he chose the smallest one, which was Shane. "Yewoh, he's after me." He thought it would be better to save his breath for running, not for complaining.

Noticing a low-hanging limb, he leaped and caught it, swinging higher than the boar could reach. The only problem was—the limb was rotten. Shane came crashing back to earth as fast as he had swung up. The only difference was that now he found himself riding bareback on an angry boar, running at full speed. There was nothing to grab, like there was during bull riding at the rodeo. He wasn't even going to stay on eight seconds, like Bowie had to do to win.

The boar was so angry about the weight on his back he was jerking his tusks back and forth, trying to hook Shane and throw him off. The grappler noticed another low-hanging limb. He caught it under both of his armpits and swung aboard, securing his safety on the stronger limb.

Unfortunately for the jungle swine, when Shane finally exited, the boar didn't have time to recover. It plowed full speed into the soft-barked tree directly in front of him, burying its tusks into its trunk. Now he was stuck. He tried to shake himself loose but was not strong enough.

Esterdo, knowing he had very little time, rushed to the boar and put him out of commission, which means he speared the pig right through the heart, and it flopped over "dead as a door latch," as Jungle Boy had said before.

Esterdo aims his spear at a wild boar as Bowie Pinetree looks on, rooting for his dinner to be obtained.

82

Esterdo roasts the boar while Marty, Erin, and Billy chat with some of the villagers

CHAPTER 11
Caiman Attack

This scarry-looking critter is a black caiman, an apex predator. It's one of six caiman species around the Amazon River. It's a close relative of the alligator, but there are no true alligators in the Amazon Basin. However, sometimes I'll refer to the animal as an alligator or gator, since that's what many of the locals call it.

There was great rejoicing as the hunting party triumphantly marched into the village, carrying on a stout pole, the biggest wild boar anyone from their tribe had ever seen. It felt like only a few minutes had passed before the boar started turning on a rotisserie over a well-watched fire for the rest of the afternoon. The dinner was more than anyone had imagined. It fed the whole village, just as Esterdo said it would.

The shaman knew he had to move quickly. The Gringos were becoming more popular each day. He set his plan in motion, getting someone from a distant tribe to do his bidding. The shaman threatened to curse him if he disobeyed. Only three days remained until the Gringos left. The shaman had to act tonight.

While everyone was satisfied after the meal, darkness fell quickly and finally. The day was done, and everyone went to their huts for last-minute preparations before resting for the night.

Meanwhile, in the Gringos' hut, always the last to blow out their candles, they had prayed for some eternal results before they had to leave in two days. The girls were praying for everyone in their hut. Linda, however, was only biding her time until she could get back to civilization.

When Batubo believed everyone in the camp was asleep, he sent his henchman to execute the plan. The accomplice took the valuable bow off the rack, walked purposefully to the Gringos' hut, and attempted to slide it under the cloth door—setting up the Christians as supposed thieves and hypocrites, just as the shaman planned. Batubo was convinced this would ruin their reputations and cause the whole tribe to turn against them.

There was a big problem with this plan. The cruel and powerful spiritual leader of his unfortunate people forgot to inform his henchman that not all of the Gringos' group were sleeping in the hut. There was one more who slept outside, for various reasons; no one needed to explain to anyone with a lick of common sense.

Just as the unsuspecting stooge was about to complete what he thought was a perfect crime, by pushing the bow under the cloth door, a huge thing came crashing down on him, pinning the poor victim to the ground, with the treasured bow under him. Needless to say, pandemonium ruled the darkness. Everyone rushed out of their huts to investigate the commotion.

It was a striking sight. Harriet, with her red hair, sat atop the stranger, easily holding him in place by her weight, appearing calm, with three bananas in her mouth and one in each hand. She seemed content to stay there, perhaps finding it more comfortable than her usual resting spot on tree limbs over the past ten days.

When Esterdo arrived at the scene, he was not only surprised but also extremely upset. Who was this stranger lying on top of his precious bow? Bowie tapped the ape's arm and gestured for her to follow him. He was waving a banana in front of her to give her some incentive. As soon as Harriett stood up, Batubo's blackmailed victim jumped to his feet and scurried into the jungle.

The prized possession was safe. Esterdo thanked the whole group of Gringos for the return of his most precious bow. Everyone was so happy the bow was undamaged and secure; they gave no thought to the man who was the source of all this commotion.

The furious shaman was pacing restlessly in his hut, clearly frustrated that his entire plan had backfired. Rather than causing the village to turn against the Gringos, the people now wanted to honor them. He was unable to sleep, agitated and alone with his thoughts.

Esterdo couldn't understand all of this, so, as before, he hung his hammock in the Gringo's hut for additional support and protection.

The next day dawned, bringing with it the familiar chatter of jungle birds. Shifting to a new activity, Esterdo planned to demonstrate his fishing skills, honed since his childhood. He invited all the Gringos to join him at the river so they could watch him spear a caiman, an event he had succeeded at many times before.

The grapplers thought this was a bad idea and said so. But Esterdo was in a good mood. He didn't think he needed advice from amateurs. They didn't know what it was like to spend a lifetime in the jungle. He also felt lucky. That's why he wore the cowboy boots Bowie had given him. They were a little big, but he didn't mind. He liked how they looked.

The Oregonians, taken aback by Esterdo's change in attitude, recognized the risk he was courting. Bowie asked permission to retrieve a bow from Jungle Boy's hut, and Esterdo agreed, seeing no threat to his own plan for the day.

Bert, Marty, and Shane went into their hut to grab their Bowie knives. These knives had nothing to do with the Nez Perce, but everything to do with Jim Bowie, who was a frontiersman who died at the Alamo. The group felt armed and ready for danger. The ladies waited at the water's edge, praying nothing would go wrong.

Esterdo entered the river up to the top of his boots. He started slapping the water with his palm. The Gringos were convinced this was a bad idea. They knew it could attract huge gators. But Esterdo wanted to show everyone how good he was at facing the jungle's most feared reptile.

Something was coming around the bend in the river. It was approaching rapidly, maybe more than Esterdo had thought possible. He drew back the spear and waited for the exact moment to launch it. But just as he let the spear fly, the gator took a deep dive. It was huge, more than anyone wanted to face, ever!

The large black caiman swept Esterdo off his feet and bit down on his Oregon cowboy boots, trapping him. A gator grabs its prey and twists until the victim is underwater and can't breathe. It keeps twisting as it dives deeper. Usually, this means the end for any creature caught in the gator's strong jaws. The muscles that close the mouth are ten times stronger than those that open it. Its jaws are filled with massive teeth.

Bowie had already guessed they were in trouble when the caiman rounded the bend. He had an arrow in the bow. Drawing back, he made his first shot count. It hit the gator right below his right eye. This stunned it for a few seconds, but didn't stop it from diving and grabbing Jungle Boy. The twisting couple was now in water up to Bowie's waist.

Bert, Marty, and Shane jumped into the river to help. They saw the gator had Esterdo underwater. Jungle Boy had little time left. He was likely holding his breath, but it wouldn't last much longer. All three grapplers lunged at the caiman, stabbing and ripping at whatever they could reach. The water turned blood red. They hoped it wasn't their own.

Multiple, deep stab wounds took their toll on the gator. Still, it looked like he might drown the kid. Loretta jumped in front of the gator and grabbed Esterdo's hands. She screamed at him as he surfaced. "Hold on to me." She pulled; the gator twisted and pulled; the grapplers kept stabbing. No one wanted to see a sight like this in a lifetime.

Finally, after more time than anyone thought Esterdo could survive, the gator must have felt it wasn't worth his life to continue the fight. He released his fortunate prey and swam away, probably to die later from all the wounds he had received from humans who hated his rotten hide.

Loretta grabbed Esterdo and began mouth-to-mouth resuscitation. The water was still thick with gator blood, making the experience unpleasant.

When Jungle Boy started to spit up red water, everyone sighed in relief. He was safe. The rescue of such a soul is very rare once the beast has started its "death roll." Everyone had to do their part for the jungle teenager to be saved from a horrible death.

Linda rested her forehead on her hand. "What a rescue! It was uncertain for a long time. Every minute felt stretched into an hour. WOW! This is the stuff they write books about. I think I'll write to *National Geographic* about it. I can imagine the magnitude of terror in one's soul to be thrashed about so and almost drowned, only a hair's breadth away from being eaten alive. It almost happened to me when the horrible, slimy anaconda grabbed my foot." She almost fainted from the stress. But, if she had fainted, she wouldn't have been able to complete her soliloquy: "Never, EVER, before in my entire life have I seen or experienced terrifying events such as these horrific happenings."

Back in the village, as the ordeal began, the cruel and powerful shaman, Batubo, was forced to watch in horror as his only son was thrashed about in the throes of a life-and-death struggle with the jungle's most ferocious and feared reptile. The beast was so huge. Batubo knew it was partly Esterdo's own fault—being so proud, even calling the gator out for battle—he couldn't help but see Esterdo as a kid who needed more training. Esterdo was 18, a man by the village's standards, but in Batubo's eyes, he would be a child for quite a while.

After the chaos had ended, Batubo returned to his hut. Ashamed of his actions, he reflected on how he tried to frame the Gringos with the precious bow and sought to turn the other villages against them. Now, contemplating his dire situation, he remained focused on his own choices and their consequences.

He was estranged from his wife and had been ever since he started the training of his son to be the cruel and powerful man to take his place. He had alienated his son by trying to make him into a person he never wanted to be. He had deceived many people into doing his bidding. He used threats and curses to get what he wanted, at any cost. What had all this work accomplished? NOTHING! Absolutely nothing of any lasting value. He was feared by his own people when he really should have been serving them. His own family despised him. His wife didn't even like him. He had even made an enemy of their only son.

He was heading toward his grave lonely, unhappy, and hated. No one would miss him when he was gone, not one bit. This disturbed him greatly. He didn't start this way. He remembered his happy, carefree childhood. What was the turning point in his life? When did he begin to become the person his tribe members feared and hated? What happened? Was there really an answer? Could he actually pinpoint the change of direction to this path of destruction?

He was doing a lot of soul searching. He wanted answers. Looking back on his whole life, he finally concluded there was an awful turning point that caused him to morph into the cruel and powerful man he was, but had not planned to be. That turning point was now clear in his mind. It was when he made a pact with the spirits of his ancestors, asking them for help. Since that day, he had never experienced one minute of peace. After that request, he had only been agitated and disturbed, without rest. He dedicated himself to a quest, making the lives of the people he purported to love miserable. He had spent the last two decades destroying people rather than helping them. Now, in the declining and most powerful years of his life, he was the most hated and despised person in all their tribal area. He finally realized that power was not the solution to his heart's true desire. This had to change, and the time was NOW.

The Gringos he hated with a passion were not bad people. Patricia and Lori did only good things for other people, and no one paid them to do this. The government didn't pay them. The state of Amazonas didn't pay them, and the tribe certainly didn't give them anything in return for their help. Yet, they were kind, loving, and sacrificial ladies who only thought of others.

These new Gringos, for whom he had nurtured a deep hatred, were just like the ladies whom he had observed most of his life. They had done no harm to anyone since they came. All they wanted to do was help, and help they did. The God they were teaching about was just like them, at least that's what they had been saying. Or was it "they were just like Him." Whatever it was, it was true. This Jesus, they were affirming to know, only did good. At least that is what everyone says about Him.

And NOW, they risked their lives to save his only son. He stood by, frozen with fear, while they acted bravely. He was the coward; they were the heroes. Everyone in the village saw this and knew he was worthless as a husband, father, tribal chief, and spiritual leader. Instead of establishing his authority, as he had been trying to do, he destroyed it with his cruelty and constant conniving. Instead of leading them toward good, as a true leader, he drove them toward evil. He knew this was, finally, the end of his influence, the total collapse of his reign of terror and submission.

Even though no one who had observed his past activities would have guessed it, Batubo had a deep, true love for his family. If he wanted to keep his wife and son in his life, he needed to act fast before these Gringos left. They were leaving tomorrow, so it would have to be tonight. He decided there had to be a total renunciation of his past beliefs and a confession of his evil ways. This was the only route to any chance of retaining his wonderful wife and restoring his image in his son's eyes.

The entire tribe was surprised when Batubo called a general meeting. This meant EVERYONE had to attend. Only the sick in bed were excused from sitting around the center of the communal living area while the shaman spoke to them.

One hour before the sun would disappear on the horizon, the meeting started. He made sure the Gringos were present. Because it was necessary to ensure the Gringos understood what he had to say, he spoke through his son, who served as an interpreter. He looked nervous, and the tribe looked scared. Usually, these meetings ended with someone getting in trouble, or worse, being punished by him for whatever he deemed an affront to his orders or authority. Never ONCE over the past 20 years at these mandatory shaman meetings did it go well for the tribe.

He started to stutter slightly as he began, something his tribe members had never seen before. He had their very utmost attention.

[*AUTHOR NOTE: Because Esterdo's broken-English translation may not convey the entire message Batubo would like you to read, I'll translate Batubo's words for you.*]

"I want to put your minds at ease. This isn't a trial. No one will be punished or exiled today." Everyone let out an audible sigh of relief, and some even started to smile, revealing rows of missing teeth throughout the audience.

"I've been cruel instead of helpful, vengeful instead of forgiving. First of all, I want to thank the Americans for their visit to our village. It must have been hard to leave their own comfortable dwellings to come here and live in a grass hut, sleeping in hammocks. I've seen pictures of their lovely living quarters. I have many people to ask for forgiveness. Beatings and punishments were all I had to maintain my authority as tribal head. Instead of being a spiritual leader, I've been a curse to my own people. For this, I ask your personal forgiveness."

Some villagers looked shocked; others were obviously baffled by his remarks. His son was tearing up, making it hard to translate these surprising remarks into his broken English. The Americans were getting glassy-eyed from all the emotion.

"I've not been totally ignorant of the teachings of Patricia and Lori. It's their understanding that this Jesus, whom they call the Son of God, is the greatest man ever to have walked this world. According to the book they brought to us, He is the only way to pass from this life to the glorious existence beyond the clouds and stars; the afterlife. I know I've done a great deal of wrong; they call it sin. And according to the book they teach us, this sin will be the reason I'll be pushed aside if I try to enter this glorious place and be condemned forever in a place of eternal punishment. I don't want this horrible punishment. I fear it greatly."

Right now, Loretta knew exactly what the tribal leader was talking about. She had to make these decisions herself. It was the only way to be forgiven. He wrapped it up by saying, "In the presence of all my fellow tribe members, I renounce my position as the leader of this tribe and any other tribe. I don't qualify as a political leader and never did qualify as a spiritual leader." At this point, many of the villagers were wiping their eyes with the back of their hands. This was beyond belief.

"I also want to say something with all the sincerity I can squeeze from my wicked heart. I renounce myself and recognize my sin before this tribe and the Holy Man of God called Jesus. I want to accept Him and receive His forgiveness. I finally recognize that He died for me, and I must do this if I want to live with Him forever in His wonderful village in the sky. I also recommend that all of you consider this for your own life. With this, I lay down my staff of authority and turn the leadership of this tribe over to my son, who has always shown the qualities of leadership this tribe needs."

Esterdo dropped his jaw in disbelief. Never in his wildest dreams did he believe his cruel and powerful father would ever say these things.

The meeting was dismissed. Everyone went to their huts and carefully pondered these things in their hearts. There was a noticeable silence throughout the whole village. It was like a tomb or a church service. No one made a noise; there was not a peep from any hut. The candles were blown out, and for the first time anyone could remember, the villagers lay down to rest in peace.

The Gringos had a meeting in the boys' hut. Loretta spoke, "WOW, I wish Patricia and Lori could have been here. They would've soaked a few crying towels with tears, for sure. What a wonderful climax to decades of working among these people. We need to raise our voices in praise to our Heavenly Father for this spiritual victory. I'm going to ask Engelbert to pray before we dismiss and get some sleep. Fernando asked me to let all of you know: it's wheels up at five o'clock. We have to get aloft during the calm morning air."

With that closing remark, Bert prayed. "Oh, glorious Father, You have shown us a great miracle today. I thought my own salvation was a wonderful work of grace, and it was. I certainly didn't deserve Your patience with me. Batubo's decision was marvelous in our eyes, the culmination of decades of work by Patricia and Lori. We're thankful You allowed us to have a small part in this very heartwarming conversion of a cruel and powerful man who spent his whole life working with and for Your enemies. We have been privileged to see this, and for this we thank You profoundly. Please give us a trouble-free flight out of here to Fortaleza. We ask these things in the name of Your Son, for Your glory. Amen."

Just before 5:00 in the morning, as the Gringos were preparing to board the plane, Batubo, his wife, and Esterdo met them at the river's edge. Each one had a present for their new American friends. The ex-shaman's wife gave each of the girls a beautiful woven blanket. Batubo gave each grappler a stone with his real name on it—Matillen.

And lastly, Esterdo handed Bowie a handcrafted bow wrapped in a blanket. He had tears in his eyes as he said goodbye. "You shoulds have dis bow because you are now family. I supposed I vill never sees yu again. I gives yu dis present so yu wills remembered me an prays for me ever times you sees it. May yu cherished it all your lifes and never forgets us. Goodbyes my friends."

Bowie took his Amazon friend aside and put his hand on his shoulder. "There's a good chance I'll be back. I believe God is calling me to be a missionary, and it may very well be right here with you." Esterdo was elated, to say the least.

The Oregonians left while they still had some tears left in their system. It was hard to say goodbye. It always is when you leave a piece of your heart behind. After all of the Gringos had entered the plane, Esterdo yelled out to them in flawless English. "I accepted Christ as my Savior, as my dad did."

Fernando, the pilot, completed his final checks. The Albatross roared to life (causing many of the tribe members to back away from the water's edge), sped down the river, and rose from the water toward the sky. Everyone in the village waved as they watched the great metal bird, containing their American friends, soar into the clouds and disappear.

Esterdo gave Bowie a hand-crafted bow as a deep sign of respect and trust, a symbol of Bowie being adopted into Esterdo's family.

A man sells cashew fruit door to door. It is very toxic and can cause serious allergic problems for some people.

CHAPTER 12
Fortaleza in Northeast Brazil

FORTALEZA, BRAZIL

Fernando skillfully guided the Albatross above the clouds and into the clear, blue Brazilian sky, leaving behind many experiences and tears. During the flight, Loretta pressed her face to the window, looking down when the clouds thinned. After several hours of flying time they reached the coast. She could see ocean on her side and land through Shane's window on the other. The Gringos and ape were off on another adventure in Northeastern Brazil. Their three-week stay with Esterdo's tribe in the Amazon basin had marked them deeply. Some might return, perhaps as full-time missionaries. Loretta prayed for God's will for her teenage charges.

They would spend three weeks in Fortaleza, a beautiful, windy, coastal city 1,500 miles southeast of Manaus. Fortaleza is known for its 60 miles of lovely beaches. It is less humid than Amazonas and wetter than Mossoró, their next stop; the semi-desert. Fortaleza has rainy and dry seasons. During the dry season, the grass disappears from many parks, but during the rains, thick, deep-green grass grows and needs frequent mowing.

After their textbook flight, Fernando landed the flying boat in the harbor. He helped everyone retrieve luggage, finished business with the harbormaster, and checked into a downtown hotel. His passengers awaited transportation to their next stop.

The Gringos would stay at a campground on the city's edge, in a town called Mesejana. The property once belonged to the state when the governor lived there, but Maranatha Baptist Mission purchased it. Mango and coconut trees covered the grounds as if they had always belonged there. There was even a swimming pool.

Linda, the dramatic one, was elated. "Now we can begin to live like all of us always wanted to become accustomed to living!" (Whatever that meant. Kosy was unsure.)

Their guides would be Jack and Luke Richerson, brothers from Alabama. Their dad had been an Army chaplain, so they traveled often. They got new passports every five years because they ran out of blank pages for visas and custom stamps. The guides arrived by bus and helped the visitors with luggage. Harriet insisted on carrying her bag of bananas.

During the short drive, Luke warned the Americans: they would see tarantulas, monkeys, rats, cockroaches, ants, large lizards, flying ants, and parrots all day. Jack added that they must roll hammocks tightly and hang them up after use, even for daytime naps. Otherwise, unfriendly creatures might be hiding in the hammock, waiting to bite or scare them at bedtime.

Everyone enjoyed the new sights along Brazilian roads and reached camp without incident. Before bedtime, Linda felt ill and vomited up lunch food. Within the vomit was a ten-inch white tapeworm, the size of the lead center of a No. 2 pencil. The city slicker saw the worm and fainted.

Loretta got a wet rag and patted Linda's face with it. Finally, Linda stirred. "It was a dream, right? I didn't really vomit a white, squirming worm, did I? PLEASE TELL ME I DIDN'T! I'll surely die if I did, I can't abide a worm in me." Of all the Gringos, she would have to be the one who hosted this ugly, sickening, stomach tapeworm.

Now the rest were in for another lesson in theater drama. Erin hesitated to break the news; she didn't want to tell her, but the better part of wisdom dictated honesty. Jack, the tour guide, stepped forward. "My dear American friend, what you have is a stomach worm, or as they call them Stateside, a tapeworm. You probably got it just by drinking water in the Amazon area."

Linda exploded, "I only drank bottled water during the entire disgusting visit, and I even brushed my teeth with bottled water. How could this happen to me? Do you think I have other worms in my system? How horrible! I have wiggly, slimy creatures crawling around inside of me. This is worse than any horror movie I've ever seen. Find a tree and hang me right now! I can't believe I've become an involuntary, warm motel, restaurant, and playground for nauseating, wiggly worms."

Luke knew worms were a normal part of life here in his hometown of Fortaleza. The Richerson families got tested every six months for worms. Sometimes the test was positive; sometimes it wasn't. Eventually, everyone faced this parasite. There was no escape. To avoid worms completely, one must stay far north of the Rio Grande between the U.S. and Mexico. These worms live in Mexico, Central America, and South America.

Linda pleaded, "What in the world am I going to do. Give me some poison or something to kill them, NOW." They assured her she only needed to drink some liquid three times a day for a week, and the problem would be resolved. The worms would die and leave her body. "And just how are they going to leave?" she demanded, noticing Jack and Luke's smirks. "NO! Don't tell me. I don't ever want to know."

Linda persisted, "NOW, tell me how I got this undesirable creature in my system if I didn't consume Amazon water in any way, shape, or form. For Pete's sake, I want to avoid this invasion of the slime species."

Jack decided to be direct and share hygiene tips. "You might have gotten the worm from taking a shower with river water or swimming in the Amazon. Did you do that?" Linda and others nodded. "Did anyone get ice with bottled water or soda?" More nods. "To avoid contamination, boil water for 20 minutes. Then run it through a ceramic filter like those red jars over there." He pointed out the three ceramic jars, each with a faucet.

"Even with all these precautions, someone in our family still tests positive for these worms every time we get tested. It's just a way of life here. You do the best you can and accept the fact that, if you live south of the U.S. border, sometime in your life, you'll host one (or more) of these local parasites and require treatment for tapeworm infestation."

Miss Deluxe protested, "I, for one, will never, ever, accept this involuntary move to Wormsville. Don't even think it for one minute. There's not enough gold in Fort Knox to get me to do that. NO SIREE! You can all paddle your little canoes down Tapeworm River if you want to, but leave me at the dock, waving good-bye." They all thought she made her point well. They gave her a 10.0 for performance and a 0.0 for flexibility.

The campground, filled with coconut trees, was also full of playful monkeys. As the group settled in, Erin noticed one young monkey miss a branch and tumble to the ground, knocking itself out. This new environment brought not only challenges but unexpected adventures.

Kosy started rushing to its side to help it when Jack grabbed her arm and pulled her back. "You can't go near that primate," he cautioned. "It's full of fleas and lice. If it bites you, which it surely will, you might lose an arm or a leg, or even worse, it could kill you."

The tender-hearted pre-teen wanted to help and took a step toward the monkey. She looked at Jack with concern. "But the poor monkey might die," she said. "Isn't there something we can do?"

Luke grabbed a towel and covered the monkey, knotting the towel. He then took the primate to a bamboo cage and threw the whole bundle inside, pulling the towel out through the bars. "It's safe in here. Then we can assess if it needs medical care. Now, no one will be in danger."

The Gringos were to sleep in hammocks as they did in the tribe. In the smaller room where the ladies slept, for lack of space, they had to crisscross the hammocks. Jack was being funny when he asked, "Does anyone wet the bed?" They all snickered. "It's important. If any of you wet the bed, you have to hang your hammock at the bottom, close to the floor. Do I have to explain why?" They all assured him he did not.

Before ending their busy day, the group ventured downtown. Luke, their guide, took two VW vans; he drove one while a camp worker drove the other. Harriet stayed behind, comfortable among the trees and monkeys. She started to enjoy mangos—and, a few large insects for dessert.

Marty noticed candles burning on the curb at the crossing. He asked the caravan to stop and walked over to it. He was reaching down to touch something when Luke yelled at him. "Hold it right there, Gringo! Don't touch anything." He seemed serious enough, so Marty drew back. All the

Oregonians followed their guide to the site where the grappler was waiting.

Billy seemed to be left out. "What's all the yelling about, anyway?" he asked. The tour guide stood in front of everyone, facing them, with his back to the candles, making sure none of them came any closer. "I know this is going to sound a bit strange to you, since all but one of you have spent your whole life within the borders of the United States. Fortunately, you've never seen anything like this. It's a high-caliber Spiritist offering."

"This offering has a dead chicken, cigars, bottles of beer and whiskey, popcorn, candles, baked potatoes, and money. Obviously, the Spiritist who put this offering here has some money to burn. I didn't want you to touch it because we understand these offerings are not to God but to demons. I didn't want you to touch any of it. It would be very UNWISE to do so."

Shane wanted information. "Why do they put these expensive offerings on the corners?"

Luke was serious. "They're always placed at corners where paths cross because they represent where the decisions of life have to be made. It's a symbolic gesture. These offerings are given to the spirits for several reasons: 1) ask for a blessing, 2) give thanks for a blessing received, 3) put a curse on someone, and 4) take a curse off oneself.

Basically, they're asking the spirit world for help. It could be to win the lottery, get a job, find a wife, or pass an exam. They also place these offerings at the corners to give thanks for any blessing they believe the spirit world is responsible for. They might have an enemy they want cursed, or someone they actually want to see die. If they think someone has put a curse on them, they will put this offering out to get the evil curse removed."

Bowie was flabbergasted. "Whoa, Partner! This is really serious stuff. My Indian tribe talks to spirits and ancestors, but this is way over the top. It is like an extreme exaggeration of what the Nez Perce do. Man, this offering is interesting. Do you know any Spiritists personally?"

Luke just shook his head. "Not really, none that would give an offering like this. I know some Brazilians who believe this way, but their main emphasis is reincarnation."

On the way back to the campground, torrential rain started pouring down in buckets, beating on the van roof so loudly they couldn't hear each other. It was so heavy it obscured the road, and they had to pull over.

When it subsided a little, Luke pointed to a toad crossing in front of them and asked Marty to grab it behind the back legs. He wanted it for a biology class at the Christian school.

After the heavy rain stopped, Erin spotted small frogs hopping across the asphalt. She asked Luke if he wanted some of those, too. He said he did and asked Marty to get them. The grappler handed the toad to Shane, jumped out, and swooped up two tiny frogs, each about twice the size of a jellybean. The tour guide said he wanted to put them in his glass jar with the rest of the critters he had collected.

About one mile from the campground, Luke's van was stopped by a police blitz. The other driver in the group, having lived in Brazil for his whole life, thought it was the better part of wisdom to keep on driving, as if he didn't even know the people in the other van.

Just as the van pulled over, Luke told Shane and Marty to put the big toad in the glove compartment along with the two small frogs. They didn't understand, but since the tour guide lived in Brazil, the Oregonians did exactly as he wanted. The policeman asked to see Luke's ID card and driver's license. He handed the officer his ID card; unfortunately, he had left his driver's license at home.

The patrolman told Luke he would get a ticket for driving without a license unless he had $50 to pay for their lunch. The guide thought he might have left his license in the glove compartment, so he asked the policeman to come around to the other side of the van and shine his light in to see if it was there. The kind policeman was glad to accommodate him.

When Marty flipped the door open, the two tiny frogs jumped into the back seat, but the big, ugly toad just sat there staring at the light, like he was hypnotized. The policeman jerked his head back and dropped the flashlight. "What in the world are you doing with this big, ugly toad in the glove compartment? Close it quickly, NOW!" Marty obeyed the officer.

Luke said he was going to use it for a biological experiment at the school. The policeman had a ten-minute pow-wow with his partner. He then returned the ID Card and told them to head out, pronto. Not wanting to disobey the officer, Luke popped the clutch and was off like a rabbit.

Back at the camp, everyone wanted to know what had happened, especially the other Gringos in the van that had not stopped. After Luke explained the drama, he put his hand up with his forefinger pointing upward, as if he had just gotten a new revelation. "I couldn't figure it out at first, but now I know why the officer let us go without giving me a ticket or try to force us to give him a $50 tip.

"He must have overheard all of you speaking English and presumed you were students or teachers at the University of Fortaleza, which was only one mile east of our location. He and his partner probably didn't want the political fallout from giving important people a ticket or extorting them for money. The toad got us off the hook, because only 'important' people do experiments."

The two small frogs that had tried to escape were placed in the glass jar. It was a survival experiment. The jar already contained a tarantula, a huge moth, several cockroaches, a two-headed gardener snake, and some grasshoppers. The idea was to see who would eat whom first. They set the jar on the porch and went to bed.

The next morning, they checked the jar and found that their scientific experiment had not turned out as they had expected. Fire ants had sent out scouts and found the jar. Crawling in through the small air holes on the lid, they devoured every species trapped inside. And, as Kosy commented, "They weren't even invited to the dinner party!"

The campground was peppered with mango trees. They produced so much fruit it would fall to the ground and rot before the residents could eat it all. They made mango jelly, mango popsicles, mango ice cream, mango cake, mango juice, mango dessert, and even mango candy. The Brazilians would grab a mango bigger than a softball, squeeze it until the pulp was all squashed, cut an X on the peak, and squeeze it, sucking all the juice out, then throw the peel and the enormous seed on the ground.

Shane decided to climb a huge tree and get the biggest, ripest ones. Reaching the top, he began to feel something crawling on his legs. He knew he was in big trouble. Yelling and slapping his legs, he began to descend as rapidly as possible. Everyone heard his screaming; they came a-running. He hit the ground and headed straight for the swimming pool. His whole body was covered with red fire ants.

Hitting the water, he stayed under until they drowned or gave up to get some air. When he came up, he was still scratching and pulling off the die-hard ones. Some of them were actually standing straight up, held vertical by just their biting of his flesh. Loretta was the first one to come to his rescue. She was slapping and pulling off the remaining, stubborn ones.

"Son, I guess these fire ants thought they were going to eat you alive or take you to their nest. I am dreadfully sorry. I know, by experience, their sting is very painful, and the agony will last a few hours." Which it did, too!

When the drama subsided, someone suggested they visit the local park. Shane was somewhat recovered, so they took off in the two VW vans. At the park, Kosy, Erin, and Linda got separated from the rest. A very beautiful, olive-skinned lady began speaking to them in rapid-fire. Of course, they couldn't understand a word. She was using hand gestures and getting more excited.

The Brazilian lady mimed that she wanted them to take her picture. So they did. Finally, Linda pulled a pen and a pad out of her purse and handed them to the nice, excited lady. Then the lady wrote something down. She hugged and kissed each American before turning and leaving, waving and smiling as she rounded the corner.

The girls took the note to Jack, and he burst out laughing before he translated it. This certainly got all of their attention.

Bert was dying of curiosity. "Okay, enough of your good-time laughter, what does the note say?"

Jack translated it. "I know you are Americans. Could you take my picture to Hollywood and see if they would give me a job making American movies? I would love to do it. Can you help me?"

Spiritists offerings to demons are placed near corners of roads.

Luke's informal "critters in a jar" experiment yielded a surprisingly unexpected result. It conclusively demonstrated that tiny Brazilian fire ants are, collectively, apex predators.

CHAPTER 13
Erin to the Rescue

A jangada is a simple home-made fishing raft, with a sail, used by Brazilian fishermen near Fortaleza, Brazil.

The male monkey they had retrieved, unconscious, would be kept in a bamboo cage while Jack and Luke watched for signs it needed medical attention, mainly to appease Kosette. Had Jack and Luke chosen alone, they would have left the primate on the ground, confident its relatives would help. Still, aiming to please as good Christians and hosts, they adjusted to fulfill the tourists' wishes.

Obviously, the monkey thought he was in the human's jail. He didn't like it at all. He worked on the door and couldn't get it open. He then tried to chew through the hemp cords holding the cage together. He finally figured he didn't have strong enough dentures to finish that job. Finally, after failing twice, he decided to suck in his chest even more and try to squeeze between the bars. This worked. He was free at last.

His tricky escape would have been brilliant, except that, like most properties in Brazil, this one was guarded by the canine corps. To be more specific, four huge, barking, panting sniffers. They were turned loose at night to keep undesirables away, including animals that tried to claim property rights.

The tree swinger ran freely across the back yard and took a right turn when he got to the swimming pool. He saw the bushes and trees just ahead. To humans, it was only short manzanita bushes alongside tall, swaying coconut trees, but to an escaping primate, it was the promised land. All he had to do was to scamper quickly and silently across a small open patch of ground about the size of a tennis court.

How could he have known that stationed at the south end of this little piece of the planet was a canine corps team? And how could he have ever guessed that these four-legged guardians of human property and life took their responsibilities very seriously? He couldn't have been abreast of any of this information because he had just arrived on the premises ten minutes before he took a nose-dive into the hard-packed ground under the mango tree he was trying to swing aboard.

Just before he was going to leap onto the bush, the monkey was blocked by four black, moist noses that appeared between him and his escape route. Each nose belonged to a dog with two rows of large, sharp, drooling teeth and strong, unpleasant breath, all accompanied by fierce barking and panting. Seeing the dogs' aggressive stance, the monkey concluded it was trapped.

Then, suddenly, out of the darkness, there descended rapidly, with great grunting and kiss-squeaking, the biggest monkey any of them had ever seen. With arms swinging and feet stomping, Harriet pounded the ground and glared menacingly.

The undefeated canine corps had never seen a monkey this size. (They didn't know Harriet was actually an ape, not a huge monkey, but they didn't care.) The four of them had viciously dominated the campground, and never before had any primate even made them wince. But this was a whole new zoo now. It was time to be the runner, not the chaser. A solution to the situation was put to a quick vote by the canine committee. The unanimous decision was to turn tail and head for the barn at full speed!

With the backyard quickly returning to calm, Harriet relaxed and watched her small, distant relative resume its original escape plan. She made no move to follow, content with her effortless victory. Shane motioned in her direction. She hurried to the VW van to join the Gringos and the scene shifted to the coastline, where a different set of dramas was unfolding.

Fortaleza boasts 60 miles of beautiful, pristine beach. Sometimes, the only occupants are a few swimmers who don't have regular day jobs. The permanent residents are the bravest fishermen in the world. They live in houses along the beach and have fishing boats called "jangadas." Some are fancy, but most are only wooden planks nailed together with Styrofoam or recycled, plastic water bottles between them. They use a small sail to power the boat with the heated winds of the Atlantic.

The fishermen head out in the early morning and fight relentless waves all day. Most days, they bring in fish to sell, making enough profit to support a family of seven. At times, they're caught off guard and have to spend the whole night at sea, sleeping on a boat about the size of a large canoe. If they aren't careful, they can fall overboard and never make it back to the beach. It has happened more times than anyone wants to remember.

Jack and Luke set up a volleyball net so the Americans could experience beach volleyball. In Brazil, two styles of vollyball were popular sports. Brazil had recently won gold in indoor volleyball at the Pan Am Games.

Only a few families swam nearby, and several jangada sails were visible on the horizon. After hours of play, everyone decided to swim. Harriet had already been in the water for over two hours, energetically wading and attempting to catch fish. She was doing a pretty good job of it too.

At the beach, they were getting ready to head back to the campground. They noticed someone running toward them, yelling frantically. Jack sprinted to intercept the runner and find out what had them so excited. Jack listened carefully, then translated the urgent plea for help: "It appears their father has fallen off the jangada, and it sailed away from him. He's about 500 yards out into the waves. He can barely keep afloat because he injured his shoulder and hip yesterday when he fell. If he doesn't get help, he'll drown in a few minutes. He's in that direction."

Erin, understanding the emergency, quickly pulled off her shoes and ran to the shoreline. Without hesitation, she entered the water, running until it was a little higher than her waist, then began to swim toward the distressed fisherman.

Billy, always the planner, thought quickly. "Even if she finds the fisherman, Erin won't have the strength to return to the beach, especially not while dragging another person. We need another jangada to get out there and bring both of them in." Bowie and Bert split up to search for another raft-like sailboat.

The rest of the group formed a tight circle and began to pray. Shane took the lead. "Lord of the sky and sea, we don't know who Erin is trying to save out there. We need grace, help from above. This person may not be a Christian, and to lose him would be a tragedy. Please give Erin the ability to find him, the presence of mind to hold on, and the strength to bring him in. In our Lord Jesus' name, Amen."

The water was warm, and this was not going to help. If the fisherman swallowed any seawater, it would be double trouble, being warm and salty. Erin was an excellent swimmer on her high school varsity team. She always placed well in state competition but never won the gold. Going for the gold now occupied her mind. She prayed, between each freestyle stroke, that she was heading in the right direction.

The waves were about one foot tall; that's a lot for a swimmer. She took a little seawater into her mouth but managed to spit it out. It still wasn't helping her; she needed fresh water instead. In the distance, she could see the sail of the jangada as it drifted further out to sea. She figured the drowning fisherman had to be between the jangada and her. Certainly, he was still trying to catch the raft-like boat.

Finding him was only one of her concerns. She knew dangerous sharks, searching for a quick snack, patrolled these warm waters. Also, other sea creatures were nearby; some, almost as dangerous as the sharks. There were sting rays and jellyfish, either of which could kill her with just one prick of their stingers. She also prayed for protection from them.

Bowie and Bert located another jangada, but Bowie hesitated, unsure of how to handle it. Bert, confident, pushed the raft into the waves and urged Bowie, "Climb aboard! I can operate a sailboat." Surprised yet trusting, Bowie joined him without delay, realizing urgency outweighed questions.

Even if Erin could save the fisherman from drowning, it was almost certain she wouldn't be able to retrace her path and drag him to shore. She'd be exhausted by the time she reached him. She knew it when she dove in; they all realized it after seeing how far out the jangada had drifted.

The varsity swimmer was wearing down. She knew that even if she found the fisherman, she'd still have several obstacles to overcome. He may be in panic mode, and instead of surrendering to her for rescue, he could take both of them down to the depths. She might be able to do it. She had practiced with Marty, pulling a dummy across the school pool. The second item occupying her tired mind was the stark reality that she did NOT have enough strength to make it back to shore pulling a heavy fisherman.

If her friends didn't realize she would need a boat for rescue, Erin knew she would not make it back. She trusted them to act, wondering if Billy or someone else would think quickly enough to help.

Swimming in the pool at Lebanon High was a piece of cake compared to fighting ocean waves and the tide. She could swim the 100-yard freestyle in less than one minute, but that kind of speed was not important here. The 2,000-yard freestyle was more like what she was doing now. In the pool, she never had to fight ocean waves or refrain from swallowing any of the water surrounding her. Here she had to adapt to both of these obstacles. There would be no medals and no ribbon ceremony after this ordeal.

If the boys weren't up to snuff, the only meeting marked in time would be a few sad funerals for a drowned American swimmer and a poor jangada fisherman from a small beach in Fortaleza. Her optimism and faith in God kept her arms pounding when she thought she couldn't manage another stroke.

Suddenly, she could see a hat floating in the waves directly in front of her. There was no one under the hat, so she pushed on towards the sailboat. Finally, she spotted the Brazilian about 20 yards to the right. He was barely keeping his head above water. She knew no Portuguese but could at least say, "socorro," which meant "help." She had learned this word in the Amazon village when the women asked for drastic medical help for their children. She said it over and over until he looked her way.

The surprise on his face was evident. He must have thought he was seeing an angel swimming towards him. A red-headed white girl who couldn't speak Portuguese. How did she get to him? The beach was over 600 yards away by now. He was exhausted and hoped she wasn't. Erin swung him around and put her arm under his right armpit and across his chest. Then, she started heading back for the shore, knowing she wouldn't make it. It appeared her prayers were answered as the surprised fisherman lay still in her grasp.

If the boys didn't catch on and didn't make it to her soon, both of them would be fish food for sure. Just when she thought there was not even an ounce of strength left in her 120-pound body, she spotted the sail of a jangada coming towards them. She managed a weak call for help, hoping it was enough to draw their attention. Bert spotted her and turned the rudder towards them.

When the grapplers reached Erin, she was going down. Bowie jumped in the water and held her head up. Bert let go of the rudder long enough to pull the lucky-duck fisherman aboard. Then he turned towards Bowie and grabbed Erin. Bowie climbed aboard first to help Bert pull the varsity swimmer onto the deck. There was a lot of hearty huffing and puffing going on, but some very relieved looks coming their way, too!

After she regained a little strength, Erin began to cry. She was so thankful Bowie and Bert had the common sense to find another jangada. "It was Billy's idea. I'm not sure any of us would've thought about it. We were all in a daze, but since he's blind, his mind isn't cluttered with visual distractors. I suppose that's why he's always so alert. We owe him a lot. It looks like we got here just in the nick of time." And they certainly had.

The choppy ride back to shore was filled with deep gratitude, first to God and then to the boys on the beach for their sharp thinking and quick action. The reunion at the water's edge was one to behold. The beach was filled with fishermen and their families. They are a unit, a community force, working together to eke out a meager living from the dangerous waters off the coast of Fortaleza.

This daring rescue would be talked about for decades. These brave Gringos would be remembered by all the families along the 60-mile coastline. The Americans weren't looking for fame, but it always seemed to come their way without even thinking about it. Bowie took a photo of all the happy children in the crowd on the beach.

The kids began to consider God's plan in all this. That's why they invited all of the fishermen and their families to attend a church service in town honoring the efforts of Erin, Bowie, Bert, and, of course, the quick thinking of Billy. Most of them said they would be delighted to attend. It was scheduled for Sunday night, just three days away.

Loretta was so glad to see Erin, whole, rejoicing, and ALIVE. She had her doubts, but never doubted God's will. The ex-runaway mom was feeling elated, joyful, and extremely thankful to the Lord Almighty for His loving grace, allowing the Gringos to be at the beach at the exact moment necessary to save the fisherman's life. She had seen His perfect timing on various occasions over the last year, bringing her rebel heart to its knees and putting her faith in Christ. She was now seeing these same circumstances working out in the lives of her children and these teenagers dedicated to Him. It was a great privilege to be a part of His plan.

Loretta wanted to have a meeting when they got back to the campground. It would be a time of praise and prayer. Praise to Him for His protection and guidance. Then, much prayer for the upcoming church service, that some of these brave, wonderful fishermen and their family members would come to know Christ and receive eternal life.

It was the Gringos' custom to find Harriet before they went to bed so they could be sure she was safe and to supply the ape with a load of bananas to last her until sunrise. It was Kosy and Bert's turn to push the loaded wheelbarrow to the usual spot and leave it there. Every morning, the same two would return and bring back the empty wheelbarrow.

They weren't sure if she was the one eating all the bananas; it seemed like a bit much for a single orangutan to consume in eight hours. Perhaps she was sharing her bounty with the little folk that decorated the trees like Christmas ornaments. Maybe she was using the fruit to bribe them into getting coconuts or mangos for her. It really didn't matter; bananas were easy to get here, since they literally grew all over the city. In the USA, people said, "It's dirt cheap." Here in Brazil, the saying was replaced by, "It's cheaper than a banana."

Kosy and Bert delivered Harriet's load of bananas and went to bed. The next morning, as the grappler waited for Kosy, he noticed an unusual quiet throughout the area where the monkeys lived. Usually, it was chaos as the primates raced from tree to tree, trying to beat each other to the mangos and coconuts. That was not the case now.

He mentioned it to Kosette. "There's something wrong, my little friend. I don't see the herd of hairy noise-makers like we usually do. What do you make of it?" Kosette was still rubbing the sleep out of her eyes and could hardly think with her head still full of nocturnal cobwebs. "I can barely function at this time in the morning, Bert. What do you think is wrong?"

It didn't take them very long to discover what was amiss. They called and yelled their lungs out, and not one primate came to investigate the racket. Both of them raced back to the house and turned the corner into the dining room.

Kosy spoke first, "Harriet is gone!"

Erin got to the fisherman in time. She grabbed him and started back to the beach.

CHAPTER 14
Finding an Ape

Harriet, the orangutan, was missing. All the Gringos wanted to find her and reunite her with their group.

"What do you mean, Harriet is gone?" Linda demanded. "If that hairy troublemaker is just hiding, I'm going to start rationing her bananas." The rest of the group, realizing Kosy wasn't joking, quickly split into pairs and methodically searched the premises. Some scoured the bushes behind the buildings, while others swept through every room and corner. There were absolutely no monkeys on the property—not a single one. This was very strange.

Jack shrugged. "She probably just walked out of the campground for a little stroll, right? She has done this before, correct?"

Shane, who knew her best and longest, replied, "She's never disappeared like this before. It's unlike her. If she left, something's wrong. There are no primates on the grounds. That may indicate she was taken or is fleeing something—or someone."

Marty donned his detective hat. "Did anyone hear anything unusual last night?" Everyone shook their heads, except Billy, who tilted his head, lost in thought, and poised to speak. At least, this is what Bowie observed. "I think our Blind Sherlock has something to share, right, Billy?"

Billy, the pint-sized grappler, said, "I heard three sharp pops around 3:00 AM. I woke and checked my Braille watch. I thought it was gunfire, but since silence followed, I went back to sleep. The lack of primates now suggests someone shot at Harriet."

"Why wouldn't she just come to the house where we are staying?" Kosette asked. "She's familiar with these buildings and has come here often. It would seem logical that she'd just run for cover here."

Marty nodded. "Kosy is right! She would've, normally. Then it must be that whoever was shooting at her was standing between where she was and these buildings. This would cast suspicion on an employee at the campground. We know not all of them are Christians."

Luke assembled all the workers and discovered that Edwardo Fonseco Silva dos Dores dos Santos was missing. He'd only been here three days. While searching his file, they found that he'd given a false address and phone number. Sherlock Holmes would be proud. Their only question: "Where do we start looking for her?" Nothing else mattered until the orangutan was found.

Breakfast was on the run: a piece of French bread with cheese and baloney, lubricated with mayonnaise, washed down with coffee or Guaraná. The team decided to organize the search by splitting into four groups: one group would cover the zoo, another would search downtown Mesejana, a third would look in the park behind the campground, and the last would head to the beach. Each group knew its assignment. There were two groups in each VW van. To improve coordination, two additional interpreters joined Jack and Luke. This way, someone could communicate and translate at every search site. Bowie was paired with Shane for the downtown area search.

Brazil has more pharmacies than any other type of business. In downtown areas or on crowded streets, you might find four per block. The grapplers started there. They failed at the first three. The fourth promised intrigue. Its clerks started at midnight, as it was open 24 hours. Around

3:20 AM, they heard a commotion and stepped outside their barred store to investigate.

Commuters at the bus stop half a block away were beginning their morning rush to the hospital. Their conversation buzzed, so a pharmacy worker wandered over and returned with a story. Apparently, a huge red-haired creature raced by—they'd never seen anything like it. Its hands almost brushed the pavement. It reached the end of the block and veered left.

Relieved to be on the right trail, one group member returned to the campground to update everyone so all could join the city search. The other members stayed downtown to follow up on new leads. According to witnesses, several men had chased Harriet down the street and turned at the end of the block. The searchers debated why these men would pursue her, noting that capturing an ape would be difficult for anyone unfamiliar with orangutans.

<START OF HARRIET'S FLASHBACK>

Harriet drifted in and out of sleep, dreaming she lay on a bed of bananas, until something jolted her awake. Someone clattered with a stick in hand. She hated that sound. She wanted to reach her humans, but the noise-makers blocked her path. The banging persisted. One human's strange stick spat fire at her.

She high-tailed it away from the bad humans with the noisy stick. Jumping from tree to tree, she finally landed on the thick wall surrounding the campground. Letting herself down gently, she took off running down the street towards the lights. Maybe there she would find more kind humans who would keep these bad humans from harming her. When she got to the bus stop, she didn't see any friendly faces. In fact, those humans were waving their arms and shouting at her. It was all a bit confusing, and she didn't like it when humans shouted at her, so she kept on a-trucking.

<END OF HARRIET'S FLASHBACK>

Edwardo Fonseca Silva lied to secure a job at the campground. He'd learned they sheltered an animal unheard of anywhere else in Brazil. His harebrained idea: capture it and sell her for enough money to buy a motorcycle. With transportation, he could get around and maybe even start robbing pharmacies regularly.

Running away after a robbery was not as successful as he had hoped it would be. He had been arrested twice already. Luckily for him, the new Brazilian laws were very lax. Since he hadn't used a gun and had really not harmed anyone, he had been released twice. He figured capturing the strange animal would be his way of winning the lottery, in some strange twisted way of thinking.

The would-be gangster recruited three buddies, each with an even duller wit, who took to his plan. He promised them a 6.23% share if successful, or lunch if not. It was the rainy season, boredom prevailed, so they threw themselves into the plan. How hard could it be? Surely any animal must be dumber than them. In reality, these four made dirt look clever.

They "borrowed" an old shotgun from a neighbor who was out of town, and his new, "vicious" guard dog was asleep. Then they headed to a new money-making venture. Climbing over the wall of the campground was easy enough. They could spot the large animal in the upper branches of a mango tree. It appeared to be sleeping. They figured if they just wounded it, maybe stunned it, and it fell to the ground, they could put a few ropes around it and be off and running to the bank with their money in hand. It appears they had spent too much time watching Curly, Larry, and Moe on a television in the local bar.

Their first shot missed, and the creature darted toward downtown, much faster than they'd imagined. They raced after it. Their big chance to be rich was slipping away from them. They'd luckily brought some twine for binding her arms. All Edwardo had to do now was get close, and he kept promising it would work. (THESE GUYS ARE IN FOR A BIG SURPRISE)

The people at the bus stop looked amazed as Edwardo and his crew approached them. After getting directions, they told the crowd not to worry or call the police, claiming the animal had escaped from the zoo and they were handling it.

Harriet was still on the run, but didn't know where to go. She just kept following her animal instincts and continued going forward, toward the unknows. The sun rose at 5:30 AM and set at 5:30 PM every day of the year in this part of the planet, only 350 miles from the equator. So, like every day before it, the sun came over the tree tops promising its blazing heat to the beach-loving people of Fortaleza.

The ape scaled a brick wall, sidestepping shards of glass cemented atop it. Nothing here was familiar, and she had no idea how this would end. She only knew she was lost, hoping her humans would find her before the men with the fire stick did.

Maybe the humans in this odd treehouse would be friendly and give her bananas to quiet her empty stomach. She hammered on the door, expecting a welcome, like at the campground. The woman inside took one look, screamed, and collapsed. This clearly wasn't working for the ape.

She turned and headed towards the backyard. Maybe they would have a banana tree there. To her pure delight, they DID have a banana tree and a mango tree. She took down a big bunch and started peeling them, stuffing one after another into her mouth. Then, a Great Dane turned the corner of the house and came straight for her. Using long strides, it only took a few seconds for the unfortunate canine to slam into the bottom of Harriet's left foot. This was the first time something it wanted to chase didn't try to run away, so it was not prepared for such an abrupt stop. It went flying east and landed in the swimming pool.

Feeling rebuffed, Harriet decided to move on. She climbed the mango tree, swung over the wall, and landed in the yard next door. Another banana tree! She snatched a bunch and didn't stick around to apologize to the man mowing, who bolted, waving his arms and yelling. Whatever— humans were hilarious.

The disoriented ape was unsure which direction to go now. She was walking down the street when she decided to cross the road. She noticed many of those noisy, moving machines with people inside. When she stepped out into the road, all of them came to a screeching stop, and some even bumped into each other. She didn't give a lick about how much confusion and damage she caused. Why would she? She didn't even understand what was happening.

Edwardo and his cohorts were following the confusion. They thought this was the way to grab the ape, as they would eventually call her. They arrived at the street, chaos was evident, clear proof that she had been there. Brazilians had both hands on their shaking heads, jabbering about some huge red-haired monkey causing all the rear-end collisions. They were hoping their insurance companies had this coverage in their policies.

The capangas (Portuguese term meaning "henchmen, thugs, or hired gunmen" in English) still had hopes of capturing the ape and selling her carcass for enough money to make their thieving lives a little more comfortable. Maybe they could get a 125cc Honda motorcycle. Then two of them could ride by old ladies and abscond with their purses. Or they could rob small corner stores using the bike as a quick getaway. They would have to fold the license plate up so no one could read it. They couldn't remove it because the police would notice and impound the bike.

They saw Harriet turn the corner a block away. Believing she had just entered a dead-end alley, they grabbed their twine and zoomed to the entrance. Edwardo spotted her climbing a fire escape ladder. He took one shot at her, trying to wound the ape enough to subdue her. He got off a lucky shot and hit her in the head. It was a very superficial skin wound, but enough to knock her off the ladder. She hit the cobblestone street and was out cold.

<BACK TO OUR HEROES>

All the Gringos stopped in the middle of town for a quick prayer. Kosy asked to pray. "God, we care a lot about Harriet, and we need help finding her. Please give us the help we need." It was a simple prayer but effective because it was, as the Bible calls it, "the effectual fervent prayer of a righteous man," or, in this case, "of a righteous twelve year old."

They followed the chaos, like the bad guys did, just a little further behind. They heard a shot from the alley, but didn't get there in time to rescue the ape nor even learn what had happened to her. All they knew was that she wasn't there; probably with the bad guys. Everyone was concerned about Harriet's well-being, for sure. But the safety of the men dealing with something they had no experience with also worried them. Billy sounded off, "These idiots have no idea what they've gotten themselves into. If Harriet gets mad enough, the people who find her captors will have to call the police or the paramedics to rescue them from her."

There was nothing more they could do for the huge ape. Waiting for someone to complain or for the police to contact them was the best they could hope for. With this in mind, they all returned to the campground for supper and bedtime.

Linda didn't think it was important to roll up her hammock as she'd been told. She hated the thought of obeying rules. Rules were for weak-minded people, souls who couldn't think for themselves. People didn't comprehend how independent she was. She considered herself a free spirit, above most people's understanding. This was bound to get her into a lot of trouble in her third-world environment, and it already had.

When the three teens and Loretta got to their dorm room, Linda went right to her hammock and laid down at a 45° angle, as Esterdo had taught her. This allowed her to extend perfectly straight rather than lie parallel to the cloth, which would make her back curve all night and give her aches and pains the next day.

Just as she was about to close her eyes, a huge black, hairy tarantula crawled out from under her pillow, reached up, and slid thousands of tiny hairs connected to its foot (called a "paw") across her left cheek. She let out a yelp and sprang up from the hammock like no one could believe she was ever capable of doing. It was like she was blown out of bed. Loretta came to her rescue, throwing a towel over the spider and gathering it up to take it out to the grassy grounds, far from the building. She said she did this because the huge fright machine ate things she hated more than she hated the spider.

Linda was in shock. At first, she couldn't speak. When she did, it was *Anne of Green Gables* time again! "How ... how utterly horrible that was. The hairy tarantula was on my face. He could have bitten me. How poisonous are tarantulas, anyway? I've seen movies with these creatures. If it had taken a bite out of me, I'd have only had a few hours to live. What would they have said of me? 'She died in Brazil by the fangs of a huge, hairy, black spider, called a tarantula.' The *Lebanon Express* readers would've felt sorry for me, but that wouldn't and couldn't make a difference. I'd still be stone dead! A goner before my time, a wasted life, for sure!"

<RETURN TO HARRIET'S SITUATION
Are you still following the story?>

Harriet was out cold on the cobblestone street in the dead-end alley. The "lucky" thugs were elated their shot had only wounded her and she was still their prize, a way to get rich quickly, to fund other capers. Because she was out cold, they didn't need to use the rope. They just placed her in a wheelbarrow they found leaning against the wall. They felt their boat had finally come in, that their lucky star was finally shining down on them. Unfortunately, for them, that boat is about to sink and that star is about to blow up!

Rushing off with her in the wheelbarrow, they avoided the arrival of the Gringos. Their hideout was only three blocks away. They were sure they could make it there before anyone got suspicious of their huge, red-haired, bleeding cargo. Arriving at the two-story shack, they bound her hands behind her back and deposited her in one of the first-floor rooms and closed the door behind them, securing it with a cheap slip latch. They were smiling and backslapping while they looked up the phone number of the black market dealer in town. Their gravy train had finally arrived at the station.

Pacho Gilherme Cardoso de Oliveira was a sleazy, crooked, slimy, black-market dealer of anything with some value. He'd take exotic animals from the Amazon and sell them as pets or for food; it did not matter to him. He was a low-life Brazilian who cared about nothing except his bank account. He worked with the capangas and marginals of the worst part of Brazilian criminals.

He told them the ape was worth about $10,000 American money. They were rubbing their greedy hands together.

Harriet woke up with a very bad headache. If anyone had ever thought she was a little bit dangerous, unstable, or unpredictable, they might have been right, but none of the Gringos ever saw her in this state of mind. She was normally very docile and playful, even to the extent of playing a practical joke on them when they least expected it. None of them had the slightest inclination that she was capable of harming a human, without a VERY good reason. That reason just hit midnight on the clock of doom.

The angry primate broke the bonds they had secured her with as if they were tissue paper. She looked around and got her bearings. It was time that some knuckleheads found out what a red-haired, infuriated primate could do when she had a good reason. The four happy-go-lucky, would-be-rich criminals were sitting at a round table, talking about how each would spend their share of the bounty. They were not prepared for the battle of their lives, which was about to begin.

The first thing that startled them was when the door to Harriet's room came crashing down flat on the wooden floor. They all went bug-eyed when they noticed her hair was not the only red thing. Her eyes were blazing with anger. She had been shot, and she didn't like it one bit. They ran for the front door but forgot they had locked it and stored the key in the freezer.

There was no time to get it, as the furious ape stood between them and the freezer. She grabbed the neck of the closest one to her, lifting him, and gave the unfortunate soul one huge blow from one of her feet. He went through the bathroom door as if it were a Japanese paper wall and landed in the ceramic tub. He was still conscious, but thought it best to pretend he was not. He just slunk down into the tub and laid there motionless.

The other three capangas thought if they all charged at once, they could confuse and dominate her. They apparently spent too much time watching cartoons instead of the nature channel because they had no idea how strong orangutans really are. She caught two by the waist and knocked their heads together, then threw them against each of the walls. The third one thought he heard his mommy calling him and hightailed it out of there.

When the two regained their senses after being flung against the wall, they decided to zoom out of there before they were toast. They ran to their vehicle praying they could escape with their lives. The only problem was their imported 1946 Larmar 249cc from England was no match for the strength of an enraged Borneo orangutan.

Harriet flipped the Larmar mini-car like a fluffy pancake. The occupants burst out of broken windows, headed in whatever direction they were facing when they escaped from the car, and were never seen again by anyone near Fortaleza.

During all this chaotic battle, Edwardo was convinced he had escaped. BUT ... Harriet followed him to the beach area of town and found him hiding behind a rock close to the water's edge. He still had the shotgun and was aiming it at her. Just then, a wave hit the rock and knocked him down. Harriet grabbed the gun and smashed it into the rocks—ensuring that the shotgun could never harm any living creature again. Then she gripped him with both hands, raised his unlucky carcass over her head, walked into the sea up to her knees, and threw him into the oncoming waves.

The last she saw of him, he was swimming out to sea to save his miserable, now much poorer, hide.

The ape was sitting on the beach trying to recover her senses when she heard the police sirens approaching. She never liked a lot of noise, so she took off towards the buildings along the boardwalk. No one knows exactly how she found her way home, but she did.

Jack and Luke came to breakfast with the news that the police had been called to a suspicious hideout because of all the noise of a tremendous battle. They found the place broken to pieces, but there was no one present to take the blame. The authorities thought all of this seemed to be a little strange.

There was also a report from the Coast Guard. They had rescued a wanted criminal who had swam about two miles out into the bay. His name was Edwardo Fonseco Silva da Cruz dos Dores dos Santos. They were baffled at his delirious babbling. It didn't make sense to them. What was he planning to do, swim to Miami? He wasn't giving them any information to explain his weird actions.

They all wondered if Harriet might have had something to do with all these stories. They were about to pray for food when Kosy ran into the room. She was hardly able to blurt it out, "Harriet is back! She is sitting in the mango tree eating bananas."

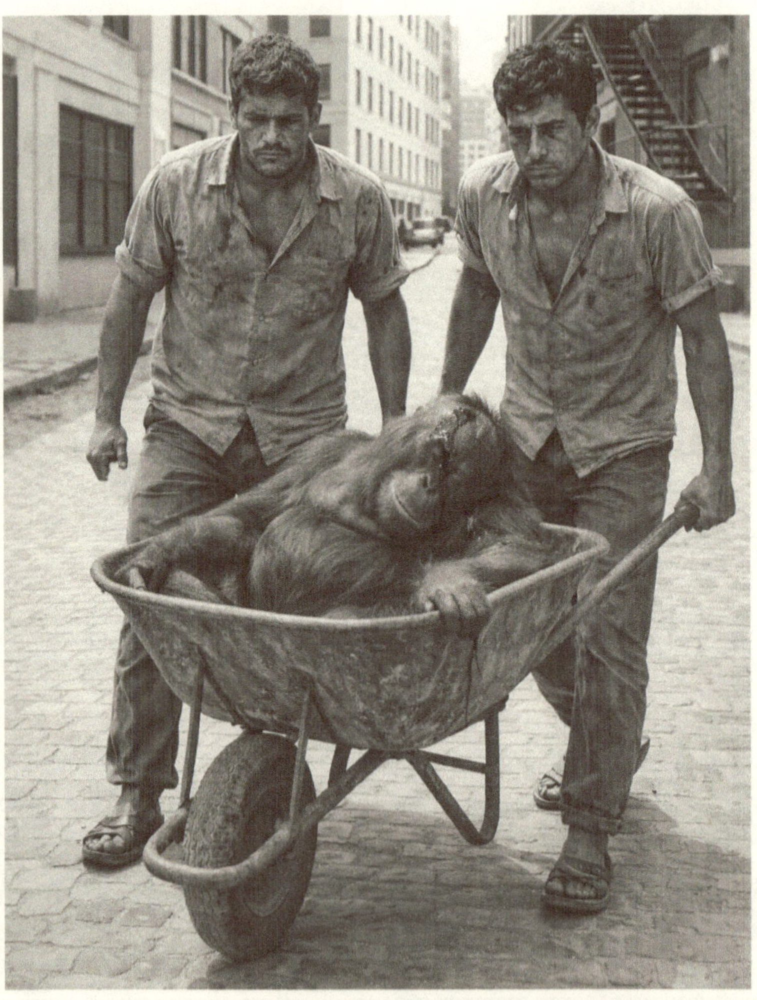

Harriet was out cold on the cobblestone street in the alley after falling off a fire escape ladder. The two thugs put her in a wheelbarrow and rushed toward their hideout.

CHAPTER 15
A Cardboard House

Many homeless Brazilians, including children, live in cardboard shacks like this.

All the happy Gringos and the two tourist guides ran out to the coconut trees after Kosette alerted them. Sure enough, they found Harriet balancing on a limb in the mango tree. Shane coaxed her down, then noticed a wound on her noggin. They brought Harriet into the house, cleaned her wound, and put a bandage on her head. If she looked scary before, now she resembled an unshaven pirate!

Bert spoke up. "We'll probably never know what happened last night unless we talk to that lunkhead in jail, who thought Harriet was a monkey. I'm not keen on that today. It's enough to see her safe. Still, I wish I'd seen their faces when they figured it out."

After resting at the house, the Gringos began planning how to make the most of their remaining time before the Wednesday night church service marking the end of their stay in Fortaleza. First on their list was a trip to the Christian bookstore. They invited some Brazilian Christians from outside the capital to the bookstore.

At the bookstore, the Brazilians from other towns asked TJ, the owner, where he was from. "I'm not an American," he said.

They stared. "You must be! No one speaks English that well unless they're American. Are you sure?"

TJ shook his head. "I'm not an American." He smiled and returned to the counter.

They couldn't believe it. "No one speaks English that well unless he's an American. You're just kidding us, aren't you? You're really an American, right?" He insisted he was not and walked away. They were smirking and smiling. They knew he was joking. They knew for sure NO ONE speaks English that well unless they were raised in the States.

He returned to his position behind the counter, smiling as he usually did when this conversation came up, and it came up regularly. He never told anyone, not unless he had to—he was Canadian! Most Brazilians think that in Canada, they speak Canadian (whatever language that may be). They didn't know anything about the English and French spoken there.

Jack noticed a newborn baby in a stroller. Having five kids of his own, he was attracted to the little tyke. He asked the mother what the baby's name was. Louisa, the proud mother, said, "My daughter's name is 'Feemallie'," as she pronounced it.

Jack frowned. "I've lived in Brazil for 35 years and never heard this name. Where'd you get it?"

Louisa agreed. "Me neither. It's not Portuguese or Brazilian."

Luke asked, "So, how did you choose it?"

She replied, "I saw an American hospital film. The baby's wristband said 'Female.' I liked it and used it for my daughter."

Later, Jack joked to Luke, "If she has a boy someday, maybe he'll be 'Mallie.'"

Linda was looking at various Portuguese books when she noticed a girl dressed rather poorly standing very close to the book rack. Feeling suspicious, Linda kept her eye on the girl. When she saw the Brazilian slip a book into her jacket pocket and start toward the door, Linda ran to find TJ and told him the girl was stealing a book.

TJ hurried out and caught the girl in front of the store's large display window. "Would you mind emptying your pockets, please?"

The girl panicked and tried to run, but TJ gripped her jacket. He said gently, "Please, empty your pockets." She bowed her head, tears coming. TJ softened, knelt, and hugged her. "Why did you take from our store?"

The girl trembled, pulling a small New Testament from her coat. "I heard this book tells wonderful stories of God and love. I can read a bit. I wanted to learn about this God, because no one loves me."

TJ struggled not to cry. On his knees, in front of the bookstore, he asked her, "Where do you live? What's your name?"

The girl was dressed in rags and smelled bad. Her brown scraggly hair was lightly blowing in the wind. She also carried an aluminum cup to beg for money. "I live in the ditch behind the docks, about three blocks from here. My mom died last year, and there was no one to take care of me."

By this time, the Gringos had come out to the sidewalk to listen to the conversation. Jack was interpreting for the group. Some of the Americans were in tears, especially Kosette, who was the most tender-hearted. Billy wiped his eyes with the back of his hand. Loretta, wanting privacy to compose herself, returned to the store to avoid being seen weeping. The scene was heartbreaking for them all.

After listening to the girl's gut-wrenching story, Luke wanted to see her living conditions for himself. He invited her into the VW van, and together with the rest of the group, they drove toward the docks.

The Americans continued down the pier until they came to that dock. They all descended, and the girl took them to the far side where she lived. On the way, the boys stepped on several huge cockroaches, and Shane kicked three ugly rats into the bay, hoping they flunked Rodent Swimming 101. This was an intolerable situation.

Erin tried to explain everything to Billy, who had not stopped crying since they left the bookstore. Billy had experienced homelessness, but hearing about this was more than he could comprehend. The tragedy, the desperation, and the utter hopelessness were difficult for him to process.

The girl was eight years old and had no one, absolutely NO ONE, who cared for her or wanted her. Jack and Luke knew there were kids like this in the city; they had heard of them and read about their dreadful plight in the city newspaper. However, until now, they had never met any of them or seen where they lived. For these veteran missionaries, this was an entirely new experience.

The Americans were informed that almost nothing had been done for children like her; city, state, and federal services seemed nonexistent. This deepened their concern as they processed the situation.

Her house was a large cardboard box, once holding a refrigerator; it read "Electrolux." The top was bowed, likely pooling water when it rained, and the bottom was damp.

In the corner was a dirty blanket, empty Coke cans, and plastic bags. No food or water was in sight. Marty thought, "Where does she spend her days? Nights I can see."

Bowie spoke his mind. "I have relatives who live on the Nez Perce reservation in Eastern Oregon. Their situation isn't very good; it's actually rather poor. BUT, I've never seen anything like this, and am deeply moved. Is there something we can do for this little tyke?"

Bert, the rich boy, was the most moved by the scene. He knew how good he had had it all his life. He was pampered, spoiled, and yet he had been such a rebel, a bully, and a brat. His well-to-do parents were ashamed of him for most of his teen years. It was only the testimony of these goody-two-shoes, these religious fanatics, as he used to call them, that had brought him to Christ and eternal life.

He had heard some people in the world lived like this. He never thought he'd see it himself. The Indians on the Amazon were better off than this poor little girl was.

Erin was upset. "How can the guards let this happen? They know about her. Don't they care?"

Jack, not trying to defend the guards, explained, "Most Brazilians know about situations like this. There aren't any social programs like in the USA." He turned: "Your mother is gone. What about your father?"

She was so shy and didn't want to answer the questions. "My dad is a drug dealer, and he cares nothing for me. I see him now and then. Sometimes he gives me some money, but he has too much to do and lives in a big fancy apartment downtown."

Linda wiped her eyes. "I'm not moving until we help her. Living like this—cockroaches, rats—it's horrible. She's eight! What can we do? I mean it; I won't leave her like this."

Luke asked her what she owned. "Is this all you have in life? What's here?" She nodded, affirming it. "Would you be willing to go to our campground and stay with us for a few days?" She looked surprised, a little suspicious in fact. No one had ever asked her: "How long have you lived here? What's your name?"

She was warming up to them. Maybe they COULD be trusted. "My name is Rosa Maria Santos de Coelho, and I've lived here for a year, ever since my mom died. There are hundreds of children like me living all around Fortaleza, homeless, hungry, and abandoned. Some don't even have a cardboard house, as I do; they sleep on the street. Did you not know this? Have you never heard of us before?"

Jack and Luke were a bit ashamed to admit they had known about these street kids, some of whom even lived in the sewers beneath the city streets. They wanted to do something for Rosa and needed her to agree. "Will you come with us and stay at our campground for a few days? We're going to do something for you."

She consented and grabbed her two torn plastic bags, all the belongings she had in the world. The ex-homeless girl gave the cardboard box a swift kick, and it caved in; a rat and two cockroaches fled their collapsing abode. She stomped on the roaches with all her scorn and threw her aluminum cup at the runaway rat. Turning her back on it all, she put her hand in the outstretched hand of Bowie Pinetree, "I'm ready, let's go!"

[AUTHOR NOTE: Real-world house in Fortaleza, former governor's home, purchased by Maranatha Baptist Mission. The campus was converted into a campground for missionaries to stay. My family stayed in the house while attending Portuguese language school.]

Rosa was happy to have met more friends than she had in her entire life. She was introduced to Harriet as the ape was sharing bananas with her miniature primate friends. Bowie looks on and smiles.

CHAPTER 16
Church Service in Portuguese

The people listened intently as Pastor Rudenei Carvalho Silva dos Santos spoke at Faith Baptist Church of Mesejana. Francisco and his wife sat in the front row with their eldest daughter and her boyfriend.

At the Christian campground, Rosa quickly became the center of attention, welcomed with open arms. The group, eager to help her, notified the authorities about her move from her cardboard box on the docks. Jack and Luke, attentive to Rosa's needs throughout, anticipated no difficulties with the process. Now, as Rosa began her journey toward a better life, Jack and Luke focused on finding her a home, ideally with a family that already had children.

Later that same day, the Sunday evening service at Faith Baptist Church of Mesejana was organized by the Gringo group, who planned to give testimonies and present special music. Pastor Rudenei would deliver the message, with Jack serving as interpreter for the Americans present, ensuring both Portuguese and English-speaking groups could participate.

Shortly before the service began, 38 visitors arrived from the beach, led by Francisco, the fisherman whom Erin had saved from drowning. Francisco and his family of eight were surrounded by their extended family and friends. The crowd—mainly fishermen and factory workers—gathered in support of Francisco, who was recognized in the community for his dedication as both a husband and father.

Francisco's children, all doing well in the nearby public school, reflected their parents' commitment—Carla helped them with daily homework. Their desire for a better life for their children united them as a strong family. Even if Francisco had drowned, they believed their family would not be broken, an attitude shared by other families in the close-knit fishing community.

The pastor shifted focus to the Americans, asking two from the Gringo group to give their testimonies of salvation. Their group agreed that Loretta and Bart had the most dramatic stories to share.

Loretta began by recounting her personal story. She described how addiction drew her away from her children and responsibilities, ultimately leading her into severe hardship. Loretta's journey included dramatic turns, such as time in a Russian Siberian prison camp, where she encountered a pastor's wife who explained God's forgiveness. This personal transformation story established Loretta as a central figure in this part of the service.

She explained clearly, "My good works could never be enough to pay for my sins. Only the applied blood of the Lamb of God, Jesus, could release me from eternal condemnation. The pastor's wife said I needed to invite Christ into my heart for salvation because He comes only by invitation.

"In my heart, I knew these words were true, so I accepted Christ. He saved me and gave me eternal life. I'm so thankful and want to serve Him. I hope you'll realize your need for salvation before it is too late. God bless all of you."

Jack, the interpreter for the Brazilians, added a few comments after wiping tears from his eyes. "If you want to talk to us about your own need for salvation, please come up to any one of us after the service. The most important thing for us to do today would be to help you come to Christ."

Bert spoke next. "I was born into a wealthy family, surrounded by luxury—houses, cars, vacations. I became spoiled and rebellious, making life difficult for others. My main goal was to lie and cheat my way to the top. I saw good people as my enemies. I had little respect for the law or for others.

"This group of Christians (pointing at the Gringos) never stopped praying for me, though I resented it. When I was arrested for selling illegal liquor, my only phone call was to Shane. I realized what he had was what I needed—God's forgiveness and peace. In jail, I read a tract from a policeman that made it clear my good works could not save me. I needed to invite Jesus into my life to be forgiven. I did, and He truly saved me.

"I was changed as the Bible says: 'If anyone is in Christ, he is a new creation; old things have passed away, everything has become new.' My parents noticed the change right away. I didn't set my mind to improving; I was changed from within. I hope you can also be freed from the penalty of sin by coming to Christ and asking Him to save you.

"This is what's called 'being born again' or 'being saved.' God bless you, and I pray you'll make this decision to have your name written in the book of life and secure your eternity with God."

The visitors listened attentively as the testimonies ended and the pastor prepared to conclude the meeting. Shifting the focus from the personal stories, he emphasized the message of salvation and invited reflection. "If you were to stand in front of the Pearly Gates and God asked you, 'WHY SHOULD I LET YOU INTO MY GLORIOUS HEAVEN,' what answer would you give Him to make the gates open and allow you to enter?" This was a good question that anyone could relate to. It didn't insult anyone and made each person come up with an answer.

"If you said it was because you were a good person, the gates would not open. Perhaps you might say you were no worse than anyone else; the gates would remain closed. Maybe being a church member would be your answer. The Pearly Gates would not open for this reply either.

"The only answer that will make the gates swing wide open is: 'I've accepted Christ as my only and sufficient Savior to apply His blood sacrifice to my sin. I'm born again, by faith through grace.'

"Do you have assurance that you're going to heaven? If not, and you want that assurance, then please talk to any of us after the service. We're here to help you come to know the ONLY way to be saved, Jesus Christ." With that invitation, the pastor closed the meeting.

As the evening drew to a close and the service concluded, the atmosphere remained charged with hope and change. Francisco and his wife worked their way through the crowd to find the pastor. They wanted to accept Christ as their Savior. He took them into his office, and they were born again. Three other adults talked to Jack and Luke, and also would find their names written in the book of life. It was a glorious meeting.

After the meeting, Loretta's concern for Rosa resurfaced. Loretta, wanting assurance about Rosa's future, spoke with Jack and Luke. The group's attention shifted to discussing Rosa's options with Francisco. Together, the adults explored whether Francisco's family could temporarily take Rosa in, emphasizing the important role of Francisco and his wife in Rosa's placement.

They said it might not be possible for them to keep her for years to come; it all depended on the success of his fishing ventures. Their house was not big, but they could always crisscross another hammock in the girls' room. They promised she'd never be alone again. Possibly, they could even get her into one of their extended families with fewer children.

Francisco's wife had a brother in Aracatí who had only one child and was looking to adopt another. She was sure this would work out.

Rosa was ecstatic. "Wow! You mean I'm going to have a new home with brothers and sisters? I'm not going to sleep in the box with roaches and rats anymore. I'm so happy. Am I going to school, too? Will I be able to take showers with clean water and sit at a table to eat?" Francisco assured her that she would have all of this and more. They were glad to help her find a home at last.

A few days later, after arrangements for Rosa had begun to fall into place, the Gringos decided they wanted to go back to the beach one more time before moving southeast to Mossoró. Jack and Luke wanted to visit Rosa in her new home. They collected clothes, school supplies, and treats to give her. Rosa seemed to have wormed her way into their hearts and would be there forever. Jack and Luke needed to drive the vans.

Finding Francisco's home was easy. It was right on the beach. The simple structure had seven rooms, four of which were bedrooms. The front porch had his fishing net hanging on a sturdy pole. As usual, the beds were just hammocks rolled up and hooked to the wall during the day, making the rooms available for other uses. The Americans bought Rosa a new hammock. It was multicolored with beautiful hand-crocheted string trimming. Rosa was delighted.

The seaside experience was fascinating as usual. The warm water gently beat upon the brown sand, and the shallow depth allowed them to walk out into the Atlantic for 300 feet, with water only up to their waists. Billy was right at home in the short waves. He loved to feel the firm sandy bottom as it slanted slightly toward the deeper water.

After enjoying the welcoming home and time with Rosa, Bert and Linda took a walk along the shore. Suddenly, they came upon a chaotic scene. The sand was covered with a multitude of starfish about half the size of Bert's hand. They were trying to reach the water, but it was a long ways off, and they didn't have legs or wheels. Seagulls were swooping down and picking them up at will, hauling them off for lunch and dinner. Bert began picking them up with both hands and tossing them into the oncoming, gentle waves.

Linda wasn't going to touch the ugly, spikey crustaceans. In fact, she questioned what he was doing. "Really, Bert, do you think you're going to make a lick of difference. Look at this beach. There must be thousands of them. It's not possible to throw all of them in. The seagulls are still going to get most of these unfortunate creatures."

Bert continued working without pause, increasing his speed as he picked up starfish. Meeting Linda's eyes, he tossed two into the sea and said, for each one he helped, it made a difference. He picked up two more and said, "That mattered for them, too." Though acknowledging he couldn't save them all, Bert remained determined to help as many as possible, asking Linda to fetch the others for assistance. Finally catching on to Bert's enthusiastic attitude about the starfishes' survival, Linda rushed back to bring help.

Everyone pitched in, and it appeared they were gaining ground on the seagulls. Even Billy could help. He felt around, and when he found a starfish, he picked it up and heaved it in the direction of the noise, the constant, rhythmic soft beating of the waves against the beach.

Kosette had to stand closer to the water as her pitching arm wasn't as powerful as the others. Marty, being a good baseball hurler, took his place at the highest point on the beach and was flinging them like frisbees. It was quite a sight to behold.

When Harriet started tossing starfish, it was time to be ready to duck. She wasn't interested in which way she was throwing them. She just thought it was a fun human game. They were flying straight up and coming back down on the beach, some even ending vertically as one of their tube legs sunk into the soft sand. She was flinging more than they were, but not making much of a difference to the starfish's survival.

Shane tried to help her understand that the starfish she was launching high into the air needed to end up in the ocean eventually. She seemed to comprehend a little. At least she started hurling them in the general direction of the ocean.

Billy, the brains of the outfit, was enjoying being able to participate and contribute more than just good ideas. While he continued to lob starfish into the water, he made a mental note. "This whole ordeal would make a great sermon illustration. I'm going to have to talk to Pastor Ballentine about it when we get back to Oregon."

Bert starts throwing starfish into the ocean to save as many as he can before the seagulls eat them. Linda told him he wasn't going to make a big difference.

CHAPTER 17
Semi-Desert in Brazil

Sloths are great climbers, but they move very slowly. In Brazil, sloths are frequently seen in cashew trees, eating both the leaves and the nuts. They always appear to be smiling at you.

It's hard to imagine any part of Brazil as semi-desert. Yet, some regions escape humidity entirely. Mossoró sits 350 miles south of the equator and 35 miles from the ocean. Five years could pass without a single drop of rain. Moisture-laden clouds drenched Natal to the east and Fortaleza to the west, leaving Mossoró dry. Everything died—no green grass, no public flowers.

Thermal activity simmered beneath Mossoró; well water reached 155 degrees—too hot to touch or bathe in, but perfect for coffee without a kettle.

Residents daily faced extreme heat from above and searing heat from below, like living in a double-roasting oven. When temperatures dropped to 80 degrees, locals wore coats and sweaters.

The sun rose at 5:30 AM and set at 5:30 PM year-round. Daylight Savings Time came to Brazil, but not Mossoró—it wasn't needed. The heat was suffocating, like an oven. Many stores closed at noon for lunch and a quick siesta, reopening at 2:00 PM. Most closed at 6:00 PM.

Even at midnight, heat lingered above 90°. No season brought relief. In Fortaleza, it was sweltering and dry or sweltering and wet; here, it was hotter and harsher. Residents faced a higher skin cancer risk than anywhere else in South America. Some dubbed Mossoró the armpit of Brazil. Over 90% of low-income people lacked air conditioning. Many lay in hammocks, soaking shirts for coolness, with bedwetters on the bottom tier.

Early the next morning the Gringos and one banana eater grabbed a public bus to Mossoró, leaving Jack and Luke behind. Tom Ballentine, the Oregon pastor's brother in Rio Grande do Sul, had some missionary friends in Mossoró who would provide housing and tour-guide assistance for the Americans.

Halfway to Mossoró, the bus stopped. Locals sold field corn baked on a metal can that had been turned into a camp stove. A side hole allowed for charcoal—just pre-burnt branches—to be added.

The Americans, unused to field corn, found it tough to chew with some burnt edges. Women also sold tapioca made in tin cans.

Before they could finish chewing the hard corn, the bus driver told everyone to get aboard. The Gringos took the corn with them.

Every mile toward Mossoró increased the heat: cracked earth, dead trees, shimmering air over blistered asphalt. The discomfort was painful. The bus had no air conditioning; open windows brought only scorching blasts that whipped their hair around—well, at least the girls' hair.

Mossoró is halfway between Fortaleza and Natal, the capitals of Ceará and Rio Grande do Norte. Intense heat slowed the city. Main industries were rock salt, pineapples, cashew fruit, and nuts. A hotel drilling for hot water for its pool struck oil, instantly turning Mossoró into a boom town.

Huge sums of money flooded the area. Every bank became a fortress of cash. This wealth drew criminal syndicates. The Mafia arrived, and bank robberies surged tenfold. Police responded by posting two armed guards at each bank. Life in this formerly-peaceful city turned nightmarish.

The Mossoró mayor said, "Money isn't what people claim it is. We're in dire straits and need federal help to control the Mafia's influx. They're involved in oil, salt, liquor, drugs, and money laundering—too much for local police to control."

Each town had police checkpoints at entrances and exits. All vehicles slowed to 20 mph. This is where they checked truck documents and sometimes weight. If a violation occurred, sometimes lunch money would get the car or truck back on the road quickly.

At other places around town, some were stopped for document checks, called a "blitz." Random stops often yielded tickets and impounded vehicles. Brazilians disliked it but could do nothing about it.

At the checkpoint, new missionaries met the Americans and led them to their housing annex at the town's main church. Breakfast and lunch would be served there. Every night, they were to eat with different Brazilian hosts to taste local food. Pastor Donn Kittle would meet them later.

After settling in, they planned to visit the zoo. Harriet perched comfortably on the roof, shaded and near banana and mango trees—close, but not too close. Off to the zoo she went, leashed.

Few cities in the Brazilian interior have zoos, but Mossoró does. Its spot on the main highway between Natal and Fortaleza made it a commercial hub for truck traffic from São Paulo and Rio de Janeiro. Via large outdoor ads tourists were encouraged to visit the zoo.

The zoo featured an anaconda, monkeys, parrots, and a sloth. Linda boldly claimed no interest in the anaconda, and no one argued. Harriet was fascinated by the primates, trading faces and grunts as Marty let her get close.

Kosy asked the zookeeper about the sloth. He said it was in the big tree. She replied that the group had looked, but hadn't seen it. He assured her, "Have patience. It's there."

They returned and stared up. Bowie suddenly spotted it: "It looks like a large bump on the trunk. Keep looking." Finally, everyone saw it.

Billy asked how long the sloth took to descend the tree. The zookeeper said 40 minutes, noting it was the animal's only defense. The group lacked the needed time to see it happen. Marty joked that it reminded him of Erin getting out of bed, earning him a warning look from his sister.

Before returning to the dorm, they aimed for fresh ice cream. The flavors were unique and local—green corn, cashew, passion fruit, and guava. They sampled all of them. Linda loved them until she tasted the passion fruit. She quickly spat it out.

Linda's eyes swelled and watered. She grew very uncomfortable. It would be her! The group rushed to the dorm. Before arrival, Linda was already puffed up; her body signaled a severe passion fruit allergy. Her eyes swelled shut, her lips doubled in size, and blistered. She was miserable and wanted a mirror, but Erin thought otherwise.

She wasn't in pain, just terribly puffed up and swollen. "Geve me a mirror, peas." Even Bert thought better of it, but still she insisted. Finally, she squinted out of her left eye and almost fainted. Her words came out slurred. "Whaa happen me? I'm a monster. Yook at my farce! Awo deadful. Don anone take my pitcure now." No one would have dreamed of it.

Passion fruit, guava, and cashew fruit have strong smells and flavors. If allergic to one, it usually means the person will also be allergic to the other two. A person can even start reacting to the odor even from across the room or on the highway if a truckload is ahead of them. These people avoid even getting close to the fruit section in the stores.

Jack told a story: "A visitor cut open a raw cashew nut, and pulp juice touched an open sore. It was toxic—they nearly lost their arm and needed hospital care. Factory workers wear gloves and wash up every hour. Raw nuts are toxic, but roasted, they're delicious and shipped worldwide."

The Gringos dined without Linda, who lay nearly unconscious, face swollen, barely able to speak. When ready, she'd surely give a dramatic account; everyone eagerly awaited it.

Kosy leaned over and asked Erin about a trail on her arm by her elbow, shaped like half a circle. "What's THAT?" They all looked at it and couldn't figure it out. They showed the missionary and asked him what it was. He said it was a worm. This didn't sit well with Erin. "What! I have a worm wiggling around under my skin? What kind of worm is it?"

"It's called a geographical worm. It comes into your system from the outside of your skin. It's from an insect that bites you and leaves its egg under your epidermis. The worm moves, making that trail just under the skin's surface. If you want to cut it out, we can. Its body is the lump you see. If you can wait a few days, it can be killed by applying a cream. All the pharmacies carry it. It's a standard item you can get without a prescription."

Erin opted to have it cut out. "I can't stand a worm under my skin, not for one minute. It's a horrible thing to think of. Cut it out, NOW." She was warned it would leave a little scar. "I can handle the scar, I can't, and will never be able to accept a parasite making my arm its private freeway." It was cut out promptly. Linda's artistic descriptions apparently were contagious.

With the recent skin problems, Missionary Kittle decided to have all of them check each other for any other skin infections, a thorough going over, from head to toe. Marty came up with a black spot about the size of a BB with a white center. This was diagnosed as a "foot worm." Bert also had one. These infestations were just above the back edge of their shoes.

Donn informed them, "We'll have to cut this out. It's rather painless— almost. Those who don't take care of this will lose their whole leg. It can kill you if you don't cut it out. I can show you a man in a wheelchair. He lives only three blocks from here. He didn't take care of it. Now, he has lost both legs. Another neighbor didn't take care of it and died with 110 in his body. This is serious. "

Marty and Bert had them cut out immediately and were glad they had been told to look for anything under the skin.

Bowie had asked to take the pastor's motorcycle for a ride. He took Erin in the sidecar and Kosy on the back seat. They zoomed around the city, across the river that divided the metropolis, and out to the police checkpoint at the outskirts of the town. On the way back, Bowie felt something painful on his right wrist and bicep. When he got back to the dorm, he felt like the spots were on fire, and he had a fever. The skin on his face began to feel like leather.

Donn took one look and knew what it was, "This is from a potó. It's an insect, like a mosquito, that urinates on you and burns your skin. If the fluid hits your eyes, you'll be blind for life. You're lucky to have been wearing a helmet and a clear plastic face shield. It probably saved you from being hit in the face. We'll go to the pharmacy right away and get you a shot for this. It'll be cleared up by tomorrow night."

Billy wanted to know if the Gringos had determined to experience ALL the infectious insects in the area? "It appears that we're magnets for these weird creatures."

Donn said it had something to do with the year-round hot climate. When you get to Rio Grande do Sul, where it's colder, even freezing in August, with snow, these insects won't be found there. They don't like cold weather, except for the "foot worm," which likes it everywhere in Brazil.

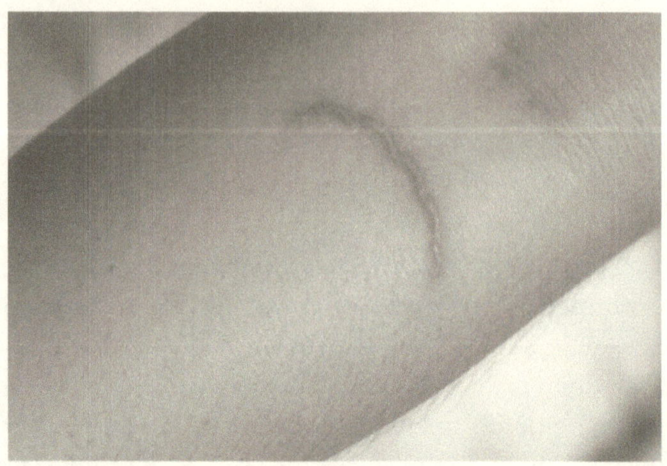

Erin had a geographical worm (Cutaneous Larva Migrans or "Creeping Eruption") under her skin.

Erin, Billy, and Bowie observe a northeasterner barbecuing corn on the cob in the semi-desert between Fortaleza and Mossoró.

CHAPTER 18
The Opposition

Because Mossoró is located 350 miles from the equator and is sitting above something causing a lot of heat, it's the hottest city in Brazil. Well water is 155° and even at 2:00 AM the ambient temperature is still around 80 degrees, making life miserable for the 200,000 people living there.

Grace Baptist Church in the Pedro Velho neighborhood was started 27 years earlier. In fact, its building was considered by the state as a historical landmark. When the present missionary arrived on the scene, the church was closed because it had seen some difficult years. The last missionary working there had to go back to the United States because of severe health problems.

Donn Kittle had been in town for only three years. Reflecting on his early days, he described his first experiences to the Gringos. "My Portuguese was not that good, having just graduated from language school in Fortaleza. The five ladies who remained in the area wanted to reopen the church building and resume services. About halfway through the sermon, struggling with my Portuguese, a few bats started swooping down around the congregation.

"If that was not disorienting enough, sometimes one would hit the overhead fan. Everyone would duck, unsure where the body might land. If I hoped to keep their attention, I had to deal with the bats. The prior missionary had left me a fox skin, with a note suggesting I nail it to the rafters to deter the bats. I tried it, but it didn't work.

"Finally, we had to remove ALL the roofing tiles, stacking them on the roof's wooden supports. When we did this, it disrupted all of the nocturnal mammals' nesting sites. During the three days it took to finish the job, we used barrel lids and tennis rackets to whack them as they flew around the auditorium. We were able to kill 180 of them. That gave us a better 'batting average' than the Chicago Cubs.

"Another problem we are experiencing right now is that halfway through the service, our electricity goes out. All our neighbors have lights, but we don't. Some of our people are getting nervous, saying we're having problems with the Spiritists in town—curses and all—you know what I'm talking about. I really don't have an explanation."

Billy wanted to know whether there had been any recent improvements to the building. Donn, glancing at the newly coated walls, explained that whitewash had been thrown on the building just a week ago. Billy, leaning forward, asked if the problem existed before the paint job, prompting the preacher to reply, "The lights going out in the middle of the service started just after the paint job. I never considered that. Do you think it has something to do with the problem, Billy?"

Billy, the group's small but clever thinker, evaluated the situation. Suspecting an electrical wiring issue, he asked the missionary to take him where the wires entered the building. "Is the connection a clamp or a box?" he asked.

Donn fetched the ladder and climbed up to inspect the connection. He called down to the group, "It just has one wire doubled over the other. Is this a viable problem?"

Billy, experienced with technical issues from his studies, instructed, "Shut off the power at the street first." After confirming the power was off, he advised, "Now, take a pair of vice grips or pliers to separate the wires." Donn followed these instructions. Billy then prompted, "Are there some black burnt marks around the connection?"

There were. "Here's your problem: when the paint hit, whitewash seeped into the connection. After 20 minutes, the wires overheated and separated at the blackened areas. Clean those spots with sandpaper, twist the wires together, and clamp tightly for now. Later, add a proper connection clamp."

Billy always tried to find the physical reason, the logical solution, rather than attributing every abnormality to demons or every wonderful occurrence to God. "I figured there was some connection problem, some logical explanation." He was right again.

Later, as the Gringos were going downtown to the central market, Marty spotted another Spiritist offering. It was quite elaborate, like the deluxe one they had seen in Fortaleza. He had learned his lesson; therefore, he didn't touch anything on it. He did take photos of it, quite a few in fact.

Donn disapproved, but Marty had already taken several photos. As Marty noticed Donn's gesture to stop, he put the camera away. However, several nearby people had noticed, and their unfriendly stares revealed their displeasure.

There are various forms of Spiritism in Brazil. The highest form doesn't require these bloody sacrifices. The lower types do and say these are necessary if a blessing is to come from the spirit world. Usually, chicken's blood is used. There are leaders and co-leaders for these followers. They have weekly meetings in their own buildings, just like churches do. They expect their followers to give money to support the leaders, just like churches do.

Pastor Kittle was very clear. "The Bible leaves no doubt. These offerings are not given to God. Even the followers of these religious groups know and teach that. They're reaching out to the spirit world. The Word of God teaches that these offerings are given to demons. "The Apostle Paul says that because of this, we should be aware and keep far from these evil things. There is NEVER, EVER supposed to be any mixing of their ideas or practices with our faith."

After this conversation, the Gringos wanted to know just how these Spiritist things, curses and such, could affect the lives of believers. Because of Pastor Ballentine's preaching and teaching in their home church back in Oregon, the Americans already knew a demon couldn't live in the same body where the Living Christ abode. Their questions were in the area of what ELSE a demon, or a herd of them, could do against any believer.

Donn was adamant that the only viable information a Christian can glean must come exclusively from the Word of God. So, he gave them many examples of what Satan or his demons did in the Bible. "Satan and his army of evil soldiers can only do what they are permitted to do by God. The devil sent thieves to rob a man named Job, a wind to kill all of his children, and even sickness to his body. BUT, he was always limited because God still had a divine plan for the rest of Job's life.

"We know a demon can never possess a believer, but he can be oppressed. Demons can camp all around him and cause havoc in his life. If a believer is walking carnally, it gives the evil forces a better chance to send in scouts and attackers to ruin his life. It's happened many times on this mission field. It's very dangerous to mess around with these evil icons, and foolish not to take them as a serious threat. It's very risky for a believer to walk carnally. That kind of behavior is dangerous to his health, well-being, and even to his life."

Billy, the thinker, the analytical mind, wanted some specific examples of what these demons or spirits could do in Mossoró. The missionary continued with the doctrine class. "They can burn your house down or send thieves to rob you. They can wreck your car, give you a flat tire, blow up your motor, or have someone steal your motorcycle.

"They can send unbearable temptation your way. Satan can kidnap your children or give you a sickness that will send you back to the States. I could go on and on. I've seen it all happen to believers and to good missionaries. I've seen it occur in the lives of both spiritual and carnal people. God said Job was a righteous person, and look at what Satan did to him."

Following this, Linda, the only non-believer, was shocked. She had never heard of this before. She was shaking her head. "What in the world are you talking about, anyway? Do you mean to tell me I'm in mortal danger every day of my life? Are you saying that Satan, if he really exists, can do all of these things to me? This is too much to fathom. It seems like a fairy tale to me. If there IS a God, I believe He's full of love and will watch over us, sending His angels to protect us. I can't imagine believing what you've just told me is true. If it is, I'd be scared to death to get out of bed. Even walking across the street would be dangerous. I'd be petrified to drive a car or fly in a plane."

In response, Loretta believed every word the pastor said. "It doesn't matter if you believe it or not, Linda. The Bible is the Word of God, and every truth He wants us to know about Satan and his army is in this book. I was often protected from the dark side. I know my life would have been snuffed out if it weren't for the grace of God and His guardian angels who watched over me.

"God IS love, Linda, but He is holy, too. This holiness has to be satisfied before He can allow us sinners into heaven. The life of Christ and His death met all the requirements necessary for us to be saved. That was God's part. Our part is to recognize our sin and condemnation before Him, repent of our sin, and invite Jesus Christ, the only and sufficient Savior, to come into our hearts and save us. Then we'll be saved and have eternal life. He protects His children from the enemy of their souls."

After this exchange, Linda shrugged and went to her room, making it clear she was not easy to convince. Erin wondered, since even a horrific event like the recent anaconda attack could not change her mind, what would it take for Linda to consider her eternal destiny?

Linda was tough to reach after seeing too many hypocrites—people who carried Bibles but didn't live up to their message. Though she did not consider these Americans hypocrites, she harbored considerable skepticism. Right after she had tried to kill herself by jumping off the Waterloo Bridge, her dad quit drinking and the whole family started going to Lacomb Baptist Church. But that didn't last very long. Right now, the three of them moved back to Atheist Avenue.

What she found hard to digest was the fact that if their God was as good as they said He was, why was there so much pain and misery in the world? In Linda's mind, if there was a God, He could make it better, but it seemed to be getting worse. She hadn't experienced a lot of it herself, but had seen it in magazines and on TV; misery that was the dirt-poor and dirt-floor kind. Children born with defects, the cruelty of wars, and the horror of floods, blizzards, tornadoes, and tsunamis bothered her humanitarian feelings. These terrible things killed hundreds of thousands at a time, even millions in wartime.

If God is love, even as Loretta just said He was, how is all of this evil and misery explained? In her logical mind, there was no way of just sloughing it off, ignoring it totally. Someone had to have an answer; she just hadn't met this person yet. Until she had some satisfaction in this area, she was not interested in making any spiritual decisions, as she had just seen these poor and ignorant people in Fortaleza make. No siree Bob, it would take someone of great intelligence to persuade her to convert.

<FADE TO HARRIET AT THE COMPOUND>

Harriet always slept on the roof, under a shelter built especially for her. It was more comfortable where she was than it would have been on the ground or in a building. At least, she got some breeze now and then. Also, she could throw her banana peelings on the ground from where she was sitting. She often tried to hit the huge guard dogs wandering the property at night. They had two German Shepherds, a Great Dane, and a Black-and-Tan hound dog for tracking.

The grounds were surrounded by a high, thick brick wall with glass embedded in the flat top. Above the broken glass it also had electric wires running the full length of the walls. Many Brazilian homes had the same security measures. It wasn't foolproof, but it was better than nothing, which is what most people had.

Security was an important issue in Brazil. Many companies provide guards to protect both businesses and homes. These guards take classes for two months, and some even wear guns. They guard the entrances to apartment buildings, banks, stores, hospitals, gas stations, and schools. These are not government employees. The security companies are privately owned and operated.

Some guards ride motorcycles and patrol an assigned eight-block area of town. They start at 10:00 PM and ride their bikes up and down the streets until 6:00 AM. Some residents pay the guards a monthly salary. Since there may be 100 homes or businesses on his route, he doesn't need to charge much per person. Usually, these guards are not armed. They have whistles and know where the public phones are. They can call 190 to have the police come quickly. Police are generally very responsive to calls from these roving security guards—a kind of professional courtesy.

Most homes have guard dogs. When the mailman is walking from house to house, just his presence agitates the dogs, and they start barking. One dog is the catalyst for the next one. The mailman hears these dogs all day long, every day on the route. It is torturous to the ears. He can't enter the yard. He must put the mail in a box located high enough so the vicious dog can't bite his hand.

The local Spiritist club was not a bit pleased with the Gringos being in their territory. They were messing with their clientele. Their sales were falling off, and they were losing the authority they had maintained with fear and curses. Some of the people who accepted Christ were their previous customers. They had already put several curses on Pastor Donn Kittle, but until now, nothing had happened to him. Maybe they needed more chicken's blood or more drum beaters.

They wanted to do something to put the skids on their declining business. The local leaders decided to send a message to the Americans: get out of town, and get out NOW, while they were still in one piece. The four thugs that were sent to give the message left their headquarters at midnight and headed straight for the Gringo's dorm. They had planned on spreading chicken's blood all over the building and breaking a few windows.

The capungas arrived at the property on four small Honda motorcycles. They decided to throw a blanket over the electrical wires, which would also provide a way to get over the embedded glass on the top of the wall. It worked well, and they were over in a flash. The distance to the dorm was about 50 yards. They figured it would be a breeze; no problem. They'd be done with their dastardly deeds and be gone before anyone was the wiser. They figured there might be some dogs, so they brought some poisoned meat to throw at them.

When they were just 15 feet from the dorm, the four dogs came around the corner woofing and barking. They were about to take the poison meat out of their backpacks to throw at the dogs when the ground shook under their feet. They were eyeball to eyeball with the biggest monkey they had ever seen. It didn't look friendly at all.

The light from the porch lit up the monkey's grinding teeth and its glaring eyes. Since fighting with a huge monkey for property rights was not what they signed up for, all four of them turned tail and lit out for the blanket on the wall. They would have all made it, too, if it hadn't been for that red-haired creature who could move faster than they could.

Just as they got to the wall and started pushing each other over, Harriet landed square in the middle of them. She had taken to the trees and arrived there before them. Now the fun really started. She was swiping the air with her long arms and knocking them over like bowling pins. The only thing that saved them was the Gringos' arrival, which called her off.

Donn grabbed one of them by the nape of the neck. "Well, well, well, what do we have here? Some local yokels want to befriend Brazil's only orangutan. Did you have a good introduction to our nightguard? She's a real loyal friend if you get on her good side, but I think you all got off to a bad start."

The rest of the gang didn't move. Donn kept them in the yard until the police arrived and hauled them off to the calaboose. They could see Harriet watching them from the roof, and they didn't dare try to escape. It appears they all agreed—jail would be safer than another encounter with the red-haired giant.

[AUTHOR NOTE: This is the real-world church that inspired the Mossoró bat story—notice the tile stacked on the roof. It REALLY happened to me.]

CHAPTER 19
Street Evangelism

The missionary used metal barrels and slabs of plywood to build a makeshift pulpit. People would gather around and stand there for a couple of hours listening to special music and preaching.

Bowie borrowed the pastor's 500cc Honda and drove Shane and Marty to visit Luciano Barcellos da Cruz on the north side. Bowie and Luciano exchanged nervous words in hesitant English. Outside, the hidden slash of a knife ruined the Honda's front tire. Frustrated, the group left the bike at Luciano's house and trudged home, anger simmering on every step.

Shane spotted a drunk staggering toward them. Tension knotted his stomach. Bowie and Marty stepped aside. The man ignored them and lurched straight into Shane, his weight pressing onto the grappler's shoulder. The sharp and overwhelming stench of liquor filled the air. Shane's voice trembled. "What do you want? Do you know us?"

In broken English, the drunk slurred, "I ham fends to Luciano." The others brought him to Luciano's house. Luciano told his wife to make coffee. The man, Valmir Sousa de Oliveira, owned the store across the street from Luciano's house. His wife had been saved for a while but couldn't convince Valmir to go to church with her. Their children sometimes went to Sunday school. Luciano and his wife had been praying for this man for quite a while.

Luciano wanted Valmir to drink at least ten cups of coffee before the service. They got eight down. Valmir sobered up quickly. Pastor Kittle was pleased—Luciano was his best soul winner in 39 years in Brazil.

The message was on the prodigal son, and Pastor Kittle explained its meaning. Valmir, sober enough, came forward during the invitation. A deacon took him aside and showed him how to accept Christ. The rest of the church stayed, curious about the neighborhood drunk. When Valmir returned, he gave them a big smile and two thumbs up. There was clapping and backslapping. If they weren't Baptist, they'd have danced for joy.

There's always doubt when someone this deep in the ditch makes a decision. Was it real? Will it last? How soon will they know? Churches and believers hesitate because they had seen some pretend to make decisions to gain something material. No one at Grace Baptist wanted Valmir's conversion to be one of those.

They weren't disappointed. The next morning, Luciano watched Valmir take all his liquor off the store shelves and pour it down the drain. "That should give the cockroaches a reason to go to the next AA meeting. I won't sell this devil's juice. It destroyed my life; I won't let it hurt my neighbors. I'll stock fruit juice and soft drinks instead."

Cristina, Valmir's wife, entered singing a trembling verse of the religious song Donn recognized as "At the Cross." She rested her hands, warm and shaking, on Donn's shoulders. "I have a new husband," she whispered, voice thick with emotion. "He came home sober last night—the first time I recall. Our five children just stared at him, wide-eyed. I sent them to school singing 'Jesus Loves Me.' Now, they can't wait to get home."

When Loretta heard Valmir's story, she couldn't contain a grin and a few joyful tears. "Glory to God! I've felt the choking grip of liquor and the sweet relief from it. Witnessing this change fills me with hope—it will transform his family and spread through the neighborhood. Everyone knew what a drunk he was. Now they'll know hope."

Valmir's decision upset local suppliers. The neighborhood knew about his store, but not that he was the main middleman in the state's black-market liquor trade. He kept this secret from everyone.

State liquor taxes were 45%, but the black market operated under the table, pocketing that extra profit. In Mossoró, this illegal business generated about $3 million per year. Valmir was deeply involved with the Brazilian Mafia.

A missionary in Juazeiro do Norte, John Paulson, had faced this group before. He helped many people with addictions to convert, so the Mafia retaliated—burning his church and shooting him. Crippled, John returned to lead from a wheelchair. Some take their calling seriously. John is one.

Valmir knew the risk and John's story. He hid his past ties from his wife to spare her worry. Instead, he confided in Pastor Kittle, explaining his role in the liquor trade.

The pastor was shocked and called a special meeting of the deacon board to decide how to help Valmir.

Next Sunday night, Valmir's neighbors filled the service, curious about his change. Three women approached the pastor. Grace spoke for them, "We know what a drunkard he was. What happened? Did he get religion?"

Donn answered briefly, since the service was starting. "This isn't a religious club or reform group. We preach Christ, His crucifixion, and resurrection. A new life comes from being born again. If you want more, my wife will talk to you after the service." They seemed satisfied and sat in the front.

After the service, the women talked to Isabelle, the pastor's wife, and prayed to accept Christ. Isabelle told them they now had eternal life, reminding them of John 3:16 and other Bible promises.

The three women offered Grace's house for an outdoor meeting. They set up a stage from five steel barrels and plywood, lit by a 100-watt bulb. Total darkness fell at 6:00 PM; the meeting began at 6:30 PM.

That night, the three women shared their stories. The women had invited many friends and neighbors. Over 150 people came out of curiosity. The Gringos sat up front. All three husbands spoke with the pastor and accepted Christ.

To keep momentum, Donn planned another meeting for the next

night. The Gringos proposed using Harriet as the main attraction—an ape's exebition of tricks and strength. Donn, surprised by this request but willing to cooperate, agreed and announced to the crowd that a huge Borneo ape would appear.

Daytime was for tourist activities. The Americans toured the salt flats at the beach, 35 miles away. Sea salt production, driven by heat, was a major industry in the area. Flats were flooded with seawater, then left to evaporate. When dry, bulldozers collected and mounded the salt. It was packaged and distributed for making ice cream and seasoning churrascaria-barbeque meat across South America. That meat, turned by electric rotisseries, was roasted on long knives over charcoal. This tradition started in Rio Grande do Sul, the Gringos' next stop, where Pastor Ballentine's brother lived.

With well water at 155°, locals built a hotel with nine pools. Water cooled as it flowed from one pool to the next, with temperatures decreasing in each pool until it reached the air temperature by the time it got to the last pool. The hotel was called Thermos Hotel.

The Americans spread out in the pool area because each wanted a different level of heat. Harriet was not allowed in the pool, for obvious reasons. It didn't seem she minded.

The evening service began with Shane and Harriet on the plywood stage. Shane, the grappler, demonstrated the ape's tricks. Harriet waved flags from Brazil and the USA. As Shane counted out loud, Harriet used her fingers and toes to count to twenty, just as he had trained her. She also bent a one-inch rebar until both ends touched—something no normal human could do.

Near the end of the exhibition, a tomato flew at Harriet from the back of the audience. She caught it, and popped it into her mouth, and downed it with a single swallow. Shane made it seem like part of the act, "We thank the generous Brazilian in back for donating to Harriet's food bill."

Suddenly, there was a lot of commotion behind the audience. Everyone thought it was part of the show, but they were wrong. When they turned around, they saw something no one would have expected to see.

The local Mafia sent real culprits there to break up the meeting, but it didn't turn out the way they'd hoped. When the invaders saw Harriet, they turned around and slipped back into the darkness. They'd wait for a better time. A time without a one-ape army guarding the outdoor meeting. This was just the beginning of unwanted problems. The Mafia goons were not the only problem facing the Gringos and the missionaries.

CHAPTER 20
Genuine Conversions

Brazilians are friendly and kind to Americans. The people in this northeastern part of Brazil are humble and polite, making it easier to see more results than in the southern part of Brazil, where most of the people are decendents of Europeans.

Valmir's story of salvation and lifestyle change quickly became the talk of the desert. Soon, people from the surrounding cities flooded into Mossoró to check out what was happening. They arrived crowded onto a truck called "the beast." Since there were no rules on loading or seat belts, locals continued to pack passengers and luggage until the truck was overflowing.

The three wives and three husbands who accepted Christ as their Savior were in Church the following night. Their presence heightened anticipation among the congregation, as everyone eagerly awaited details of their experiences. Each of the ladies gave a glowing testimony about how they came to realize their condemned condition before God and who was responsible for bringing them to Christ. The husbands also wanted to speak.

Paulo spoke first through an interpreter so the Gringos could hear it, too. He began, "When my wife, Carla, accepted Christ, I wasn't very happy. I didn't want a religious fanatic as a spouse or mother. She was just fine the way she used to be. I was very upset with the pastor and this church. But I had my eyes opened dramatically.

"Carla used to lie all the time. If someone wanted her to do something she didn't want to do, she would lie and say she was sick or too busy. I knew she was lying. The problem was, I never knew when she was telling ME the truth. It was troubling, but I was willing to let it go because lying served us well when we needed it.

"In the last two days, I noticed she went out of her way to tell the truth; it was very clear that something wonderful had happened to her. I wanted to know what it was. If it could change my wife that much, I wanted it, too."

Next up was Ricardo. His wife was Isadora, Grace's best friend. This husband took the mic and started to tear up. "My wife has always been a very wonderful person, kind, generous, loving, and sacrificial. She started smoking when she was just 12 years old. I knew this when I married her, but I always thought I could talk her into quitting. Now, we've been married 20 years and have four lovely children. No matter what I said or how much I harangued her, she never could quit. Whenever she wanted to quit, and actually went a few days without smoking, a crisis would appear, prompting her to light up a cigarette to calm her nerves. I kept telling her if she didn't quit, I was going to be left alone to raise these marvelous children.

"After she came home from church last week, she told me she had accepted Christ as her Savior and Lord, and now she was going to quit smoking once and for all. It has only been three days since she quit. Usually, that wouldn't be enough time to evaluate whether she was really going to quit. BUT, I know she's done puffing on those coffin nails because I can see the determination in her eyes. I thought, any Savior who could do this for my wife was worth following."

Roberto was the last to speak that evening, following his friends' heartfelt confessions. "My wonderful wife, Edete, permitted me to give this story to all of you. Although she's a marvelous wife and mother, my beloved companion has had a serious problem over the years. I would find small items all around the house, new knick-knacks or clothes. I'd ask her where she got them, and she'd say they were gifts from her friends. I knew she was lying, but I never wanted to confront her about it because I lacked the courage and wanted harmony in our home and marriage. She was shoplifting these items from various stores around the city. I knew it, and she knew I knew it. This problem was a mum subject between us, by mutual unspoken consent.

"After she accepted Christ, things changed. She gathered all the items, and I mean ALL of them, and took them back to the stores. She didn't just put them back on the shelves. She took them to the managers and put them on their desks along with a gospel tract. She told them the only thing that could have changed her was being born again by faith through grace. Accepting Christ as her only Lord and Savior was the motive for returning the items. She volunteered to work for free to pay for any items that they couldn't sell now. This really blew my mind. She also apologized for the inconvenience and asked for forgiveness. Religion and hoping for the best never made this change in my wife. I needed to know this Man who gave my wife, not only a motive to change, but the courage to make things right, when nothing else could."

With the congregation still absorbing the power of these stories, Donn thought it was wise to say a few closing words. After all, these testimonies were enough of a sermon for the evening. "All these stories support the biblical teaching in II Corinthians 5:17. This passage tells us that when a person really accepts Christ as his Lord and Savior, their lifestyle changes. It's not normal or biblical for a new convert to continue in their sin. There has to be a new person the world can see, and this new person is the catalyst for bringing many others to Christ."

The pastor reminded the congregation that all these results of evangelism began when someone punctured the tire on the motorcycle that Bowie and the Americans were riding. First, Valmir was saved. Then, like a domino effect, one person accepted Christ, prompting others to follow. Now, the pastor encouraged the congregation to seek out others whom God has placed in their path, so they, too, could accept Christ as their only and sufficient Lord and Savior. He concluded, "Is there anyone here who wishes to do this tonight?"

The congregation gasped as a well-dressed man stood up in the back of the church. Only a few people had noticed him slip in and quietly sit in the back. Everyone knew this man, and that made them feel uneasy, as he confidently walked forward in his expensive suit and costly shoes. He then asked the pastor for permission to address the people. Donn hesitated, recalling the man's reputation as "THE FOX," but a sense of duty, and a nudge from the Holy Spirit, compelled him to allow the man to speak: "Our visitor has the floor."

He started with his head up high, almost in an arrogant stare. "My name is Escobar Villa da Sousa Raposo, but I think all of you already know who I am, and I believe I've caused most of you to fear for the lives of your children."

Then he lowered his head and looked directly at them. "I know these three men, Roberto, Paulo, and Ricardo. I went to high school with them. I often cornered them and took their money. They never had a chance. My capungas always surrounded me.

"I dropped out of high school when my drug business started to grow. I became a very rich person and someone the whole community despised and even feared. I've seen the deaths of many people who were involved in this drug business, as well as the deaths of innocent people who got in our way. I'm guilty of many sins, and for this, I knew I was bound for hell and an eternity of punishment.

"I knew Valmir; he was not a drug dealer, but he was involved in our illicit liquor business. When he got saved, we all thought it was just a religious attempt to squirm out of our deal. We all believed he was either lying or afraid to keep doing business with us. Actually, it was neither of these things.

"I needed to be sure, because I was responsible for his section of town. I followed him and observed his every movement. He didn't know I was doing this. I saw him pour all the liquor down the drain in his house. I followed him to the park where he sat on a bench and read the Bible. I noticed he was giving out little pieces of paper to strangers. I accosted them and ripped the papers out of their hands. They were some messages about how to know this Savior of his.

"I kept close behind him when he came to church with his family. I decided to come in to see what was going on, and maybe to cause these people a lot of harm, physical harm. But I was always restrained from doing so. It was like I had lead feet; they wouldn't move into the church building. Finally, I walked away, into the darkness with my dark soul.

"I came back tonight with a completely different motive in mind. I sat through the speeches of all three of my former classmates, and I was glued to their every word. I've kept watch over these three and their families over the years. Even though I've been responsible for the ruin of many a person and some whole families, I never wanted this horrible tragedy to put its slimy claws on these three families. I figured I owed these men something for all the pain I had caused them in high school.

"So, I know very well what they were speaking of. I knew their situations intimately. They're all speaking the truth. I followed Edete to the stores where she returned the things she had stolen. I stood outside the offices when she told the managers how sorry she was for what she had done. Each manager was amazed that someone would do this, even to ask for forgiveness. Needless to say, I was absolutely blown away. This was so marvelous to see, someone actually sorry for what they had done, sorry enough to make restitution and ask for forgiveness.

"Outside that last office, I suddenly felt goosebumps and weakness, unable to stand from the intensity of the moment. Something extraordinary was happening, and I realized I was the only one observing it. Sitting in a chair, I debated speaking to her as Edete left the office and hurried past me, but instead chose to speak privately to her God.

"Right there, in that chair, I realized my condemned condition before her Holy God, and I asked Him to save me by the cross of Christ. I admitted my sin and asked Jesus to come into my heart, right there. This is a message I had heard all my life, but never wanted to do anything about it. Now I did, and here I am to tell all of you that I'm a Christian, just like you. Thank you, Edete, for your courage. Thank you, my friends, for your faith."

Tears filled many eyes in the church. Some people were joyful, others doubtful, and a few remained fearful. The fearful ones, most aware of the situation, understood what might happen now that Escobar planned to leave his Mafia partners behind. They remembered the fate of missionary John Paulson in Juazeiro do Norte.

Escobar looked directly at the pastor. "I want to be baptized as soon as possible. Can you do that for me, please? When the thugs of my organization find out what I've done, my days on this planet WILL be numbered, if you know what I mean." The pastor knew exactly what he meant. The baptism was scheduled to happen during an emergency service at 6:00 PM the following evening. "Good! I have a private security team outside to guard me until I return tomorrow night and then to escort me to Fortelaza so I can fly somewhere the mafia will never be able to find me." The whole church dismissed with much excitement and some fear.

Unbeknownst to the pastor or anyone in the congregation, the Mafia sent two men to spy on the following night's proceedings. They were to see if Escobar was going to open his mouth and squeal on the whole Mossoró chapter. They were dressed like poor folk and mingled well with the large crowd. Since there was no more room in the auditorium, the thugs stood outside looking through the windows. This is where the overflow crowd and latecomers always had to watch.

The baptismal was filled with water from the street. No one seemed to notice that it hadn't had time to cool off before they got into it. [*AUTHOR NOTE: Remember, only very hot water came out of the ground.*] Donn stepped into the tank and Escobar followed closely behind. When Donn realized it was way too hot to stand in, he rushed out with the Mafia dude right on his heels. Both stood on the podium and looked at the tank.

Escobar tried to talk to the pastor, but the full house was laughing so loud Donn couldn't hear him. The congregation had never seen anything quite so funny at church. Some were laughing so hard they had tears in their eyes.

Even though the capungas watching outside didn't know what a normal baptism was, they were sure this wasn't it. They were laughing too. They decided the whole thing was a joke and left to inform their bosses not to worry; Escobar had become a laughingstock of the community. But the bosses in Rio were not appeased. They started the ball rolling to eliminate him. NO ONE left the Mafia and lived to tell about it.

Finally, Donn could hear the new convert. "I've never seen a baptism quite like that. Is the water supposed to be that hot?" Donn assured him it was a big mistake. He asked the music leader to sing a few songs while the water cooled down a little. He also sent some members to the corner store to buy 10 bags of ice cubes.

The song leader, Mauricio, led the congregation in singing "Shall We Gather at the River" and "On Jordan's Stormy Banks I Stand." After half an hour, the water had cooled enough for them to withstand the heat. The baptism continued without the Mafia's messengers looking on.

The Mafia thugs were not the only unsavory visitors to the church service that night. The local Spiritist group had also sent their capungas to see whether they could do any damage, because so far they hadn't succeeded in causing any. What they had planned was to grab one of the Gringos and make off with her. A girl would be much easier to shanghai and hogtie. All they needed was an opportunity.

They returned to their lair and talked to the head honcho about the best way to carry out their diabolical plans. They all decided it would have to be tomorrow, as they had heard the Americans were leaving the day after tomorrow. They set the plan in motion by stealing a VW van.

Right after breakfast, everyone had an opportunity to get alone with their Bible and keep in touch with their Lord and Savior. All the Gringos appreciated this time, but it was totally voluntary. That's why Linda usually did her nails during this quiet time. Today, she was feeling much better after her unfortunate encounter with the passion fruit. Most of the swelling had gone down, and she could see out of both eyes fairly well. She still didn't want anyone taking photos of her.

She waved good morning to the cook and motioned that she was heading to the front gate to buy some pineapples from the vendor ringing his bell. The cook just smiled and said something in Portuguese that Linda didn't understand. Getting to the front gate, the cheerleader turned the corner, which hid her from the cook's view.

After ten minutes, Sonja, the cook, looked out the window, expecting to see Linda coming back with an armful of big, ripe, yellow pineapples. When she didn't appear, the cook found it strange. She put down her dish towel and walked to the front gate. Perhaps the Gringo girl needed some help with the translation.

Seeing she was not there, Sonja noticed Linda's coat on the ground. This wasn't good. She grabbed the coat and ran back to the dorm. Finding the Gringos she started yelling something they couldn't understand. Donn was quick to translate what she said, "Linda's been abducted!"

Donn stepped into the tank with Escobar right behind him. When Donn realized it was too hot to do the baptism, he scurried right out of there. Escobar, never having seen a baptism and also realizing it was too hot, followed Donn right out of the baptistry.

CHAPTER 21
Kidnapped

The kidnappers used a VW van, called a Kombi, because the open double doors gave them enough space to get a kicking and punching victim into a getaway vehicle.

Linda walked to the gate, opened it, and stepped onto the street. At the sound of the bell, she expected to see the pineapple vendor. Instead, someone threw a heavy black cloth bag over her head and pushed her into a rusty VW van with trash bags on the roof carrier. She tried to scream, but a hand covered her mouth. Horrified, she realized she was being kidnapped.

The stolen VW van sped off. Linda was thrown onto the cold steel floor. She realized she was in deep trouble. What would happen to her? Would anyone realize she was missing in time? Even if they did, chasing the van in this traffic seemed impossible. She felt hopeless.

Linda's coat was left behind, but a thug grabbed her purse and sped ahead on a motorcycle to clear traffic. Linda's purse waved in the breeze—a strange sight.

Of all the Gringos, she alone was not a believer. Her beliefs didn't acknowledge God. She had resisted every attempt to instill faith in her. Now, everything changed. If she were to be found, "The Man Upstairs" (as she so often, disrespectfully, called Almighty God), would have to grant her mercy.

It was hot under the hood, and she yelled for them to take it off, unsure if they understood English. She realized they were not paying any attention to her, so she decided to change her actions. She determined to pay attention to sounds and smells for clues about her surroundings.

She kept quiet to listen for sounds and remember smells. They passed a train station—an important clue. She smelled the cashew plant and heard the 8:00 AM Catholic Church bells. These observations helped keep her mind active. She thought of Billy and appreciated his abilities now that her vision was blocked.

<AT THE MISSIONARY COMPOUND>

After the Gringos finished their devotions, they looked for Linda. It was just then that the maid came running in holding Linda's coat. She was jabbering something, looking horrified. They got an interpreter and discovered Linda had been abducted. They also noted that her purse was missing. The missionary debated notifying her parents. Loretta and the adults agreed to wait 24 hours to avoid shocking them if it wasn't necessary.

The only plan they had was to grab the black-and-tan hound and Harriet and try to follow her scent. Harriet alone would not do, but with her and the hound dog working together, perhaps they could pick up a trail. They really had no other option. First things first, though. They had to pray about this. Erin asked to pray, "Lord, we've been attacked by Your enemies. Linda is the only one of us who doesn't know You. We need to find her and quickly, too. Give us success. Send us help, we're lost without it. In Jesus' name we pray. Amen"

They needed to find her trail, and quickly too. Shane coaxed Harriet down from the roof and handed her Linda's clothes, sniffing on them so Harriet would do the same. After the dog got a good sniff, the ape led the way to the gate because she knew that was the way out. The hound was close behind, following Linda's scent. Bowie said, "If they threw her in a vehicle, it's impossible to find her trail. We can't catch a scent if she's inside."

Billy knew Bowie was right because the pint-sized grappler read a lot and was up on these things. He had an extensive collection of Braille detective books at home.

Shane called from the front, "The dog is onto something. Listen to him. Let's get transportation and keep Harriet and the dog in sight. Bowie and I will ride the Honda motorcycle behind the dog to avoid contaminating the scent."

Donn grabbed a city map, jumped into the church van, and followed. Bowie drove the Honda, Shane rode in the sidecar, and Kosette held on behind Bowie. The black-and-tan hound headed down the main street with Harriet close behind. Brazilians might have thought a circus was in town, but these Gringos were not amused.

Kosy wore a helmet to protect her noggin, but it didn't keep the wind out of her face. She had no plastic face guard. Once in a while, a bug would smack her in the cheek or lips. This was distasteful, so she kept her head behind Bowie. She vowed never again to ride without a plastic face guard, not only to avoid possibly eating bugs, but also because she wanted to see where they were driving. The motorcycle stayed in front of the van.

The hound howled and sniffed east, toward the city's edge. Billy, in the van's front seat, was puzzled. "How can we be following Linda's scent? Maybe they're hanging her purse out the window. Could anyone be that dumb?"

Bert and Loretta debated. Bert, concerned for Linda, wanted to notify her parents right away, but Loretta, as a mother, preferred to wait 24 hours. She knew a drastic message they couldn't act on would be unbearable.

Marty sided with Loretta but promised Bert, "If Linda isn't found in 24 hours, we'll call her parents. Cross my heart and hope to die, stick a needle in my eye. That's a promise you can take home and put in your dad's bank."

Erin, sitting by Billy, asked, "Billy, do you think we'll find her soon, within 24 hours? Can you imagine how horrified she must be? Maybe this ordeal will change her beliefs."

The Jewish wrestler nodded. "We spent four days on a Montana ledge before I accepted God's existence. Maybe this is God's way for Linda, too. It would be wonderful."

<BACK TO THE KIDNAPPERS>

The kidnappers grew frustrated—Linda wouldn't stop yelling. Even under the heavy black hood, someone might hear her screams. They removed the hood and put duct tape over her mouth. Linda, fueled by Judo training, began using her limbs. She kicked a thug in the jaw, sending him flying. She kneed another in the midsection. The kidnappers had had enough—they overpowered her, tied her feet, bound her arms, and put the hood back over her head. She'd be held tight until drop-off.

Their luck worsened—a police blitz was stopping every car to check for required documents. The motorcycle thug, signaled by the van driver, turned right onto a dirt street. It would delay the drop-off, but no one was in a rush; if caught, they wouldn't arrive at all.

Linda refused to cooperate. Determined, she'd do her best to make the kidnappers pay a high price to complete a successful kidnapping. But now, bound tightly, numbness crept into her feet and hands. This was not good. She began to cry, seeing her plight differently.

She recalled going to church with her parents as a child. She liked the Bible stories and the cheerful songs. But during high school, her parents stopped attending church, so she followed. During her first year of high school, she mostly tried to impress boys.

She dated Engelbert Farnsworth III because he had money and a beautiful car. He was a jerk, but weren't all boys? While working at the Dairy Queen, she met the Lacomb kids. When Bert bullied them, she stood up for the kids, telling the rich kid to take a long walk off a short pier.

Only a few weeks later, she was back with Englebert for the same stupid reasons. With Bert, she partied and drank. Bert was a bully and a knucklehead. He held his liquor much better than Linda could. It annoyed her that when she was almost falling-down drunk, he still danced like he was sober. She finally dumped him and struck out on her own.

Because Erin caught her drinking, the lead wrestling cheerleader reprimanded her at the State Wrestling Tournament and got knocked in the noggin by Linda's flying whiskey flask. Linda stormed out of the gym and caught a ride back to Lebanon.

At her lowest, Linda left a note at home and went to the Waterloo Bridge. She tied a rope around her neck and to the bridge railing. She climbed onto the railing and was prepared to jump. She paused, but was startled when Shane came toward her waving an ax in the air, having just burst out of Bowie's Nash. Determined to end her suffering once and for all, she jumped. Shane cut the rope with the ax just before it tightened. Erin jumped into the water to help. Bowie grabbed his spare tire and threw it into the water. Both Erin and Linda grabbed the tire. Linda's life was spared.

All these painful memories flashed through her mind as she bounced on the van floor, going who knows where. She needed some inner strength, now, more than ever. Again, she was at the end of herself. She started praying silently. "God, I've denied You ever existed. I'm in dire straits now. It looks like I may not survive this ordeal. Please accept my apology for ignoring You all these years. I beg of You to help me. I believe in You."

<JOIN THE RESCUE TEAM>

The Americans kept up with Harriet and the black-and-tan hound, who seemed hot on the trail of something. They arrived at the police blitz and saw a long line waiting to be inspected, with violators being ticketed. They knew for sure the abductors were not dumb enough to stay in this line and be arrested. They must have veered off. Bowie stopped and got off the motorcycle. He motioned for Harriet to follow him. The hound stayed at their heels.

Walking alongside the parked vehicles, they finally came to the street where the crook's van had turned. Bowie spotted the tire tracks as the hound started baying and took off down the dirt road. It was back on the scent again. Was this a stroke of luck? Not really. Bowie knew quite a bit about tracking, having sat at the feet of his Uncle Elk Looks Back, the best Nez Perce tracker in Oregon.

It was nearing noon; the hottest part of the day lay ahead of them. The temperature was already 90°, and it was expected to hit at least 101°, according to the radio. They knew Linda would be in deep trouble if she had no water or air circulation. It was hot enough in their van; they didn't even want to think of how miserable she must be at that exact moment.

<BACK WITH LINDA>

Their fears were not unfounded. The cheerleader was suffering greatly in the kidnapper's stolen van. She hadn't completely recovered from the allergic reaction she had from eating the maracujá (passion fruit) ice cream. Her face was still a little swollen. Now, under this hood, with the extreme heat, her face started to throb.

Her situation was more dire than before, so she continued to pray. "God, all during this trip I've called you 'The Man Upstairs' with as much contempt as I could get by with. The others knew I was being as disrespectful as I could. I remember what I learned about You in Sunday school as a child. I recall hearing of Your mercy and grace. Lord, I need this now, or I'm not going to make it. Please send me some help."

One of the capungas was João Pedroso da Villa Lobos, a teenager with no living parents. He never thought it was important to go to school. Now that both of his parents had passed away, he was on his own. None of his relatives liked him, and even if they did, they still wouldn't have had the financial means to help the orphan. He was alone!

His best friend, Pedro Roberto Carvalho Filho, was still going to school and lived with his loving parents. This friend tried to help João when they were in grammar school. He would always say, "My Friend, we both need to study hard, get good grades, learn to read well, and obey our teachers. If we don't do these things, we're going to be hauling 100-pound sacks of cement on our heads, like you see the common workers do every day we pass the construction site. I've even seen some carry three sacks at once."

João knew he was right, but always came back at him with the same answer. "I'm just a kid, I want to have fun, play soccer, chase cats, and swim every day. You're too serious. You need to get a life, lighten up a little. You never have any fun; you're always studying and being serious. Life is short, and we have to have fun while we can."

Yup. Pedro was right all along. João knew his best friend was on the mark with everything he told him. Look at his life now. He was in a van with kidnappers, and his future looked about as bright as a mouse at a cat convention. He only wanted some friends. These guys offered him a place to stay if he wanted to hang out with them. They were deep into Black Spiritism. It appears they were following their spiritual leader's instructions by kidnapping this American girl.

He was in the pig slop up to his eyeballs now. He had dug a ditch too deep and was sinking in it. When they left for the morning, no one told him they were going to kidnap someone, AND AN AMERICAN TO BOOT. The United States Marines were probably on their way to rescue her right now. He had seen enough movies to know you don't mess with American citizens. Their government defends them, unlike the local government, which leaves its citizens to always fend for themselves.

He actually was a fairly good kid, with no police record and never expelled from school. BUT, now he was in deep trouble. He had no desire to go to jail because he knew how horrible the penal system in Brazil was. If you had no one to bring you food, you just ate the scraps the other prisoners threw at you. Now he had this poor Gringo lady lying in front of him, kicking and squealing, mouth taped shut, suffering under the black hood, and tied up like a pig going to the barbecue pit fire. He had to do something, anything that would maybe get him off easy.

His other three "friends" were all in the front seat, driving or playing lookout. Now was the time to move. He took off Linda's hood. WOW, her face was swollen. He didn't know what had happened. They hadn't hit her, that he knew for sure. He ripped off the duct tape on her mouth. She squealed quietly, trying not to get him into trouble, since she sensed he was trying to help her. Next, he took the ropes off her wrists and feet. He noticed she was feeling better, giving him some eye language, saying "thank you" with just her lips moving. He knew a few words in English.

The driver looked into his side mirror and didn't like what he saw. "What the devil is going on," he complained. "The big ape is only two blocks back, and a dog is right next to it. How in the world did they find us? The dog would have to be following a scent from an article of hers that's in our possession. Certainly, they can't follow her scent when she's in the van."

He started looking for something that fit the description he had in mind. Then he noticed his cohort on the motorcycle in front of him had HER PURSE around his neck. "What! He's so dumb he couldn't pour water out of a boot even if the instructions were on the heel." He pulled up to the biker and told him to get rid of the purse, PRONTO!

Spotting another similar van nearby, the motorcyclist drove behind the van and hung the purse on the handle above the engine compartment of that vehicle, and sped past their van. He splashed water on his jacket from a bottle he had with him, and scrubbed the area where the purse was touching. He looked back to see if the boss approved. The driver nodded and motioned for the bike to turn left immediately. The thugs vehicle followed the bike, and both faded out of sight down a street lined with trees hanging over the road.

<FADE BACK TO THE RESCUE TEAM>

Bowie was right behind Harriet and the dog. The black-and-tan sniffer seemed very excited, which made the ape speed up. The heavyweight wrestler knew the dog's reaction was due to his getting very close to the object he was tracking. When they rounded the next corner, Pastor Kittle was surprised to see Linda's purse hanging from the back of a van, which was stopped at a red light.

Donn pulled next to the van at the light and asked the driver to pull over when the light turned green. Since Donn had a kind face and the other van was full of teenagers, the surprised stranger decided there was no real danger and pulled over.

Shane jumped out of the sidecar and retrieved Linda's purse. It was hers to be sure. But the driver assured them he knew nothing about it. After a peak in the van's window, they all believed him. BUMMER! Wrong van. They were off the trail and didn't have any idea what to do now!

The well-trained canine sniffer was doing exactly what it was trained to do: follow Linda's scent. Unfortunately, the rescue crew was tracking the wrong van.

CHAPTER 22
Rescued

Harriet and her canine partner raced down the street sniffing and panting as they searched for the kidnappers.

The criminals had been instructed to take Linda out of town toward the east, then turn north and leave her inside a dry well in a fenced-in field full of nasty, mean Brahma cattle. Following these directions exactly, they obeyed the holy man's instructions. They believed his threats. He claimed to have extraordinary power in the spirit world, capable of casting an effective curse on anyone who disobeyed. If he wished, he could even arrange for someone's death.

One of the kidnappers, referred to as the "good" kidnapper, had given Linda a short break. He was preparing to give her some water when the lookout, seated next to the front door, turned and saw what was happening behind him and shouted, "Hey, what are you doing! Boss, he took off her ropes and the hood. Now he will think the next generous thing to do will be to give her water!"

Hearing this, the boss slammed the brakes, jumped out of his door, and ran to the van's side doors. Flinging them open, he grabbed the teenager who had freed Linda and threw him out onto the dirt street. The teen tumbled a few feet, scrambled up, and ran as fast as he could. He didn't pause to check himself to see if he was injured, he just ran away from the van and the criminals—leaving Linda behind. He had done what little he could, but now his priority was his own escape.

The gang's boss, Lamar Coelho de Sousa Siva, was not a good man. At 22, he already had at least 24 major police records. Usually, he was released as a minor. Organized crime used minors for crimes since minors weren't jailed. Brazilians hated and suffered under this system. For the last five years, Lamar had been the head henchman for Vitor Mendoza Silva de Ribeiro, the holy man of the largest and most dangerous Spiritist organization in the state. Their headquarters was in Mossoró because the other holy man in Natal, the capital, was more powerful than Vitor. There was always bad blood between these two holy men. Just between these two, curses in the state were more common than cockroaches in a sleezy diner.

Now Lamar was in charge of the biggest crime of his life. Most of his activities before this were just small store robberies, using a motorcycle as a getaway vehicle. He had been caught a few times, but because he only used a toy pistol, he was released to continue his criminal career. This was yet another example of flaws in the justice system. Kidnapping was a huge leap from his usual crimes. This could put him in good standing with the holy man and off the boss's naughty list. The list tracked all those Vitor wanted to control. Many tragedies in Mossoró came from it, though to outsiders they seemed normal. Insiders knew the truth.

The holy man, Vitor, was the most powerful person in this part of the state, even more than the chief of police and top politicians. These leaders of the city had already been the target of this holy man's wrath. They all knew he was not to be trifled with.

The only people Vitor had no power over were the Christians. They seemed to have a circle of protection preventing him from controlling their lives. He worked hard at it but had very little success. His only claim to fame in this area of accosting them came when he could get something going in the life of one of their "more or less" followers, the ones who went to church very little and didn't take their religion very seriously. That was fun to watch—the downfall of the whole household because of the sins of only one adult.

Disappointing Vitor was NOT on Lamar's agenda; the risk was too great. Determined to follow instructions exactly, he had thrown the weak, vacillating Pedro out of the van and onto the ground. He retied Linda and put the hood back over her head. He had no intention of crossing Vitor to invite a curse.

Linda begged them not to do it, but even if they could understand her English, they didn't care about her crybaby pleas. They were much too independent, too macho to listen to a whimpering American girl. Unlike Pedro, they were hardened criminals who showed no mercy. She would only be in their care for a few more hours. Then they would be free from their obligation to the holy man, at least for a while—they hoped.

It appeared they had lost the Gringos; at least as far as they could see. There would be NO chance the Gringos would find the girl now. All they had to do was deposit her in the well and drive away. What happened to her after that would be on Vitor's conscience, if he even had one. No one could verify he actually did, and NO ONE wanted to ask him! They liked their miserable lives just the way they were, without getting on Vitor's bad side.

Their fear of Vitor stemmed from more than belief in black magic. The henchmen they replaced died when their stolen van's steering failed, crashing into a power pole. The pole toppled another pole, which fell onto the van. Large water containers from a vendor's shelf next to the van burst. Water splashed into the window, soaking everything inside, as live wires struck. Electricity from the wires on the pole surged through the van like an electric chair, killing the four inside. Even though this was truly just a freak accident and these unfortunate souls had been among Vitor's best crews, he saw an opportunity to tighten his stranglehold over his followers. He told everyone the crew had disappointed him and claimed responsibility for the results of his powerful curse. NO ONE in his circle of influence doubted his explanation, not even the chief of police. The accident report details section was a single short sentence: "It was an unavoidable act of God."

The group drove into the countryside and located the field Vitor had described. They took Linda, who still had her hood on and limbs bound, out of the van. All the black vicious Brahman cattle were at the far end of the enclosure. They knew they could drop the girl in the well and high tail it out of there long before the cattle could get to them.

After tying a long rope under her arms, they carefully lowered her into the dry well, following Vitor's orders to ensure she was unharmed. Linda tried to fight back, but she couldn't prevent them from lowering her to the bottom. After dropping the rope in after her, they drove away. Later, Linda would see this careful treatment as an act of God's grace, though the henchmen's real motivation was fear of Vitor's wrath if she were harmed.

Linda was terrified. When her feet touched the bottom of the well, she tipped over and landed on her stomach. She knew she was in a brick-lined dry well, having felt the walls with her feet.

Although she thought of many places she'd rather be, she thanked God she wasn't dropped into water. In pain and scared, she managed to roll over, slip her hands under her feet, and get her arms in front. Soon, the ropes were off. She took off the hood and foot bonds and stood up. It was past noon. There wasn't enough light to see the bottom of the well.

She sat down and covered her face with her hands. Her face had returned to being a little swollen, but the pain was quickly subsiding now that she had removed the suffocating hood. She leaned against the well's circular wall and began to cry; tears flowed freely. She knew her situation was desperate. How was she ever going to escape this well? Were the others having any success locating her?

The kidnapper's journey across town had taken them through many streets and turns. Linda had lost track of the landmarks she was trying to remember. Her chances of survival were almost ZERO as far as she could figure. She knew her only hope of escape or rescue was going to have to be in the hands of the God she had forgotten, ignored, and belittled her whole teenage life. She wiped her tears with the soiled blouse, now soaked with perspiration.

She was very scared and sincere. "God, I know I don't deserve Your attention, but I also know You are listening. I believe all the things my Sunday school teacher taught me years ago, when I was still very young. I know You love me. I'm also absolutely positive I'm still alive because You are merciful."

She paused to sigh deeply. "I've sinned against You and failed to acknowledge Your ownership of all of Your creation, including ME. Erin and her friends have done their best to lead me to a place where I could see You clearly, but I refused to give them the satisfaction of their efforts. They've been very kind and patient with me. But not as much as You have been."

Her prayer was interrupted when a large, bald-headed vulture perched on the top of the well and leaned forward to peer into the darkness below. It knew there was something down there and was trying to smell if it was dead yet and ready to become an easy meal. Linda knew exactly what that awful bird had in mind. It looked like it was going to stay there until suppertime, with her as the main course. She shuddered at the thought.

A dramatic presentation of her feelings about that subject would have to wait until later. Right now, she was trying to square away her life with the only Person who could save her: the Divine, Holy Creator of all humanity.

Trying to ignore the uninvited dinner guest at the top of the well, she continued to plead her case at the throne of grace. Her demeanor was completely different from what it had been during the group's past prayer times. She always tolerated what they were doing but strongly held to her unbelieving heart. Sometimes she would even walk out of the session and find some place to do her fingernails, trying her best to display her total disdain for their pleadings to the "Man Upstairs," as she liked to call Him.

Her face was still pounding. She could hear her heart beating through the pain in her head. The cheerleader was not done praying yet; there were still some areas she needed to clear up. "Lord, I'm sorry I've shown so much disdain for You and for Your servants, the kids I've called my friends. I've seen a real change in Bert's life. He used to be a bully and a brat, causing a lot of damage and pain to the kids from Lacomb, especially Bowie. I saw such a change in him. He's actually a nice guy now. Lord, I want what Bert has. I want to be different. I abhor the person I've become. I know how to be saved, I've heard it many times. "I confess my sin and ask Jesus, Your Son, to come into my heart and live here."

Linda put her hurting hand on her heart. "Forgive me, Lord, and save me, now. I love You and am thankful that I'm in this well right now."

She knew in her heart it had to be this way. She had to come to the end of what she could do for herself. Looking up at the sky, she saw through the well's round, faraway mouth and teared up again. "God, my Savior, Jesus my Lord, I give my life wholly to You, lock, stock, and barrel. I'm already Your child by grace through faith. I promise you, Lord, if I get out of this well, I'll serve You anywhere in this whole wide world You send me, ANYWHERE!"

THIS IS A PROMISE LINDA WOULD KEEP.

She continued looking up, staring at the vulture, who wasn't aware of her religious conversion and was obviously contemplating American cuisine for its next meal. There was a certain peace she felt as she leaned against the well wall and slid down. She spread her hands to steady herself against the dizziness. She felt something cold to the touch under her hand. Picking it up by what felt like a handle, she realized it was an ax—she could barely make out the shape in the dim depths of the well. What was it doing here? How long had it been here? Who threw it into the well? She spent time in the Pioneers, a girls' outdoors group. She knew how to use an ax.

Without wasting time, she used the edge of the ax to start carving out a brick about knee high. Since it was a narrow well and she could spread her legs to reach both sides at once, she loosened and removed a brick on the other side, a little higher up. Putting her foot into the hole left by removing the brick, she carved out another one higher up. She repeated the process until she was about halfway up the wall. She paused, feeling too weak to continue. Concerned about slipping and falling, she climbed back down to rest for a while, with the confidence that, eventually, her escape was certain. "Thank You, Lord, for this ax. I believe it's Your way of saying You heard me and accepted my offer. I won't renege on it either, LORD. You can count on me to keep my word."

<JOIN THE GRINGO RESCUE PARTY>

The Gringos seemed out of options. If they didn't come up with another plan, there was nothing more they could do. They decided that Bert, the closest one to Linda, would pray. "Lord, we need some help. We're out of ideas for finding Linda. She's suffering greatly, and we need to find her soon, or she'll not make it. Please send someone to help us. We love You, Lord. Amen." No one was expecting someone to ride up on a motorcycle with a written message from God. They all looked at each other and chose to head back to the campground; maybe something helpful would be there. They stuffed Harriet and the hound in the van with them and headed back.

The traffic was very heavy at two o'clock in the afternoon. They were stopped in a line of cars that stretched over six blocks. A policeman strolled up to the van. "I know you're looking for Linda. You can find her at these coordinates. I see you have a city map. Use the aerial map on the back." He handed Donn a piece of paper, walked into the backed-up traffic, and was gone. Loretta was sitting next to Donn. He was dumbfounded. "Who was that? I've never seen such a strange thing happen." The ex-runaway mom just smiled and opened the paper. She knew who he was. She had seen him several times before. The note clearly listed coordinates. Donn took out his city map, flipped it over, and located the exact spot the policeman had given them.

Donn motioned for the motorcycle to turn around and follow him. "I know where this field is. It's a cattle farm just outside of town to the north. After we lost the kidnappers, they must have changed directions from east to north. That's where we're going. It's pedal-to-the-metal time." He punched the van and zoomed out of there. It took them thirty minutes to arrive at the edge of the field. It was almost impossible to see the ground because the whole area was filled with mean-looking Brahma cattle.

<QUICK FADE TO LINDA>

The cheerleader had revived her body and spirit. She took to the walls again. It only took her one more hour of carving out bricks to arrive at the top of the well via her ingenious set of steps. After throwing a few bricks at the vulture, it decided to find a meal someplace where bricks were not the appetizers; maybe at the local dump, for example. Off it flew. "Good riddance to bad rubbish," as Linda was used to saying.

She pulled herself onto the edge of the well and sat there with her legs dangling over the outside. She realized her quest for freedom was not quite over yet. Before her, she could see what seemed like a thousand Brahma cattle, including a lot of bulls. They were black, brown, and white; very menacing with all the dust embedded in their hides. She could wait it out unless she fainted and fell backwards into the well. She leaned forward and started praying again. She knew, for the first time in her life, she was now on good praying grounds with the Lord of the universe.

<BACK TO BOWIE>

Bowie was quite resourceful when it came to bulls and such. He ushered Harriet and her canine partner out of the van. Climbing over the fence, he motioned for the ape to imitate him. She did, with the hound following by slipping under the fence instead of climbing over.

Bowie started waving his hands, yelling, and running back and forth. The simple-minded primate thought this was a new human game, and she was liking it. The hound always barked and howled at these kinds of gestures.

The largest bull started to charge toward Bowie. When Harriet saw this, she jumped between them and growled, baring her green teeth. Waving her hands and running full speed at the bull made it skid to a stop, turn tail, and scoot in the opposite direction. It was only a few minutes until the herd dissipated enough for them to see Linda sitting on the edge of the well.

Bert had joined Bowie and was also yelling and waving his arms. When he saw Linda, he broke into a full-speed run and grabbed her in his arms, making sure she didn't fall back into the well. "We're so glad you're okay. "Wow," he exclaimed, leaning over the edge to peek into the darkness, "were you at the bottom of this well?" How'd you get out?"

Linda fell limp in his grasp. "It's an interesting and harrowing story I'll have to tell all of you tonight. Right now, I want to get out of here, hit the shower, and take a long nap in a soft bed. By the way, big guy, I'm now a Christian just like you are." With that, she faded away, and Bert carried her to the van.

There was a lot of rejoicing at the campground that night. The whole group of Gringos and missionaries was sitting around a campfire roasting marshmallows on sticks. Harriet even had one in her hand, but she had no idea why. She let it stay over the fire until the stick burnt through and the white delight fell into the flames. She didn't care; she was enjoying the camaraderie.

Linda slept for six hours. When she awoke, she was ready to share her story. "First of all, I'd like to ask forgiveness from all of you, especially from Bert. I've been a brat, a spoiled kid. I mocked you and insulted your faith and your God, calling Him 'The Man Upstairs' whenever I got the chance. Your patience has been admirable, while my behavior has been deplorable. I really believe God allowed this kidnapping to occur so I'd be down looking up.

"I started praying in the kidnapper's van. I was suffocating and in a lot of pain. I knew my goose was cooked if God didn't help me. He showed me mercy all along the way. How did you start searching for me?" Bert filled her in on the purse story.

"The teenager in the van took off my hood and the duct tape on my mouth just in time. I thought I wasn't going to make it. God used him to help me. Then, when I thought I was never getting out of the well, and I finally realized I might never see another day, I sought God and beseeched Him to save me through the cross of Christ. I was born again at the bottom of that dark well." She finished telling them about the vulture, the ax, and all the frightening details of her ordeal.

By now, there wasn't a tearless eye in the group, except for Harriet, of course. Linda continued, "My sins were forgiven by grace through faith, and Jesus gave me eternal life. I also promised God, if He got me out of the well, I'd serve Him anywhere in the whole wide world—ANYWHERE."

Bert was paying very close attention. This was wonderful, and he was glad to be a part of it. He closed by praising God for it all.

The next day, after a tearful goodbye to their friends in Mossoró, the Gringos packed their bags and caught an early bus back to Fortaleza. Luke met them at the bus station and transported them to the docks. Fernando was at the harbor with the Albatross, fueled and ready to depart. The other missionaries and a few Brazilian friends were there to see them off. These departures were always difficult on the tear ducts. With a lot of Brazilian-style cheek kisses and hearty backslaps, they said their goodbyes.

Two 9-cylinder, piston-powered, radial engines simultaniously shattered the silence and brought the Albatross to life with a mighty roar. The flying boat took off and headed south on a perfect 180° compass heading. The next stop would be Gaucho Land—the State of Rio Grande do Sul. COWBOY COUNTRY!

THE OFFICIAL FLAG OF THE CITY OF GRAVATAÍ

The group sat around a campfire, roasting marshmallows on sticks. Linda gave her dramatic presentation, giving God what He deserved. Bert closed the meeting by praising Him Who made it all happen.

Rio Grande do Sul is cowboy country, filled with rodeos, horses, and Gauchos (both male and female). They love to ride their horses in prades.

CHAPTER 23
Introduction to Southern Brazil

FIVE REGIONS OF BRAZIL
Gravataí, Rio Grande do Sul, is located in the South.

The Albatross left Fortaleza with an extra-happy group of Gringos on board. Linda had not only been divinely rescued from the kidnappers, but also gloriously converted. Her decision to follow Christ to the ends of the earth was duly noted by all of the Americans, including Fernando, the pilot. He had been listening to all of their religious discussions, especially while floating on the Atlantic.

There were no secrets among them about her feelings toward God, whom she used to call "The Man Upstairs." Now, she was talking non-stop about her conversion—a complete turnaround like the 180° heading on the plane's compass. She declared, "This cheerleader is sold out to God, lock, stock, and barrel!"

She could hardly wait to get home and share her newfound faith in Christ with her parents. Her description of how the whole kidnapping went down would have made the author of *Anne of Green Gables* jealous. "I was roughed up, hooded, and thrown into a nasty, smelly WV van. The horror of it all. Trapped in that sweatbox, I was certain rescue would never happen. Imagine the stupidity of the motorcyclist in taking my purse and allowing the tracking dog to follow his trail. Then, I started to place God in the equation, and things began to change in my favor. The hood over my head was causing my unfortunate face to swell up again, and the duct tape on my mouth was suffocating me. You all know I can hardly breathe through my nose. Don't share that with anyone, please.

"The fact that the young man took off my hood and duct tape was a definite answer to prayer. I wasn't going to make it, I knew it for sure. He was punished for his act of kindness, but I think he really wanted out of the whole thing and was glad he got thrown out on his keister.

"Imagine being hog-tied and lowered into a dry well. Proof again: God sent His guardian angel. And SAVED I was, gloriously redeemed. The ax I used to chip my way out was marked 1861—maybe it landed there a century ago, the year the Civil War started.

"Last but not least, how did the policeman who gave you the coordinates of my location know my name? This whole story smacks of divine intervention. Yes siree Bob, the Lord Almighty, the Creator of the universe, had His loving and merciful eye on me. He looked down on a poor, sinful cheerleader like me and redeemed my soul from the grip of my spiritual enemy. I now have my name written in the book of life and will spend my eternal days praising Him and enjoying His presence forever, with all my wonderful friends who prayed for me and demonstrated true Christian love. This is my story, and I am sticking to it."

Bert noted to himself, "I'm glad some things have not changed. I wouldn't want the pendulum to swing the other way. I want her to channel these dramatic abilities to spread the gospel for the salvation of souls."

This was a marvelous change from the doubting, disrespectful teenager she had been. No one doubted her commitment to the "ends of the earth" promise. Linda was never mediocre—always the extreme exaggerator.

The flying boat touched down in the harbor of Porto Alegre, the capital city of the state of Rio Grande do Sul. The state had 8,000,000 residents, of whom 2,500,000 lived in the capital. This was the cowboy country of Brazil. This part of South America was like Texas in the USA, with a lot of cattle and leather products, including shoes, coats, gloves, and car seats.

Tom Ballentine was the pastor and had been here for 40 years. He had established four churches. The first had been in an inner-city area, the second in the town of Restinga, the third in Cachoeirinha, and the last in Gravataí, where he was still the pastor. He lived six miles from the church, in a rural area.

Tom and his wife Susana met the Gringos at the docks. It was still a 40-minute drive to his house. All the Americans were able to stay at his home because it was a retreat center. The whole backyard was a sports complex used by many public schools because they had basically nothing.

Once the group arrived, Billy, always the astute one, piped up, "I'm surely not the only one who noticed the drastic drop in the local temperature. It was 100° when we left Mossoró, and now we're grabbing our overcoats. It must be only 40° right now. Can anyone see my breath?" He exhaled, and everyone assured him they could see the vapor emerging from between his lips.

Kosy joined in. "Why, it looks like it might get cold enough to snow. Does it ever snow here, Dr. Ballentine?" Kosy asked.

Turning to Kosy with a smile, Tom enlightened her. "First of all, Princess, call me Uncle Tom. This is a practice that all Americans have. We want our children to feel we are a close-knit family. Mr. Ballentine, or Dr. Ballentine, is too formal, and just 'Tom' lacks the required respect. We opted to use 'Uncle' and 'Aunt' instead."

Accepting the suggestion, Kosy tried again. "Okay, Uncle Tom," she asked, "does it ever get cold enough here to snow? This is Brazil, for Pete's sake. I never heard of it snowing in Brazil! No one would believe us if I told them."

Tom was smiling at Kosy's surprise, fully aware this was incomprehensible to most Americans: snowing in Brazil. He explained, "You just came from the only semi-desert region of Brazil. Now you are in the only part of this massive country that can produce snow. It might even snow while you're here, imagine that, Princess!

"Besides being a pastor at Central Baptist Church," Tom said, "I also coach wrestling at a public school three blocks away. It's the most effective evangelistic tool I've ever used. One-third of our congregation is from this ministry. I believe the next pastor, who will follow me, will be a seminary student who came to the church to wrestle. How cool is that?"

The Americans were getting settled in when Shane noticed an ugly toad crossing the road in front of the missionary's house. He thought it would be the right thing to do to give the little green guy a helping hand. It appeared he was not going to make it before he was squished into a crack. Grabbing the wiggly reptile behind his front legs, Shane reared back and threw him into the bushes. Immediately, he felt some liquid hit his lips and go into his mouth. It was very distasteful. Tom saw the whole thing but didn't have time to warn Shane before he picked up the toad.

The missionary rushed into the house and returned with a glass of water for Shane. "Here, Shane, rinse out quickly. It's not poison, but it'll make your mouth numb for a few hours. We could take you to a dentist right now if you want a tooth pulled, and you wouldn't feel a thing! This liquid is the toad's only protection from predators, and it works extremely well. He's not molested by ANY local predator, not even by snakes. I'm sure he was frightened AND surprised when you grabbed him."

The other Gringos tried not to smirk at Shane's twisted smile, courtesy of Dr. Toad's lidocaine. Clearly, there was still much to learn about Brazilian culture and animal safety—Billy hoped for fewer inconvenient firsthand lessons.

Tom spotted a cockroach trying to get away, running for the front door or anywhere to hide. Stomping on the big, red, ugly insect, he waved the rest over. "We're going to meet here when you hear our bell ring so you can see a real-life show in survival, anatomy, and teamwork."

When the bell rang, they returned to the squashed roach. Apparently, a "scout ant" had located dinner and sent out signals to the rest of the army. About forty of them got under the roach, raised it, and headed straight up the wall, unconcerned that they were being watched. When they got to the entrance of their nest, every attempt to put the whole body through was without success. Then, the cutters got to work. They sliced and diced the roach right there on the wall, letting the carriers take the parts inside. After about 15 minutes, the wings, the only inedible part, fell to the floor. The ants had their supper on the table.

Tom laughed. "We have a zoo in town, but who needs to go. Our home here offers plenty of entertainment without an entrance fee. I have a few other very interesting shows to take you to yet. By the way, DO NOT leave the front door or any upstairs window open. If you do, things will come into the house that will hunt you down and get donations to their blood bank, leaving you with the joy of scratching for the next week."

The missionary invited the boys to accompany him to wrestling practice at the public school while the ladies all took showers, except Loretta. He asked her to come so they would have at least one lady present to help coach the girls. This was a rule he never violated, for his protection and the testimony of his church.

Before pulling out of the driveway in his 1963 Mercedes-Benz minibus, Tom gave his wife last-minute instructions on what to fix for supper. "Let's have shish kabobs. We might as well give the Gringos the full nine yards while they're here!" She nodded and smiled in agreement. Off they went.

Tom spent ten years pulling a trailer to 18 different public schools to coach Olympic freestyle wrestling. He had to arrive at the school after 5:00 PM, when all the afternoon students had been dismissed. He always hoped some would stay to learn the fairly new sport in Brazil. One problem was that he was left in charge; no one from the school stayed around. He was given the gym keys, or the practice was held outside in the weather. This left him vulnerable. If some brat broke something or hurt someone, the parents could sue Tom. He was willing to take the risk for the benefits.

He usually started in each new school with 40-45 participants, boys and girls. After six months, or so. the number usually dwindled to a meager group. (Wrestling is a tiring and demanding sport.) He said when it got down to five, he would have to find another school. It was way too much work for such a small group.

On tournament days at the church, he would rent a bus to pick up the brats from four different schools and be responsible for their conduct on the bus and at the church. This again put him at the risk of being sued if something went wrong. He did this for ten years, and because God watched over him, he was never sued. This reinforced Tom's claim to the wrestler's parents that God was watching over all his activities, because Brazilians are litigious. Many historians claim Brazil is one of the most litigious countries in the world.

Finally, Neusa Rosane Modinger, the director of Jeronimo, a public school only three blocks from the church, invited him to serve as a PE teacher and coach the wrestling team during school hours. This was a real boon to the project. He was an unpaid school employee working within the school program. No one would be able to sue him now, with an entire public school district as a buffer. He even had to write a paper explaining the project, present it to the city and wait for their approval. He did it and the city officials approved it.

Practice was on Tuesday and Wednesday afternoons. He got to the school at 3:00 PM, pulled the mat sections out of the trailer parked there, and assembled the pieces to make two mats in separate locations. Usually, he had Carla Menezes da Silva and a few teenagers helping him. But since he had the Gringos, he gave his coaching staff time off.

Practice was for the second and third grade boys and girls. Bowie and the others laid out the singlets (wrestling uniforms) on the mats. At 3:30, right after recess, the second graders ran to the mats and put their singlets on over their school clothes.

Tom let Bowie and Shane show the excited kids a move that included a countermove. Then the kids separated, and the girls went to one mat with Loretta, Bowie, and Bert. The boys stayed with Shane, Billy, and Marty at the other place. The students were called in pairs and given a chance to try the move. As soon as one wrestler was down on the mat, they stopped, and two more stepped forward. It had to be quick, so each one would have at least two full minutes of wrestling before they returned to the classroom.

After thirty minutes of practice, they were sent back to class, and the third graders came running to take their place. The school had no other extracurricular activity for the kids, no art, music, or sports programs. The kids only went to school for half a day: one group in the morning, another in the afternoon, and the GED students studied in the evening. These few hours of study were because, across the whole of Brazil, 50% of the population is under 35 years old. In the city of Gravataí, with a population of 200,000, there were 90 public schools.

After practice, the mat was disassembled and stored in the trailer. The coaches left the area before the students were dismissed. The ride back to the retreat center was over six miles and 20 speed bumps. They passed a police blitz just two miles from the house.

It appeared the authorities were pulling all motorcycles off the road to check documents. They already had two mounted on a tow truck, pulling out to deliver them to the pound across town. They were lacking the proper documents or it had been stolen. If it were just a lack of documentation, the owners had to pay for it, along with a fine, before they could redeem the bike from the impound lot. This was a real pain in the neck for motorcyclists who used the bikes for business or delivery.

Getting back to the house, Tom invited all the Gringos to the front yard to explain some cultural things. Sitting in a circle on the grass, he began his instructions. "The most important thing to Latinos (everyone living south of the Rio Grande River on the U.S. southern border) is saving face. This isn't so important to Americans, but here it's inexcusable to ignore it. I'm explaining this to you because an offended person is much harder to win to Christ.

"Don't use the words stupid or idiot when talking among yourselves. The Brazilian words are almost the same, and they might think you're talking about them. Our words are idiota and estupido. You can hear how close they are!

"Don't whisper to one another in public places. It doesn't matter why; the people close by will think you're saying something about them, and they'll presume it's not flattering. Also, you don't open the door when you leave someone's home. This indicates that your visit was unsatisfactory and that you don't plan to return. Let the host open the door. If the host doesn't open the front door, it might mean they don't want a return visit!

"On the other hand, don't be afraid to refuse something you can't eat or don't want to eat. Here, in this state, these Gaucho's don't have a problem with this. They're mostly composed of Italians, Germans, Russians, and Polish immigrants who arrived after World War II. They chose this part of Brazil because it's cooler, as you are aware.

"Also, don't use these gestures." (He showed them some using his hands.) "These are very offensive to them. Most of the time, they would understand and give you the benefit of the doubt, but we want to avoid any chance of offending people, especially visitors to our church.

"We have four teenagers in our church who speak English fairly well. They're prepared to help you converse with our church members. Use their services as much as possible. Also, I'm giving you a list of the most common words and phrases you'll need to know to start and finish a conversation. My wife, Susana, will go over these with you after dinner.

"Every morning after breakfast, I'll have a missions class with you, for about an hour. I'll be teaching you from the first two chapters of my doctoral dissertation on why missionaries quit. It's titled *Missionary Problem Areas*. We've seen many give up, and some so quickly, that I decided to give this subject some thought and developed a doctoral program around it.

"We'll talk about the culture and its many facets, some good and some bad. The missionary attrition rate and its causes will also be explained, with many examples. The second chapter is on the VERY important subject of interpersonal relationships between the missionary, his coworkers, his bosses, and the local nationals.

"According to the survey I conducted of all the major mission boards, 24% of missionaries quit because of medical reasons, and 23% give up and go back to the States because of interpersonal or cultural problems. Most causes for those reasons, almost 50%, could have been avoided with sufficient preparation, proper in-country actions, and a Sprit-controlled temperament."

While they were still talking among themselves, two motorcycles zoomed by, the drivers yelling something the Gringos didn't understand. The one who was not doing a wheelie threw a brick over the iron fence. It hit Bowie on the side of the head, and he fell over, knocked out cold.

[AUTHOR NOTE: This team of 2012 Freestyle Wrestling State Champions inspired the true public school wrestling stories in this chapter. I'm the coach on the right side of the front row.]

CHAPTER 24
Clunked in the Noggin

The retreat center was used for various activities, including inviting public school children to spend the day jumping on trampolines and running back and forth on the white, wooden playstation.

Susana and Loretta rushed to the kitchen to get some warm water and towels. Linda and Erin got to Bowie first. They lifted his head and put it on Erin's lap. Bert was trying to wipe the blood off the back of his noggin so they could see how bad the wound was. Shane was helping him, "What in the world happened? Maybe if we knew what they were saying, we could figure out what is going on."

Tom had knelt to have a look. The missionary had served in the Navy as a corpsman and electrician. "It appears to be just a flesh wound. It might not even need stitches; we'll know in a moment, just as soon as we can get this thick black hair out of the way."

Linda was flabbergasted. "What's going on here? We were sitting on the grass, minding our own business, and these thugs zoomed by at a hundred miles per hour, yelling and throwing bricks! I knew Brazil was sometimes a dangerous place to park your life, but this is just a little too much, don't you think? It's a bit over the top. If that brick had hit Bowie in the temple, we wouldn't be wiping off the blood; we'd be calling a hearse. Man, I for one am wearing a crash helmet from now on any time I'm outside."

Kosy was more interested in helping Bowie than getting excited about it. Linda was a new Christian, and it was good to know that some things NEVER change. The youngest Lacombite was praying silently for her heavyweight, Nez Perce hero.

After cleaning off the blood with warm water, Susana brought out cold water. With a lot of cold water and an abundance of TLC, the Native American finally came to. He was shaking his head, trying to clear his vision. "Man, what happened. Where am I? Who are all of you?" Whoops, someone got more than a skull cracking. We have memory loss here.

Tom realized it was imperative to get the Gringo to a hospital ASAP, and assured Bowie, "We're friends, here to help." Marty and Bert helped Bowie into the van, and off they headed to the Dom João Becker Hospital in downtown Gravataí. The 17 speed bumps had to be maneuvered slowly to avoid more shaking than the Nez Perce could handle.

The Hospital was divided into two parts. The nice, modern section, was where Brazilians entered if they had insurance. The other part was broken-down, rusted-out, and had badly painted hallways. It was overloaded with adults and children. This is where the unlucky, unfortunate, poor citizens went to be attended by the sad and unbelievable social medicine program.

Bowie went into the new section. Tom filled out the paperwork while the doctor looked at his head. It didn't need stitches because it was just a flesh-wound, an abrasion. What the doctor couldn't understand was how such a small, shallow wound could cause amnesia, which was exactly what Bowie was experiencing.

If the Nez Perce had not been docile, the Gringos could've had a problem on their hands. The doctor recommended they see a neurosurgeon as soon as possible. The x-rays proved there was no internal damage, not even a small subdural hematoma, but they wanted to do all they could to help the grappler get his memory back. There was no serious damage to any part of his anatomy, not even his head. He just lost his memory.

The doctor insisted that he not fly until all conditions were normal. This would make returning to the States unwise for the time being. All indications were that he could return to the retreat center, but couldn't drive a vehicle or participate in any sporting events. And under no circumstances could he swim or water ski.

Even though he didn't know who he was or where he was, the heavyweight grappler still entrusted his life to the Gringos because they looked like a nice group of folks, and he had no other choice. So, back to the house they went, driving slowly again over the 17 speed bumps.

It was an interesting ride back to the house. Bowie was asking questions a mile a minute, and Billy was chosen to answer them all. "You're in Brazil."

"What's Brazil, and where's Brazil?" Bowie inquired. This was going to be harder than they had originally thought!

Kosy scooted over closer to her Native American friend and put her hand on his big shoulder. "We'll help you get your memory back, Bowie. I'm your very best amigo. You call me 'Princess' and sometimes 'My Little Friend' with a great deal of feeling. We know this'll all work out. We believe in God, and He's going to get you through this."

Tom knew it was imperative to contact Bowie's parents, and he did this via his ham radio. He called Pastor Ballentine, his brother in Lacomb, who made a phone patch to the Pinetree residence. Travis was informed of all that the doctor advised. He spoke to his wife, and they agreed it would be best for their son to stay where he was.

Travis was not nervous but cautious, "We know Bowie is in good hands. Perhaps, being around so many people he knows intimately, his memory will come back sooner. We understand the flying restrictions. We'll keep him in our thoughts and prayers. Tell him we love him. OVER."

Pastor Ballentine was about to sign off. "Tell Bowie the Lacomb Baptist Church will pray for him. This is WB0SQO in Lacomb, Oregon, signing off with PY3ZBA in Porto Alegre, Brazil. 73's and 99's to you, Tom."

Tom thought he had some explaining to do, so he called a meeting at the house. Everyone was present, even the wrestler with the white bandage on his noggin. "When the motorcyclists rode by, they yelled, 'This is only the beginning. Get out of town and stay out.' This was a message from the Gaucho Mafia, which controls all the drugs and liquor in this area of southern Brazil.

"We've had so many drugees and drunks saved lately, the big bosses in Porto Alegre have taken it personally. We're messing up their profits big time. Not only have we seen users and alcoholics come to Christ, but some of them were more than that. They were middlemen and suppliers, high up the chain of command.

"There was a cocaine house right across the street. Anselmo Cardoso Pinho dos Patos was their chief man in this area. He and his wife, Leila, were saved. We baptized them last month, and they're now hiding in another town until things cool down here. It was a dangerous business he was in, and it's still very precarious for them. They should be unseen and unheard of for the time being."

Linda wanted to know what the missionary was planning, since it was going to become so dangerous for his church people. "I know God is merciful and loving. This, I found out just recently. But, I also know He gave us common sense and PF FLYERS running shoes. So, what's the plan for surviving?"

"My fine American friend, that might be the $64,000.00 question for some people. It's still up in the air right now. One thing I know we're NOT going to do is tuck our tails between our legs and catch the first flight out of here. We're here for the long haul. When I volunteered to be a missionary, I never thought it would be anything but a lifetime passion. It never occurred to me that I'd go back to the USA for any reason whatsoever."

"What about a medical problem, would that make you go back to the States?" Billy wanted to know. He knew how insurance worked because his dad had a lot of it for the jewelry stores and the family. The pint-sized grappler handled much of the bookkeeping in Braille and then had it transferred to the accounting office.

Tom was happy to tell them. "We have excellent hospitals and doctors here. We've given English classes to many of the doctors, and they give us personal attention. We can call at any time, night or day, and they'll meet us at the hospital for emergencies. We could never get this good treatment in the States. Besides, it costs about one-tenth the price here. We have excellent insurance to pay all our bills with no deductible.

"When I accepted Christ, I gave my whole life to Him, lock, stock, and barrel. I never once thought there was a place God could call me where

I wouldn't be willing to go. And when I decided on Brazil, I never for a minute considered my tenure here would be anything less than a lifetime. Our bones will be buried here.

"I love the Brazilian people, and they love us, as you'll see when you attend our church services. When Brazilians ask me if I like it here, I say I like the same things they do, and I don't like the same things they don't.

"I don't like corrupt politicians, and they don't either. I detest dishonest police officers, and so do they. I hate being robbed, and they hate it too. If they have to live here under these conditions, so can we. It's a WHOLE lot better here than most mission fields in Africa, India, and China.

"When Brazilians ask me why I stay here. I always tell them that I've stayed for 40 years and will stay for the rest of my life, because God called me here and He never told me to leave. Besides that, I love the Brazilian people, and they know it too."

Marty, the doubting Thomas of the Gringos, wanted a more definite answer on how the missionary would handle the problem. "Apparently, these threats are for real and coming your way. I have a philosophy of life: 1) plan way ahead, 2) get an early start, 3) do the hard job first, 4) take time to smell the roses, 5) work as a team, 6) never quit, and 7) give God the glory. Using these principles, how can we help you?"

Tom was glad for Marty's principles and enthusiasm. "The planning part can start now, with prayer. We're up against forces much more powerful than we are. BUT, they're not even a drop of water in the ocean of God's power. It's silly beyond imagination for these anti-God groups to think they can actually go up against Him and come out unscathed."

Harriet was housed in the bocha court. It's also called Italian bowling or lawn bowling. It's a covered court, 12 feet wide by 72 feet long, with a sandy floor. The ape liked it because the sturdy rafters let her swing. Since they were too high off the ground, a hammock was hung for her to sleep closer to terra-firma.

Bowie was cooperating with his memory recovery program, but there hadn't been any meaningful progress yet. It was like a new, blank sheet of paper. It had to be filled in with information. He just hung around the others and asked a lot of questions. He particularly liked the ape. "Wow, she's really big and so friendly."

The Gringos were using all the photos they had and telling all the stories they knew, way back to when they first met him at the T.P. Oil Company. They even went through the trouble with the Outhouse gang and his winning All Around Cowboy at the rodeo in Eastern Oregon.

He didn't remember any of these instances. What he did remember was being lost in a cave where it was dark and cold. He also remembered something about a pitcher throwing a spitball. These two instances really had no connection whatsoever, at least this is what they thought, but they were not experts in this field. The doctor would be able to tell them if this meant anything at all.

Susana made an appointment for Bowie with the best neurosurgeon at the Hospital de Monhios de Vento in Porto Alegre. Maybe he could give them some hints on how they could help the Nez Perce bring back memories that would be the catalyst for his complete recovery.

Shane and Bert were playing two-person volleyball when a huge, black and tan tarantula started crossing the grass. They rushed into the house to get a container to catch it, since neither of them wanted to reach down and pick it up!

Tom was also interested in capturing the ugly, hairy creature. When Shane started to make a move to use a dust pan to push the spider into the Tupperware container, Tom yelled at Shane, "Don't get close to it!" The grappler dropped the dust pan like it was a hot horseshoe and backed away.

"I don't know anyone who's been bitten by a tarantula. But, that's not their most dangerous tool." Everyone looked at him like he was from another planet.

Billy was the first to question the veteran missionary's statement. "Really! All the movies I've ever heard have always portrayed the tarantula as a deadly killer. What are you referring to when you say it has something else, much more dangerous than their bite? Please fill us in, we're all ears and dying of curiosity."

Linda was dumbfounded. "Do you mean to tell me that the hairy, ugly, nasty, scary, universally hated tarantula has something more dangerous than its bite. This is unbelievable. I've seen a lot of movies about Africa and South America. Every time they put this horrible creature in the script, it's given a role of attacker and biter, and it always ends with the funeral of the attackee. I'm going to keep my distance if it has a weapon more dangerous than its bite."

"Alright, already," Tom smiled, "I get the idea. Now for the free Biology 101 lesson. The tarantula has hair like porcupine quills. Each hair is similar to an arrow. It can shoot this hair like a weapon, reaching up to six feet. If the hairs hit your eyeball, they will blind you for life. They're so small your eye can't see them coming, and your eyelid won't close.

"I was cleaning its cage once when a tarantula tried to escape. I did what Shane was doing with that same dustpan. It peppered me with its red, flying hair, hitting me in the face. If I hadn't been wearing glasses, I'd be blind in my right eye. The miniature hair spears also hit my arm and shoulder. It was quite painful for a few days. Now do you understand?

"Susana is deathly afraid of the smallest spider. She'll see one during the night and start screaming, or wake me up to kill it. I'll come into the room and ask where it is. She'll point to it, and sometimes I have to get a magnifying glass to see it. The scary creature is half the size of a BB.

"I smash it with my fist and go back to bed. I've read that no matter where you are in the world, you're only three feet from a spider. After living here for 40 years, I believe it's true. Daddy longlegs can be seen in a few of the corners of our house every day. I really don't mind them there because they're trying to trap mosquitoes, which are hoping to hunt me down and suck my blood. But for Susana's sake, I twirl the webs around the broom, and that's the end of their reign of terror!"

Tom was drinking something from a gourd, using a metal straw. Shane approached him and wanted to try it. "What have you got here? It looks like chopped up alfalfa."

Tom poured more hot water into the gourd. "It's what we call 'chimarrão.' The straw is called a 'bomba,' this gourd is called a 'quia,' and the green stuff is called 'evra.' It's just green tea. It's a very traditional drink here. The Gauchos make it early in the morning, mid-morning, at noon, mid-afternoon, after work, and before they go to bed."

Nothing got past Billy. "Then, it appears they drink it all day long!"

"That's about right. It has 59 times more caffeine than coffee. That's just at the beginning, as more water is poured into it, that number goes down rapidly. If you have to stay up late to study for exams or finish a term paper, this is the stuff to drink. You'll be wide awake for the rest of the night. The custom is to pass it around; each person has to finish all the hot water in the gourd, fill it up again, and pass it to the next person."

Erin was surprised. "You mean I'd use the same metal straw as six other people? I find that a little hard to accept, you know, germs and such, bad breath, slobber, and unidentifiable yucky stuff!"

Tom was smiling, "My fine American friend, that's why we give it to the Gringos first. They're usually appalled at having to share the same straw. Actually, the water is so hot that when it goes through the metal straw, it'll kill all the germs."

Linda took a look at the end of the straw. "Okay for the dead germs, but what about this accumulated gunk on the end of the metal straw. That's slobber glued to it, and I, for one, am NOT going to put my lips on top of the slobber of six or more people."

Tom understood perfectly, so he pulled out a dozen metal straws and gave each Gringo a new, clean one. He was flexible; that's what made him a great missionary.

They all tried it with their OWN straw. Billy thought it was too bitter for him. He wanted to add some sugar. Tom told them the macho Gaucho never added sugar, but some more sensitive souls did suck on a mint the whole time, which is basically the same principle.

They were eating dinner in the dining room when the doorbell rang. Tom went to answer it, as he always did. He never approached the gate, 50 feet from the house. He always verified who it was. It was dangerous to approach the street unless you DID know. Thugs were always accosting Brazilians at their front gates, robbing them and taking their cars.

The man was large and broad-shouldered, with a deep voice. He wanted to know if Loretta was here. Tom found it strange that another American, not of the group, was looking for her. He still didn't go out to the front. "How do you know this lady? Are you a friend of hers?"

The stranger repeated his question without inflection, indicating he was not losing his patience. "I was told she would be here—at Tom Ballentine's home. Is this his home? Pastor John Ballentine, from Oregon, told me I could find her here."

It was getting more interesting. Tom went halfway to the gate and felt a bit safer when he noticed the stranger was not at the gate, but to the side, holding the bars of the fence. "I need to know how you're connected with Loretta. Are you a relative of hers or just a friend?"

"If she's here, tell her Rocky from The Crab Shack on Fisherman's Wharf in San Francisco is here to see her. I'm sure she'll know who I am, and we'll not need to continue this conversation out here on the street in the cold."

CHAPTER 25
Rocky's Arrival

Rocky Hartung, an ex-professional wrestler, followed Loretta to Brazil, checking up on her wellbeing. She introduced her friend to the gang and he became a part of their remaining adventures.

Tom returned with an inquisitive look. "Loretta, do you know a fellow named Rocky who worked at The Crab Shack?" Loretta's eyes widened, and she stiffened, her voice tinged with surprise. "Rocky? From The Crab Shack? What are you talking about?"

Tom continued, "There's a tall, burly man at the gate named Rocky Hartung. He says he knows you from San Francisco. Do you know him?"

"Of course, I know him. But what's HE doing HERE?" Loretta stammered, stunned and unsure what to do next.

Susana grinned, "Well, if you know him, we can't leave the hunk on the street outside in the cold."

Loretta caught her breath. "Of course not. Let's go get him." The three hurried to the gate and opened it. There he was: the man who'd once defended and befriended Loretta at The Crab Shack last year.

He was 6 feet 5 inches tall and weighed 280 pounds. Some might say he made Mr. Universe look like one of those kids bullies would kick sand on at the beach.

Loretta shook his hand and motioned for him to come in. "I suppose you know by now, my name isn't Linda, like I told everyone at The Crab Shack. I was hiding from Vini the Fin, the gangster, as you probably already found out. I have a lot to explain to you ... but how'd you find me here, in Brazil?"

Rocky responded, "Well, when you didn't return to work, my wife and I were very worried about you. We drove all over the Bay Area trying to find you, but we only ended up getting hit by a drunk driver in Oakland. That accident took my wife's life and left me alone. After the funeral, I worked for another eight months at The Crab Shack, but I knew that wasn't what God wanted me to do forever.

"The Lord told me in no uncertain terms that I had to find you. I was at my wits' end after searching in vain for so long. Last month, out of the blue, your friend Gloria, a high school classmate from Oregon, called The Crab Shack. She followed up on a phone call you two had while you were still at The Crab Shack. Someone there called me and gave me her number. I called her, and she told me where you had lived in Lacomb, Oregon. I left right away, and soon I had a great conversation with your dad.

"He told me you were in Brazil, supervising a group of teenagers who were spending their whole summer here. I asked for your itinerary, and that's what brought me to Porto Alegre, then here to Gravataí. I'm so glad you're okay."

Loretta nearly fainted, and Rocky steadied her. "Rocky, I'm so, so sorry about your wife. I feel responsible since you were looking for me when it happened."

"Linda—Loretta, don't blame yourself! Karyn and I were serving the

Lord. God chose her time. Even if she could, she wouldn't want to come back."

"Rocky, this still doesn't answer my question of what you're doing here? I know you came to find me, but why? Certainly, I didn't gain a special place in your life or heart during the short time I worked at The Crab Shack, did I?"

Rocky hesitated for a moment, caught off guard by the vulnerability in Loretta's question. He shifted his weight, struggling for the right words, his voice softened. "Not really, Loretta. The truth is, I never let myself admit how much I wondered about you, or how often thoughts of you crossed my mind. Karyn was always sharper than I was about those things. She saw you were hiding something, maybe in pain, and she put you on her prayer list. She spent hours praying for your safety and soul. Karyn had an intuition about people. Toward the end, she seemed to know she was about to leave this world. Some people get that feeling, you know.

"About a week before she died, Karyn made me promise to find you if she passed first and help you find Christ. I didn't know it'd be my last promise to her." Rocky's eyes teared up, but not quite enough for a tear to escape and slide down his chiseled cheek.

"So, here I am. Now it's your turn—how did you get here? I've got plenty of time to listen. By the way, who's this big Native American kid? He's almost my size."

After a quick introduction to Bowie, Loretta found a quiet place to converse. She told Rocky her story; the whole nine yards. When she finished, he was so happy it was hard to hold back the tears. He didn't want her to see him cry, so he said he needed some air and quickly went outside. She followed him to the back of the house. He had just finished wiping his eyes with his hand when she caught up to him.

She gently reached up and touched the back of his shoulder. "If the real reason you came is for more than friendship, say so. I haven't heard a man say that, and mean it by proving it, in years. I can handle it—really."

Despite his imposing and muscular build, the former professional wrestler was, in fact, quite a shy person. Years of staged wrestling matches and ring trash-talking bravado never really reflected his true personality.

Turning to look her deeply in the eyes, he spoke, "Okay, I'll be honest. I came to help you find Christ—but you already have. And, WHAT a story: mafia, coffins, angels, spies, warships, even the White House. I couldn't write a more interesting novel than that!"

She smiled. "Me neither. But it's what it took for me to see my sinfulness. I'm saved, and I can't stop sharing it. My family is back, and my father sleeps well." Loretta insisted. "I still didn't get an answer!" She yearned to receive a response her heart wanted to hear.

Rocky knew what she was talking about. He broke their deep gaze and looked down at his shoes. "It's true. I came all this way to see if you were okay and to lead you to Christ. You ARE okay, and you ARE a Christian. Based on my original plan, I wouldn't have any other reason to stay after learning that. But, YES. I want to stay long enough to see if a meaningful relationship could develop between us."

She was visibly relieved; her face beaming the euphoria she felt in her heart. For 23 years, she'd never felt so happy—except when she found salvation. Now that the question's response was tucked away in their mutual history, they shared a brief, yet meaningful, hug and planned to revisit it soon.

Rocky wanted to know more about what happened to Bowie. Marty filled him in on the details.

Even though he had been a professional wrestler and knew what they did on the stage was 100% planned, and many times, just impromptu fakery, he was no dummy. Rocky had a degree in psychology from the University of Minnesota in Minneapolis. Living there for 10 years, he regularly participated in professional wrestling events on WCCO-TV.

He was going to write to some of his Christian professors at the well-known university and ask them for their opinions about Bowie's condition. This might be helpful; at least it was worth a try. He knew it would take several weeks for his letter to reach them and their reply to find him. But that would be a better option than waiting, seeing that the local medical professionals had run out of ideas. They had concluded Bowie's condition might be permanent.

The letter to the U of M experts could wait until tomorrow. First, he wanted to meet everyone in the group. After introductions with hearty Brazilian backslaps from Tom and the boys, it was proper introductions all around.

Tom told Rocky about his identical twin girls, Camila and Tiffany. They were three years old and spoke no English but understood it perfectly. They wouldn't speak anything but Portuguese.

Meanwhile, Susana was upstairs trying to get Camila into the shower, gently urging her through the shower stall door. Camila hesitated, leaning into her mother's gentle nudge, small fists balled at her sides, her wide eyes darting back and forth from her mom to the shower stall.

As Susana nudged her forward with a little more force, Camila suddenly stopped dead and stared into the shower. Her face went pale, and she backed away, repeating, "cooob, cooob ..." Her voice trembled, fraying with each syllable. Susana, puzzled, leaned closer, hearing only the urgency in her daughter's voice. She thought perhaps the water was too cold, but she had checked it herself and knew it was actually on the warmer side. She watched as Camila clung to the edge of the opening with both hands, refusing to go further. With her arms stiffened, her eyes grew even rounder and she whimpered like a frightened puppy.

A ripple of anxiety pricked at Susana as she replayed Camila's sound in her mind. "Wait a minute! My daughter doesn't speak English. What's she trying to say? Cooob ... coooob, cobra. COBRA!" (Cobra is the Portuguese word for snake.) Susana cautiously peeked past the shower door, and sure enough, there were two red and black striped, dangerous-looking snakes slithering around, trying to get back out.

She wrapped a towel around Camila and called Marty and Shane to capture the reptiles. They threw a towel over them and wrapped them up, then took them to the back of the property and turned them loose. They didn't want to kill the snakes because the sneaky, squirmy creatures ate things they disliked more than the snakes.

After the snake ruckus calmed down, everyone headed for bed, still murmuring about the night's adventure. Just before the Gringos slipped into la-la land for the night, a sudden movement startled them—a bat swooped past the bedroom door, down the stairs, and through the living room downstairs.

Linda, sleeping on the couch, immediately jerked upright in fright, pulled her blanket over her head, and let out a sharp yelp. The hairy mammal flapped back up the stairs, creating chaos. Everyone jumped to their feet, hearts pounding. Tom quickly took charge and told the boys what to do. "Bowie, you stay here at the bottom of the stairs and don't let it pass this way again. Just put up your arms and wave them back and forth like a fan. It won't try to go through you.

"Now, we have to start isolating it so it stays upstairs. Someone must have opened a window." Tom, Billy, Marty, Bert, Rocky and Shane went upstairs and closed the sliding door behind them. Now they had it stuck on the second floor. Upstairs, they split up again, leaving Billy at the end of the hallway, waving a towel. Since the bat was still in the large game room, they closed all the doors except the one to the boys' bedroom.

The fang-tooth, flying mammal headed straight for blind Billy at the end of the hall. Rocky yelled at him. "Wave the towel higher and faster, lightweight." Billy did just that. Loretta, Erin and Kosy poked their heads into the hallway and Billy told them to close the door and pray for help from above to get rid of the bat. They did just that, too!

The ugly, hairy bat swung to within a hair's breadth of the grappler's head, but because he was blind, Billy only felt the wind's aftershock. When he did feel this, he ducked to the right and hit his noggin on the wall. That did it for him; he wasn't really hurt, but he wasn't happy about what happened. He slid to the floor and put the towel over his head. They all knew he was done for the night.

Shane started running behind it, waving his arms. The bat flew into the boy's dorm room. Tom and Rocky ran inside and shut the door behind them. They had already closed the bathroom door, so the only place left was the walk-in closet. When the flying horror went in, they followed it and closed the door behind them. They both had towels. It took no time to throw a towel over the bat in the closet's confined space. They returned to the hallway and slid the door open again.

As they were hooping and a hallaring with a bat in the towel, another winged terror zoomed past the grapplers. Bowie was a little late in warning them that another got past him and was coming up. Bert yelled at Billy. "Stay seated, Billy. We have another one."

Just as Rocky held up their unfortunate prey, wrapped in a tight towel, he heard Bowie yelling again and ducked as the third bat whizzed over his head. "What's this, two more loose out here?" He was right, another hairy flying mammal had joined the fracas. Together, they quickly herded the two new invaders into the bedroom. At least both arial varmints were confined to the bedroom. The great white hunters managed to get the other two into towels—all three invaders were under control, and the aerial battle was over.

Tom was out of breath and baffled when they went back downstairs with their three prisoners, "This is too much to accept. Something's rotten in Denmark."

From across the room, they noticed the door to the front porch was partway open, a welcoming gateway for cold bats searching for a warm hideout. Tom raised his arm to slow them all down. "No one move!" He reached for the crossbow he had stored in a cupboard next to the front door, pulled back the string until it locked in firing position, and inserted a short arrow. Then he flipped on the front porch light and proceeded with utmost caution, asking Rocky to slowly open the door wide enough for him to step through with the crossbow.

Nothing happened, but they heard a lot of high-frequency squealing. What Tom saw when he stepped onto the front porch was hard to believe. The rest peeked out. What they saw gave them chills up and down their spines. There before them was a wired cage slightly smaller than a military footlocker. Inside were five bats fighting for the right to try to escape through the cage's small open door. None were taking flight. They were beating each other with their wings.

All the bats were foaming at the mouth, showing sharp, ugly green and white fangs. The missionary was flabbergasted. "My lands, these are vampire bats, and they all have rabies. Who would do such a thing? I believe someone wanted these bats to get into the house and bite us during the night. This would've been a horrible plague. God's hand must have been upon us to be able to capture three of the creatures without being harmed and keep the others in the cage."

Billy had recovered and joined them downstairs just in time to hear their comments. "Really, you don't know who's behind this? There's no doubt in MY mind who it is. It's the same capungas who threw the brick at Bowie. They wanted to infect us with rabies so we'd have to leave."

Tom nodded his head in agreement. "I believe you're right, Sherlock. That makes perfect sense. Man alive, these guys are really serious and dangerous. Can you imagine what a mess we'd have on our hands if one of these infected bats had bitten any of us? Let's secure all of them in a safe place tonight. I'll contact the animal control folks in the morning so they can pick up the creatures for study. There's a special team studying bat rabies and potential new treatments for their victims, since it's such a big problem in this area."

Bert could imagine the mess they might have had to deal with, "Yeah, I can, especially if it was Linda. Besides having a medical emergency to deal with, we'd all be privileged to witness a theatrical presentation of the highest emotional order and the utmost verbal description." All of them, except Rocky, knew exactly what he was talking about and chuckled to themselves. But if Rocky stayed around long enough, he'd find out what Bert meant.

Before they went back to bed, Tom fired up his Collins KWM-2 ham radio to contact Pastor Ballentine to ask him to call Dr. Charles Baker, head of the neurophysiology department at the University of Minnesota. Rocky wouldn't have to write a letter, and they'd get a faster response to their questions about Bowie. After sending his message, Tom and the gang waited for a reply.

Pastor Ballentine called back after about 20 minutes. "This is WB0SQO from Lacomb, Oregon, calling PY3ZBA in Gravataí, Brazil. Are you there, Tom? OVER."

The missionary answered the call. "This is PY3ZBA in Gravataí, Brazil, calling WB0SQO in Lacomb, Oregon. Roger, we are here. Can you help us? OVER."

"Yes, I can, brother. Even though it's getting late in Minnesota, I have the nice doctor on the line now. I explained your situation to him, and he DOES have some suggestions for you. Are you ready to write them down? OVER."

"We're ready. Shoot. OVER."

Doctor Baker started his lecture. "Lately, we've found there are three other ways to jolt someone's memory besides talking and rehearsing the person's experiences of life. You have to get the wheels turning in the right direction, so to speak. There are other senses you can stimulate besides storytelling. First of all, there's the sense of smell. Figure out what smells dominated his life for the last few years, simulate them, and they might bring back the memories associated with the smells. Are you writing this down? Do you understand what I am suggesting? OVER."

Marty assured Tom they understood exactly what he was saying and they already had some ideas. "Tell him to give us the other two now."

After a quick exchange over the radio, the teacher continued, "Feelings of touching something familiar can also retrieve deep-rooted memories of experiences associated with the object in hand. Find out what you have that can be placed in Bowie's hands. OVER."

Shane was taking notes, too. "I have some great ideas. Tell the doctor to keep talking; we're paying attention." Tom relayed Shane's request to the professor.

"The last sense available to us is sound. I forgot to tell you that Bowie must be blindfolded for these attempts to succeed. Now, for the last experiment, take the wrestler to a quiet place and introduce familiar sounds from his past experiences. He has to be completely isolated from all outside noise. The second part of this is to take him to a noisy place, preferably outside, and do the same thing or something similar. Do you comprehend? OVER."

They did and ended the conversation, thanking the kind doctor for his time and expertise. Tom signed off with Pastor Ballentine. "This is PY3ZBA from Gravataí, Brazil, signing off with WB0SQO from Lacomb, Oregon. 33's and 99's, my brother. OUT."

They could hardly wait to try these experiments on Bowie; all were optimistic about the possibility of a positive response. They had already figured out that different aspects of rodeo and wrestling would be the catalysts for restoring the Nez Perce's memory. But that needed to wait until morning because they were all tired, including the patient. They all agreed, including Bowie, that it would be best for his brain to be fully rested before trying to stimulate it to remember.

Before they headed back to bed, Tom delayed them a little longer. He wanted them to go outside and see something he had just discovered on his property, something he had never seen before. It was a brown ball about the size of a beach ball, with a tree limb running through it. He shined his huge flashlight on it and asked them if anyone could guess what it was.

Loretta said it looked like a ball of hardened mud. Shane said it appeared to be made by insects. Kosy put her hand on it and observed it was hard, very hard. But no one could guess what was inside. The pre-teen put her ear up to it and said she heard humming inside.

The missionary took a five-gallon bucket containing a mixture of gasoline and diesel oil from the storage shed. Before he poured the liquid on the ball, he told them it was a termite mud dwelling. It took them about three months to build it. He enjoyed watching the loathsome, destructive insects labor in vain, not even realizing they would all perish when they got done. When they come out, they'd have wings and would fly to all the surrounding homes, go straight to any wood they find, and have a banquet that would destroy all the rafters in the neighborhood, including his.

He ensured everyone was at a safe distance, then poured the liquid on the mud ball and set it afire. This was not a fire for roasting marshmallows. Tom said it would burn for a few hours. The wood eaters started coming out. Tom poured some of the mixture into a glass. He kept throwing it at them as they emerged from the ball. "They're trying to get to their union rep to sue me for unannounced eviction. This is more effective than a lawyer for me." Tom was always so funny.

While Tom stayed to monitor the fire, he sent the rest back to bed, since it was so late, a result from all their unplanned activity that had interrupted their normal bedtime. Kosy was standing next to Bowie. Just before they headed back into the house, she noted something. "Even though Bowie has lost his memory, apparently, his stomach hasn't. It still remembers to growl when it's empty."

After showing Bowie where to find a bedtime snack, they finally hit the sack and had a normal, peaceful night's rest in Gaucho land, 3,000 miles south of the equator. When they came back to reality after their nocturnal trip to Never-Never Land, they noticed Bowie was missing.

After thoroughly searching the grounds, they also discovered Harriet was nowhere to be found. This was not good. A red, always hungry, hairy, scary orangutan from Borneo loose on the general public, accompanied by a huge Nez Perce Native American who didn't know who he was.

Kosy broke down and wept uncontrollably, while Linda's silique began: "How horrible a situation, beyond anything we could ever deserve. In addition to all of last night's terrifying events, seeds waiting to germinate into horrendous nightmares, we wake up to yet another calamity. How will our group ever be made whole again, with our two largest and strongest members missing? No offense intended, Rocky."

"None taken, little lady."

Simple fact or dramatic exaggeration, this was definitely NOT a good scenario!

FLAG OF THE STATE OF RIO GRANDE DO SUL

CHAPTER 26
Lost in the City

Bowie and Harriet were lost in a large city. Without his memory, Bowie couldn't find his way home. Harriet was just happy to be near her human friend.

A Nez Perce Indian with no memory and an ape with an IQ that wouldn't scare anyone were lost in the city of Gravataí; this was not a good thought.

The Gringos, determined to find them quickly before trouble started, piled into two VW vans and headed in different directions. Half of them went downtown, driven by worry about the pair, and the other group went towards Cachoeirinha to run by the church, hoping for leads.

Unbeknownst to all of them, Bowie and Harriet were headed for neither location. Mistakenly thinking it best to get away, they were out near the main highway, trucking toward the mountains. The Nez Perce didn't know who he was, and the ape didn't know where she was; she just knew she wanted to be with her human friend, driven by loyalty and comfort. Neither knew where they were going; they just wanted to see some new territory together, driven by curiosity and a need to escape.

Bowie had the sense to take some Brazilian money with him. They tried flagging down a local bus, but when the driver saw the largest monkey he'd ever seen, he drove past without slowing down. Dealing with a giant monkey was more than he wanted to handle today.

The Nez Perce tried for a taxi next. The driver, undeterred by costumes, pulled up closely to see who he might transport. Harriet poked her head through the window, flashed her green-toothed grin, and blew bad banana breath in his face. He recoiled, pushed her face away, rolled up the window, and sped off, uninterested in any further surprises.

Harriet saw a full-sized yellow bicycle with training wheels lying in a yard. She knew how to ride a bike. She grabbed it and started down the road. Bowie was amnesic, but he remained an honest person who knew stealing was wrong. He made her take it back.

The grappler didn't have a memory he could recall, but he still had common sense. The heavyweight wrestler wondered whether it was a good idea to try to make friends with strangers while traveling with a huge, red, hairy primate with no useful brainpower. At least, this was the first impression he had of her. Although he assumed they had a meaningful past, since she was sticking close to him.

The Nez Perce thought it might be a good idea to return to the house, hoping to find safety and answers. But by now, they had meandered down so many side streets he wasn't sure which way would lead them back to the retreat center. He had some instinctive navigational skills, but no access to the training he had received from his expert-tracker uncle back in Oregon. So, practically speaking, the two of them were completely lost. One knew it and felt anxious, while the other didn't even care, focusing only on sticking with her friend.

Both were thirsty, but only one could communicate it, and he didn't think it was important to let the tree swinger know; what difference would it make if she knew, anyway?

<MEANWHILE, BACK AT THE RANCH, SO TO SPEAK>

The Gringos were searching long and hard for two living, breathing creatures who could cause a lot of confusion and potential damage if they got into the wrong situation. Motivated by both responsibility and concern for their friends' safety, they feared that someone with ulterior motives could take advantage of these two less-than-responsible beings. It was imperative to find them ASAP. Each group had a Brazilian translator.

Linda, Kosy, and Erin checked stores, asking if anyone had seen the pair. Describing Harriet was particularly difficult, as few people there had seen an orangutan. The translators referred to her as a "big monkey," while Kosette used gestures. This scenario amused many locals, but the Americans remained serious and concerned.

Loretta, Bert, and Rocky stayed on the streets, each one covering one side of the avenue, while the third stayed at the beginning of the search route in case the lost duo passed that way.

Shane, Tom, and Marty took to the downtown parks — there were many. Some even had monkey bars with no humans or primates swinging on them when they passed by. Billy just stayed in the van, hoping no one would steal it while he was inside. Right now, he couldn't handle the stress!

With no success, Tom decided to notify the police. Their headquarters was located only a few blocks from the downtown park. Captain Marcos de Oliveira das Cruzes was in charge. The missionary explained the situation to him. The Police Chief found the whole story hard to believe. "You mean to tell me, we have an orangutan and an amnesiac Native American running around loose on our streets. This is a pretty weird story. You're kidding me, aren't you? Tell me this is a late April Fool's joke. Humor me, please."

Tom assured the surprised Captain it was certainly NOT a joke. They had been searching for them all morning but had not seen hide nor hair of either one. He asked the Captain to notify all his patrols to keep an eye out for the pair.

The Captain said he could try, but doubted his officers would believe such a story. Their experience was with small monkeys. Tom asked him to inform them anyway, hoping for some help finding Bowie and Harriet.

The Brazilian policeman decided to humor the Americans. He radioed his patrolmen on the various beats, explaining the situation. The Gringos heard a lot of laughing that didn't require any translation. When the hilarity died down, the Captain explained it again. The laughter continued. Finally, he gave up and told the entertained crews to get serious.

Captain Marcos turned to the Americans. "I tried. Those officers are my worst clowns. They think everything is funny. They think I'm funny, and that's not funny at all! If anyone calls in and asks me who left the gate open at the zoo, I'll get a hold of you. This is the best I can do for you."

<REJOIN THE WANDERING BOWIE AND HARRIET>

Bowie and Harriet were still on the streets. They had all the dog divas going out of their minds. Each house has at least one four-legged guardian on the premises. When one starts howling, the whole block becomes a canine choir of the barking, panting, and snarling type. It drives mail carriers and door-to-door salespeople into early retirement. A believable English translation of a German word for dog could be "barkingpantingsniffer."

The duo needed liquids, but Bowie couldn't speak any Portuguese, and the ape wasn't any good at it either. They came to a lady watering her lawn with a hose. Even though he couldn't remember anything from his past, Bowie was still a gentleman. But Harriet was nothing close to this and never would be. She rushed up, grabbed the hose out of the woman's hand, and started slinging it around. After getting drenched, the lady let out a scream and headed for the house. After Harriet slurped her fill, she passed the hose to Bowie. He felt terrible for the lady, but couldn't do anything to calm her down now. Because he was so thirsty, he followed Harriet's example, but his slurping of water was MUCH more refined. He turned off the water and thought it would be best if they moseyed on down the street. He didn't have a memory, but he DID have a brain and self-preservation desires.

The street they walked was in a rough area of the city. Drug dealers loitered, and caring families with the means had already left. Buildings were defaced with graffiti, streetlights were broken, and mailboxes were damaged.

Many poor Brazilians had to stay despite daily disturbances from druggees using abandoned properties. Bowie and Harriet didn't realize the danger they walked into. Of the two, only one might be considered wise in such situations.

A little further down the street, Bowie saw a few thugs roughing up a poor lady who just wanted to water her flowers. The ruffians had their backs to the strangers, so they didn't see them sneaking up from behind. Bowie, still motivated by a buried sense of justice and a hatred for bullies, hadn't forgotten everything from his past. There seemed to be a recollection of one who had hounded him a lot in the past. What was his name, Burnie, Bart...whatever, these guys harassing the nice lady would pay for what Burnie or whoever had done.

When Bowie tapped the tallest one on the shoulder, all three of the hoodlums turned around to take care of the intruders. Neither one of them could imagine seeing anything that could challenge their domination of these poor people.

What they actually saw made them drop their jaws and take several steps backward. One even tripped over the lady's garden hose. When he got up, the bully turned tail and headed for higher ground. The other two were braver or maybe dumber. Whatever! They grabbed the woman's water hose and squirted Harriet with it. Now, it was time for them to pay their overdue "stupidity tax."

The primate did not particularly like water, and NEVER liked it in her face. She grabbed both of them by the nape of their necks and began dragging them down the street. The capungas tried to wiggle their way loose, but Harriet had a vice-like grip on them like they had never felt before. Each thought the top of their head was going to blow off from so much pressure.

The happy neighbors came out to their front yards and were cheering the local heroes on. Booing, clapping, and hooting, they expressed both their disdain for the teenagers and their admiration for this huge monkey, acting as a police officer should have all along.

Apparently, the drug-gang leader didn't like what was happening. His vision of the whole scene was partially blocked. He only saw a big monkey roughing up his henchmen, and this made him mad. He grabbed a rope and started to swing it toward Harriet's back to teach her a lesson. That was NOT a smart thing to do!

The Nez Perce heavyweight wrestler intercepted the whip before it struck his friend. And a good thing he did too. The drug dealer made a mistake, as many ignorant people do, who spend no time watching the National Geographic channel on TV. They have NO idea how immensely strong an orangutan really is. Nor did this person have any idea what legitimate wrestling was. Bowie put a double-leg takedown on the unfortunate dealer and flipped him over, pinning his hands under him. Bowie sat on his back. The weight alone was very uncomfortable for the hapless criminal.

The neighbors had all come out, armed with pans of hot water and pig slop. Bowie forced the boss to join his crew, while the locals had a real neighborhood party, dousing the teens and their boss. This was too much for the would-be Mafia members, so they zoomed out of there like a rabbit that just found out it had woken up surrounded by angry foxes. They were threatening to tell the big boss about this as they sped away. The neighbors just gave them the wave off.

The thankful crowd didn't take long to show their appreciation. They brought cold soda pop for Bowie and a bunch of bananas for Harriet. Noting the big guy didn't speak any Portuguese, and neither did the redheaded, hairy one. They called one of the public school kids out who knew some English. The seventh grader could speak English fairly well. "We can like to tank you ford getty rids of da bad guys. Whose are you? Wheres are you froms? My name is Maurício Pedro Lopes dos Lobos."

Harriet let Bowie do the talking. "I've been told my name is Bowie, but I don't know if I have any other name. I'm an American. I hurt my head and don't remember very much. I don't know where I live or how to get back there."

Since it was getting close to noon, the neighbors got their heads together and invited Bowie to stay for lunch. The nice lady who was watering her flowers was Carol Maria dos Coelhos. She had Bowie escort the ape to the backyard, where she could swing in the tree and pick as many bananas as she wanted.

Carol had a son, Valdmir Camara Lopes dos Coelhos. He was a real Brazilian Gaucho, riding in the rodeos and living most of his life on a cattle ranch about five miles outside the city limits. Since Bowie didn't know where he lived, the Gaucho decided to take him to the ranch. An advantage to this arrangement was that the cowboy could speak English fairly well. Apparently, he had the God-given gift of language ability.

They left in a Ford pickup, with Harriet standing up in the back, holding on to the holes where the windows should have been, as 45-mile-per-hour winds blew her red hair all over the place. It was quite a sight.

The EL RANCHO PARADA was a big spread with 1,232 cattle, including 34 bulls. They also had 24 bucking broncos used in the rodeos.

<FADE TO THE GRINGOS AND MISSIONARIES>

The Gringos and missionaries had no success in finding either Bowie or Harriet. They were looking north when, in fact, the lost duo had gone south. No one figured they would go in that direction because it is so sparsely populated and includes many bad neighborhoods. After searching all day, they had to call it quits due to the weather. Lightning was illuminating the dark sky. They didn't want to quit, but it was not safe to be out in a thunderstorm the size of the one looming above them.

Tomorrow was the start of a two-day rodeo competition. They thought it was a good chance they might find Bowie and Harriet at that event. Feeling Bowie might be drawn to that kind of activity, they began to pray the duo would find out about it and show up. It seemed like a long shot, but they really had no other options.

Tom met with the whole crew. "Tonight I'll have to call Bowie's parents and tell them he's missing. This is not going to be a pleasant chat. We were responsible for monitoring him during his memory problems. I expect his dad to chew me out royally. We need to pray he'll show up at the rodeo tomorrow. Other than that, we have no further leads. The police will contact me if the two are reported anywhere in the city. They can't assure us they can help us at all if he is not in the city. Their rural police coverage is very sparse."

Tom radioed Pastor Ballentine and asked him to make a phone patch to Bowie's parents. The missionary was right. He got a real haranguing from both Pinetrees. They said this was too much to handle. They were booking flights to Brazil in the early morning, probably leaving in two days. If Bowie showed up within two days, they wouldn't make the flight.

They felt this was not a problem that would be repeated after Bowie was found. Tom assured them they were right. Tom was a very conscientious person and just hated being irresponsible, which is exactly what this whole episode seemed to suggest he was.

The prayer meeting before bedtime was longer than usual. Rocky asked to be the last to pray. "Lord, I don't know this Native American boy. I want to get to know him, though. We need Your guidance and protection for both him and the ape. To avoid a lot of trouble and hassle, we need to find him soon. Tomorrow would work for us; then his parents would be relieved and wouldn't have to come here. Please, Lord, give us this grace. We ask these things in the name of Your only Son, Jesus Christ. Amen."

Kosy had her own prayer she wanted to give, but decided against it. She would pray alone for her big friend just before she went to sleep. She had been the most affected by Bowie's absence because he had always called her his "Little Friend," and she loved him for it.

<BACK TO BOWIE ON THE REAL RANCH>

Bowie liked the ranch. It had familiar smells. The horses, bales of hay, barns full of stalls, and horse manure, LOTS of horse manure. These smells seemed familiar; he was enjoying this visit. There were also sounds he knew he had liked his whole life: the rhythm of running horses, the neighing of mares and studs, the slapping down of saddles on horses, and the rebellious prating when a bronco didn't want to be ridden.

Valdmir wanted Bowie to experience all the good things about being a Gaucho, letting him handle everything in the barn related to the horses: reins, ropes, saddles, and blankets; even the nice sheep's skin to sit on. The Gaucho enjoyed his new American friend. After the rodeo tomorrow, he'd go by the police station and find out if there were any Americans around here who were missing someone. He was enjoying this company too much to go today. It was a selfish decision, but he decided he could live with it to spend more time with Bowie.

The ranch was a lonely place for Valdmir. He was the only person on the grounds during the week because the owners were bankers in Porto Alegre. When they came for the weekend, he left to spend time with his family.

In conversing with Bowie, he concluded that the American knew a lot about the rodeo. He asked him if he would like to ride a bucking bronco tomorrow. Bowie said he thought it would be worth giving it a try.

The Gaucho got out his meanest horse and let Bowie give it a try. Because he was programmed to stay on, the Nez Perce had no problem finishing the ride, with an impressive professional style the Brazilian Gaucho had never seen during any of his rodeo competitions. The ranch hand was stunned.

"Man, yous is relly grets on da bronko. Tomorrow you vill rides witch our teem - OS GAUCHOS VALENTES."

CHAPTER 27
Creative Thieves

A fake moving company had a horrible surprise for the recipient of new bedroom furniture.

The Gringos had two days to find Bowie before his parents arrived from the USA to help. The Oregonians were not happy. Travis put it this way, "Bowie is as big as a tree, and you lost him. What are you running down there, a lost and found department? This is unbelievable, and you also lost Harriet! We couldn't schedule a flight earlier than two days from now. If he doesn't show up, we're coming down there as very unhappy parents."

Tom gave the Pinetrees his full attention. He understood their feelings were justified. He never tried to save face. That was not his way of handling mistakes, because it never resolved anything and only made matters worse. Fessing up to errors always helps resolve them faster.

"I'm deeply sorry we allowed Bowie to wander off like that. He must have gotten up before any of us and apparently went out to see the ape. For some unknown reason, Bowie and the ape appear to have left. We're going to the rodeo tomorrow to see if Bowie shows up. We all agreed this would be our best option. I think you two must agree, right?" They both agreed.

The rodeo arena was only one mile from the retreat center, in Brazil's cowboy country. The state of Rio Grande do Sul borders Uruguay to the south, a ten-hour drive from Porto Alegre. Argentina and Paraguay meet Brazil at the world's largest waterfall system—Iguaçu Falls, more than one and a half miles wide, with 275 individual drops, is a twelve-hour drive from Gravataí.

This part of South America, called "The Pampas," is often dubbed the "Texas of Brazil." The state's residents have many rodeo grounds spread across the area. Every weekend and holiday, the Gauchos would ride their favorite horses in front of Tom's house. Residents ride large horses with worn saddles and sit on sheepskins. Cowboy Day is September 20, a state holiday, but not in the rest of Brazil.

The cowboys and cowgirls rode horses a short distance to display them in parades. For longer trips, they used trailers. The Gaucho wore his special outfit on these occasions or whenever he wanted. The ladies showed off their "prendas"—full-length dresses with hoop skirts and bright colors.

Gravataí's parade featured over 300 horses, ridden by Gauchos ranging in age from 5-year-old beginners to veterans over 90. No one was ever too old to show off his Gaucho outfit or to ride in the parade.

During September, they'd bring portable sleeping shacks to Porto Alegre and set them up in the park. For 30 days, there were nonstop rodeo activities. The young ladies had barrel races just like their counterparts in the USA. Numerous stalls sold cheese, bread, jelly, and sausages.

Some cowboys traveled more than 50 miles in trains of small Conestoga wagons pulled by two Brahman bulls. Entire families were crammed into some of these wagons. This is the only state in Brazil with such traditions. It made these people feel like a big, happy cowboy family.

The rodeo that Valdmir told Bowie about lasted only two days, Friday and Saturday. The American had explained to him about vague memories of riding in several events somewhere, sometime in his past, but couldn't put it all together.

Harriet was enjoying her time at the ranch. She ran up and down the fenced fields, startling some of the horses. Valdmir was unconcerned about this behavior, knowing these horses spooked easily at sudden movements such as a passing crow or rabbit.

This area wasn't much different from other parts of Brazil; teens used drugs and robbed homes to keep their supply going. Before bedding down in the boss's house, Valdmir set all the alarms in the adjoining buildings, including the elaborately decorated home where the boss and his wife lived. They kept many valuables inside.

The cowboy was uncomfortable with all these expensive temptations in one place. He thought it was too much of a lure for the capungas who lived in homes along the route to the city. Everyone knew what kind of home he was guarding, and it made him nervous.

The owners did all they could to secure the grounds. They put a high, thick brick wall around the buildings, but not the fields. On the flat, concrete-covered top of this wall, shards of glass were embedded. Above the glass was circular, razor-sharp barbed-wire. Above that, was a triple-wire electric fence three feet tall. Most Brazilians don't even have ONE of these precautions.

Besides this, they had five ugly, vicious, huge Rottweilers, which were only fed the bare minimum. They were lean and mean, always looking for someone to add to their menu. Many Nationals have dogs, but not like these four-legged guardians. These dogs think that anything moving is infringing on their property rights and deserves to be on their dinner plate.

Valdmir's employer sent him to security school, where he learned how to use a gun. He was always packing. The academy also taught him the arts of Karate and jiu-jitsu, in which he earned black belts. He was not shy about protecting his life and the possessions for which he was responsible.

In addition to all these security measures, they had an alarm system so advanced that the one at Fort Knox seemed like a plastic whistle in comparison. Bars and sensors covered every window. Each door had both a sensor and a magnetic lock. Should anyone open a door or window while the alarm was set, chaos erupted: alarms blared like a battlefield while a signal rushed to the police station only two miles away. When the alarm sounded, a squad car arrived within five minutes.

After all, these were important people and deserved the very utmost consideration from the police. The fact that they hosted an annual picnic for all the local police officers and their families really had nothing to do with it, at least that's what they wanted everyone to believe.

It would seem that all of these expensive precautions would be enough. But if anyone thought this would provide 100% protection, they must have lived most of their life in the USA, because Brazilian thugs seem to have more creativity than most other capungas around the world.

The neighboring apartment buildings have bars on all first-floor doors and windows. This is standard anywhere in Brazil and is required by law to be installed by the building owner. The second-floor windows lack bars. The lady of the house usually puts her laundry out the window, hanging from an expandable metal rack.

Cheap, good-for-nothing thieves catch unprotected cats and tie thin nylon ropes to their waists. They toss the terrified felines up to the second-floor clothing rack. Seeking anything to dig their claws into, the flying cats latch onto the clothes and are pulled down, bringing the loot with them.

When this story broke in the local news outlets, everyone wondered why these creative, industrious thugs didn't use their talents to do something productive for themselves and society. The only answer they could come up with is that these capungas were just plain lazy and worthless.

When Valdmir arrived at the ranch house in the afternoon, he immediately noticed a large, new closet sitting in the living room. Since most Brazilian homes require stand-alone wardrobes because bedrooms lack closets unless specially built, this wasn't unusual. Still, he found it odd, even though the lady of the house often replaced furniture, giving older pieces to less fortunate families. Here's how the closet got into the house.

Earlier that morning, while Valdmir was away, a truck from a well-known high-class furniture store pulled up to the front gate. The delivery crew had cut the telephone wire on their way in. The driver, knowing Valdmir was absent, rang the doorbell and waited. No one came except the four barking dogs.

The barking and snarling were at max volume. The delivery boy didn't look worried. He just meandered over to the neighbor who lived about half a block away. He got her attention, along with the disdain of HER attacking, irate canine corps. Trying to explain what he wanted was nigh on to impossible with the barking and howling at higher decibels than a jet plane motor. The patron was Victoria Inez Roberta de Madeira, a very close friend of Valdmir's lady boss. She said one quick, boisterous word, "Quieto," and the dogs ran back to their lairs. Now they could talk.

The delivery person said he was from a well-known upper-class furniture store, but the side of his truck read "Coca-Cola" instead of "furniture store." Victoria had already noted this. When she asked him about it, he said all their trucks were in use, and they had borrowed this one.

His demeanor was not that of an uneducated person. He spoke Portuguese at a high level of proficiency. His hands were clean, and so were his fingernails. He also sported a uniform from the store and a baseball cap with the store's logo—all these things she needed to confirm before she could even start a meaningful conversation with him.

"May I help you?" she started with some reservations. He explained that her friend next door had ordered a closet, and he needed to leave it there now to avoid doubling the delivery cost. She said it would be necessary to call her friend first. She returned to say the phone was not working at the moment. They would have to come back another day.

He turned to go, then doubled back. "I'd like to take the closet back to the store in Porto Alegre, but it's closed now because one of the employees had suffered a heart attack and passed away on the spot. They shut down immediately out of respect for this longtime worker, whom everyone loved.

She expressed her sympathies and insisted they take the closet somewhere else, anyplace else; it didn't matter to her. She wasn't opening the door to her friend's house.

Just then, a tire on the truck blew out. How unfortunate, they didn't have a spare either. He explained the truck would have to be left there for the night. He could leave the closet inside the truck, but they couldn't guarantee it would be there in the morning. They certainly couldn't stay out here in this dangerous rural area of town to protect her friend's furniture.

By this time, Victoria was tired of the hassle. She thought this store definitely needed better customer service. She got the key to her neighbor's house and let them leave the big closet inside for the night. "There, that should be enough arguments for one day, don't you think?" With that, she waved "good riddance" to the workers, feeling she had done a charitable deed for her neighbor.

Valdmir was surprised to see the closet, but paid it no attention because his lady boss was always doing this kind of thing.

Because of the inclement weather, he decided to let Harriet sleep in the enclosed garden area in the middle of the house. He always slept in the boss's house when they were in Porto Alegre. This arrangement was strange because most upper-class folks didn't trust their servants this much. This cowboy had proven he was completely trustworthy in every aspect of life. They knew he'd never lie to them or steal anything from them. This kind of confidence has to be earned; it doesn't just come with the territory. The property owners thought this kind of honesty needed to be rewarded, too. So, they let him stay INSIDE the house.

Hanging a very well-built hammock between a coconut tree and a banana tree made a comfortable bed for the ape. She could actually reach up and grab bananas without getting out of bed. How good could it get, anyway?

Bowie had his own bedroom right next to Valdmir's sleeping quarters. For some strange reason, he couldn't explain, Bowie knelt beside the bed before he retired. Since he was down there, he decided to say a prayer, feeling this was something he always did. Then he climbed into the sack, and within just a few minutes, he was snoring.

The capungas, posing as delivery workers, convinced Victoria's neighbor to let them leave the closet in the living room. This was a big mistake on her part. Inside the armoire was a small capunga. He planned to gather all the valuables in the house and put them in the closet. The next day, the delivery workers would return, change the tire, and inform the neighbor they had mistakenly delivered the furniture to the wrong house. They needed to get it out before the nice lady came home, lest she get mad or even worse, jealous.

At least, this is what they were planning to do. The small thief would then walk out like one of the workers. He was hired to do the short jobs, like working under the kitchen sink. The "Small Man For Hire" was Pedrinho Souza de Marcos Araujo. The name Pedrinho means "Little Peter," which fits his situation just perfectly. He was only 14 and was just three feet tall, weighing just 67 pounds, and wasn't going to grow any taller. Even drinking yeast yogurt and eating spinach wouldn't help this runt.

The criminals like to use minors and small people because they would never be put in jail, no matter what they did. It was just the way the crazy justice system was in Brazil. It infuriated the nationals until it was THEIR teenager or small person who was in trouble, then they liked the senseless law.

Pedrinho was going to start in the main bedroom because he knew no one would EVER be sleeping in there. He had dropped out of school and decided to try his hand at thievery because he was tired of being made fun of there. So far, he hadn't made enough money to even buy a small bicycle.

When he returned from the owner's bedroom, he had his arms full of jewelry he had found in shoe boxes under the dresser. Did they think he was dumb or what, that he would never look there? He also had some money he had pulled from the fake soccer ball in the corner. These people had been watching too many cop episodes on TV. They were too predictable. He was laughing inside.

With his arms full, he turned the corner of the hallway, expecting to store his loot in the closet, when he came face to knee to the stinkiest person he had ever smelled. The problem was, it wasn't a PERSON. He looked up and stared into the most unfriendly face he had ever seen. Only it wasn't just a face. It was a big set of green and white teeth smiling at him, blowing its bad banana breath all over his face. The half-pint thief dropped his jaw. Bug-eyed and knees a-knockin', he tried to tell his feet to get a runnin'.

He didn't wait to see if the massive, revolting creature had friends. He just wanted to instantly run from the terrifying sight. He tossed the loot aside and took advantage of his small size by diving between Harriet's legs. The ape bent down, looked backwards under her own legs to follow the noise maker's path. It was a comical sight, to be sure. Harriet thought these humans were always so funny.

The noise from the falling loot woke up one angry cowboy and one dizzy-headed Native American. Valdmir saw the loot scattered everywhere and noticed Harriet sitting on the floor, staring out the window at a coconut tree. Looking toward the top of the tree, he saw a tiny person clinging to the trunk with all his might.

Bowie and Valdmir waited around until the police arrived with a tow truck to haul away what turned out to be a stolen truck. They gave Tiny Tim a ride to the clink in their squad car. Valdmir insisted the closet stay as a little payment for all the hassle they had to go through. Because the police officers didn't want to move the closet, they agreed to it. The Cowboy knew, as soon as they got to the police station, short stuff would be turned loose. After all, he was a minor, living in the minor key.

Because of the attempted robbery and their dealings with the police, Valdmir and Bowie arrived at the rodeo later than they had planned. Valdmir had already registered the American for two events, bull riding and bronco busting. They arrived seconds before the officials would have scratched Bowie from his first event. Valdmir signed him in as Bowie grabbed a participant bib and ran to the stalls while pinning the bib to his shirt. He mounted his assigned bull, grasped the belly rope to hang on, and flew out of the gate with a one-ton furious Brahma bull between his legs.

Because the announcer was German and didn't know Bowie's last name, he called him "The Gaucho Hovie." When Bowie and the bull broke out of the stall, things got a little exciting.

Some of Americans had been milling around the rodeo grounds looking for their two missing friends. It never occurred to them, and why would it, that Bowie would be participating, riding a bull. Kosette, Erin, Billy and Bert had wanted to watch the Gauchos, so they were leaning on the rail when the heavyweight wrestler broke out of the gate.

Kosy yelped and jumped down, leaving the other three there. She ran full blast toward the rest of the gang. "You'll not believe it, BOWIE IS RIDING A BRAZILIAN BULL!"

Billy, Kosy, Erin, and Bert are at the rodeo hoping to find Bowie. Kosy was the first to recognize it was her friend trying to stay on the bull.

CHAPTER 28
Bowie's Back

Bull riding is one of the most popular events during Brazilian rodeos.

The Americans rushed to the fence just in time to watch Bowie finish his bull ride as the buzzer sounded. Then things got ugly. He couldn't free his hand from the rope quickly, as he hadn't gripped it properly before the handlers opened the gate. The ride lasted longer than it should have. He should have been off by now.

The Gringos were getting nervous, yelling and praying at the same time. Kosette prayed hard for her big friend, Bowie. Suddenly, Bowie broke free, went flying, and landed on his shoulder, his head plowing into the dirt.

The bull stopped on a dime and turned towards the Nez Perce. With Bowie's head tucked in the dirt, the bull took off full speed towards the Gringo it hated. The Brazilian clowns are as good as the American ones. They pushed the wooden barrel towards Bowie and shoved him inside.

The clowns rolled the cowboy out of the way, leaving the bull with nothing but dirt to plow as it sped past the clowns and Bowie's barrel—its head and horns slammed into the wooden fence. Spectators right by the rail scattered and ran for higher ground.

When the dust cleared and Bowie was pulled out of the barrel, the Americans were right there to help him up. The Nez Perce, took one look at Kosette and blurted, "Did I ride the whole eight seconds, My Little Friend?" Kosy ran up and hugged him, exclaiming, "Bowie's back, my Big Friend is back!" It'd be a huge understatement to say this was a great relief to all concerned. The heavyweight wrestler said, "I don't know what happened after we sat on the lawn."

Bowie glanced around. "Did those clowns just save my hide?" Linda nodded in confirmation, assuring him that was exactly what happened. The group then recounted the events of the past few days to him.

Erin sized him up. No lost pounds, apparently. "You must have been eating well. By the way, where's Harriet?"

When they got to her, she was entertaining the Brazilian kids at the rodeo's edge, right where Valdmir and Bowie had left her with a basket of bananas. When they rounded her up, the local kids groaned in disappointment. Valdmir assured them, "She'll be back tomorrow, same time, same station."

Contacting Travis Pinetree was the number-one item on the Americans' priority list; it had to be NOW to keep Bowie's parents from catching their flight to Brazil tomorrow. Tom went home to contact John Ballentine via ham radio and tell him to relay a message to the Pinetrees that Bowie had been found and was just fine. Bowie has complete memory recovery.

Bowie looked sheepish. Had he embarrassed himself while lost in Never-Never land for so many days? Bert reassured him: "You did just fine. For being 'out of your mind,' you did really well. We kept our eyes on you. But getting up before us and sneaking out—that worried us because you're usually the LAST one to roll out of the hammock."

Valdmir was glad the Native American stranger found his tribe. With Tom present, Valdmir chose to speak through an interpreter. "Bowie and Harriet were good companions for the day I spent with them, except my boss lady has no more bananas in her backyard. The small marauder didn't get the items he wanted to sell, so he could buy himself platform shoes, but the tiny crook did get released from the Police station before the paperwork was finished."

Rocky wanted to know if there was more to the rodeo. Maybe he could join Bowie in working together to win a trophy or two. Valdmir volunteered, "Tomorrow is the last day. Bowie has already qualified on the brahma bull. Would you like to try on the bronco this afternoon?"

Loretta eyed the newcomer with skepticism. "I knew you were a professional wrestler, but I never heard you rodeo, too. Are you really this multitalented?"

Rocky replied, "My family is from Broken Bow, Oklahoma; everyone out that way is involved in the Rodeo. My best friends from Broken Arrow got me interested in rodeo during high school. We all participated in local events. A few times, we went to the national open at Broken Back Lake."

Billy, always the astute one and wanting to be a part of conversations, asked, "For Pete's sake, is everything out that way broken?" Rocky laughed, finding the pint-sized wrestler hilarious, as he usually was.

Valdmir signed up the pro wrestler for the next bronco ride. Many Brazilian cowboys thought this was a mistake, since he could get hurt, and they didn't want to be responsible. After seeing his size, they changed their minds and worried about the horse instead.

There was one other event both Gringos wanted to try. It's only found in Brazilian rodeos. A mid-size cow is turned loose and starts running to the other end of the corral. The cowboy has to lean over and grab the cow's tail, tripping it in a marked-off area that has three sections. If he can trip it in the first slot, it's more points; each further slot has fewer points.

Rocky went before Bowie. He had never done this before, but watched several who went before him. Reaching down on the right side of the horse, he grabbed the tail. When he yanked it upward, trying to knock the cow off her feet, he was left holding the tail of a tailless cow that was running away from him. The Brazilians said that only a person with superhuman strength could do that.

Bowie had a little more luck. He managed to tilt the cow but not knock it off its feet, so he earned zero points. Rocky spent the rest of the day preparing himself for day two. When the pro wrestler mounted the bronco, the poor horse seemed to bow more than usual under his 280 pounds.

The horse didn't have a chance. It tried to rear up and flop over on its side, but was unable to because of the extreme weight on its back. Rocky had no problem staying on for the required time. The clowns needed to rescue the horse from the cowboy this time. They had heard of it happening before, but this was the first time they had seen it.

That night, the Gringos went to a churrascaria with a show. Meat was the main course—plentiful and varied. As folklore dancers performed, sparks flew from their spear-hop and sword fights. Servers appeared at each table, offering ten types of meat on long swords and slicing it to every guest's preference. Only Rocky dared try the barbecued chicken hearts. He thought they tasted like a cow's heart; their texture was gummy.

The bolhadeiro was Edson Silva Cavalho Schmidt, whose dad was German. He was one of the best in the world, having performed all over Europe and Asia. He used two round stones tightly wrapped in leather with three-foot leather cords. He swung them around his head in various directions. It was amazing. He even clamped the ends of the cords between his teeth and swung the balls all over the place.

He asked for a volunteer. Because Tom had visited many times, he arranged for Edson to call Erin, Bowie, and Linda to the stage. Edson put a white bandana on Erin's red hair, covering her eyes. Then he twirled the bolas near her head, closer and closer, until the cords grazed her bandana, sending it flying. Erin sat back down, her hair in a tangled mess.

After Linda's part, she returned to her seat and began her dramatic explanation of what happened. "Wow. After seeing what he did to Erin, I worried less about my own head. I felt the light breeze as the bolas passed just a fraction of an inch from my skull. I couldn't help but imagine what might have happened if those balls would have hit my head. Those concrete-hardened balls would've knocked my noggin halfway across town. If he'd called Harriet up there, things might've turned out differently—she probably would have eaten the bolas."

Edson sat with the Gringos, speaking through the restaurant's interpreter. The interpreter's English was good but not perfect. "I wan to welcomes all of youse Americans to our lovely cities. We has many atrackings downtowns dat youse mike like to sees. I also wants to asked

Tom if he is still teached Greco-Roman fighting? He is da worlds champion, did youse knowed dis?" Edson nodded toward Tom.

Every time Tom brought a tourist group here, Edson said the same things. He was a bit confused about some of the details of Tom's wrestling ministry, but the coach never thought it was worth fussing about, especially the part about him being the world champion!

On their way out of the restaurant, the Gringos noticed beggars beside the parking lot—cold and hungry. Rocky, moved by the sight, slipped off his shoes and handed them to the biggest man. One by one, the Americans followed his lead; they all went home barefoot. Before leaving, Bert asked the parking lot guard to buy $100 worth of barbecue for the hungry crowd.

After arriving at the retreat center, Tom asked the Gringos to meet in the living room. He wanted another hour of instruction on surviving as a missionary. He taught the first two chapters of his 1960 doctoral thesis about why missionaries quit.

"Adjusting to a culture isn't easy. Here, it's not as primitive as the Amazon or much of Africa, India, or New Guinea. You've been in Brazil for two months. What do you like or not like about the culture? Be honest; you're among friends."

Marty was the first to answer. "I don't like the fact that the Brazilian people feel uncomfortable when they see policemen. When I'm in the States, and I see a police car or an officer, I feel good, safer. Apparently, Brazilians don't feel this way, and I am sorry it's like this for them."

Bert commented, "I really like the way people greet each other. The Bible does say, 'Greet the brethren with a holy kiss,' not a holy handshake. I shake hands with people I don't even like. This kissy stuff is a very intimate way to greet each other, and I really go for it."

The dramatic one got wound up, "I, for one, am shaking in my boots most of the time. If a mosquito isn't stalking me, then a cockroach is running under my feet, or a tarantula is closing in on my personal space. The fact that there are insects that want to bite me or carry me off to their lair is a frightening thought. The horror of it all is that these problems are year-round here. Snakes in the shower, bats in the bedroom, alligators and anacondas that want to digest you slowly, it's just too much to process."

Bowie was recovered enough to participate. "I like the extreme contrasts within the borders of Brazil. We wrestled with Indians on the Amazon, ran from alligators, fought anacondas, fished for piranhas, swam in thermo-swimming pools, climbed mounds of rock salt, and participated in the rodeo."

The ex-runaway mom had her opinion, too. "I like the friendliness of the Brazilian people. They're kind, generous, and loving. Everywhere we went, even on the Amazon, we were received with open arms and treated like kings and queens. Of course, that doesn't include cruel and powerful shamans, kidnappers, or mini-marauders. I've noticed that Brazilians love Americans and talk kindly of our home country."

Tom was pleased with their input. "I'm so glad that, for the most part, you've spoken kindly of your host country. I've lived here for 40 years and agree with everything you've mentioned. There are people, even those who would count themselves as dedicated Christians, who wouldn't even consider living here. It's mostly the corruptness, robbers, and the bugs that keep them in the USA.

"I believe I'm immortal until God is done using me here. Tarantulas are scary, without doubt, but I don't know ANYONE who that spider has ever bitten. When I see a cockroach in our house, I buy an item at the store. It's called "Check-in but Don't Check-out Housing." We keep all our doors and windows shut (the Brazilians don't) so we can keep the flying and crawling critters outside. I even put towels at the bottoms of the doors, as you noticed.

"We were working with a family to come here. But when the wife found out Brazil has cockroaches, she told her husband she'd never live in a place that had roaches. For Pete's sake, there are roaches in every building in the States, not just here. I wonder where she's been living all of her life, anyway, in Fantasy Land?"

Before they finished the discussion on culture, Kosette wanted to add her two bits. "I love the children here. Even though they have so little, they're very friendly. From the children in the tribes to the little tykes in Fortaleza and Mossoró, I found the families united, even in their poverty, their dirt-poor, dirt-floor poverty. I find this amazing."

Shane didn't want to be lacking in thought. "The people are Brazil's finest asset, without a doubt. The economy, the weather, and even the wonderful food are not the greatest things about this country. I've made many friends here, from Indians to fishermen to cowboys, and they're all wonderful people, easy to love and hard to forget."

Billy never liked to be left out of any discussion. "The whole experience, in all three parts of Brazil, has been marvelous, discounting the 'run for your life game with an alligator,' of course. The hosts have shown us wonderful hospitality and flexibility. We know their schedules are busy, yet they took the time to be tour guides for us, and even more, to help us adjust to Brazilian culture."

Tom continued, "Adjusting to Brazilian culture is important. But there are things we as Americans will never be able to adjust to. These are the same things that nationals complain about every day. Just last year, inflation was 125% a month. No one can adjust to life like that.

"The constant fear of being robbed or mugged is no way to live. Fearing even the police, who are supposed to protect you, is absurd. No Brazilian will ever be able to adjust to that. The rich and famous having their children kidnapped is a part of this culture that NO one wants to see continue, yet it's in the news almost every day.

"Some of these people tell me they hate living here for these exact reasons. They'd like to go to the USA to work as maids and gardeners. I don't blame them. We stay here, but not because we love the living conditions or the food. Our lives are embedded here for life because God called us, and He has not told us to leave yet. We enjoy living here because of our love for the Brazilian people. They're our priority and always will be."

Susana, Tom's wife, closed the meeting with a cute story about what happened while they were at the rodeo. Their daughter, Tiffany, one of the identical twins, is three years old. She was lying down to take a nap with her sister when the little tyke saw a huge roach climbing up the wall. She yelped, "Look, Mommy, a huge, ugly cockroach climbing on the curtain. Daddy isn't here to kill it. What are we going to do?"

"I told her we could pray about it." She came back with, "Praying is always good, Mommy. But I want to know who's going to go over there and kill it?"

Marty was snickering and finding it hard not to bust out laughing. "As Billy always says, 'there is a good sermon illustration in this story. I think I'll have to talk to Pastor Ballentine about it.' At least that's what Billy always says." The pint-sized grappler was nodding his head in approval and wondering how he managed to let Marty beat him to the punch.

The Americans were invited to a costume party that night. The party was organized by Antonio Chagas Silva Rodrigues, a well-to-do person who had just started attending Tom's church. He was celebrating his daughter's 15th birthday. This is VERY important in any country south of the Rio Grande River. Some families spend half a year's wages on the party, others, who have no such means, make the most of their humble conditions.

BUT no father would ever consider failing to have this party for all his daughters. It's necessary. Any father who failed to give his daughter her 15th birthday party would basically be declaring that he had no love or respect for her; she was worth NOTHING to him!

Everyone bought an outfit except Harriet. She was going "au naturel," and everyone felt that would be enough. The party was to be in a rented room.

During the festivities, everyone was milling around, grabbing finger food and soft drinks. Loretta was hanging onto Rocky's arm most of the time. She meandered over to observe the huge, beautifully decorated cake. She grabbed a soda and took off her mask to drink it. Just as she was about to return to Rocky's side, a tall man sauntered up to her and spun her around.

At that same moment, he also lowered his mask. The ex-gambler gasped, panic filled her eyes, and all color drained from her face. She found herself looking straight into the eyes of Vini the Fin, the Mafia boss who had been stalking her for a whole year.

Loretta was spun around by someone who pulled down his mask. When she realized who it was, it made her heart begin to race. There looking evilly into her wide-open eyes was the dreaded Vini the Fin.

CHAPTER 29
Mafia Closing In

Even Gravataí had their share of Mafia thugs ready and willing to make gullible Brazilians pay a hefty price for not being mindful of details.

Loretta dropped her drink and ran toward Rocky. Vini the Fin shouted, "Aha! I've found you, Loretta! Pay what you owe, or your life won't be worth a nickel." He hurled his mask to the floor and rushed out.

Rocky met her near the patio. "What was THAT all about?" He saw her trembling and speechless. Kosy and Shane came quickly to her side. All the Americans surrounded her like a wall of protection; Bowie, Marty, Bert, and Harriet made an impressive barricade, backs toward Loretta.

Loretta tried to explain. "That ... that ... per ... person was Vini the Fin. HE'S HERE! How did he get here?" She was still shaking, and Rocky steadied her. Tom brought the birthday girl's father to the circle of Americans, with Loretta and Rocky in the middle, protected by the others.

Tom pressed through and put a hand on her shoulder. "Who was that? What did he mean? I only heard part of it—sounded like a threat. Can you explain, Loretta?"

She struggled to speak. "He's a Mafia boss from San Francisco. Before I was a Christian, I gambled a lot and owed him over $10,000, with no ability to pay. He threatened my kids and me. I took it seriously—many people who crossed him disappeared. That's why I ran and left my kids, thinking I protected them by sending them to my dad's farm in Oregon."

Tom asked Antonio about the tall man who yelled at Loretta as he left. Antonio replied, "I don't know him. He came with a friend of a friend. I'll find out. This ruined my daughter's party. I spent so much—what a mess!"

Rocky tried to calm Loretta. "I saw him once at The Crab Shack. How did he get here? This can't be a coincidence. Some Mafia business must've brought him to Porto Alegre—and to this party."

Shane and Kosy embraced their mom as she trembled, heart pounding with memories she'd tried to bury. She thought the nightmare had ended. Yet here it was again. Teenage choices, lovers with cruel faces, a life on the run—her children's fear and flight, her own misery in a Siberian camp. Redemption had seemed possible. But the past's shadow stretched long, threatening to dilute her happiness.

Now, after turning her life around and loving God, she was back at square one. But this time, loving friends, her children, and even Rocky stood by her. It was a new game—but still frightening.

The Americans decided the party was over for them. They kissed the birthday girl, filled two VW vans, and headed to the retreat center. Dark scenarios played through their minds. What were they going to do now?

In the van, Rocky spoke softly. "This ends here, in Brazil. We won't leave until we see this finished. We have to trust God. Only He can end this now."

There was a great deal of contemplation and prayer at the retreat center just before bedtime. Loretta asked Rocky, "Do you have any idea how we can end this? Now I've involved all my friends with the Mafia. I feel awful—so low I could do jump jacks under a dime."

Rocky had known Loretta only briefly, most of it spent unsaved and on the run. Nine months after his wife died, he found her. From now on, his only priority was to protect her and the kids.

The upcoming and final day of the rodeo was going to differ from the first. This time, Bowie would be joined by all of his American friends.

They planned to be extra vigilant: keeping one eye on the rodeo action and the other on the lookout for any suspicious people who might be connected to the mob.

Bowie and Rocky were still on Valdmir's team. The Brazilian wanted to know why all the Americans had their heads on a swivel, as tourists do. He said that even though there are many German, Italian, Russian, and Polish immigrants living in this state, it was still easy to spot a tourist. They always have a camera around their neck, and always looked around.

Tom updated their Gaucho host on Vini the Fin. He wasn't surprised. Tom interpreted for Valdmir. "The Mafia's presence here is strong—lots of Italians, police are lax, and laws favor criminals over victims. The Mafia uses minors because they know the kids will just be released as soon as they hit the station; police barely report their crimes.

"I'll tell my friends. We'll keep watch for any stranger—anyone who's not a cowboy or seems suspicious. We Gauchos, know all locals and their families. We'll spot outsiders fast."

Bowie was up next on the Brahma bull. He drew "Black Fire," one of the orneriest, biggest, and fastest bulls in the state. Kosy frowned. "If Bowie hits his head again, will he go back to being mindless?"

Gaucho mania has infiltrated every aspect of life in Rio Grande do Sul. Doctors, lawyers, politicians, teachers, policemen, and firemen all dress up in the traditional clothes and make the best of living in cowboy country. A medical doctor sitting near them overheard Kosette's concern about Bowie. "I know about yours friend, the Indian. We ark going to has him wear a helmet when he ride. We does not wants him to have another problem. Does dis make you feels best now?"

Kosy thanked him and complimented him on his good English. She told him, "Bowie means a lot to us, and even more to me. He calls me 'My Little Friend,' and I love that."

Valdmir explained to Bowie, "Black Fire is the most fear bull around dis area. Not only vill he gives you a very rough rided, he vill make almost a 180° turn and then come backs on you. That suddn, violent jerk has trown the best of us off on our backs. Also, he his hateful, always vants revenge. So, if he succeeds in trowing you off, run for the barrels. He has mauled tree of us and even kill one."

Bowie replied, "Thanks. That helps. I rode a bull like this before—almost didn't make it. Now that I know about the jerk, I'll brace for it. You probably saved me a lot of embarrassing pain. How can I thank you?"

"Youse cans buy me a pieces of pizza if youse can still valk and talk after dis ride," he joked, "oh, and by da vay, no one has ever ridden dis bull for the wholes timed to get score. Just thoughts you might like to knows dat." Now, Bowie WAS starting to develop a little anxiety about the ride.

The heavyweight wrestler drew gate #4. He could see the large name plaque printed in both Portuguese and English: **"FOGO NEGRO— INVENCIVEL / BLACK FIRE—UNDEFEATED."** The grappler thought to himself, "I have to end this winning streak today, don't I?"

Kosy quit crossing her fingers after she became a Christian and had almost stopped chewing her nails; almost is but to fail. She was praying for her hero. The gate opened, and Black Fire blew out of there on a well-rehearsed mission of destruction!

The bull's first move was to jump to the left. The action was so swift, powerful, and perfectly executed that he even surprised himself; it brought him to his knees. This caused the Nez Perce to lunge straight forward, between the horns. Black Fire paused in that position for just a second and then was back up on his feet, taking poor Bowie with him and throwing the Native American backwards, almost parallel with the bull's back.

Bowie was having the roughest, toughest, scariest ride of his life. Suddenly, the bull jerked; the 180° jerk Valdmir warned him about. Bowie was ready for the yank. It twisted him violently. It wasn't in perfect competition form, but he stayed aboard without any disqualifying actions. The buzzer's blast ended his self-imposed torture atop the one-ton fury. Breathless and shaking, Bowie Pinetree had done what no one else ever had: conquered Black Fire in public, where legends are born—on the precarious precipice, straddling terror and triumph.

All the cowboys and cowgirls loved the ride. Now came the hard part: dismounting without being trampled or gored. The Nez Perce caught the jump just at the right moment, let go of the rope, and, without wanting to, flipped backwards, landing on his feet.

When his boots hit the ground, he zoomed across the hard-packed dirt like a 100-yard dash sprinter. It made the whole ride seem magical. He was an instant hero, a true Gaucho for sure.

A few people present would have preferred a different outcome for the ride. All their names ended in O or I; they ate a lot of spaghetti and grew acres of grapes, indicating that their ancestors came from the same county where the Pope lives. They had wanted to see Bowie get gored or trampled, actually wagering with each other about how many seconds it would take for the large, sweaty, windowmaker to end the Gringo's rodeo career.

Vini the Fin was disguised as a cowboy. One thing he forgot was to walk like his legs were parentheses, which is not a choice most Gauchos have, but rather a result of riding so much. Also, his thugs were anything but Gauchos. They looked like a bunch of kids who got their duds at the local used-clothing store. They thought this facade was good enough to hide their identities.

Rocky was up next: bucking bronco riding. Loretta was shocked that, in addition to being a pro wrestler, he also participated in rodeos. She was hoping he could prove that mold or rust had not accumulated on his spurs. How long had it actually been since he played the part of a rodeo junkie, anyway? He said it didn't matter; it was like riding a bicycle. Once you get back aboard, you never forget.

The horse he drew was "Double Trouble." He asked Valdmir why this jet-black horse had such a fearful name. The Brazilian told him, "He is named dis cause only one peoples has ever riddens him, ME. Dere are two tings youse have to know if youse are to stay aboard for eight seconds.

"One is dat he vill not comes out of da gates jumping. He firsts runs straight ahead for about ten meters (30 feet), and den leaps up to da left. The seconds ting youse need to knows is dat he vill tuck his head almost betweens his front legs, hoping da rider will slides off past his ears.

"So, when he does dat, bow with him and youse can stays on. If youse try to compensate by leaning backs, as some novices do, he vill dump you right off his backside vhen he comes back up. Do youse understand me?"

Rocky was glad he talked to Valdmir. The Gaucho knew what he was doing; he knew each horse and bull well. The pro wrestler blew out of gate #6. Double Trouble did exactly what the Gaucho said he would. When the bronco went down forward, Rocky went with him and came back up with him. The buzzer sounded, and the pickup riders swiftly and safely pulled Rocky from the bronco, which was still bucking a little.

The rodeo was over. Bowie took third in bull riding, was awarded the blue ribbon in the barrel-rolling race with the clowns, and received a sign that had been in place for many years: "FOGO NEGRO—INVENCIVEL / BLACK FIRE—UNDEFEATED." The rodeo award committee voted unanimously to present the sign to Bowie in honor of his record-book achievement. Besides, BLACK FIRE would need a new sign anyway. The bull's owner initially protested because he wanted to give the sign to one of his nephews, but committee members convinced him that Bowie had earned the honor—and he agreed.

Rocky took the blue ribbon in the bucking bronco contest. Loretta was stunned. "Wow, do you have any more hidden talents I should know about? Maybe some black belts or world titles. Don't hold back, give us the whole nine yards, now."

"Okay, I'll fess up. I also have black belts in Karate and Jiu-Jitsu. And I make a pretty mean omelet to boot. Do you like anchovies on yours?"

Billy was not surprised at Rocky's multitalented personality. "I know about type-A people. People like you have strong choleric personalities. Many were great leaders of history, and take-no-prisoners war generals. Alexander the Great was almost a pure Choleric. You're a hard driver, hate to be late, don't mind bossing others around, plan way ahead, and always get an early start. Am I right, or not?"

Rocky assured him that he had pegged him very close to the truth. "How come you know so much of these things, being blind and all, no offense intended."

The grappler just shrugged his shoulders, "No offense taken, tough guy. I read a lot and listen well. Our local library has an amazing collection of Braille books. I see with my ears and notice more than sighted people do. Many say my other senses are sharper, tuned better. I'm not sure that's the whole truth. I have no visual distractions, so I listen with an alert mind. I pick up things others miss because visual things can distract them."

There was a ceremony to give away ribbons and trophies. Valdmir won the All Around Gaucho trophy. All of his American friends were cheering and hollering to beat the band. All the lovely Gauchas liked the attention showered upon their hero, Valdmir.

When everyone was milling around after the events, Vini the Fin and his cohorts planned to make a beeline for Loretta, hoping to grab her and leave the premises quickly. She had just come out of the snack bar with five hot dogs, one in each hand and three running up her arms.

Slithering out from under the bleachers, the snake, Vini the Fin, accompanied by some of his meanest minions, planted his feet right in front of the ex-gambler, blocking her path.

CHAPTER 30
A Gaucho Gets Saved

A Gaucho is the same as an American cowboy. Many people in Southern Brazil participate in weekend and holiday rodeos.

Loretta let out a yelp and dropped six hot dogs. She couldn't run. It was like her feet were on strike or went SOUTH for the winter. It didn't look good for her. Vini thought this was going to be a successful caper at last.

Like all previous attempts, he was wrong!

Valdmir and all his rough, tough cowboy buddies had been watching Loretta closely. When they saw the mobster make his move, they rushed between Vini the Fin and his intended victim. The impenetrable wall of Gauchos seemed to appear from nowhere and was impressive. Tom translated for Valdmir, since the Mafia dude had flunked his Portuguese 101 class.

"Valdmir demands that you desist now and forever. He said it would be VERY harmful to your health if you started a rumble here and now. Let's face it, DUDE, you're not only outnumbered, but you're also in a foreign territory. It'd be very unwise for you to do anything except run away as fast as your fancy shoes can take you. NOW! He also recommends that you run due east until your hat floats. If you don't do this in the next few seconds, you'll prove what he thought about you all along: if we removed your brain and put it in the head of a flea, it'd roll around like a BB in a boxcar. Oh, by the way, I added that last part about the BB, but you get the idea how we both feel about you."

The criminal may have been out maneuvered, but he wasn't dumb. He understood and respected the overwhelming force confronting him and his crew. As he backed away from the pending one-sided conflict, he made sure they knew the situation was not resolved. "I've not finished with her yet. We'll be back, and THEN you'll experience our capabilities."

With the threat lingering in the air, the mobster and his henchmen took a few more steps backward, turned like a precision military squad, and walked away from the cowboys. The Gauchos grinned from ear to ear, pleased they were able to do a meaningful favor for their American friends. Valdmir said it well, through Tom, "We love Americans, despise people like Vini the Fin. We already have too many 'Vinis' here in Brazil. He should go home to the USA soon! No one I know will miss him."

The Americans were very thankful for the protection and kindness of the rodeo cowboys. A trip to Gramado was scheduled for the following day. The Gringos invited Valdmir to join them and help with interpreting. He gladly consented. They planned to leave Harriet at the retreat center to guard the banana trees. She heartily concurred with that idea.

Valdmir was half German and half Brazilian. He loved Gramado, the German settlement 50 miles into the mountains. He knew how important a city it was to Brazil as a whole. It had taken Rio's place as the #1 tourist city in all of South America. He asked Tom to explain how that actually happened.

"Rio de Janeiro used to be the second most popular tourist city in the world, bested only by Paris, France. But the Brazilian crime rate had soared, causing tourists to go elsewhere, and Rio no longer showed up on any of the top-ten lists of popular destinations it had been on for many years. The Brazilian tourist association wrote a letter to all travel agencies worldwide. 'We have resolved the problem; you can now send your citizens back to our wonderful city with lovely, sunny beaches.'

"The Americans, always suspicious and wanting verifiable proof, asked the association exactly how they made the situation better. They replied, 'We've indeed solved the problem. We put a small police cabin every 100 yards on Copacabana Beach. Now it's easier to report a mugging without having to go downtown anymore. You can take care of the paperwork right there on the beach. Forms are available for multiple languages, including English.' I don't think many Americans rushed out to buy plane tickets to Rio, do you?"

That night, Tom had a prayer meeting at his church. He invited Valdmir and his cowboy friends to come. The Americans would sing songs and play some instruments. The Gauchos had nothing else to do and enjoyed spending time with their new American friends, so most of them promised to show up. Billy was going to play the guitar, Bert the harmonica, and Marty the saxophone for special music.

Tom liked to start services on time, but out of respect for latecomers, mostly visitors, he frequently began ten minutes late. He always insisted, "People are more important than programs."

He gave this illustration to the Gringos the night before. "A conductor complained to the directors of the train line. 'We could make a lot better time if we didn't have to stop and pick up these people.' Unfortunately, this is the attitude some of our missionaries have had, and the hurting and needy can easily detect it. Our priority is the Brazilian people. Our interests, hobbies, and schedules take second place to these tasks God has given us."

The missionary asked Billy and Bowie to give their testimonies so the cowboys could get a clear picture of salvation by grace.

Billy went first. "I was raised in a very well-to-do family. My father, Solomon, insisted on hiding the fact that we were Jewish because he was afraid of the backlash hurting his jewelry stores. Because of the German holocaust horrors, he didn't even believe in God. This attitude trickled down to all of us; we were atheists. These friends of mine (pointing to the Gringos) showed me what real Christians were like. Last year, we were stranded in a crashed plane, on a ledge in the Montana mountains, during a white-out snowstorm. All we could do was converse and wait. It was enlightening. I did my best to hold out, clinging to my unbelief. But their many prayers, along with the indisputable facts of the Bible, were hard to keep denying.

"I know Jesus Christ is the Messiah, the proofs are many and irrefutable. He said if any person came to Him, admitted he was a sinner, and received Him into his heart as his only Lord and Savior, they would be given eternal life. I did this, and now I'll live with Him forever. He can also give YOU eternal life if you put your faith in Him. It's salvation by grace through faith, and not by good works. If you want to accept Christ, it's simple. Just talk to God honestly. Admit to Him you're a sinner and need His forgiveness. Believe that Jesus died for your sins and rose again. Then ask Him to come into your life as your Lord and Savior. Trust Him to save you. That's what I did—and you can, too. He promises to hear anyone who truly calls on Him."

Bowie was next, glad to give the story of how he came to Christ. "I was raised as a Spiritist, worshiping and seeking the help of my ancestors. We lived on the reservation in Eastern Oregon until I was eight years old. My dad, Travis Pinetree, wanted us to have a normal lifestyle, so we moved to Lebanon, where he purchased a gas station.

"I didn't believe anything: nothing, nada, zilch. Shane and his friends from Lacomb stopped at the gas station and became my friends. I saw how real Christians lived when I visited the Lynch's ranch and Shane's farm. I found it hard to believe the Creator of all humanity was interested in me. I always accepted the existence of a higher power, but never had that defined into a person. After attending church with my friends, I heard Pastor Ballentine clearly explain salvation. I always liked free stuff!

"Shane and Marty helped me understand that although salvation was free for me, it cost Christ everything. He took my place on the cross and paid the penalty for my sin because I couldn't do it myself. I realized if I didn't receive Jesus as my only and sufficient Savior, I wasn't going to be allowed into heaven. I went against the teachings of my family and my tribe when I accepted Christ. Some of them haven't been very happy with me for this decision. I really am sorry for them. I know for sure I'm going to heaven when I die because I did what God said I must do. I put my faith in Christ, and HE saved me by HIS grace."

The Gauchos had their interests piqued. Valdmir had a few questions for Shane and Bowie. Tom took the three of them into his office. They sat down to talk. Shane looked right at Valdmir. "What's the question you have? Is it about something that was said tonight?"

The cowboy waved off Tom's offer to translate and tried to explain himself. "I wants to know ifs a person can real know he vill goes to heaven or is dis just a good guess? I has been a religious person all mine lifes and I do not feel dat I ams going to da heavens dat Billy e Bowie spoked abouts. I have heards dat Jesus is da Savior buts I do not think He is MY Savior. I don'ts tink I vould goes to heaven vhen I dies, buts I do vant to goes. I ams a very sincere persons, isn't dis enough to gets me into heaven? I have always heards from our religious leaders dat if I do da best I can and am sincere, dis is enoughs. Is dis okay, it is isn't it?"

Shane thought he had a story to clear this up for him. "I'll tell you a true story I heard at church. In 1868, a lady named Joyce was traveling in a train across the state of Montana with her newborn baby. She wanted to get off the train in Belgrade, so she asked the conductor, Mark, when it would stop there. He said he would let her know when they arrived and ensure the train didn't depart until he had confirmed she had gotten off.

"Paul, a nice gentleman sitting next to her, told the lady not to bother the conductor. He often traveled on this train, and he could tell her when they stopped in Belgrade. As the train continued down the tracks, it began to snow so hard no one could see out the windows. It was very cold outside, but comfortably warm inside the train.

"When the train stopped in Bozeman, Paul advised Joyce that the next stop would be Belgrade; he was sure of it. The train moved forward for a short time, then stopped. He told the lady she could get off the train. She asked him if he was sure of it. He said he was absolutely positive this was Belgrade; it was always the next stop after leaving Bozeman. She could get off here. It was snowing so hard she couldn't even see her hand in front of her face.

"Joyce descended, and the train moved on. The conductor returned and asked where the lady was. Paul said he told her to get off at Belgrade, the previous stop. The conductor looked horrified and pulled the emergency cord. The train stopped immediately. He ran to the front and told the engineer to back up. He never liked backing the train, especially when he couldn't see down the track behind him, but did what the conductor ordered.

"Returning, Mark shot a stern look at Paul. 'You sent that lady and her child to their deaths in this freezing blizzard. We didn't stop in Belgrade. It's still five miles in front of us. We stopped in the middle of the prairie to investigate an unusual engine noise. I hope she's still alive.' After several minutes of searching near where they had stopped earlier, they found her and the baby, less than 30 feet from the tracks ... frozen to death. Paul was sincere when he told Joyce to get off the train. The mom was sincere when she followed his sincere instructions. Both of them were sincere, but BOTH were sincerely WRONG.

"Paul gave her the best advice he had, and she was following the best advice a very sincere man gave her. So, you see, Valdmir. Sincerity was not enough. This story ended in tragedy because all the decision-makers were sincerely wrong. Many people, like you, believe that doing your best and being sincere is enough to get you into heaven. They can find many religious people, including pastors, who will agree with them. Sincerity is NOT enough. People did their best and were very sincere before Christ even arrived on earth. If good works and sincerity could save your soul, then Christ died for nothing."

Valdmir was nodding his head. He understood perfectly what Shane was trying to point out to him. "I understoods now. Good vorks and sincerity cannot saves a soul. Den it is only as youse said, I needs to ask Christ to comes into my hearts to have my sins forgaven and He vill gives me eternal lifes, Right?"

That cold winter night, in the city of Gravataí, at Central Baptist Church, one Gaucho named Valdmir confessed he was a sinner and needed a Savior. He accepted Christ into his heart and was given eternal life. It was a glorious night in cowboy country.

Rocky shared a lesson in God's planning. "The fact that Bowie and Harriet wandered away from the retreat center was in the archives of divine planning. Without that event, a Gaucho would never have come to Christ tonight. It's a matter of good coming out of misfortune. It's marvelous to be part of God's plan and to be doing His will."

All the Americans went to bed rejoicing that Valdmir would spend eternity with them, in God's glorious habitat with Christ and the angels. His name would be found in the Book of Life, and he would escape paying the eternal penalty for his sins. The plan was to leave for Gramado at 6:00 AM. Tom always liked to get an early start.

During the night, drums started pounding at the small creek beside the retreat center. The missionary had already warned the Gringos about the noise. Everyone dozed off with the sound of these drums calling for the spirits to appear and do something for the seekers. It was more than just a strange custom; this was a local Spiritist ceremony, with people hoping to connect with spiritual forces for help or guidance. The contrast between these noisy Spiritist rituals and the quiet, prayerful seeking of God that the Americans had experienced earlier was striking. It was a reminder of the different ways people seek meaning and salvation, and of why sharing the message about Jesus' gift of salvation was so important.

Everyone else in the compound may have drifted off to sleep to the rhythmic drum beat, but Harriet hadn't joined them. She found it a strange noise, disturbing to her peacefulness, which she guarded with much vigor. When the noise continued for more than 15 minutes, the ape decided someone needed a lesson in manners. She meandered through the woods, following the noise. It was louder and more irritating as she got closer. When within spitting distance, she stopped and stared long and hard at the violators of her cherished sleep time.

Without warning, she burst through the bushes and curled her lips to reveal her white-green teeth, roared, and waved her arms like a windmill. Drums stopped. Drumsticks went flying. Dancers stumbled all over themselves, racing toward the multicolored van 50 feet away.

The leader, dressed in a white robe with a white turban wrapped around his head, threw a string of beads at Harriet as he ran past her. The ape grabbed the beads as they flew toward her, spun them around on her index finger, let fly, knocking the turban off the leader's head, leaving him bald and bewildered, as he ran for his life.

His assistant was just as scared and befuddled. Since Harriet was standing alongside the only path out of the woods, the unfortunate assistant had to pass within a few feet of the ape. Harriet, being the constant clown she was, stuck out her foot and tripped the Spiritist, sending him tumbling headfirst into the filthy, cold creek water. A few of the slower followers also ended up in the drink and had to pull themselves out, because no one was sticking around to see what this huge monkey would do next. It was a comical sight, to say the least. Some of the slower Spiritists were left behind because the van wasn't waiting for stragglers. The abandoned worshipers scattered and disappeared into the dark forest.

With the area clear of humans, Harriet threw all the drums and paraphernalia into the creek and waved bye-bye to it as the current dragged the items out to the bay. With the unpleasantness concluded, she returned to her hammock and to her dreams of ransacking banana orchards, instead of hearing annoying drum assemblies.

A Brazilian breakfast was first on the morning agenda, because it was fast and easy to prepare. It usually consisted of various types of sliced cheeses and lunch meats, small loaves of French bread, a variety of diced melons, a chocolate or vanilla cake, pitchers of orange, mango, and pineapple juices, as well as the best coffee in the world; beans hand-picked by Juan Valdez. (Just kidding—Juan was from Colombia). Harriet was given a choice of three different types of bananas. Looking at the human's food spread, she was interested in the mangos she smelled. When she saw it was just juice, she decided to be happy with the carefully curated selection of fresh bananas in front of her.

Tom told the Gringos to take some chewing gum on the day's excursion, because they would climb to about 3,000 feet, and their eardrums might need some readjustment due to the drop in air pressure. He also insisted that each one bring a snow cap, scarf, and gloves. "It's going to get very cold, and might even snow today." SNOW, in Brazil? Who woulda thunk it?

It was 25 miles to Taquara, halfway to Gramado. The steep climb wouldn't really begin until after they passed the toll booth, with only 10 miles to go. After driving three miles, the vans pulled over at a 'scenic overview,' so the Gringos could take pictures of the men cutting sandstone blocks from the mountains. They used chainsaws, which required the chains to be sharpened every hour. The stone blocks were used for sidewalks and house foundations.

The closer they got to Gramado, the more the Americans noticed German- and Italian-style homes. The facings and verandas were peppered with designs carved by skilled craftsmen using expensive scroll saws. The names on building signs didn't seem very Brazilian: like Schmitz, Haas, Muller, and Goring.

Gramado is South America's chocolate capital. Linda revealed her expertise on the dark delight. "When chocolate was first discovered, it was used as an antidepressant. It still works that way for me. I've had low blood sugar all my life. If my count gets down to 65, throw a Snickers bar at me, 'cause I'm about to pass out. It's a wonderful way to recover! There are few pleasures greater in life than popping a chocolate-covered cherry into your mouth and sucking all the juice out of it, slowly dissolving the chocolate coating, then slowly chewing the cherry until the pulp slides down your throat." When she paused longer than normal, everyone noticed her head was tilted back, her eyes were closed, and she had an incredibly satisfying smile on her face.

Bert chuckled, snapping her back to reality. "Hey, I think even roaches and grasshoppers would be edible covered with thick milk chocolate."

The German city is also known for its picturesque waterfall and for leather goods, coats, gloves, hats, and rugs. Kosy wanted to know how many cows had to die to make leather coats for Rocky and Bowie. "I'll bet you it was a dozen or more." Then she broke out giggling, as she usually did. This is one of the reasons why Bowie loved her so much.

In addition to chocolate, a waterfall, and handmade clothing, Gramado is the shoe capital of the world. Factories pepper the landscape. Workers live in wooden houses constructed on company property, alongside the enormous buildings. These shoes are shipped to destinations worldwide. Erin wanted to know if this is where the 'Old Lady in the Shoe' had her house made? Now everyone was laughing.

After arriving in the city, the Americans went directly to a fondue restaurant. First, they serve small potatoes, veggies, and pieces of French bread to dip in a pot of three different melted cheeses heated over a Bunsen burner. After you're done with the cheese dip, they bring a hot lava square, and a black pot of extremely hot oil, both heated over a Bunsen burner. They offer thin slabs of chicken, beef, pork, shrimp, and fish to stab and cook in the oil or fry on the lava slab. The table is crowded with 10 types of sauce for dipping the cooked meat.

When your stomach is already full, they bring out the hot, melted, smooth, dark chocolate. They offer slices of mango, pineapple, apple, pear, orange, grape, banana, and strawberries, as well as wafers. Already stuffed customers usually double-dip to make the fruit taste even better.

All the Americans left the fondue restaurant holding their aching stomachs, except for Bowie and Rocky. These massive bodies that block the sun could have eaten more. But everyone else was done, so they surrendered their silverware, wiped their mouths on their napkins, and swished their mouths with Guaraná for one last swallow of sweet goodness.

Hand-carved furniture is a big business in Gramado. Tables, chairs, sofas, and beds can be handcrafted in the buyer's preferred style: European, German, Spanish, or Italian. They can also customize them to fit any room size. On the way back to the vans, Loretta was window shopping with Rocky. He wouldn't leave her side after the scary incident at the Rodeo. The two of them were coming out of a cheese store when Vini the Fin blocked their path to the sidewalk.

This time, he had six capungas at his side, each as big as or bigger than Rocky, each with a scowl broadcasting that they meant business. The Fin was determined and extremely confident this time. "We've followed you all over the city and finally isolated you from your other American friends. It's payback time with no Gauchos within shouting distance."

Rocky knew they were toast this time. There was no way he could protect both of them from all six of the huge thugs! And all his friends were too far away!

The gringos enjoyed riding on the ski lift as they took in the majestic scene of the Caracol Waterfall in the city of Canela in the state of Rio Grande do Sul.

CHAPTER 31
A Scary Thought

The Gringos and their Gaucho friends drove up a treaturous mountain road to visit a popular Brazilian German tourist city.

It looked hopeless for the American duo. Vini and his massive hoodlums loomed over them with overwhelming numbers and merciless faces. Fear tightened in the Gringos' chests as they braced for the worst.

But suddenly, the meter guy and the street cleaner came running, swinging clubs. At the same moment, the eight-member all-male choir setting up for a singing performance on the corner rushed to help. Four of them carried steel microphone stands, weighted bases still attached. As this was happening, a passing taxi screeched to a stop; the burly driver and his fare, who looked like a professional bouncer, jumped out and joined the defense. In an instant, Rocky and Loretta found themselves shielded by a dozen rough, tough cowboys. (Guess what, Vini, many men in the state, even on this mountain, are Gauchos.)

When all but one of his hired henchmen quickly ran off, the Mafia dude looked very frustrated. He snarled and left mumbling under his breath. "What's happening to me? Every time I have her in my clutches, there's always a way she escapes. It's like the cards are stacked against me. CAN SOMEONE PLEASE TELL ME WHAT IS GOING ON?"

Hammerhead [*Obviously, this wasn't his real name.*] followed. "Boss, if youse didn't have bad luck, youse wouldn't have any luck at all. Have you considered that maybe the stars might be aligned against you? When was the last time you checked with your astrologist, you know, your horoscope, anyway? I'm leaving now. Calls me if you need help with a noder job—juss not wit her."

"Thanks," Vini muttering to himself, "that must be it. Since The Crab Shack in San Francisco, I haven't been able to lay my hands on her. She lives a charmed life. But if so, why was she such a bad poker player? Did something change after she lost so much money to me? Who has the answers?"

All his thugs, henchmen, and capungas combined couldn't put Humpty-Dumpty back together again, even if Vini could get THEM back together again. He fell off the wall and was cracked, heading towards becoming a scrambled egg. He was a type-A personality, a choleric, take-no-prisoners type. The problem, which he didn't know, was that HE WAS DEALING WITH HEAVENLY POWERS beyond his strength and comprehension. He headed back to Porto Alegre to seek solace from his Mafia friends there.

Rocky and Loretta were stunned. Where did these warriors come from? They were all just about the same size as the pro wrestler. By this time, Valdmir had caught up with the duo. "Aha, I sees dat my plan vorked. I asks mine friends to follows us up heres and day stayed closes to youse liked I vanted dem to dos."

Loretta was teary-eyed. "Thank you, friend. My past haunts me. We must end this threat, or he'll catch us off guard—or hurt the teenagers traveling with us."

Shane and Kosy rushed over. "What happened, Mom?" Shane asked.

Loretta replied, "Valdmir and his cowboys saved us from the mobster again. I'm so tired of running. I'm asking God for help because we have no solution. Valdmir's posse can't protect us forever."

The cowboy had good news he hoped would shake Loretta out of her funk. "I wants youse to know dat last night, afters da church meetin I explains to tree of des Gauchos vat I did, to asks Jesus to saves me, and day dos it too. Is dis not good news?"

Billy heard the cowboy. "That's VERY good news," he said. "Knowing our Gaucho friends will be with us for eternity brings joy—just like the Bible says when someone accepts Jesus as Savior." Valdmir asked if he could ride back with the group so he could spend more time with them. They consented.

With that fiasco behind them, the Gringos and some invited Gauchos decided to relax and took to the mountains for a ski lift ride. The route passed very close to one of Brazil's most beautiful waterfalls. Since only two riders were allowed on each lift, Bert sat with Linda, Shane with Erin, and Rocky with Loretta. The rest formed pairs as well, with Kosy insisting that Bowie ride with her. When they both sat down, the lift tilted greatly toward the Nez Perce's side. [*Anyone surprised?*]

A walk around the Lago Negro, which means "Black Lake," was the last item on the agenda before descending the curvy mountainous road. There were small swan boats to paddle around the lake. It was called "Black Lake," but actually it looked very green. Ducks, geese, and swans honked and quacked their way around the lake, getting popcorn and bread crumbs from happy tourists.

After the lake outing, a caravan of four VW vans wound its way down the treacherous road. Tom was driving the lead van and soon got a little ahead of the group. Checking his mirror, he realized he couldn't see anyone following. It was late, and the separation made him uneasy. In Brazil, there's a certain safety in numbers. His fears were confirmed when, just as he made a 180° turn, sawhorses blocked both sides of the road. Several men dressed as police officers forced him to stop. Something felt off—these men looked too burly and unkempt to be real officers.

Just as the armed impostors approached Tom's van, three more vans barreled around the corner. Valdmir's van led. He immediately recognized the scene as a setup rather than a police stop. Flashing his lights, honking, and flooring the gas pedal, he charged ahead, the other two vans closely following. The would-be robbers realized their plan had failed and scrambled back to their own van to escape. The Gauchos jumped out and shook their fists, shouting after the retreating crooks.

Marty, trembling in Tom's van, was pale with shock. "We were doomed, absolutely doomed! I never imagined we could be ambushed like this—robbers disguised as police. They're shameless, heartless thugs. I hope the real police catch them before they disappear." Relief and gratitude flooded the group when, just ten miles later, they saw the thugs finally caught—lined up, hands raised, as real officers took control. The Gringos and

Gauchos cheered, pouring out praise to their true rescuers as they drove by, hearts pounding with lingering fear being replaced with gratitude.

Linda spoke up. "This place is dangerous. I felt safer in the Amazon. Here, being in a group has saved us. Most Brazilians aren't so lucky. My family's never been robbed. In fact, I know that none of my relatives have either. I wish I could help these people."

Engelbert Farnsworth III was impressed. Linda had been a Christian for only three weeks and was already expressing herself this way. "You've changed a lot in only three weeks—from drunk, to mocker, to philanthropist. I'm also troubled by the daily stress these wonderful people face—always alert or they're robbed, or worse."

Bert continued, "Last week, Valdmir told me about when his sister and brother-in-law came home, two robbers put guns to their heads and stole their car and his wallet. His wife ended up in the hospital with a nervous breakdown.

"They're members of Faith Baptist in Porto Alegre. The congregation prayed. Amazingly, the car was found intact, with no missing spare, and no bullet holes in the car. Usually, crooks use stolen cars for bank robberies."

Erin, sitting behind, said, "That's horrible. A nervous breakdown, just because of robbers. Will this ever change for Brazilians?"

The cowboy shrugged. "As longs as ve has des politicians who do not holds persons responsible for der crimes it vill continue. Minors can rob days after days and are turned loose agains. If a minor entereds my home to rob me and I hurts him I VILL GO TO JAIL. It is as you Americans say, a stupid tax ve all pay for voting for des politicians."

Later at the house, just beforetime bed, Tom told them one more story. "Robbers enter the front of the bus, pull a gun, and take everyone's wallet and watch. Then they open the back door and exit the bus. They rob everyone, young and old. A lady named Veronica, a member of our church, is a nurse at a hospital in Porto Alegre. She was riding home on the bus last week.

"The thugs came in the front door, brandished their guns, and began robbing everyone. She started praying. 'Lord, I just got my salary. I can't pay my rent if I get robbed. You made blind eyes see, now, please Lord, make seeing eyes blind.' She was next to the window, keeping absolutely still, not moving a muscle; she didn't even look at the thieves. They robbed the lady in front of her and the poor lady sitting right beside her. Apparently, neither of them saw Veronica. Walking right on by, the two robbers jumped out the door at the back of the bus and casually walked away. This is an amazing story. I wish that, if it had to happen, it had happened that way for all our believers.

"We do have divine protection, I know that. But if nothing bad ever happened to believers, everyone would want to be a Christian to have these obvious advantages. Unfortunately, the rain falls on the saved and the unsaved alike. Christians get hit by drunken drivers just like non-Christians do. Rocky confirmed that fact. I don't have all the answers to this difficult theological question that goes all the way back to Job in the Old Testament. "Even though Christians suffer in this world, just like unbelievers do, we do have an advantage, a great and awesome advantage. We have a God who can replace whatever is stolen and wreak vengeance on the perpetrators of crimes against us.

"Our Lord can comfort us in our stress and pain. The unbeliever doesn't have this Comforter. The Bible calls Him the Holy Spirit. He comes and lives within us the very moment we accept Christ as our Savior, and never leaves us, NEVER. Just because we have divine protection doesn't mean we should be careless. We need to use our seat belts and crash helmets. We should secure our house as much as possible and remain alert at all times. There's no such thing as being too careful here in Brazil. A lack of security and vigilance can get you robbed very quickly.

"We have theft insurance. We don't buy it here in Brazil because it would cost us a whopping $1,000 a year to be insured for $3,000, with a $500 deductible per robbery. This is stupid. We purchase our theft insurance from Lloyds of London. It comes through an agency in the States. We pay only $550 per year for $20,000 in coverage, with a $500 deductible per robbery. This makes more sense.

"When we go on vacation, even for two days, or to the States for furlough, we have to get someone to stay in our house. When I tell Americans this, they think it's because of robbery. While it's true, it's not the only reason. It's also needed because of squatters. If a family with children invades my house while I'm away, I can't simply go to the police and have them run the family out. NO SIREE BOB, I have to get a lawyer, and it takes a full two years to extradite them. By that time, they've sold all my belongings and trashed my house. It's called 'Squatter's Rights,' and it's beyond comprehension in an American's way of thinking.

"Maybe I'm scaring some of you by telling these facts about living in Brazil. I can imagine that because I'm scared, too. YES, I'm scared because we've been robbed over 100 times, three times at gunpoint. It's a frightening experience. It leaves you feeling violated and vulnerable. This isn't a place to live for people with weak constitutions. The last time our house was robbed, we were in Gramado. The thieves spent two hours ransacking our place, taking everything that caught their interest. They took my Harley-Davidson, Ford car, and other items for a total of $50,000. Fortunately, we had theft insurance. But unfortunately, most Brazilians don't.

"Some of our relatives and friends stateside have insisted we leave here immediately and return to the States, where we can live in a more secure place and have the protection every person deserves to have. I assure them that we're NOT going to do that. Our beloved Brazilian friends, believers and unbelievers, have to live here their whole lives. We aren't going to abandon them just because we've been robbed or are scared. They all have been robbed, too, and they are scared most of the time. We'll live here the rest of our lives, like they have to, and we'll leave our fate to God, who loves us and is with us at all times.

"God didn't call Susana and me to serve Him only if the situation was safe. We answered God's call to serve Him here in Brazil. It's much safer here than in Africa or other primitive places where missionaries have served their whole lives. Some of those missionaries, like David Livingstone and Adoniram Judson, served in dangerous places and died in those places. Some died of old age, and others of diseases that took them early. We'll live here and be thankful for the comforts of life God has given us and for the police that give us some protection.

"We know we are immortal until God is done using us. We can't leave this life without His personal call. No one can harm us without His permission. We have a million angels surrounding us, protecting us from evil and our spiritual enemies. We know this from Job's story and from the rest of what the Bible teaches us. This is a comforting thought, don't you think?"

All of the Americans went to bed pondering this lesson in doctrine and Brazilian culture. They all had a lot to think about as they contemplated their future in God's will.

CHAPTER 32
Vini's End

Vini the Fin was angry and frustrated about his incessant failures to trap Loretta. Was he fighting against some unknown force?

Vini the Fin still schemed for revenge against Loretta, her kids, her friends, and even the ugly ape. He refused to leave Brazil without some satisfaction. It infuriated him that someone of lower stature could keep besting him. After more than a year, his efforts had accomplished nothing. His henchmen always failed, and their plans unraveled. It felt like Loretta had an invisible shield against him. If he could break it, maybe he'd finally have peace seeing her suffer.

All his Brazilian Mafia friends told him to go home and forget her. She wasn't worth it. Write her off as a cost of doing business, close the ledger, and move on. One of the semi-religious dudes even recounted a Bible story he had heard in Sunday school many years ago. A queen named Ester and her uncle Mordecai had a mortal enemy. A powerful man named Haman tried to destroy all the Jews, Ester's people. He also wanted to hang Mordecai on a gallows. The story ended with his whole family being destroyed, and HAMAN was hanged on the gallows.

The dude ended his story and looked at Vini the Fin, "Maybe you should consider yourself lucky you still have your head on straight. Go home and forget this vengeance before it's too late. Sometimes vengeance is too costly, too painful."

Vini scoffed as his Mafia colleagues quoted Bible stories. Religion? That was for the weak, he told himself. The idea of higher powers meddling in earthly affairs seemed absurd—yet somewhere deep inside, a flicker of doubt gnawed at him. Was he really above consequences? He quickly dismissed the thought. He would prove to everyone, including himself, that no one—not God, not angels, no invisible shields—could stand in his way. But his bravado felt thinner with every new failure.

Ricardo Pacheo Keppler Vastanii, the kingpin of the Porto Alegre Mafia, had invited Vini to discuss a collaboration with the San Francisco Mafia. Ricardo noticed Vini was nervous and confused—not traits of a real leader. Vini was disappointing everyone. If he didn't improve soon, he would be told to leave before harming their reputations. Public image mattered greatly to these men.

The Mafia grapevine spread news that a 120-pound unarmed woman had outsmarted Vini and his gang on several occsssions. Rumors said a Nez Perce Indian and a red-haired, ugly, female orangutan had made a mockery of Vini and his men. This was humiliating for the supposed San Francisco Mafia leader.

The Mafia committee, representing all factions, called a meeting. They voted 12-0 to give Vini one last chance. If he failed again or refused to leave, he risked being fitted with cement boots. These were serious men, not to be trifled with.

Vini planned his final caper: isolate Loretta again, hiring 24 of Porto Alegre's worst. No price was too high to restore his reputation. The plan would happen today. He believed this would end his troubles and he could return home in triumph.

Just as he was about to board his thugs onto the bus, one ran up waving *Zero Hora*, Rio Grande do Sul's most popular newspaper. "Boss, you need to read this before you leave."

Vini snapped, "Are you crazy? I can't read Portuguese. Throw it away. Are you all idiots?" The nervous thug persisted. Vini grabbed the paper and glanced at the article.

"Vini the Fin, Yes, YOU, Vini. I witnessed you steal $50 from your mom's purse on March 7, 1935, while she was distracted on the phone with your Aunt Sally from Chicago. I also know you cheated on your final history exam on January 22, 1942. I am aware of the woman you are targeting. Stop IMMEDIATELY. You will write her a note confirming all debts are settled and promising that she and her friends will not be bothered again. Failure to do so will result in consequences far greater, especially when you face your final judgment. Consider this your ONLY warning—a message from someone who sees beyond what others can."

Vini's face turned ashen. His whole body shook, knees knocking so loudly his men could hear. Vitor, his chief henchman, moved quickly to steady the boss, who was hyperventilating.

"How ... what ... for Pete's sake. Where did this newspaper get this information? I want someone who speaks Portuguese to call them and ask who paid to have this article in the paper. NOW, move it!"

They did just that as fast as they could. It was never a good idea to irritate Vini. They knew that getting the boss mad might mean cement shoes. Within ten minutes, they had an answer. "Boss, the newspaper guys said they don't know what you're talking about. They don't have any English articles in today's paper. In fact, it's against their policy to print anything in English."

Vini sent them out to buy another copy. When they opened it to the exact page, there it was again. He was livid. "Call them again and ask them again. NOW!"

The henchman came back with the same answer. "They say that in this exact spot, there's a picture of a local clown juggling papayas. They claimed again, almost yelling at me, that it's against their policy to print anything in English."

He sent them to buy all the papers they could find. The capungas came back with 53 copies. All of them had the same English article.

Since the *Zero Hora* headquarters was only five blocks away, he decided to go there himself. When he pigeonholed the man in charge of editing the final preprinted copy and showed him his copy, the Brazilian was baffled. Through his interpreter, he carefully explained it to Vini. "I know absolutely NOTHING about this article. It's a complete mystery to me. I've been in this paper business for 50 years and have never seen anything like this. It appears to me that it's the hand of God. If I were you, I'd take this as a personal message from the man upstairs." Then he showed Vini a stack of papers in the lobby with the clown picture in the same spot as Vini's mysterious letter.

Vini's mind reeled. No one alive knew what was printed in that article— no one but him, and all others were long dead. His skin prickled as panic surged through his body. For the first time, he realized that maybe not everything could be controlled or bought. It was a feeling he despised, this primal fear, but now it overshadowed even his cherished anger. For a moment, vengeance no longer mattered at all; he was simply terrified, forced to confront the unimaginable.

Rattled to his core, Vini acted quickly. He had to get out—away from this city, away from whatever unseen force was watching. He marched his men onto the first flight he could arrange, desperate to hide the article before any Mafia leader could see it. Every muscle trembled with the urge to run. He supervised as the damning papers were destroyed, determined to erase every trace, though he knew the real problem was one he couldn't pulp or burn away.

Since he knew where Loretta was, he caught a cab and started writing a note while the driver was headed for Gravataí. When he arrived at the retreat center, he asked to speak to Tom, the white American missionary. When Tom saw Vini, he was a bit nervous. But the mobster motioned for him to come closer. Vini didn't look good, not good at all.

"Mr. Tom, please take this letter to Loretta and tell her she will never see me again. I promise this on my mother's grave. Please do this for me." Vini looked absolutely terrified.

As soon as Tom took the note, Vini quickly turned, got in the cab, and disappeared down the road.

The group was in the living room discussing a Bible passage. The missionary handed the note to Loretta, who read it. Tears began to flow freely down her cheeks, tears of joy, of relief, of utter astonishment. She asked Rocky to read the note to the whole group. Rocky was shaking, hardly able to finish reading the letter. It was just what they needed to hear.

LORETTA, THE DEBT YOU OWE ME IS PAID IN FULL. I AM DREADFULLY SORRY FOR ALL THE PAIN AND SUFFERING I HAVE CAUSED YOU. I AM LEAVING NOW, AND YOU WILL NEVER HEAR FROM ME AGAIN, NOR FROM ANYONE ASSOCIATED WITH ME. PLEASE FORGIVE ME FOR MY SINS AGAINST YOU AND YOUR FAMILY. SINCERELY, VINI ROBERTO MASSTROTTI.

There wasn't a dry eye in the room. A loud shout of "HALLELUJAH" came from the back. It was Billy. He stood up and jumped with joy. He knew this was a glorious victory, and it was all of God. No one in the room had any logical explanation for the letter from the mobster.

Tom was so relieved, "He looked absolutely terrified. His face was ashen, almost like he was going to pass out. When he returned to the cab, the driver had to get out and help him, or he was surely going to collapse right there on the road. I'm absolutely convinced this letter is legitimate. I believe God has solved our problem in a way we'll never know."

Suddenly, Susana came into the room, waving a *Zero Hora*. She was ecstatic, "I think I know what happened. Let me read an article printed in today's paper. It's in English, if you can believe that. I know it's their policy NEVER to print anything in English." When she read the article, everyone got goosebumps. The article was the same one that had frightened Vini. It was even more mystical when Susana said she checked the neighbor's, *Zero Hora*. In the neighbor's copy, at this same spot, there was an ad with a clown juggling; some circus promotion. It just didn't make sense. No one could figure it out, and that didn't bother them the way it did Vini.

Loretta now had Shane and Kosette hanging onto her shoulders. It was a wonderful moment for the Woods family. No more debt, no more mobsters, and no more running. They could return to the farm in Lacomb with a completely clean slate. This was marvelous, and they thanked God for it. Jack Woods was going to be the first one Stateside to hear the good news. The kids knew it would give Grandpa goosebumps galore.

The chief of police rang the doorbell. Tom escorted him into the living room, where everyone was still drying their teary eyes. Tom translated for the officer. "We want to know what that member of the American Mafia was doing here. We've had our eyes and ears on him since he came here three weeks ago."

Rocky spoke for the whole group. "He's been harassing us for the last three weeks. He came from San Francisco, California, and is working with the Mafia in Porto Alegre. If you send some of your men to the airport, you might have an opportunity to talk to him before he escapes."

The kind officer thanked them for their helpful information. He said they must rush to the airport to apprehend Vini the Fin so he can give them all the information he has on the Mafia leaders running amok in Porto Alegre. He assured them all that it wouldn't go well for Vini and his henchmen if they didn't cooperate.

Bert stood up and clapped. "Wow, now the hunter is going to be the hunted. The fox is going to be caught. This is truly what I've heard called 'divine retribution.' The chickens have come home to roost. The caper is over. The skunk is in the bag." When he noticed the questioning looks, he paused. "What? Too many similes?" Everyone laughed.

Shane was elated. "It does seem to be a bit ironic. Vini the Fin comes here to show off his Mafia skills, finds Mom, and spends his whole time trying to wreak vengeance against all of us. Now he's going to experience what it's like to deal with the Brazilian police force. I've heard they're not an organization to mock or trouble in any way, shape, or form."

Valdmir arrived at the retreat center just in time to hear the shouting. He wanted to celebrate, too; he just needed a reason. When Tom informed him of the morning's news, he threw his cowboy fist in the air and did a Gaucho victory dance. He tapped his spurs on the ceramic floor like he was Bojangles [*heralded by many as the best tap dancer ever to grace the stage*].

He said it would snow in the afternoon, and he came over to invite the whole crew to his ranch so they could build a snowman and have a very rare snowball fight. He was so excited, he asked Tom to translate. "It gets cold enough here to snow, but as Marty and Erin know, living in Montana, it requires more than just cold to create snowflakes. This afternoon, we'll have all the right conditions. This wonderful winter phenomenon only happens about once every forty years here in the valley. We have a nice fireplace burning and some excellent filet mignon on the grill. Are you all ready to have some Gaucho fun?" They all said they were ready.

Someone even woke Harriet so she could go, too. They piled in the vans, threw in a few bushels of bananas for her, and off they went. On the way there, Tom told the Americans they had to have their bags packed tonight before they went to bed. He also wanted to see their passports tonight. These were practices he had always insisted on because so many things had gone wrong over the years while traveling back and forth between the USA and Brazil.

After building a snowman and a snowwoman, the snowball war began. Harriet got into the fracas and was doing well. She seemed to miss the point that it was all in fun. Her snowballs were bigger than the others, and she would get up close to lower the boom on them. It was getting a bit painful for the non-primates! The whole ordeal came to a halt when someone noticed the ape putting rocks into some of her snowballs. Apparently, she missed the Primate Fair Play 101 class given at Orangutan Good Conduct School. For a finale, all the Americans and Gauchos threw huge snowballs at the ape, knocking her over and almost burying her with snow.

She got up and shook herself off, but wasn't smiling as she usually did. It was time to run for the house and close the door behind them. That's exactly what they did, leaving her out in the cold to contemplate her unsportsmanlike behavior. She stared at them through the big bay window, scratching her belly button. When she began to throw rock-filled snowballs at the bay window, they decided to let her in. It was the lesser of two evils.

Valdmir wanted to say something before everyone headed off to bed. Tom translated for him. "I was a good Gaucho, never been arrested, never took drugs, and never stole anything. I was even a religious person, going to church now and then, for first communions, weddings, and funerals. Like every other Brazilian, I thought I was doing the best I could, and if God required more than this, then He was unfair.

"I never had much contact with REAL Christians before. I had only heard they were a bunch of goody-two-shoes. If you're wondering, Bert taught me that phrase. They always condemned everyone else. When I found Bowie and Harriet on the street, things began to change for me. I saw what a real born-again Christian was like, AT LEAST IN BOWIE." Everyone smiled at his humor. "I even felt the sin I had committed was enough to keep me out of heaven.

"At the church service, I listened carefully and discovered I needed to have my sin problem resolved before a holy God. He wouldn't allow anyone who didn't repent and accept Christ as their only and sufficient Savior to pass through the Pearly Gates. I did that and have had a peace in my heart I've never had before. Now, I know for certain that I'll see you all in heaven, even though I may never see you again on Earth. I thank you for coming and for being my friend." With this, he took his Gaucho handkerchief out and wiped the tears from his cowboy eyes and cheeks before heading out the door.

He wasn't the only teary-eyed person in the room. Kosette wanted to give a little speech. "I'm the youngest. I can't imagine another twelve-year-old having the experiences I've had. Man, wait until I get back to Green Mountain Grammar School, I'll have a lot of stories to tell. I want to say how wonderful it is to travel with all of you. I love all of you and especially my Big Friend, Bowie Pinetree." With that, she rushed over and kissed her mom, Shane, and Bowie.

The main luggage was inspected and approved before bedtime. Upon receiving Tom's thumbs up for their bag, each member of the vacation team headed to bed. When all had successfully passed Tom's inspection, he checked to ensure they were safely tucked in for the night (yes, even Harriet), then locked the doors, set the house alarm, and turned off the extra lights. Then, he headed to bed himself.

After an early morning wake-up call at 5:00 AM, all morning activities were completed quickly, and everyone scarfed down their final Brazilian breakfast. Tom conducted a final inspection of all quickly-packed, carry-on bags. Tom had rented a trailer to take all the luggage to the docks. With all the large bags, plus carry-on items, no VW vans would do the trick, carrying the passengers to boot.

There are two levels at the airport, and on each level, people are crying. At the one on the first floor, Gauchos were crying with joy upon receiving their loved ones. On the second floor, Gauchos were also crying, but for a different reason: their loved ones were leaving.

This was not the case at the docks inside the airport grounds, their destination. There was only one level, and both Americans and Gauchos were using their crying towels. It was a sorrowful departure, as it always is when loved ones are left behind or going away. Luggage loading and customs checks were complete. It was finally time to head back home.

With all the Gringos safely tucked into the Albatross flying boat, including one grinning ape from Borneo, Fernando nudged the throttle forward and taxied away at precisely 6:00 AM. Brazilians on the dock and Americans peering through tiny airplane windows waved goodbye to each other. The final leg of this epic summer vacation, filled with exciting Brazilian Adventures, was in the air, cruising through cloudless skies, heading north.

About the Author:
Dr. Tom Latham

Dr. Latham's full name is Harry Thomas Latham, but to his friends, he is Tom. His Brazilian friends know him as Pastor Thomas. He publishes under his pen name, Dr. Tom Latham. His remarkable career as a missionary in Brazil spans more than 50 years. Many factors contributed to his success, but above all, his resolute faith in Jesus Christ, his personal Savior, had the greatest impact.

Tom became a Christian while serving in the U.S. Navy, where he began holding Protestant Divine Services whenever his ship was at sea. After completing his naval service, he spent the next four years at bible college to further his spiritual journey. Graduation from Central Baptist Theological Seminary earned him a Master of Divinity (MDiv) degree. He achieved a significant milestone in his studies by earning a Doctor of Ministry (DMin) degree from Luther Rice Seminary.

Tom met Penny Stimpson, and together they began a mission to serve God in Brazil. Their family grew to include three children, six grandchildren, and ten great-grandchildren. Together, they started four churches in Brazil.

Tom led extremely successful wrestling programs in many public schools for more than 20 years, including training and coaching. His church team won the Brazilian National Title in 2010 and the State title in 2013.

Although Penny was promoted to glory, Tom continues to serve Christ in Brazil.

Read many details about Dr. Latham and his educational journey, at www.brazilwrestler.com.

This is the last photo of the entire Latham family, taken in 2023, a few months before Penny was carried by angels into the arms of her loving Savior.
Last row: Thomas, Kossette, and Shane. Front row: Penny and Tom.

Acknowledgment & Thanks

I acknowledge Jesus Christ, my Savior. Without His guidance and grace lifting me from a spiritual ditch, this book would not exist. I owe Him more than I can ever repay.

I thank my three children, Thomas, Shane, and Kosette, for making life an adventure as we faced the challenges and joys of the mission field in Brazil. Their companionship gave us more experiences than those in my more than 70 manuscripts, which may eventually become published books.

I also thank Dave Carlson, owner of DynoTech Publishing, a proper 'jack of all trades' and 'master of many,' for his invaluable contribution to the editing and publishing process. His tremendous efforts far exceeded what I could have accomplished alone, and I am deeply grateful. His excellent command of the English language helped bring my words to life. Dave, a brother wrestler who resides in Colorado Springs, Colorado, stays busy during retirement with consulting projects related to computer technology, computer-aided illustration, book editing, and publishing.

This my favorite photo of my kids: Thomas (L), Kosette, and Shane.

I did barbecue shish kebabs for the police, firemen and some store employees from downtown.

BOOKS by
Dr. Tom Latham

www.brazilwrestler.com/book/

AUTOBIOGRAPHY

This is an exceptional opportunity to examine a 50-year professional journey, brought to life through 130+ vibrant color images.
Into the Light: Half-Century as Missionaries in Brazil
(ISBN 978-1-885708-19-9)

SHANE WOODS SERIES

Book 1: *The Snow Peak Robbers* (ISBN 978-1-885708-51-9)
Book 2: *The Strawberry Fair* (ISBN 978-1-885708-52-6)
Book 3: *The Buzzard Butte Poachers* (ISBN 978-1-885708-53-3)
Book 4: *The Eastern Rodeo* (ISBN 978-1-885708-54-0)

Planned for 2026-2027

Book 5: *The Linn County Vandals*
Book 6: *The Nez Perce Treasure*
Book 7: *The Mountain Lion*
Book 8: *The Precarious Plane Ride*
Book 9: *The Empty Coffin Mystery*
Book 10: *The State Championship*
Book 11: *The Baseball Problem*

Other Books

Brazilian Adventures (ISBN 978-1-885708-25-0)
Missionary Problem Areas (ISBN 978-1-885708-27-4)

Future books will depend on reader interest. More book sales may motivate me to publish more of my 60+ existing manuscripts.